D1553225

Corgi Cove

DAWN L NOLDER

Corgi Cove

Dawn L Nolder / published by the author

For information address:
Dawn L Nolder
dawnlnolder@gmail.com

ISBN-13: 978-1542487368
ISBN-10: 1542487366

Version _1

Cover Illustration and Copyright © by Chris Roger Aquilio

DEDICATION

To my parents. Without them and their love of reading that they passed down to me, I would never have been able to write this book. Thank you, mama and daddy.

ACKNOWLEDGMENTS

There are a few people that I need to thank for helping me make this book happen.

To my beta readers: Sally N., Michelle M., Suzy M., Cathy H., Susan M., Cecelia H., Laura K., Courtney T., Sheenah F., and Julie S. You ladies rock! Without your support and understanding, and of course reading, I wouldn't be where I am today. Thank you!

To my editor, Cecelia H. There are no words. Just a heartfelt and sincere, thank you.

To Jeffrey M. Poole, thank you for answering my endless questions on how to write and publish. Without your help, I'd still be trying to figure out this whole process.

To Chris Rogers Aquilio, thank you for the amazing cover art! You captured what Corgi Cove looks like perfectly.

PROLOGUE

Three months ago

She became aware of the pain first. The kind of pain that when it hits you, it takes your breath away. Then came the panic because no matter how much she tried to move, her body didn't seem to understand her request.

So, she laid there on the cold concrete floor and tried to remember why she was in so much pain and why she was on the ground in the first place. Had she fallen? That didn't seem right. Something bad had to have happened, though. That, she was sure of. She knew that because of the knot of fear in her stomach. She was in trouble.

She tried to focus her mind on listening, and after a moment, she heard a voice. A voice that she knew and loved. It was her boyfriend. Oh, thank God. She had to let him know that she needed his help. It felt important for her to let him know there was danger. Danger? Why would she think that word? Had someone attacked her? Is that what had happened? Her brain was foggy, but she felt like someone had hurt her. And badly.

She tried to move her arms again, but nothing. She tried to make a sound. Oddly, she couldn't remember how to do that either. The only thing she seemed to be able to do was to breathe and listen to her boyfriend and the other man. Another man? The voice was familiar, and it scared her, deep down in her chest. But why? He sounded familiar so why would he scare her? Her head hurt so bad. She focused on the words and tones and realized that her boyfriend and the other man were arguing. But, about what? And why didn't he come over to her? Why didn't he come to check on her?

"What the hell did you do?" her boyfriend screamed, striding up to the other man and smashing his fist into his jaw.

"I had to. Your girlfriend was getting too close to knowing the secret." He rubbed his jaw but didn't return the punch. "She fucking went and got the tattoo. That goes against the code. You know that. I had to. If I didn't do it, one of the others would have. So, fucking calm down and help me fix this."

Rubbing his fist from the punch, her boyfriend slowly nodded his head. "Okay. Alright. You're right. But dammit! I cared about her. There should have been another way of doing this. Maybe I could have talked to her. Maybe I could have convinced her that the tattoo meant nothing. But, none of that matters now. What the hell did you hit her with anyway?" Glancing over at the body that was face down, he rubbed his face with both hands and paced.

"A shovel." Pacing now to match the other's stride. "We have to get rid of it. And her. You *have* to help me. This is your fault, after all. If you hadn't started dating her, a goddamn professor, none of this would have happened. You got to help me. Family first, cousin."

"I know the code. But goddammit cousin, I cared for her." Walking over to the body and kneeling, he didn't touch her, just looked at the wound to the back of her head. "How did this happen?"

"I saw our tattoo on her arm, and I got pissed. So, I asked her why she got it, and she said she liked yours, so decided on your vacation to get a matching one. You know you're going to have to answer to the families about that, right?

That tattoo belongs to the families only. It's bad enough that she saw it, but you were with her when she got the damn thing. That was stupid, cousin. You should have stopped her. She was your responsibility. The families are going to have your ass for this. They might even kick you out.

"Anyway, I told her that she didn't have the right to get that tattoo and she got all high and mighty and said to mind my own damn business. Then she turned her back to me like she was dismissing me. That really pissed me off. That bitch dismissing me. ME! A member of the original families. Being dismissed by an outsider. So, I grabbed the first thing I saw, the shovel, and swung for the cheap seats. She went down and stayed down. Then I called you. We need to get rid of her." He nudged her in the ribs and after he was satisfied that she was dead, walked over to the other man.

"Shut up and let me think for a minute." He paced and stroked his jaw as he occasionally glanced at his lover's body on the floor. "Okay, I got it. We'll take her to the cove and put her in it. You come over here to talk to her about something. I don't know what but think of something. Anyway, you can't find her, so you walk around all the buildings and yard, then you finally go to the cove and find her. Make sure you do walk all around and look like you are looking for her. You need to make tracks in the snow. Make the story look real. Then, you call it into the Sheriff's Office, and it will be all legal and whatnot. Okay? Can you do that? You need to hide that fucking shovel until you can take it out on the boat and lose it way offshore. Then, we forget this ever happened."

Grabbing the other man's arm, he looked him in the eye. "You need to let the families know that I helped fix my mistake. You have to. I don't want to be thrown out. This is all I've ever known. You got to stick up for me. Family first, cousin. And whether you like it or not, I'm your family."

"I'll make sure they know that you helped right the wrong you did." Walking over to the body and grabbing her legs, he looked at the other man and jerked his chin toward her head. "You can take her head. After all, she was your girl so you should have to see her face while we get rid of her."

"You're an asshole, you know that, right?" But he grabbed his girlfriend under her arms, and the two of them made their way to the cove.

They had to take their time because it was January in Maine and there had been a recent snow and ice storm. Reaching the cove, they put her down at the water's edge and leaned over to catch their breath.

"Make sure when you walk around, you walk over our tracks. Really mess up the snow so that it's hard to see any real tracks in the snow."

"I know what to do, so stop telling me. I'll clean it all up nice. No one will know what happened once I'm done."

She knew she was in serious trouble and that her boyfriend wasn't going to help her. She had to try to save herself. But how? She could hear the water as it lapped at her and that put her into a panic, not only because of what it meant but that she couldn't feel the water on her.

Concentrating as hard as she could, she tried to once again move her legs or arms. But, as before, her limbs were refusing to listen to her. Frustrated and panicking, she next tried to yell or scream. Not that it would help her being so far away from town. She couldn't just lay there and let them kill her without trying to fight. But she couldn't make a sound, not even a whimper. The only thing she would muster was a single tear. Just one single tear. That was all. So, her fight to the death would be with a tear. She had been a fighter her entire life, and her last moment on earth, all she could do was lay motionless and cry one tear.

As they picked her up and loaded her into the canoe that one of them had taken out of the boat shed, she fought to show any sign of life. A jerk or a sound. Anything that would let her lover know she was alive. If he were aware that she was still alive, maybe he wouldn't follow through with the plan.

She felt the canoe rock as it left the beach of her cove. She knew she was running out of time and with a last-ditch effort, she got her eyes to open and focus on the man in the canoe. Her boyfriend. He looked down into her eyes and smiled. Leaning over he kissed her lips, whispered *I love you*, and *I'm sorry* into her ear, touched her cheek then pushed her into the icy water of her cove.

The last thing she saw was her lover's eyes as he used the oar to push her down into the cold water of her cove.

CHAPTER ONE

Present Day

She was completely bat shit crazy. That was the only explanation. After all, a sane person didn't do what she had done in the last two months. First, buying property in Maine, sight unseen, and with a 'Buy It Now' button on a real estate website, in the middle of a sleepless night. Then to uptick the level of insanity, Tara McDowell had quit her safe, steady job in Ohio, packed the few things she wanted after 20 years of marriage, took Connal, her corgi, and headed to a state she had never been to. She was freaking nuts. Certifiably crazy.

Tara was brought out of her internal mumbling and grumbling when Mick, her Irish GPS navigator, informed her that she would be turning into her new property in five miles. In the middle of nowhere. With bears, mooses, and bigfoots. Moose? Moosies? Whatever. Big frigging animals that would probably be picking her and Connal out of their teeth by the end of the week. She felt her stomach knot up, and the taste of the acid filled her mouth.

Her new life was beginning, whether she was ready for it or not. Tara took several deep breaths and cracking the windows of the SUV, she could smell the ocean which made her smile.

Her new home had the ocean in the back yard so she could die happy, in the middle of nowhere.

Connal, her corgi of three years, decided to wake up from his upside-down sleeping position in the back seat, and after stretching in the classic downward dog pose then moving into the more advanced one leg stretch, he yawned, arroooed and was now standing and sticking as much of his head out the window as he could. He knew when the car slowed down, it would be stopping soon.

Glancing in the rearview mirror, Tara smiled when she saw Connal's little nub wiggling. She was still amazed how lucky she was that she had found him. He was a red and white Pembroke Welsh Corgi. With his four white socks, belly and chest, he was adorable. To add to his cuteness factor, he had a white streak between his ears and a white blaze that ran from his white muzzle to between his eyes along with a small white spot between his shoulder blades. It was hard to imagine that he was a rescue, after being picked up, roaming the corn fields in Illinois.

Shaking her head to bring herself back, Tara whistled, and when Connal looked at her in the mirror, she smiled. "Well, this is it, Connal. This is where we're going to be living from now on. Let's see what your crazy-assed mom has got us into."

Connal, sensing Tara's nervousness pulled his head back into the car and placing his front feet on the center console, leaned over to lick Tara's ear. Laughing, Tara returned the affection by wrapping her arm around his neck to hold him to her cheek for a moment.

"Thanks, buddy. You know just what to do to make me feel better. We'll be okay. I'm just freaking out because this is such a huge thing. But, we'll be fine."

Mick interrupted the moment to inform her that her turn was on the right. As she made the turn, it hit Tara that she was pulling onto her new driveway. That was paved. That had to be a good sign, right? She had driven for about 75 feet before she came to a road on the left. Slowing down to look down the road, Tara saw a cabin tucked back into the trees.

"This must be the smaller house that is on the property. We'll check that out tomorrow, but I really want to see our new house. Don't you, Connal?"

Connal's answer was another lick on the cheek before he hopped back on the arm of the car door to stick his head out the window.

They had continued another 100 feet before a gated entry stopped them.

"A gate. That has to be a good thing right, Connal? People don't generally gate places that suck. Right? I wouldn't. Okay, so how do we get in?" Tara picked up the folder of papers that had been in the passenger seat and began rifling through the tons of legal paperwork that had been sent to her after the closing. She had found the key to the house earlier, and that was now tucked into the cup holder of the SUV, but the gate had a number pad. "Crap, there has to be a code on one of these papers."

The selling real estate agent had wanted to come meet her to show her the property, but Tara wanted to do this by herself. With no one watching her. She hated an audience and feeling rushed when all she wanted to do was look, so she had said no. Now, she wasn't so sure that was a good idea.

"Ah ha, bingo!" Tara grabbed a sticky note out of the folder and drove closer to the gate to enter the newly found code on the number pad. "Oh, thank God that was the right code," she sighed as the gate swung open. "So far, so good. First, a paved driveway and now a gated entry. This just might be a good deal, Connal."

Connal added his low purrish growl and jumped back and forth between the center console beside Tara, and the armrests on the doors in the back seat. He was getting as excited as she was to get to this new stage in their lives.

Once Tara had pulled through the gate and watched it close behind her, she continued driving slowly, looking left and right and getting her first glimpse of her property. Shaking her head, she still couldn't believe she had done something so big and huge and stupid and crazy and insane. "Quit it," she told herself and turned her attention to what she was driving past. Since it was the middle of April, the trees didn't have leaves yet so Tara couldn't tell what the trees were, but they were big, mature trees and there were tons of them. She had done some research on this area of Maine, so she knew that some of the trees would be birches, oaks, pines, maples, and elms and those were just the ones she remembered off the top of her head.

Finally, as she came around a small bend, the house appeared. Tara stopped the car, sat and stared. "Oh, my God," she whispered. "It's beautiful." Tears of excitement, relief, joy, and several other emotions leaked from her eyes.

"Let's go explore our new place, Con!" Tara jumped out of the car, opened the back door to the car and grabbed Connal's leash before releasing his seatbelt.

Connal wiggled and grumbled all the while shaking his little nub but waited for Tara to pick him up and put him on the ground. He immediately pulled Tara to the nearest bush and lifted his leg.

Shaking her head, Tara walked over to the garage. "We have a four-car garage, Connal. Damn. My SUV is going to be lonely in there all by itself, isn't it? Might have to go on a car buying spree to fill that up. Maybe a couple of classics. That would chap Wyatt's ass, wouldn't it?"

Turning her head to the right, Tara saw the house. Her house. Smiling, she turned to the left and saw a large barn. But it didn't look like a real barn. "Odd looking barn there, bud. We have a lot of exploring to do, so what should we look at first? I'm thinking the house. What's your vote?" Since Connal started pulling her towards the house, the decision was made. "Okay, we'll go into the house. Lead the way, little dog."

Tara followed Connal to what appeared to be the main entrance of the house. Pulling out the key, she unlocked the door and pushed it open to let Connal be the first one into their new home.

Stepping inside, she realized that this was just a small

entryway into the main house. It wasn't a big area, but it wasn't small either. There was a small closet to the left that would hold coats and boots for going out. Walking past the closet and through the open archway, they entered the actual house and stopped. Mouth hanging open, she actually pinched herself.

The layout of the house was a large, rectangular common area, with an open floor plan. She had walked into the dining room and directly in front of her was a solid wood dining room table, that was currently set for eight people and was a dark, rich brown. The chairs that surrounded it were just as solid and heavy looking like as the table. The seat cushions of dark gray softened the look of the set.

"I don't know eight people that I would invite to dinner," Tara mumbled to herself. To her left was the kitchen area and oh, what a kitchen. But what got her attention was from where she was standing, she could see straight through the living room, to the ocean beyond. And that's where she walked next instead of the kitchen.

"We'll look at the kitchen in a bit. But we have to see this living room and view." However, as they walked toward the living room, she saw there was a hallway on either side of her that separated the kitchen/dining room and living room area. Hesitating, Tara waffled between continuing into the living room and to the cove beyond or to see what the hallways led to. The interest in the hallways won and Tara, followed by Connal, turned into the hall to the right.

Immediately inside the entrance of the hallway, Tara and Connal saw two doors, one on each side. "Well, which one should we open?" Connal just sat down and looked at Tara. "Oh, so I get to pick this time, huh? Such a gentleman." Tara leaned down to scratch Connal under his ear, then standing back up, chose the door to the left.

It was a bedroom that was large enough to have a sitting area. Along both outside walls, there was a set of French doors, with one set opening out to an incredible view of the cove. The other set of doors provided a view of the woods beyond. Walking over to the cove-side doors, Tara saw that there was a large deck that she verified went around to the other set of doors. The hallway wall held a large walk-in closet and a full bath. "Damn. This is nice, isn't it, bud? Let's go see what is behind door number two."

Opening the door across the hallway, Tara saw that this was another bedroom. It was the same size as the first room, but instead of two sets of French doors, this room only had one set. Walking over to the doors, Tara saw the wooded view again and that the wraparound deck from the first room continued to the end of the house to the right. Along the wall that faced the garage, there was a large bay window that had a window seat just crying to be sat on. The hallway wall held the same size walk-in closet and full bath as the first room. "I don't know which of these rooms is classified the master, Connal. They're both amazing, but so far, the cove bedroom wins."

Heading back into the living room and to the hallway on the other side of the house, she opened the right door.

Tara stood there and smiled. "Ah. There is it! This has to be the master bedroom." Set up similarly to the first room, this one had the cove view through a set of French doors. Following Connal to the doors, Tara saw that the porch wrapped around to this side as well. "Holy shit, that's a huge porch. You're going to love running laps on that, aren't you?" Turning back toward the room, Tara saw that where the other cove room had a second set of doors on the outside wall, this one didn't and that there seemed to be another room. Walking over Tara saw there was a small hallway and opening the first door on the left, she discovered the bathroom. The master bath was larger than the bathroom in the other two rooms. Coming back out and continuing to the left, the next set of double doors opened to a walk-in closet that was bigger than some of the apartments she had lived in. "I don't have enough clothes to do this closet justice. What the hell do people buy that much of, that they need a closet this big?" Shaking her head, Tara turned to the room directly across from the closet.

Opening the door, she now saw why the room didn't have the second set of French doors.

"Oh, an office!" And not just an office. It had a microwave and mini fridge, along with a sink and cabinets. "There's too much to see, Connal. Let's leave the office to later."

Stepping back into the main part of the bedroom, they walked out the French doors of the room and Tara finally got to see, feel and smell her cove.

Turning to head back in, Tara glanced down at Connal, who was refusing to come in. "We'll go down to the water in just a bit. I promise." On the promise and a treat that Tara had produced out of her pocket, Connal walked into the house to continue with the tour.

Since she had a good idea that the room directly from the master was another bedroom and with the same setup, Tara just did a quick glance in and added the room to her list to look at later.

Heading back into the living room, Tara saw that it was had a double set of French doors that opened to the porch and the cove. The size of the room was large, and the cathedral ceilings made it look even bigger than it was.

Tara and Connal now headed to the kitchen and the first thing she really noticed was the large island that essentially separated the kitchen from the living room. On one half of the island, six stools surrounded the end, with room to add more, if needed. On the other half of the island was a stove, with the matching wall oven directly to the left of the counter. Opposite the island and on the outside wall, was the refrigerator, sink, and dishwasher, along with more cabinets and counter space and a door. Opening the door, Tara found a large walk-in pantry.

"This place isn't lacking in storage." The pantry was large enough to walk in and turn around, with a dog following. The three interior walls were lined with shelves at varying heights. "We're never going to be able to fill this pantry up, Connal. That's just too much food and stuff for one human and a little dog."

Stepping out of the pantry and closing the door, Tara noticed another door on the other side of the fridge.

"What the—?" Where Tara expected to see the outside when she opened the door, she saw a large tunnel that was completely enclosed. "Oh, a breezeway! Freaking sweet! And look, a mudroom and laundry room in here too."

Shaking her head in amazement, Tara and Connal headed out to see what was attached to the breezeway. The first door they came to was on the left, and after opening it, she found the four-car garage that they had parked in front of. "Nice." Closing the door, they continued to the next door, this one on the right side of the breezeway.

"I didn't see this building when we were outside. Let's see what's behind door number two, Connal." Opening the door and letting Connal in, Tara followed and actually let out a whoop. "An indoor pool! This would make Michael Phelps whimper, Connal! Let's finish seeing what else we bought, then we can come back and really look around."

Heading back to the breezeway and turning right, they walked to the end of the breezeway and to another door. "I bet this is the barn/not barn we saw when we were outside." Tara opened the door and walked in. "Holy hell! I think this is an indoor freaking riding arena, Connal. What the hell are we going to do with a riding arena?"

After Connal had finished exploring the arena and digging in the dirt, he joined Tara as she strolled from the dirt arena to the outside area surrounding the arena. On the garage side of the arena, they found four stalls, along with a large tack room and a door. Opening up the door, Tara saw that the door led to the outside. Closing and relocking the door, they continued to the long outside wall and saw three large slider doors. The other short side of the arena was a mirror of the first, but where the first had a tack room, this side had an office. The door on this side didn't open to the outside, though. This one opened to another breezeway. "Jesus. This is ridiculous," Tara said to Connal. But after glancing down, she saw that he wasn't with her. "Connal! Where are you? Come here," she called, refusing to panic. The arena was all closed up so he couldn't get out. Just as she was getting ready to call him again, she heard him bark.

Walking back into the arena, she watched and chuckled at Connal, who was currently upside down, rolling around in the dirt.

"Keep it up, little dog, and there will be a bath for you on our first night here." That promptly stopped the rolling, and Connal came back over to sit and smile, tongue hanging out of the side of his mouth. "You think you're cute, don't you? Come on, there's another breezeway to explore."

Connal followed Tara through the door into the breezeway, then stopped at another door. "God, I'm going to have to make a map if we have many more doors or breezeways, Connal." Stepping through the door into this building, she soon saw this was where the guts of the compound were located. Several water heaters, generators, heat pumps and air conditioning units took up a fair amount of space in the back corner of the building. "Ah, boring stuff. We'll look at this later, Connal. I want to see the water now."

Heading back into the arena, then to the breezeway to the house, they came back into the kitchen. This time they didn't stop to look at anything. It was time to see the number one thing that had drawn her to buying this place. The ocean. Stepping out of the doors off the living room, they walked to the water's edge and stood. She owned a cove!

Shaking her head at the enormity of the property she had bought, she smiled.

The cove was essentially a huge horseshoe and at the inlet, there was a jetty of jagged rocks which seemed to be a natural break since the water was calm and clear, with a slight lapping on the beach. The beach itself was a cobble beach, so walking on it would require shoes, but it was still a beach.

Tara stood there and breathed in the sea air. Closing her eyes, she let nature talk to her. She heard the tree branches brushing against one another, and she felt the salty air on her skin as well as taste the salt on the wind. Tara heard the birds calling to each other and the lazy lapping of the water. She was home.

"Let's get our stuff in the house before the bears and bigfoots and mooses get us, Connal." Connal actually stopped and looked around for said bears, bigfoots, and mooses before running to stay beside Tara. After all, he had to protect her and to do so, he needed to be close. More like she had to protect his little fuzzy butt, but that was just between them. No one else needed to know that detail.

After entering another PIN on the keypad, Tara moved her SUV into the garage. "I'm going to have to start a list of what needs to be done or found, Connal. Otherwise, I'll forget to change a code or something. Like the remote garage door opener. Need to find one of those."

Once in the garage, Tara grabbed a couple of small overnight bags and with Connal leading the way, they headed toward the door to the breezeway and then into the mudroom. She smiled. "This is just so fantastic!" Setting her first load in the middle of the mudroom, Tara went back to the garage, again with Connal leading the way.

"I'm going to have to figure out how to make you carry some of our stuff, Connal. It's not fair that I'm doing all the work." Connal's response was to run into the kitchen, then to the living room and lay down in front of the French doors, looking out to the cove.

"Well, that's just rude, little dog. Fine, stay there. It'll make this easier if you aren't a trip hazard every step of the way."

Tara continued the trips until the SUV was empty of all the suitcases and boxes that she had crammed into it. The little bit of furniture that she had kept would be delivered in the next couple of days, so they were basically moved in for now.

Standing in the middle of the house, Tara slowly turned in a circle and looked. Connal, who had deemed it safe to return to her side, followed her movements.

She had a chance to slow down and focus on the décor of the main part of the house. It was as one would expect of a house on the ocean in Maine. Beachy but not overly nautical. The colors of the walls were a blue/gray, and the floors were gray washed hardwood. The living room furniture that had come with the house fit perfectly into the decor of the living room. Simple off-whites and light blues for the upholstery and the wood accent pieces were mostly in the light gray family.

"Not seeing much I want to change so far in this room. Maybe later, but right now, I like it." That was a plus because she hated redecorating, and just the thought of having to remodel and refurnish this large house made her tummy flip.

She was brought out of her musings by a sharp, high-pitched bark. She glanced down at Connal, who was staring at her without blinking. "Ah, must be 5 PM, dinner time for the little dog. Is that what you are trying to tell me?"

Connal answered with multiple barks, along with bouncing up and down on his front feet.

"Okay, okay. I get it. Let's go find food. Can't have the poor Connal starving to death on his first night in our new house, now can we?"

Heading into the kitchen, Tara unloaded the bag that held Connal's food. "No green beans tonight, bud. But I'll put them on the grocery list. So, in light of that, you get a little bit more food."

On the mention of food, Connal's eyes lit up, and he wiggled his nub in celebration.

"Yeah, figured you would like that." As she stood there, watching Connal inhale his dinner, her stomach growled. "Hmm, now what about people food?"

Tara went to one of the boxes she had brought in from the mudroom and started unpacking the food staples she had brought along; cereal, Pop-Tarts, cookies, several cans of soup and a variety of quick and easy dinners.

"Really need to work on a grocery list. This is fine for tonight and for the occasional meal, but I need real food soon. God, there's so much to do," Tara told Connal as she opened up a pop tart. Munching, Tara grabbed one of the lighter bags from the mudroom and headed into the bedroom that would be hers. Connal followed, being a good little corgi vacuum, licking up any of the crumbs that might have fallen to the floor.

As Tara and Connal came back out of the bedroom for another bag, there was a knock on the front door. "Bears, moosies, and bigfoots don't knock, do they? We don't know anyone here, so I don't know who would be here. And how did they get through the gate?" Tara asked Connal as she went to the front door.

Looking through the peephole in the door, Tara saw a heavy-set woman with shoulder-length silver hair, standing there. "Well, at least it's not a bear," she muttered to herself as she opened the door to a woman that she would guess was in her late 50s or early 60s. "Can I help you?"

Taking that as an invitation to come in, the woman brushed past Tara and stopped to take off her coat, hat, gloves, and boots and took the time to put them in the closet.

"Hi and welcome! I'm Barb Ohlson. My husband, Bill and I live on the property in the little cabin just before the gate." Holding out her hand, she waited for Tara to shake it.

Tara hesitated a moment and then took her hand, returning the handshake. She could now see that Barb had blue eyes and a diamond-shaped face, with a nose that was slightly flat. "Um, hi. I'm Tara McDowell. And this is Connal."

"Oh, isn't he," Barb waited for Tara to confirm that Connal was a boy, "adorable. Come here, little guy."

But instead of going over to Barb for the prerequisite tummy rubs, Connal came to sit between Tara and Barb, and just looked at Barb. Tara looked down at him and found it interesting that her friendly little dog would rather sit and basically stare down a new person. Shaking her head to it, Tara looked at Barb. "It's been a long couple of days, he's tired."

"Yes, of course," Barb responded with just a touch of primness to the tone, then picked up the bags she had brought in and headed towards the kitchen, talking nonstop the entire time.

Tara couldn't get a word in, and if she could, she wasn't

sure she would even know what to say to this woman that had just barged right on into her new house.

She followed Barb into the kitchen and watched as she proceeded to put the groceries away that she had brought in with her. And she was still talking.

Tara felt like a fish, opening and closing her mouth. She had no idea what or where to start with this woman. So, she grabbed another Pop-Tart and leaned against the counter, waiting for an opportunity to jump into the conversation and ask just why she was there. As she got ready to take her first bite, Barb snatched the Pop-Tart of out of her hand and threw it into the trash.

"What the hell?" Tara finally found her voice.

"Grown women don't eat Pop-Tarts for dinner," Barb responded, turning around to continue putting groceries away.

"Well, this grown-assed woman does," Tara shot back, holding out her hand. "Now give me back my damn Pop-Tarts."

Barb stood with the box of Pop-Tarts behind her back, holding it hostage and stared at Tara. Tara stood with one hand on her hip, the other out, waiting for Barb to return the box, all the while staring her down.

Connal sat between the two women and looked back and forth between the two of them. After a moment, he stood up and moved closer to Barb, then barked, which caused Barb to break her stare to look down at him.

Silently, Barb put the box on the counter, walked to the refrigerator and opened it. She took a container out of the fridge and heading to the microwave, she began heating up whatever was in the container.

Tara, still holding the box of Pop-Tarts she had snatched from the counter, went to the refrigerator and opened it. There was food in it. Not just staples. But real food. Home cooked food in plastic containers.

Closing the door and turning to Barb. "Did you do this, Barb?" Setting the box of Pop-Tarts down of the counter, Tara stepped closer to Barb.

"Well, I'm the housekeeper and cook for you, so yes. And you're welcome," was Barb's clipped reply.

"Wait, housekeeper and cook? I don't remember hiring you."

Barb stopped what she was doing and turned to give Tara the perfect school teacher stare of disapproval. "I come with the property. So does my husband, Bill. He's the handyman. I was telling you all of that before, but apparently, you weren't listening."

Tara fought the urge to duck her head. She was a grown adult, in her own house. She wouldn't be ashamed that she hadn't listened to this woman that had charged into her house and somehow took over.

The microwave chose that moment to beep, which cut the unspoken power play between the two women. Barb turned and removed the container from the microwave, put it on the kitchen island and stared at Tara.

This time, Tara let Barb win the battle since she hadn't realized how hungry she was until she smelled what Barb had heated up. Sighing, Tara sat down and would have whimpered if she had been alone. The plate in front of her held three of the most beautiful stuffed cabbages she had ever seen. Smiling, Tara took a bite and promptly closed her eyes. "Thank you," she mumbled around the next bite.

Barb returned the smile and went back to straightening up the kitchen while Tara finished her first real meal in a long time.

Tara woke up the next morning to the smell of coffee, eggs, and bacon. Stretching, she got out of bed, went to the French doors and opened the blinds to enjoy her cove. Smiling, she took a deep breath and stood there. "This just might work."

Looking around, there was no Connal to be found, but she would bet a fair amount of her savings that he was in the kitchen helping Barb make breakfast.

"Connal quit begging," she scolded the dog as she walked toward the kitchen island and sat down. "Sorry about him. He is a mooch. Just tell him no and go lay down, and sometimes he'll listen," she said laughing while rubbing Connal's head with her foot.

"He still won't let me pet him, but he hasn't attacked me either. And he won't take the bacon I offered, in the way as a bribe. He's just been sitting here, watching me. It's sort of unnerving. Now eat," Barb demanded as she set a plate of bacon, eggs, toast, and home fries down in front of Tara. "Coffee?"

"Oh God, yes! Black thanks, and keep it coming. This smells and looks amazing. I appreciate you making me breakfast. And I don't want to sound mean, but I would appreciate it if this is a one-time thing. Nothing against you, but I don't know you. It's weird to have a stranger wake you up to breakfast," Tara added while holding a piece of bacon up.

"I just thought it would be nice to wake up to a nutritious breakfast, your first morning in your new home. I have no intention of just walking in whenever I want. It's your house, after all."

Tara chose to ignore the hurt undertones in Barb's voice because Tara knew she had every right to say what she had said. "So, tell me about the property Barb. You said that you and your husband live in the house before the gate? Does Bill take care of all the maintenance? Is there cable out here? Wi-Fi? I vaguely remember something about the house having a security system so I would love to know how that works. Where is the closest town? Is there a good pizza place close?" Tara rapid fired questions at Barb in between bites of her breakfast.

Barb poured herself a cup of coffee and sitting down across from Tara, smiled thinly and in what Tara could only describe as her best school teacher prissy voice, answered her questions. "As you are aware, you bought 40 acres of property along with the water rights of the cove. What you might not know, is that your property butts up to a state park to the south. You will never have neighbors in that direction. To the north of your property, there is a 100-acre piece of land that is privately owned. The owner doesn't live on the land, though. He uses it for recreational use and hunting only. You are extremely secluded out here. It makes for a nice, quiet living. The house and its buildings sit on a six-acre semi-cleared piece of land, and is surrounded by dense forest on three sides and, of course, the cove.

"Bill and I live on two acres of cleared land just outside the gate. You would have seen the turn off when you drove in last evening. We have a lovely two bedroom, 1 ½ bath ranch style cabin. It's on your property, so if you want to come over and see it, it's your right." Barb stopped to sip her coffee and look at Tara over the rim of the cup. When Tara offered no comments or questions, Barb continued.

"Bill takes care of all the maintenance for you. He is a jack-of-all-trades and can fix pretty much anything. There are generators to supply power to the house and riding arena, as well as the garage and the pool building. We have cable, Wi-Fi, and phone out here, and the reception is great.

"On your question about security, I can give you the basics, but there is a binder with the manual and all the current codes here in the island." Barb reached over in front of Tara and tapped on the front of the drawer. "That should provide you with any and all of the technical side of the security system. I can tell you that the entire 40 acres are fenced. As you saw, there is a privacy gate to get on the property, and the fence around the property is all wired, so if someone comes on, you'll know it. There are also multiple security cameras throughout the property. I'm not sure where they all are, but again," she nodded to the drawer in front of Tara, "it's all in the binder."

"The closest town is Eriksport, which is about 15 minutes north. Just turn right out of the driveway, and you can't miss it. And the best pizza place in this part of Maine is Gwenn's Pizza. She has amazing wings and the coldest beer in the area. I think that answers that set of questions. What else do you want to know?" Barb leaned back on her stool, took a drink of her coffee, and waited for Tara to ask more questions.

Tara stood up and looked at Barb. "Why don't I get dressed and if you wouldn't mind, can you walk me around so I can get a lay of the land? I know there will be tons more questions, but I would really like to see the place, and at the moment, I can't think of anything else to ask. I'm sure that will change as we walk around, though."

Nodding her head once, Barb leaned over to pick up the dirty dishes. "That sounds like a good idea. I'll just clean up the kitchen while you get ready. Take your time. We don't rush in this part of the world."

"Are you ready?" Barb asked Tara 30 minutes later when Tara came back into the kitchen, followed closely by Connal.

"Yep," Tara replied, holding up a tablet and pen. "And I'm going to take notes. Show me, Obi Wan." At Barb's blank stare, Tara added, "Are we going outside first? If so, I'll grab Connal's leash."

"No, not yet. I figured we'd start here, in the house, then we can head outside after it's a little bit warmer. So, no need for a leash or a coat for this part of the tour."

Barb cleared her throat and, in her best teaching voice, began. "I'm sure you did a walk through last night, but let me actually show you your house. As you know, this is the kitchen. Standard galley kitchen. All new appliances. All stainless steel. The kitchen island can seat six comfortably. There is plenty of storage in the cabinets and the large walk-in pantry.

"Over here is the dining area. You can easily seat 12, but the table is currently set to seat eight. The table was custom made from wood harvested on the property, and it stores the extra table leaves when they aren't needed." Barb turned to face the living room, and much like an airline stewardess, moved her arms and hands to point to either side of the house.

"There is a hallway on either side of the house, which leads to the four bedrooms of the house. The two bedrooms on the kitchen side of the house have views of the wood line, but other than that, they are a mirror to the other rooms off the living room. I trust that you have seen those bedrooms?" On Tara's nod, "Well, then there is no need to go into those rooms then. The two bedrooms on the living room side have cove views, as I'm sure you are aware of since one is the master bedroom.

"Here, in the living room, the ceilings are 12-foot cathedrals. You have a fireplace just over there on the right of the double set of French doors. The fireplace is both gas and wood capable, and it warms up your main living area extremely well."

Barb turned to look at Tara. "As I'm sure you have explored your master bedroom, I don't feel the need to show it to you." At Tara's nod of agreement, Barb led them back into the kitchen.

Tara was quiet for a moment finishing up her notes. She wanted to remember to see how many of the other doors had alarm motion sensors, like the ones she noticed on the living room French doors. She looked up and smiled. "This is great Barb, but I need another coffee before we continue."

"Of course. We can take it with us." Barb took two travel mugs out of the cabinet above the coffee pot and after filling them up led the way to the door to the mudroom and breezeway.

Stepping into the mudroom area, Barb started up again with the tour. "This is the mudroom/laundry room/storage room. The fifth bathroom is also in here, with a shower which could be converted to a tub/shower combo if you wanted to use this room to wash Connal."

Tara hated to admit it, but the way that Barb talked at her annoyed the hell out of her. If she hadn't been a school teacher, Tara would eat Connal's kibble for a week. Glancing down at him, Tara saw that Connal was staying between Barb and her. His body language let her know that he wasn't relaxed and having fun. He was on duty. Reaching down, Tara rubbed his ears and only then did his nub wiggle, and he gave her an open-mouthed smile.

Barb had stopped and stood there, with her arms crossed and her lips pursed, while Tara was petting Connal. After she was sure that Tara was paying attention, she continued. "As I'm sure you are aware, there is a breezeway that connects all the outbuildings to the house. It's very well loved in the winter when there are feet of snow outside. So much easier to move around if you don't have to bundle up and dig a path to whichever building you want to go to."

Opening up the first door they came to, Barb stepped in and waited for Connal then Tara to follow her in. "The garage is insulated and climate controlled, which is nice in the winter. You don't have to bundle up to go to the garage to get something." Walking over to a shelf on the right side of the breezeway door, Barb gestured then picked up a remote. "Here is where the garage door openers are kept. This one is programmed to the bay that you are parked in."

Tara took the remote and stuck it in her pocket. She would put it in the SUV later. She didn't have her keys on her and didn't feel up to dealing with Barb's prissy attitude if she took the time to go get her keys.

"There is also a keypad outside if you forget the garage door opener. The code is 553321, with the last number being the door that you want to open. The doors are 1 to 4 from left to right when facing the garage." Barb pulled a binder off the shelf that the remotes were on. "This is the manual for the garage door openers if you wanted to change the code. The current code is also listed in there."

Tara made a quick note to indeed change the codes, and then noted the location of the camera and security sensor that was positioned just over the door to the breezeway. Looking up, she nodded to Barb to continue.

"If we head back to the breezeway and go to the door on the right, you will come to the gym/indoor pool area. This building is also climate controlled with air conditioning and heating. The pool water is set at a constant 83 degrees, so it's always perfect swimming temperature. The depth of the pool is 12 feet, at the deep end. To the left is the hot tub and sauna.

And on the right side of the pool is the gym equipment with a treadmill, stair stepper, and a bike. There are also various loose weights. This building is all windows so that you can enjoy the view while you swim, ride, step or whatever. If that doesn't suit you, there are privacy screens that you can engage." Barb had walked over to the door to the breezeway. Tara was not surprised to see a shelf with another binder on it. Beside it was a series of switches, which were each labeled with their purpose.

"Let me guess. The binder has everything I would ever need to know about the equipment in here?"

Lips pulled thin, Barb just looked at Tara, then sniffed and turned back to the door.

Tara was getting rather bored with Barb's superior attitude, so she purposely walked away from Barb and took her time walking around the area, taking various notes. She saw that like the garage, the gym had a camera and security sensor over the door. When she and Connal walked back toward Barb, Barb turned and picked up where she left off.

"Going back to the breezeway and turning right, we come to the riding arena. Again, climate controlled with heat and air conditioning. You have eight stalls, four on each side of the riding arena. There is also a tack room on the left side. You have a bonus room, it used to be an office, on the right side."

"Did the previous owner have horses?"

"No. If we come this way, we come to a little breezeway that attaches to the equipment garage. In here, is all the equipment needed to maintain a property this size. This is Bill's heaven on earth," Barb finally smiled and chuckled. "There is a variety of riding tractors, mowers, snow blowers, tillers, etc. All sorts of equipment that is needed out here. You also have several utility vehicles for getting around the place; a Gator, golf cart, and four wheelers. There is a cherry picker for any sort of high maintenance that needs to be done, clearing of branches, removal of trees, etc. It's been used in the past to hang Christmas lights as well.

"This building is also the home of all the guts of the

property. You have water heaters, generators, air conditioning and heating equipment and basically, every other piece of equipment that keeps your complex running smoothly." Barb stopped for a moment to let Tara catch up on her notes. When Tara looked up and smiled, Barb led the way back to the door and just motioned to the shelf with yet another binder on it. Tara nodded her acknowledgment and shook her head. At least the previous owner had been OCD enough to have everything organized. It was rather annoying.

"The breezeways are also heated and cooled. So, the house, breezeway, and the outbuildings are all climate controlled and secured, as I'm sure you noticed. All the doors are alarmed, and there are motion detectors in all the buildings. I do know that all the sensors are set for five feet off the floor so Connal or any other animal won't be setting them off. Unless he climbs?" Barb looked down at Connal, then back at Tara, questioning.

Tara chuckled at that. "He does have some mountain goat in him. But I'll leave the sensors alone for right now. He really shouldn't be anywhere I'm not." Barb nodded once, then led the way back to the kitchen.

"That concludes the tour of the main buildings of your complex. Why don't we take a bathroom break, get a coffee refill, and then I'll take you to the cove and the boat house," Barb said.

"That sounds good. I have to say that I'm really impressed with the security I've seen so far. This place is like Fort Knox. What did the previous owner do to warrant this level of isolation and security?" Tara asked and was promptly pinned with one of the coldest stares she had ever seen. She could actually feel the chill in the air.

"The previous owner is a subject that I will NOT discuss. Now, if you'll excuse me, we'll continue the tour in ten minutes," Barb quietly answered then turned on her heel to go out to the mudroom.

"Wow. I think I hit a big, ugly nerve there, Connal. It definitely has my Spidey sense tingling," Tara whispered.

Exactly ten minutes later, Barb handed Tara the refilled travel mug. "Now would be the time to put on your coat, hat, gloves, and boots and leash your dog, if you so wish." Since Barb was already prepared for outside, she stood at the living room French doors, tapping her foot. As soon as she saw Tara and Connal heading in her direction, she stepped out onto the porch.

"The porch is a full wrap around, and each of the bedrooms has access to it," Barb said while walking down to the cove.

"The cove is protected by rocky cliffs that form natural jetties. You have the tides, and they are very pronounced, so you need to be careful until you get used to them. One benefit of the big tide changes is there is always a chance of finding sea glass and sea shells on your beach walks. There is a tide chart on the fridge, and I update it weekly so that you will know when is the best time to find sea treasures. The beach itself is a cobble beach, with coarse sand. It's not a good barefoot beach, and there is usually a fair amount of seaweed that washes in. But it's still your own beach and cove. I must warn you that the water is cold. Always. Even in the summer. So, be careful about that for you and your boy there. Folks have died from hypothermia in the middle of summer up here. Might be wise to invest in a wetsuit if you are going to do any kayaking or canoeing."

Walking toward the right side of the horseshoe cove, Barb continued. "Over here is the dock and boat house. The boat house is large enough to store various water toys; kayaks, seadoos, canoes, and the like. It also has a boat lift for maintenance on a boat, if you decide to get one. Of course, the boat house is also climate controlled."

Barb was in non-stop talking mode, fast and curt, so Tara just listened. She had hit a nerve with the question about the previous owner, and she knew it.

Barb led the way back to the middle of the cove, and there she stopped and sighed. "I love this view. There's just something about an ocean to calm you."

Tara, Connal, and Barb stood there, enjoying the view of the cove. It was cold, and the breeze coming off the water was frigid, but it was fresh and alive. Connal's nose was working overtime, smelling all sorts of smells that were new to him.

Smiling, Tara leaned down to pet him and enjoy the cove with him. Looking out she could just make out fishing boats heading in or out for the day. They weren't close enough to really see well, but occasionally, voice or laughter could be heard from one of the boats.

"I'm going to have to buy a telescope." Barb smiled in response and nodded. Tara took that as the possible beginning of the thawing of the ice wall that Barb had erected.

In unison, Tara, Connal, and Barb turned around and slowly walked back to the house.

Once inside, Barb went to the kitchen to make up a lunch platter, and Tara and Connal headed to her bedroom.

As Tara made short work of unpacking her clothes and toiletries she talked to Connal, who could have cared less since he was very comfortable in the middle of the king-sized bed. Upside down and with all four little stubs in the air and snoring. Well, at least she could say she was talking to Connal. Better than talking to herself.

"We lucked out, buddy. This place is gorgeous and big and quiet and ours. Now we just have to figure out what we want to do with it and what we want to be when we grow up. Do I want to find some sort of job out here? It would probably have to be a telecommuting job. I don't know if I want to do that, though. I don't know what I want to do and it's frustrating, buddy."

Tara stopped from hanging her clothes in the closet and looked in the mirror. Playing with her short hair, that she had recently got cut into a pixie cut, she saw just the first few hints of gray. Leaning closer to the mirror, she saw the beginnings of crows-feet around her dark brown eyes. Her mama's eyes, that's what people always told her. She had a round face, with a straight nose and full lips that she had always classified as decent. She didn't see herself as pretty or beautiful, but easy on the eyes. Her cheekbones were courtesy of her father's people, as was her black hair. She was an interesting mix of Native American, Irish, Welsh, and English, with just a smattering of Scandinavian and German thrown into her DNA. Taking her study of herself down to her body, Tara sighed. She was 5 foot 3 inches tall, and heavy set and she hated it. Tara turned from the mirror and looked at Connal.

"Jesus! I'm 45 years old, and I feel like I'm more lost now than I was when I was 18 and just starting out in the world. Nothing really seems to thrill me or make me excited about trying it. I know, I need to relax and quit overthinking it. Something will come to me, it always does. Until then, we'll just sit and eat bonbons."

Connal had been ignoring Tara during much of the conversation, but at the mention of eating, his eyes started tracking Tara.

"You are such a food whore," Tara told him while walking over to the bed and lying down beside her best friend. "Time for corgi cuddles. Be a good boy now, I need snuggles. It's not all about you, little dog."

Connal grumbled and mumbled about the horror of being cuddled and loved on, but he also didn't try to get away, and there was the occasional nose bump to Tara's nose as a thank you for the belly rubs.

"And what about Barb? I'm going to whisper since she's still here. She seems okay, I guess. But I don't think I like her much. She's very prissy and prim when she's talking to me. And she's very good at putting on the hurt face if she doesn't get her way." Rubbing Connal's belly, Tara looked at Connal. "You don't like her that much, do you?" Connal's answer was a small growl deep down in his throat. "Yeah, I didn't think so. Just don't bite her, okay?"

Connal, who was now on his side and facing Tara, answered with a series of grumbles and huffs. Along with a lick to Tara's chin.

"I'm going to have to see how long the contract for Barb and Bill is in the house papers and then be a grown up and sit down to talk to her. There's going to have to be some changes about her just coming in and out. That would be expected, right? A new owner, new rules. I hate being an adult sometimes. You've got the life, bud."

Connal was Tara's lifeline. Her best buddy. Her confidant. That would seem weird to most people, but then most people liked other people and had friends. Tara didn't, and she was all right with that. She was an introvert, plain and simple. Oh, she liked people, but in small doses. People had a tendency of wearing her out, emotionally and mentally. She felt other people's emotions more than the average person, and that caused her to burn out around people faster. And when that happened, she needed her cave time as her mother had called it. She would retreat to her room and read and recharge her batteries. If she didn't get a chance to do that, she became irritated and short and standoffish. She wasn't an easy person to really get to know because she didn't let her mask down for many people. Only those who were very close to her. Which she didn't have many of. And that was her choosing. She did better alone. It was safer and easier for her mental and emotional state. And she was happy with her life. Mostly.

Yes, she had married. And she had loved, and still loved, Wyatt. But now she considered him a friend. A close friend. He was family. But she wasn't in love with him any longer. She was upset about the divorce, yes. But more about the loss of many years of effort put into something that didn't work. She hated losing. And to her, a divorce was admitting defeat on something. They had separated mutually and on good terms and still texted, emailed, and called each other. It was weird, she knew. But it worked for them. Granted, Wyatt had wanted to get her head examined when she had finally told him that she had purchased property in Maine. Online and with a 'Buy it Now' button. She would have to get around to taking some pictures and email him, so he didn't worry about her, or send the men with the huggie jackets to take her away.

CHAPTER TWO

The next two weeks were filled with unpacking and rearranging furniture to meet Tara's needs. The rest of her household goods showed up, and that took some time to unbox her items and to find each item's place in the new house.

There were also many walks around the property, beach glassing along the cove, swimming and using the gym equipment and generally getting the lay of the land. All of this was done with just her and Connal.

After the initial show of the property, Barb was not around as much. She seemed to like cooking the meals at her cabin, then bringing the finished product to Tara's. She would come over to the house on Thursday and Sunday to clean, and drop off groceries and meals on Thursday, Sunday, and Tuesday. But Tara didn't really see Barb all that much which she was all right with since it gave her time to settle into her routine without an audience. Tara knew she still had to discuss these arrangements with Barb, but it wasn't that hot of a priority at the moment.

Now with dinner finished, for both Connal and herself, and the dishes in the dishwasher, Tara took her cup of tea to the sofa in the living room. Turning on the TV for the white noise, she got comfy on the couch and picked up her laptop.

Connal immediately jumped up to settle against her side, and after some rearranging of pillows and Tara's elbow, he settled down with his head on the laptop.

"Are you all comfy, now? Ready to check our email? I bet if you got email, yours would be more exciting than mine." Opening up her email, she saw that she had very few emails. "And nothing. Shocker. Let's play on Facebook and see what folks are up to tonight."

Tara spent some time scrolling through her news feed, liking and commenting on various posts. She was about to log off and play toys with Connal when she received a private message from an online friend. Upon opening the private message, she was welcomed with the saddest little corgi face she had ever seen.

"Oh, Connal, look at this poor baby. She was turned into a shelter because her *family* didn't have time for her anymore. And she's in Maine, Connal. About two hours away. What do you think? Nothing is holding us back from adding to the pack. Well, other than you."

Connal lifted his head and looked at the corgi on the screen. He slowly looked up at Tara and put his paw on her hand, then looked at the corgi on the laptop.

"Do you want her as a sister? Are you sure? Will you be a good brother?"

Connal stared at Tara, then at the picture of the corgi on the laptop. Sitting up now, he leaned over to lick the screen, then turned his head back to Tara and barked in her face.

"Geez, okay, let's see what we can do." Tara laughed and after rubbing his ears, exchanged a series of replies with her friend about where the girl was, and in the process found out that a rescue was pulling her tomorrow, and that her online friend was friends with the rescue owner. Before she knew it, Tara had agreed to go to the rescue tomorrow to meet the little girl.

"Well, damn if that didn't happen fast. Guess we're going on a road trip tomorrow Connal."

Tara was not new to corgis. She had corgis before Connal

and had it in her mind to eventually get Connal a brother or sister. But the timing was never right. Taking care of her parents, Wyatt not being a big fan of dogs, her parents dying, the divorce. There had always been something that had stopped her. But now? Connal was a good boy. So, why the hell not?

Early the next morning, Connal and Tara were up and getting ready for their road trip to see Connal's potential new sister. They were to meet the rescue contact at 11 AM, and Tara didn't want to be late. She hated being late, and she absolutely despised someone else being late on her. She didn't understand why everyone couldn't stick to a time if it were scheduled.

Tara didn't want to admit it, but she was excited about possibly bringing a new dog home. She was trying to keep calm about it, but the little corgi girl was already a member of the family in her mind. That was unless Connal and the girl decided they didn't like each other.

"Okay, bud. Let's go meet your new sister. You're going to be a good boy and not be the least bit snarky with her, right? Hey, are you listening to me?" Tara added because Connal was ignoring her, snooting bushes instead of listening to her pep talk.

As if on cue, Connal chose that moment to lift his leg and pee on a bush, all the while looking over his shoulder at her.

"Not nice, brat. That had better not be your opinion on this matter. After all, you're the one that said you wanted her."

The drive to the rescue was a nice one. Not too long, not too short. And the bonus was that it was a sunny day, so Tara took a chance that the sun equaled some warmth and put the windows down some. "Perfect time to uncorgi the car, Connal. It really is gorgeous here, isn't it? All the trees and plants are starting to bloom, and you can smell spring in the air."

She was interrupted from her musings by Mick announcing that the destination was on the left.

As they pulled into the driveway and came to a stop in front of the house, Tara decided one more discussion with Connal was in order.

"Alright, little dog. Some ground rules." Tara held Connal's head to get him to look at her. Nose to nose, Tara said, "You will be a good boy. You will not be snarky or grumpy or jealous. You will be loving and cute, and please, just to show off a bit, you will listen to me. Okay?" The answer was a series of grumbles, growls, and a burp while Tara unclipped Connal from his seat belt harness.

Just as Tara and Connal got to the front door and got ready to ring the doorbell, the door opened and out came a gaggle of corgis. All sorts of colors, sizes, shapes, wheeled, three-legged and the standard model of four legs. Poor Connal was beside himself. With all the barking and growling and arrooing, there was no way to introduce herself to the lady that stood at the door. After the initial attack, the herd of corgis went farther out into the fenced yard and with the new found quiet, the lady introduced herself.

"Hi, sorry about that. Bad timing on my part. I'm Clare. If he's friendly, he's more than welcome to join the monsters in the yard while we talk."

Tara reached down, undid the leash and Connal was gone, barking and arrooing and joining into the frapfest.

"Come on in. They're fine out there. It's fenced in, and we can watch them from the breakfast nook. Coffee?" Clare gestured to the small table with a bench and a chair.

"Please. Black, thanks." Tara took a seat on the bench where she could keep an eye on Connal.

"So, tell me about yourself Tara and why you think you would be a good home for Gizmo," Clare said after sitting down across from Tara.

"Well, I'm Tara McDowell. We just moved to Maine about three weeks ago. Bought 40 acres about two hours northeast of here, on the coast. So, there is plenty of room for the dogs to run and play and snoot and snort. I'm recently divorced and both my parents are gone. No siblings. So, Connal, and

34

hopefully Gizmo, are my family. I have some casual friends, but Connal is my life. I'm financially stable and have money in savings, God forbid one or both of the dogs need expensive medical help. And I understand the corgi mindset and love the breed. I've had several corgis as an adult and have had dogs my entire life. That's about it. Please tell me about this baby girl that her owners got rid of." Tara leaned forward on her elbows and took a sip of coffee.

Clare nodded and leaned forward to mirror Tara. "Well, the sweetie's name is Gizmo. She's eight years old. Spayed, up to date on shots and heartworm negative. She could lose some weight, but that's pretty normal for a corgi. She's a red headed tri colored. Gorgeous pup. She was taken care of and loved, which makes it so much harder to understand why they just got rid of her. Knows the basic commands; sit, stay, come, down, when she wants to know them. Again, very corgi. She's great with other dogs. Cats. Birds. Horses. Has a great little personality. Her owners didn't want her anymore, didn't give a reason, and in my book, there would be no good reason to not want her, or any dog, anymore. I'll never understand how people can throw away any animal, let alone one that's been a family member for eight years. I just don't get it," Clare grumbled before taking a sip of her coffee.

Tara nodded her head and raised her cup in a toast. "I completely agree. Pets are family. Period. I don't understand it. Never will. So, can I meet her now? See if she and Connal can be friends?"

"No need to worry about that. Connal and Gizmo are playing outside right now. Look." Turning to glance out the window, Tara saw Connal and Gizmo in the grass, neck wrestling.

"Well, I guess that answers that question. I'd like to meet her, though. Since I'm the upright that has to put up with those two," Tara remarked, as they headed outside.

Connal came over, panting and smiling when Tara called him.

"Good boy, cookies when we get home," she whispered

when she leaned down to pet his head.

Gizmo had followed Connal over and proceeded to sit on Tara's foot. Looking down, Tara saw that Gizmo was a mostly black corgi, at least on her back. Her little belly, chest and bottom halves of her legs were white, while her back end was the same color as Connal. But instead of having a black head, the black stopped halfway up her neck so that her head and ears were red. The white from her chest followed up to her chin and wrapped around to include her muzzle. And like Connal, she had a white blaze between her eyes, that ended between her ears.

Tara sat down on the ground in front of Gizmo and looked into the little girl's eyes, and that's all it took. She was in love. Gizmo must have felt the same because she stepped forward and curled herself up, as best as she could, in Tara's lap and let out a sigh. That sealed the deal for Tara. Petting Gizmo, Tara looked up at Clare. "I want her. What's the next step?"

On the drive home, Connal and Gizmo shared the back seat. Since Gizmo didn't have a seat belt harness yet, her leash was seat belted in. Both dogs were out cold, upside down, in true corgi fashion. And snoring.

"Oh, this is going to be a blast. Two corgis are better than one. I should stop at a pet store for some supplies, but I don't know this area. You know what that means, right? I get to shop online." Tara knew she was talking to herself since both dogs were sleeping, but she was excited, and she actually felt bubbly. So, she went with the feeling and talked out loud the rest of the way home.

"I want pizza. And beer," Tara announced to the two corgis sleeping on the couch. She said this into the refrigerator while trying to find something to eat. Yes, there was plenty of food in the fridge. Barb made sure of that. But Tara wanted pizza. She had been in her new home for almost a month and except for the occasional run into town for something for the pups, and the road trip to get Gizmo, she hadn't been out to eat since they had moved in. It was a Wednesday afternoon, and pizza and beer sounded good. Damn good. But to have said goodies would require getting cleaned up and going into a restaurant. With people.

"Hm. What do you think guys? Should I try to be somewhat normal and go into town, see people and get beer and pizza?"

This had always been a big issue for Tara. She didn't like to seek out social interaction, even if it was just going out to a restaurant for a meal. Granted, once she got into a social event, she usually did okay, and generally had fun. For a while at least, until the social interaction became overstimulating and that's when she would try to find a quick exit. And she always had to have this internal discussion for a fair amount of time to convince herself to actually go to the social interaction. She always felt that she had to give herself a pep talk and there were times that it was too exhausting to get herself to that point of going so she would cancel then she would feel guilty about it. That's what she was doing, and it was frustrating to her.

"It's Wednesday. At 3 PM. And it's a small town. In. Order the pizza. Grab a six pack and back in an hour? Actual people time? 20 minutes? I can do that." She kept up the pep talk since the two corgis really didn't seem to care about any of this conversation. "Okay, I'm doing this. I guess I should change into going-out-in-public clothes, huh?" Again, no response from the dogs. "Gee guys, thanks for the load of confidence. I know you don't care, just as long as there are pizza bones for you, right?" That got a response. Two heads popped up and four eyes looked at Tara.

Looking at herself in the walk-in closet mirror, Tara wondered if the old jeans, sneakers, and flannel shirt could pass as going-out-in-public clothes. "Screw it. I'm going like this. I'm not trying to impress anyone. I just want a pizza and beer."

Grabbing her keys, Tara looked over at the dogs. "You two coming?" When neither dog moved off of the couch, she chuckled. "Wow, I must have really worn you two out that you don't want to go for a car ride. I'll be back in a bit. Don't let the bears, bigfoots or moosies in."

The drive into Eriksport took the 15 minutes that Barb said it would take. The town was a true harbor town, and Tara could see the ocean to the right as she drove. As she came into town, she was stopped by a four-way intersection. While she waited her turn to continue, she saw the town's one gas station, along with police station, clinic, and school on each corner of the intersection. Glancing down the road to her left, Tara could just make out a church, funeral home, and cemetery. To her right was another road, but it didn't go far before it dead-ended into a left turn.

Continuing straight through the intersection, Tara saw that it was a small town, with the main road splitting the mom and pop stores on either side of the road. There were the usual businesses: grocery store, hardware store, general store, pet store, coffee shop, bank and pharmacy were on the left side of the road. That's where Gwenn's Pizza stood, last building on the left before you would take the road to leave town and head for Canada.

On the right side of the main road were the touristy places. Sightseeing tours to see the puffins and whales. Another one that specialized in taking tourists lobster fishing. Then the businesses that ran the usual fishing trips, along with the post office, two bed and breakfasts, a couple of gift stores, a bar, and the only other restaurant in town.

Driving slowly, Tara caught glimpses of the harbor and boats between the buildings on the right.

Parking wasn't an issue, even with it being street parking, and in no time Tara was inside Gwenn's Pizza Place, looking at the menu. She was sitting at the counter, trying to figure out what she wanted on her pizza when the waitress walked toward her.

She was a tiny thing with long, wavy red hair that reminded Tara of Maureen O'Hara in the old John Wayne movies she would watch with her parents. Add to that the green eyes and the milky white skin and she was Ireland walking towards her.

"Hi! Haven't seen you around here before. Oh! You must be the lady with the dogs that bought the old Roxbury place. I'm Gwenn Flanery, and this is my place," she said, holding out her hand.

Tara took Gwenn's hand, and hiding her disappointment in the fact that Gwenn didn't have the Irish brogue that her features screamed for her to have, returned the handshake. "Hi, I'm Tara. I didn't know that the place I bought had a name. I'm starving but everything on your menu sounds great, and the smell is killing me. And yes, I have two dogs. Corgis. Nice to meet you."

"Well, I'm not bragging, but I make the best pizza in town." Gwenn laughed. "I'm the only pizza place in town, but it's really great pizza. I would recommend a large, thin crust. Pepperoni, onion, green peppers and feta." She eyed Tara up and down like all of that was written on her.

"Damn. Nailed it. That's my go to on pizza when I don't know what I want. Done. And can I get a six pack of Coors Light to go with it? All for take out."

"Yep, can do. It'll be about 20 minutes. Sit back and relax. We aren't busy, so if you don't mind the company, I could take my break. I'd like to sit and chat you up. Get to know the newest resident of this part of Maine. If that's okay with you?" Gwenn added because she saw Tara's eyes lose some of the sparkle when she had mentioned the chatting up part.

"I'm not a big chatter. Nothing against you, I'm just not a big talker, but maybe you can tell me a bit about the place I bought. I've tried to ask Barb, but besides all the physical stuff about the property, she hasn't discussed the previous owner."

"Oh! That's a story. I'll be right back. Let me get this ticket to the kitchen. Soda?" When Tara nodded her head, Gwenn turned to head into the kitchen.

Tara was left sitting there, which was fine with her, as it gave her a chance to look the place over. It was nice. Clean. Small. But had that small town, homey feel. The wall opposite the counter had a bank of blue and beige striped booths and there were four top tables in between the counter and the booths with chairs that matched the color scheme of the booths. The walls and ceiling color reminded Tara of driftwood. Not white, but not brown or gray either. More of a mix between. It worked well with the papier–mâché lobsters and lobster traps on the walls. Just enough for you to know where you were, but not overly decorated. The wall opposite the entrance had several pinball machines. Honest to goodness, old-fashioned-'80s-style pinball machines. As she rotated back around from her survey of the place, Gwenn came back and sat a glass in front of her.

"Here ya go. Brought you a Coke. Didn't know what you would like, but Coke is usually always a safe bet." Gwenn sat down beside Tara at the counter, and after taking a long drink of her own Coke turned to look at Tara.

"Okay, so you aren't a chatterbox. I can respect that. So, saying that, let me tell you what the rumor mill has on the old owner of your property. Rumor has it that old Dr. Roxbury was half batty. Granted, she was a rich batty old woman, but still batty as hell.

"She bought the land about five years ago and made it her own Fort Knox. Built the house, added the fences and all the security and such. She didn't like, nor trust people much. At least that's how it seemed. Stayed to herself and really never was seen in public.

"Of course, that started the rumors really flying. And there were a bunch of them. She was a double agent. A Russian sleeper spy. Married to a king and ran away and was hiding. Married to the Mafia. Mass murderer. The rumors got better as time went by.

"Some of our more advanced locals," here she pointed to herself and smiled, "Googled her and found out that she was a retired professor of archaeology. A female Indiana Jones, that was what some of us called her. That really started the stories going. She was here looking for the Lost Ark, crystal skulls or pyramids. Of course, we knew none of that was true, but it's a small town, and we like to entertain ourselves." Gwenn stopped to answer a question from one of the waitresses, then turned back to Tara.

"About two years after she moved here and built the house, she had an out of town construction company come up and do something to her house. Of course, that added more to the rumors. She was all secretive about it, and she swore the company doing the work to secrecy, so she really just added more fuel to the rumor fire.

"This was all before Barb moved out there, so she knows as much about that business as the rest of us. Again, just rumors, but I did hear through the grapevine that she had work done in the master bedroom. I guess there is an office area in there." Gwenn stopped and took a drink of her soda, glancing out of the corner of her eye to see if Tara would confirm the information.

When Tara didn't comment, Gwenn continued. "So, anyway, rumors went on, and crazy old Dr. Roxbury kept to herself. Never really saw her around town at all. About two years ago, she hired Barb and Bill to help around the property, and after that, we didn't see Dr. Roxbury in town ever. Barb did all the shopping and chores for her. It was weird. I mean, I know folks like their quiet, but this was hermit quiet. That shocked everyone around these parts. Hell, from what Barb and Bill said, they rarely saw her, and they lived on the same property. Pretty much all the communication was done via email or text. Just weird. Anyway, it was poor Bill that found her dead."

On Tara's gasp, Gwenn stopped for another sip of her soda. She loved telling a story, and she had figured that no one had told Tara about the death on her property. "You didn't know? I guess the real estate agent didn't tell you then. That's just crappy. Yeah, Bill found her dead, just about four months ago. Floating in the cove. The sheriff said she drowned and Bill said there was a massive wound to her head. Some folks figured she slipped on the rocks at the cove, then fell in and drowned. Then there were rumors that the head injury looked like a gunshot wound and that she offed herself. We'll probably never know. But it's just all sad and weird. Oh, now,

I didn't mean to scare you," Gwenn said, putting her hand over Tara's. "Let me get your pizza and beer for you."

Holy shit! I bought a freaking crime scene. Well, maybe not a crime scene since it doesn't appear to have been ruled a homicide, but it's a mystery at the very least. And she was an archaeologist. How freaking cool is that? The death on the property does explain why the property was so far below market value. Tara cut off her internal dialogue as Gwenn came back out with the pizza and beer.

"How much do I owe you?"

"No, this one is on the house. Welcome to the neighborhood. Hope to see you more. Come in anytime. It's nice to see someone back on the Roxbury property. And it's great to have new blood in town." Gwenn laid her hand on Tara's arm and squeezed, then smiled and turned back to the kitchen.

"Oh my God. I can't believe we ate all of that. We need to move, you two. Otherwise, we'll just all fall asleep and wake up with tummy aches from eating so much," Tara told the two stuffed dogs at her feet.

Laughing at their lack of movement, she got up and headed to her bedroom. She had purposely waited until after she ate to go look at the office in her bedroom. "Wonder what Dr. Roxbury had done in there."

When Tara entered the office, she stopped at the doorway. She had been in and out of the office a couple of times, but not to actually look at it. Now, she took her time to take in the space.

The walls were gray-washed shiplap. At least the walls that could be seen since the entire shared wall of the bedroom was covered by floor-to-ceiling bookcases with Dr. Roxbury's books still on the shelves. Tons of books. "Well, she loved to read, that's for sure."

Looking to the left of the door, Tara saw the wall was home to a dark brown, microfiber sofa. Beside the sofa, was an end table that looked like it might have been made out of the same wood as the dining table.

Opposite the sofa and end table, the area was dedicated to a kitchenette.

But the one item that took demand of the room was the desk. It was huge. Gorgeous, old, and mahogany with a marble desktop.

Tara noticed that unlike most of the house that had been devoid of the small personal items, the office was not. This room was as if the old owner was still coming home. There were little treasures on the book shelves. A paperweight from Washington D.C. here, a snowglobe from Texas there.

Stepping into the office, Tara went to the bookshelf. "Let's see what Dr. Roxbury liked to read." Studying the books, Tara followed the titles of several with her finger. "Okay, shocker. Archaeology textbooks, research papers, journals, and magazines. Plenty of various theory books. Prehistoric, historic, archaic. The typical collection of an archaeologist. Very similar to mine. So, what was your specialty, Roxbury? First glance, nothing. But, let's see what is missing. No marine or shipwreck studies. So you bought property on the ocean and had no interest in nautical archaeology. Okay. I can believe that. I just did the same thing, and I have no interest whatsoever in water digging. I'm seeing generalized historical. But no real history for this area. Curiouser and curiouser. Ah, look at this. An entire shelf on prehistoric studies in this area. So, you liked the old stuff, huh? Good. So do I."

Tara walked over to the desk and sat down and looked at the desk. It was old, she could see that. And it had been well used at one time. But not now because there was nothing on the desk. No computer or monitor, not even a stapler or pen. Opening the top drawer, she again found nothing.

"Odd. Let's see what the other drawers have in them." After opening and closing the six drawers in the desk, she found every drawer was empty. Not even a paper clip could be found. "Okay, so all your books and your other belongings are still in here, but your entire desk is empty. That's officially weird." Tara stood up and walked around the desk to the mini kitchen.

The mini kitchen was just that. A small countertop, with a sink and a cabinet above and below. On the countertop, there was a Keurig coffee pot, K-Cups, and microwave and below the countertop was a mini fridge. Opening the cabinets above, she found canned soups, creamer, sweetener, and coffee cups, along with a canister of what looked like loose tea leaves.

Opening the lid of the canister, Tara took a sniff and then wrinkled up her nose. "Well, that smells like death. Who would drink this? Maybe it tastes better than it smells. Okay, well stocked and makes having a coffee or a snack easy if I'm in here working for any amount of time."

Turning back around, Tara looked past the desk, to the other side of the room. There, on the sofa, Connal and Gizmo sat watching her.

"Finally decided to join the party, huh? About time. So, the entire office is lived in. She has her books, knickknacks, and a fully stocked mini kitchen, but the desk is completely void of anything. Either she hid her real work, or someone cleaned out that desk."

As she stood there, leaning against the counter of the kitchenette and waiting on the cup of coffee she had started, she looked again at the desk. This time, she looked at the floor and that's when she saw it. She pushed off the counter, walked over and got on her knees. Which promptly brought the pups over to see what she was doing.

Rubbing both furry heads, Tara spoke to Connal and Gizmo. "See these? These are scratch marks. Not big ones, but definitely scratch marks. The kind of scratch marks something heavy being slid around would make. Something heavy, like a mahogany desk." Tara touched at the corner of the desk.

"There's damage here guys. Not a lot. But this desk has been slid around." Getting back to her feet, she pushed on the desk. "Yeah, that's what I thought, you weigh a ton, don't you?" she mumbled. "Okay, let's put some muscle into it."

Tara pushed, pulled, grunted, and cussed at the desk long

enough that the coffee that she had brewed grew cold. Sitting on the couch to rest and drinking the cooled off coffee, she spoke to the desk. "Fine, I call Uncle. For now. But now that I know that there is something about you and a rumor that some sort of construction was done in this area. I'm not giving up. I love a good mystery. Why else would I have become an archaeologist? You've won this round, but I'll beat you, Mr. Desk." Tara stood up, slowly and moaned. "I need a swim and hot soak after that. Back didn't like that. Come on you two loaves, it's time to work off some of those pizza bones."

Tara and the desk battled on and off for the next three days. She tried pushing, pulling, prying, cussing, hitting and kicking the desk, but it refused to move.

"What the hell?" Tara cursed during the third day of the desk battle. "Why won't you move?" She grunted out each word with a corresponding push on the desk. Giving up, she slid to the floor to lean against the enemy.

Connal and Gizmo took that as a sign to come over and get pets from Tara.

"I don't get it, guys. There are scratch marks. The desk is scuffed. It has to have been moved. But why won't it move? It's heavy and big, but damn it to hell. Come on!" Tara knew she was too old and an adult, but she seriously considered having an honest to goodness hissy fit, with kicking and screaming for just a moment.

"Okay, back to basics. Let's look at the scratch marks, again. That's a rubbed place, right?" She was back on her hands and knees, looking at the scratches on the floor. She had to move Connal's nose out of the way to look at the scratches. The scratches were evenly spaced and dirty. Very dirty.

"If this desk had been moved, wouldn't the scratches be odd and semi clean?" Turning her eyes to the scuffs on the edges of the desk. "Huh, they don't match the placement of the scratches on the floor. And they've been waxed over with furniture polish. A lot. These aren't new either. I think it's a freaking diversion. I don't think it moves."

Tara got back to her feet and started running her hands over the desk. Under the lip of the desktop. Over the top of the desk. Knocking and tapping along the way, which caused Connal and Gizmo to softly bark or boof at each knock or tap. "Will you two knock it off. It's me. Okay, nothing on the front or sides."

Moving around, she sat down at the desk. Repeating the process, knocking, tapping and running her hands over the desk. Trying to feel, see or hear something that didn't fit. She continued this process on all the drawers, sides and under the desk.

An hour later, Tara leaned back. "Damn it to hell. Okay, fine. Break time before I blow this stupid assed desk up."

After eating a forced lunch and a walk on the beach with the pups, Tara was again standing in front of the evil desk an hour later. "Okay, let's look at the floor again." Tara knelt down and slowly, methodically worked every inch in and around the desk but found nothing that felt wrong.

She sat under the desk and shook her head. "What am I missing? This can't be this hard."

Closing her eyes and breathing deeply to calm down, she finally felt it. It was small, very small, but it was there. A cool draft of air coming *up* from under the desk. Opening her eyes, she smiled. There was empty space below the office which was odd because the entire house was on a concrete slab. The entire house, minus the office, apparently. Tara just had to figure out how to open up the space to get to the empty space below.

"Okay, I've tried to manually move that desk, and it's not going to happen. So, if I had put a secret room in my house, I would have installed some sort of opening mechanism. Let's look for that."

As what was becoming the norm for Connal and Gizmo, they were on the couch and alternating between napping and watching Tara. They currently were tracking Tara as she got up and she moved her attention to the bookshelves. Systematically, she touched, moved, and replaced every book on each of the shelves.

After a couple of hours of tapping, knocking, and running her hands over every inch of the shelves, she finally sat down beside the dogs on the couch. Her back hurt and she had a headache, and she was beyond frustrated and moving quickly toward pissed off.

Reaching over to the end table to get the coffee she had made, something caught her eye. Something that looked odd in the office. Leaning closer to it, she saw that it was a vase of sea glass. Pretty, but it didn't fit the room decor. At all. She had been in the house long enough to know that Dr. Roxbury didn't have any sea glass anywhere as a decoration.

"Why would she have a vase full of sea glass in here, but nowhere else in the entire house?" Tara asked the two dogs who were now sitting up and looking at her, then at the vase.

Tara tried to pick up the vase and felt a slight resistance before it left the end table. And just like that, the desk slowly lowered down into the floor.

"Holy shit! Yes! About freaking time. Will you two shut up?" she added because Connal and Gizmo were raising the holiest of hells because the desk had moved. Petting them to calm them down, Tara stood up and looked at where the desk had been. "It's okay. Perfectly natural for a desk to disappear into the floor. Okay, let's do this smart. I need to get a flashlight and a gun. Just in case. After all, the desk just freaking went into the floor so God only knows what might be down there. And no dogs for this portion of the mystery."

After getting the dogs calmed down, the three of them slowly walked over to where the desk had been and looked into the hole that was there. But as they got closer to the opening, Tara saw that the area below was lit up, and there were steps with handrails leading down.

"So, I guess we can disregard the flashlight and gun. Okay, to the Batcave!" she told the corgis that were watching her and waiting. "You two still need to stay here until I get down there. Yeah, that was a waste of words," she mumbled as the two pups went down the steps side-by-side. Tara followed, slower and a little more cautiously.

Once in the lower room, she saw that there was no reason to be careful. It truly was another room. And it was a mirror image of the office above. The desk from above had disappeared into the floor down here, and only the marble top was showing now.

"Well, that explains why the desk was completely empty and had nothing on it. It becomes part of the floor down here." Bookshelves were in the same places as above, as well as a kitchenette and couch. However, unlike its mirror upstairs, this office had a bathroom beside the kitchenette.

Also, in contrast to the upstairs room, this one had artifacts. There were dozens of them lined up on shelves, and there were photos of the artifacts pinned to corkboards, with notes on index cards beside each individual photo. Timelines and theories were scrawled on several wipe boards around the office.

"Now, this, is what I'm talking about. This is what an archaeologist's office should look like." Tara spent a good hour looking around and getting an idea of what Dr. Roxbury had been doing before she died.

"So, from what I see here, it looks like she has found prehistoric artifacts on the property, guys. That doesn't surprise me that much, considering this area and its proximity to the ocean. There were, and still are, Native American groups around here. Looks like she has a variety of points, blades and other lithics that she has collected and cataloged. Her notes are detailed with the locations where each was found, and she has photos, drawings, and maps of the locations. What every archaeologist does, so I'm not seeing anything earth shattering here. Just a professional digger, digging on her own property. I'll probably end up doing the same thing, eventually. I see it's time for homework. Need to brush up on the history of this part of the world so that I can rule out anything huge that she might have found down here.

"Because, between you and me, I'm not sure I believe what Gwenn told me about her dying. I don't think it was suicide, as some of the locals think. And why would a smart woman be out at the cove in the middle of winter? Just doesn't make sense to me. I think something happened to her. And maybe, it was something she had found out here. Yes, I know. Over-imaginative brain, but just my thought process. Okay, let's head back up, I think it's time for a snack."

Connal and Gizmo didn't need any further invitation as up the steps they went, then turned around at the top and barked and hopped on their front legs at Tara while she grabbed several local archaeology books and came up the steps to the office.

"Should I close this up or leave it open and lock the office door? Barb isn't due tomorrow, and if I lock this room, she can't see what's in here. I think I'm going leave it open. Freaks me out a bit to know that there is a secret room below the office. My own Batcave, and it's spooking me. Great superhero I would make."

Now that the mystery in the office had been figured out, Tara, Connal, and Gizmo spent the rest of the day outside.

Tara didn't want to admit it, but the secret room in the office scared her some. What happened if she and the dogs got stuck down there? She wanted to think about the room some before they went back down there. She needed to have some sort of game plan. But right now, she needed outside time. It was the middle of May, so it wasn't horribly cold outside most afternoons. A light jacket was still needed, but you could feel the warmth in the sun. Tara and the pups enjoyed a long walk around the main complex and Tara could see the beginnings of flowers popping up out of the ground.

"So, there are flowers planted. I was wondering if Dr. Roxbury had bothered with planting pretties. It's always a surprise the first spring and fall in a new house. Never know what the previous owner had planted. We'll have to watch to see what these turn out to be."

Connal and Gizmo could have cared less about the flowers because the squirrels and chipmunks were out and about and running around. The dogs did their best, but those little animals were just too quick for the two corgis.

"Thank God. I really didn't want to have to wrestle one of those out of your mouths," Tara told the two dogs. "The colors are just amazing. Look at those reds and greens, guys. And you can smell spring in the air." Tara enjoyed walking around and discovering her property. She loved watching it wake up and bloom into spring. And she loved seeing her dogs run and play without leashes on them.

The house compound area had been fenced in so that the dogs could be off leash when they were outside. That had been one of the first projects that she had Bill complete and he had done a fantastic job.

The fence was white picket and surrounded the entire house to the tree line and just before the beach of the cove. There were a couple of gates so that they could easily get to the cove, or to the tree line without having to walk the whole way around from one gate. And the fence height was waist high, which kept the dogs in the yard but didn't take away from the house.

Bill had proved his worth to her in that one project. He had sealed the deal when he made sure that there were no gaps where the fence met the ground, without her asking. He seemed like a nice enough guy. He was very quiet, and truth be told, she wasn't sure that she had actually talked to Bill at all. All communication to Bill came or went through Barb or email. He was efficient and respectful and really seemed to know what he was doing around the property.

Bill looked to be about Barb's age, which she had guessed at 60 years old and reminded her of Popeye because he was bald and his jaw and forearms were massive. Granted, he didn't have a pipe in his mouth, but it didn't take much for her to visualize one when she saw him.

Like Barb, she didn't see him that often, but she knew he was around or had been around. She would see a tractor or the cherry picker out, and she would know that Bill was working on something. The last couple of days, he had been cleaning out gutters on the house and buildings, along with trimming dead branches off the trees closest to the house. It was nice that she didn't need to worry about how to get that work done.

Once the pups were done chasing all the woodland creatures Tara, Connal and Gizmo finished their outside time down at the cove. While the dogs investigated the seaweed that the high tide had left, Tara sat on the beach and listened to the sounds of the ocean. The sounds of the waves touching the shore had always had a soothing and relaxing effect on her. Add the sea breeze to that, and she was in heaven. She would have closed her eyes, but she didn't trust those two little dogs that much.

"I don't want anything in here. It's not that Barb doesn't bring fantastic meals to heat up and good groceries. It's just that I don't want any of it. It's all healthy. I'm going to have to mention to her that junk is allowed in the house. Or, I could get off my lazy ass and go junk shopping for myself. Anyway, it's been over a week, so it's not being a piggy to want to go in and get a pizza, right? And it's still cool enough that you guys can stay in the car while I go in and order and maybe chat with Gwenn again, right?"

On the word go, both of the dogs' heads popped up, and they were now looking at her, just waiting for the words they loved to hear.

"You two would be good doggies, wouldn't you? Okay, it's settled, let's go for a drive and a pizza." Tara grabbed her hoodie, purse and opened the door to the breezeway. "Let's go."

Those were the two words the dogs had been waiting on, which resulted in the jumping off the couch and the scratching of toenails while they tried to get going into a full run.

After loading the pups into the SUV and making sure that their seat belt harnesses were secure, Tara pulled out, closed the garage door and headed into Eriksport.

Fifteen minutes later, she took a spot directly in front of

Gwenn's pizza place.

"This way I can watch you two. Behave, and I won't be long," Tara told the dogs as she cracked all four windows, then locked the SUV and headed in to order her dinner for carry out. She was met by Gwenn as soon as she stepped inside.

"Hey! Was hoping we would see you in here again. Are those your pups? I want to meet them." Tara didn't have a chance to respond because Gwenn grabbed her arm and dragged her back out the door.

Tara laughingly obliged and unlocked the car for Connal and Gizmo to say hello to this new human. Connal immediately fell in love with Gwenn. He wiggled his nub at her and with his ears flat, put his two front feet on Gwenn's chest to lick her face. Gwenn laughed and rubbed his sides.

"Connal, get down. I'm so sorry. He doesn't usually get in people's faces like that. Actually, I'm not sure I've ever seen him do that at all. Connal. Down. Now!" Tara added as she reached into the back of the SUV to make him sit.

"Oh, it's okay. He's a lover. And so cute. Yes, you're very pretty too, Gizmo. Right? You just aren't as in my face as your brother, are you?" Gwenn said petting Gizmo who had sat and waited her turn for the new human pets.

After more yapping, barking, furring, and laughing, Tara locked the SUV up, and headed back into Gwenn's.

"Oh, they're so cute and fuzzy," Gwenn said, looking back at the car to see Connal standing on the door and making nose art on the car window.

"Yes, they are. They're my babies. Wow, I'm sorry about all the fur you just accumulated."

"Ah, no worries. That's what tape is for. So, I'm assuming you are here for food?" At Tara's nod, Gwenn said, "What sounds good for dinner tonight? Pizza again? Maybe a pasta dish? I also make killer wings."

"I'm going to be lazy and say same as last time. It was an amazing pizza, and the pups loved the pizza bones. Lots of dog owners call the pizza crust pizza bones," she explained, after the look of confusion that appeared on Gwenn's face.

"Oh, that's cute. I'll make sure that their pizza bones are extra-large then. Let me put this in, and I'll be back out."

While Gwenn was in the kitchen, Tara walked to the door and watched the car and the dogs, to be sure they were okay and weren't trying to escape or learn how to drive.

"Okay, order is in. I brought the pups a bowl of water, so we can get them out of the car and wait outside with them. If you want."

"Oh, that sounds perfect. Thank you. You really like dogs, don't you?"

"Yeah, I love them. But my life isn't in the right place right now for me to have dogs, so I'll just have to spoil these two." Tara and Gwenn sat outside of the restaurant and chatted, laughed, and played with the pups until one of the wait staff came out with Tara's pizza.

"Wow, that was quick. Thanks. I've enjoyed this. It's nice to have someone to chat with. I talk to the dogs all the time, but it's rather one-sided," Tara stated as the two of them loaded up the pups and the pizza into the car. "This is very unlike me, and I'm going out of my comfort zone here, but would you like to come out sometime and visit us?" This part was said in a rush.

Gwenn looked at her for a moment, then smiled. "I would love to, but on one condition. When the visit gets too long, you tell me, and I'll leave. No harm, no foul. Deal?" She said, holding out her hand.

"Deal. I'm pretty open with anytime, so whenever you are free. Maybe we can do a steak on the grill or something. Here's my cell number. Oh, and here's for the pizza. Thanks so much for making my dinner and for the chat."

CHAPTER THREE

"So, tell me about yourself, Tara." Gwenn had called and set up a day that she was off work to come out to visit Tara, Connal, and Gizmo.

Now, sitting in the living room with Gizmo sitting on her foot and Connal on his side beside her on the couch getting belly rubs, she wanted to get to know Tara. "Where are you from? What made you move up here? Now, don't get all wally on me, just tell me what you are comfortable with. I'm just curious to know you better," Gwenn added because she could see that those two questions had caused Tara's body language to change from relaxed to guarded.

Taking a deep breath, Tara sat down across from Gwenn, holding a glass of iced tea. "Okay, hmm. I was born in Ohio and lived there for the majority of my life. Got tired of Ohio and decided to try something different. So, bought this place. Seemed like a good idea at the time." Taking a sip of iced tea, Tara knew that was not going to satisfy Gwenn. Hell, it didn't satisfy her, but it was a start.

"Really, that's it? Well, that's damn short and sweet. Were you hatched? Dropped out of the sky? Built in a lab?" Gwenn commented, which had Tara chuckling.

"No, I wasn't hatched, and I'm not from Krypton, nor am I

a robot. My parents have passed on. They both had Alzheimer's and/or Dementia at the end, so I had to take care of them. Doctor's appointments, meds, etc. No siblings. I have a couple of uncles and an aunt or two and some cousins, but I'm pretty much it for my family. Except for those two." Tara stopped to nod to the two dogs that were on the couch and were now attempting to share Gwenn's lap. Seeing the way the dogs were with Gwenn, Tara decided to trust them and open up a bit.

"I was married, for a long time, but that went south. Oh, we're still friends, but that's it. He's moved on, and so have I. Or, I'm at least trying to. We met during college. He was studying computer engineering, and I was studying anthropology. We started dating, then moved in together. After we had graduated with our undergrads, we got married. He went on to work as a contractor for the military, and I went into the field to dig for a couple of years. Then I went back for my master's. Graduated, dug for a few more years, then did the museum side for a while but eventually followed Wyatt, that's the ex's name, into being a contractor for the government.

"We were good together when we were together. But with Mom and Dad getting older and sicker, they became my life and took most of my focus, so eventually, we just didn't talk anymore. Not talking grew to not spending time together and it all led to a divorce. It's okay, though. I'm good with it. It was all mutual and respectful. No kids in the picture, so no reason to be ugly with each other. Everything we had was material things, so there was no need to be mean to each other." Tara took a long drink of her iced tea, trying to not panic that she had divulged that much information about herself to an almost complete stranger.

Feeling the need to switch the focus off herself, Tara looked at Gwenn. "What about you, Gwenn? Where are you from? What made you open a pizza place? What's your story?"

"Nice switch there, but I'll let you have it. You gave up a

fair amount of information there, so it's only fair that I take a turn. Okay, so I'm 42 years old. I'm from here, born and raised. In fact, I live in the house that my parents owned and that I was raised in. I've never left and have no interest to go see the world. This place is my world.

"I had a husband too. But, unlike yours, mine was an asshole. He was mean. Oh no, not hitting but emotionally mean. Got his jollies messing with my head. Took me eight years to figure that out and when I did, I promptly kicked his ass to the curb. Been divorced from the jerk for five years now. No kids. We were always too busy. Now, I'm glad we were. I would have hated to raise a child around his sickness. Last I heard, he was in California, which is still too close for me. Good riddance.

"No school after high school. Again, no interest in going to school to learn anything. Only thing I was interested in was cooking, which I can do, and I do it well. So, after my parents died and left me the house and some money, I jumped in with both feet and opened the pizza place. Being local, people know me. Knew I could cook and they really took to my pizza place. I've had it open for about four years now, and I love it. My employees are my family. Like you, no siblings, but I have a smattering of uncles, aunts, and cousins in several other states, but no family local." Gwenn took a sip of her iced tea, then leaned over to kiss Connal between his ears.

Connal returned the affection with a lick on Gwenn's chin, which caused Gwenn to chuckle. "I don't know what it is about this little dog, but I'm seriously in love with him."

"I've never seen him respond to a new person like he has to you. Oh, he's friendly, but not anything like he is with you. He really likes you." Tara shook her head and laughed because Connal had finally gotten Gizmo to move out of Gwenn's lap and he was now laying upside down on Gwenn's lap.

"So, we're basically the same in that we don't have our parents or any family, really. Makes us kindred spirits in a way. I don't feel so alone knowing that you have the same thing going on in your life. I don't feel like such an oddity when I know someone else has the same thing going on. Anyway, enough of that, let me show you around," Tara stated while standing up.

"Oh, yes, please! I've always wondered about this property, and now I get to see it."

"Obviously, this is the living room and the kitchen. There are four bedrooms, and each one has their own full bath, walk-in closet, and entrances to the wrap around porch. This room is mine." Stepping into her room, she let Gwenn walk in and look around.

"Damn, this is huge! I'd have to buy furniture just to not feel lost in here."

"Oh, I know. I hate furniture shopping, but I see a trip coming up soon. There is just so much empty space in here, screaming for new furniture. And this," Tara walked over to the French doors. "This is the view that people would kill for." Tara opened the doors to her porch and the cove. Stepping out, she closed her eyes and breathed in the air.

"Oh, I'd so kill for this!" Gwenn followed Tara out and mirroring her, closed her eyes and breathed in the sea air. "My God. I had no idea that you had this view. This is heaven. Can we sit and just enjoy for a while?"

"Of course! Sit. Put your feet up. The pups are fine. The yard is fenced for them so they can run free. I had Bill put up the fence so that they can always be off leash, but still contained."

Just as she said this, Connal and Gizmo decided it was time to entertain the ladies with their acrobatic feats on short legs, running, barking and neck wrestling.

Sitting down beside Gwenn, Tara glanced over at her. "This is nice. I'm glad you came out. I was second guessing myself for inviting you after I left. No, not because of you. It's me. I'm a classic over thinker and second guesser. I don't make, nor keep friends because of my brain and its inability to shut up. But this is nice. Thanks for coming out."

"I'm glad you invited me. I could tell that the invite was a big thing for you. I'm having a great time, so try to chill out a bit, okay?" Gwenn leaned her head back on the chair and closed her eyes.

"Actually, I was hoping maybe you would feel like filling me in on Barb and Bill. They seem nice enough, but Bill hasn't said two words to me. And Barb is, well. She's a hard read. She alternates between being friendly and chatty then shifts to snippy and prissy when something displeases her. And after I asked about the previous owner, she's just sort of closed up on me."

Sitting up straight, Gwenn looked over at Tara, then turned her attention to the dogs that were wrestling in the yard. "Sure, I love to gossip. So, Barb was born and raised here, and from what I understand, her family has been here forever. She used to live in town and was a school teacher."

"Ha! I knew it!" Tara interrupted her, with a fist pump.

"Um, what did you know?" Gwenn looked at Tara, confused.

"Sorry, I just knew that Barb had to have been a school teacher when we were doing the tour, and she got all school teachery on me. I'm sorry. Continue." Tara gestured to Gwenn.

Gwenn chuckled, then continued. "Barb was basically the town spinster, and no one thought she would ever marry. That was until about four years ago, when Bill moved into town from somewhere down south. Yes, I know everything is south of Eriksport, but I mean like Texas or Florida or some state like that. Anyway, he moved up here to work on one of the fishing tour guide boats. Not sure why he picked Eriksport, but he showed up and was a hard worker, so it seemed to work out well.

"Bill and Barb started talking one day at the grocery store. So cliché, but they did. And in the produce section to boot. Soon, they were dating. We were all surprised and happy for Barb. Bill really seemed to dote on her, and she on him. Anyway, they got serious, and before we knew it, Bill had moved into Barb's place with her.

"Around that same time, Dr. Roxbury was having the

secret construction to the house going on. I remember that, because for a town with nothing going on, all of a sudden we had a construction team in and a new romance going on.

"Anyway, somehow Barb and Bill found out that Dr. Roxbury was thinking about having a couple move out onto the property with her to help take care of it. They offered, and Dr. Roxbury accepted them as her new housekeeper/cook and handyman. They got married, it's been about two years now, before they moved out here.

"You pretty much nailed Barb with your description. She's nice enough when she is getting her way, but she can be snippy and manipulative when someone challenges her. I had her as a teacher in school. She was tough."

Shaking herself to get back on track, Gwenn looked over at Tara. "But back to your questions. Truth be told, I really don't know much about Bill. He's a mystery and he's very reserved and quiet, but it works for him, you know? It's just his thing; he doesn't talk. He seems like a nice enough guy. I don't know what he did before he moved here and he's not the sort of guy that you can sit down and talk to over a beer.

"I'm not sure why Barb would have clammed up about Dr. Roxbury. She seemed to like working for her, so maybe she doesn't feel comfortable talking about the dead. I don't know."

"Yeah, maybe that's it. I did sort of just throw it out there, and maybe Barb was respecting Dr. Roxbury's memory. Just seemed weird that she didn't tell me about Dr. Roxbury dying out here. Anyway, she and Bill really do appear to make a cute couple, and I'm glad they found each other." Tara's stomach chose that moment to growl. "I think it's time for some food. How about you?"

"Oh, I can eat. I can always eat. I know you said steaks, but you live in Maine now. Have you even had a lobster yet?" Gwenn asked while they walked back into the kitchen and opened the cooler she had brought with her. Inside were two lobsters. Connal and Gizmo stuck their noses into the cooler, then jumped back and started barking when the lobsters started moving.

Gwenn leaned down to pet Connal and Gizmo, then pulling the lobsters out of the cooler, she had the dogs come closer to see them. After a cursory sniff, the dogs lost interest.

Tara watched Gwenn's interaction with the dogs and smiled. "You really are great with dogs. But anyway, no. I haven't had a lobster since I've been here. I don't know how to prepare lobster, and I haven't been in the mood for a go out and sit down meal. But, I would love to learn how to, and I love lobster. Teach me, Obi Wan?"

"Ah, young Jedi. Teach you, I will. It's really best to steam them. Boiling is okay and so is grilling, but steaming, it just brings out the best of the lobster."

Tara took out a pot large enough for the two lobsters, and after filling it with water put it on the stove.

"Good, now add some salt to the water. No need for any special seasonings, salt is all it needs. Once the water is boiling, put in Mr. Lobsters and cover to get the water boiling again. These are two pounders, so about 16 minutes for them should be good. How about a salad to go with Mr. Lobsters?"

At Tara's nod of approval, the two set to prepping a salad at the counter. With small talk in between, it was like they had been friends forever and didn't really have to communicate with what the other needed to do.

"Okay, it's been about 16 minutes, so let's pull on an antenna. If it breaks loose, they're done," Gwenn instructed Tara.

"That's sort of a barbaric way to check, but it works. The antenna popped off. Oh, these look amazing." Tara put the lobsters on plates, then at two places at the island counter. Grabbing two Coors Lights from the fridge, Tara sat down and got ready to pop the top of the beer.

"Yeah, no." Gwenn grabbed her beer from the counter and Tara's beer out of her hand, then put them back into the fridge. "You're a Mainer now, so you have to drink like a Mainer," she said as she pulled two Frye's Leap Ales out of the cooler. "Welcome to Maine."

"Oh, my God, I love Maine. And lobster. And the beer. I might even love you," Tara moaned. They had finished dinner and were on lounge chairs, overlooking the cove while Connal and Gizmo were patrolling the cove beach for anything that might be edible.

"I have made you a true Mainer, Jedi. My work is done," Gwenn mumbled. She had her eyes closed and was fighting the urge to nap.

They sat in silence and watched the dogs and the ocean for close to an hour, but Gwenn could see that Tara was working something out in her head. She would occasionally furrow her brow and shake her head. Gwenn let Tara have her internal conversation. Whatever it was, it didn't need to be poked at, yet.

Gwenn finally sat up, yawned and stretched. "That kitchen needs to be cleaned up, and if I stay like this much longer, I'm really going to go to sleep."

Tara jumped because she had completely forgotten that Gwenn was there. "I am so sorry! I've been so rude but I sort of forgot you were here."

Gwenn put her hand up and shook her head. "Hey, no worries. It was a very comfortable silence. It's nice to sit and relax and not feel the need to make small talk. Really. Relax some more. I'm on kitchen duty. Believe it or not, I like cleaning up."

But Tara didn't listen and followed Gwenn into the kitchen. After all, she had invited Gwenn out for the day, and it was her house. It would be rude to let Gwenn do the clean up by herself. As they were finishing up with the cleanup, Tara went internal again, and this time Gwenn decided to call her on it.

"Okay, what do I have on my face? You've been glancing over at me for the last five minutes, and talking to yourself. Don't deny it, I can see your lips moving. It's getting rather unnerving." Gwenn leaned back against the island and finished drying her hands on the dish towel and waited.

"What? Oh, nothing. I'm sorry. Again. I was just thinking. You don't have anything on your face. I'm really sorry,

Gwenn. Now you can see why I don't have that many friends. I'm a bit of an oddity at times." Tara mirrored Gwenn's actions but crossed her arms over her chest after drying her hands.

"I've been quiet and respectful of your, let's call them moments, but you are starting to freak me out a bit here. Tara, what's going on? What has you running all sorts of scenarios in that head of yours and staring at me like I've grown a horn?"

Tara sighed. "Let's sit, okay?" Leading the way into the living room and sitting down on the couch, Tara turned to Gwenn, who had sat on the other end of the couch.

"I'm sorry. I've been trying to decide if I want to let you in on something. When I'm trying to decide something, I go internal and close off from the world. That's what I've been doing. And it's incredibly rude of me to do. I've just met you, and I really don't know you at all, but I've been seriously considering letting you in, and that scares me. And it's confusing me too. I'm not a trusting or open person, but for some reason, I don't feel that way with you. I don't know why and it's scaring the shit out of me. I've been discussing it with myself, and in the process, I've been rude."

Gwenn smiled and nodded. "I actually get that. I don't trust either, so I get where you are coming from. Maybe I can help set your mind at ease a little. I'm a gossip, yes, on the little things. But on the big stuff, it will go to my grave with me. You can trust me. I don't have many friends. Oh, I have friends, but not *friends*. Not the kind that knows you inside and out. That know your deepest darkest secrets. So, I do understand your thought process. If you want to let me in, I would be honored. But if not, we will still be friends. I've already decided that we're going to be best friends, if for nothing else, for your little dogs that I'm in love with." That got the smile out of Tara that Gwenn was hoping for. "So, if you want to share with me, I'm here and would love to know what has been giving you fits for the past two hours."

Tara had sat there, listening to Gwenn, still trying to make a decision. Now, looking at Gwenn sitting there, petting Connal and Gizmo, Tara closed her eyes for a second, and when she opened them again, Connal had come over to her and was staring at her. Tara reached out to pet Connal, and that's when Connal looked at Gwenn, over his shoulder. Then he looked back at Tara and barked and wiggled his nub.

Smiling, Tara rubbed Connal on both sides of his head. "Okay, I get it Connal. If you trust her, I will too," she whispered into his ear and was rewarded with a full-face lick.

She looked at Gwenn over Connal's head. "I want to show you something. This stays with us, right?" On Gwenn's nod of agreement, Tara led Gwenn to her bedroom.

"Um, this isn't going to get kinky or anything, right? Because you're nice and all, and you're cute, but I don't fly that way."

Tara laughed and shook her head. "Yeah, no. You're nice and all, but you just aren't my type for kinky."

Stopping at the office door, Tara turned around and looked at Gwenn again. When Gwenn held the gaze, Tara took a deep breath, unlocked the office door and pushed it open for Gwenn to walk through.

Gwenn walked in and did a 360 to take in the room. "Nice office. Really? This is what the penetrating stares and quiet conversations in your head have been about? An office? Seriously?" Gwenn turned and faced Tara with her hands on her hips.

Despite herself, Tara chuckled. "No, it's not the office, it's what's in the office. Go over to the couch. See that vase with the sea glass in it? Pick it up."

"No, fucking way!" Gwenn yelled when the desk dropped down into the floor, and the lights came on down in the secret room. "Sorry, but NO! FUCKING! WAY! You have a fucking Batcave!" She ran down the steps and stared up at Tara. "This is what crazy-assed Dr. Roxbury was up to? Oh, my God! This is unfreakingbelieveable! Get down here!"

Tara laughed as she followed Connal and Gizmo down the steps. "So, is this a better secret?"

"Um, hell yeah! What is all this stuff? Huh, looks like she was researching the area. But for what? Lots of notes and drawings and photos. But nothing definite," Gwenn said out loud as she went from board to board.

Tara had stood there and now smiled that Gwenn was seeing the same thing she saw when she had discovered the room. "I know. It's a lot of information on really nothing concrete. I found the Batcave a couple of days ago, and I've been reading her notes. They're very detailed for the artifacts she's been finding on the property. I've been brushing up on my history of this area too, but I really can't find anything that would lead to this level of secrecy. She could have just been a crazy old lady, but something tells me there's more."

Tara glanced at the boards and books and notes. "But, first things first. I haven't been down here a bunch, mainly because I have horrible visions of being locked down here with no way to get out. So, are you up to playing finding the secret lever down here?"

"Oh, hell yeah! Go and close it up. I'll look around and see if I can figure it out. OH! And I have my cell so we can see if there is a signal down here when it's closed up."

"That's a great idea. Okay, if the call doesn't go through, try a text. If that doesn't work, then I'll open up the room in 20 minutes. Are you okay with that?"

"Yeah, let's do this. Get." Gwenn made a shooing motion with her hand.

Laughing, Tara and the pups went back up into the main office. "Okay, here goes. 20 minutes if the phones don't work. Try to call first. Then text. Good luck." Tara picked up the vase of sea glass, and the desk slid back up into its normal position. Tara and the pups sat on the couch and waited. She didn't have to wait long until her phone rang.

"Hey."

"Okay, so the phones work. It's freaky down here. No, not a bad freaky, so don't you dare open up the floor yet. Just freaky. I'm going to try a text while I have you on the phone. There? Did you get it?"

"Yep. That's a relief. I'm going to have to make sure you have the codes and keys to get in here. God forbid I'm dumb

64

enough to get stuck down there, I'll need you to come rescue me."

"I'm going to take some pictures so you can see what it looks like down here when it's closed up. It's really rather brilliant the way the stairs move to let the desk go up."

"Oh, good idea. I hadn't even thought about how the desk went down when the stairs were in the way."

"Okay, let me see if I can find the release to open it back up from down here. See ya in a bit," Gwenn said then immediately hung up.

"I might have just created a monster here, guys. But I have to admit, it's cool to have someone else on this adventure. And you both really like her, so I think I made the right decision to show her this."

Tara poked around and basically wasted time looking at her watch until the 20 minutes were over. Just as she was walking over to the vase, the desk slid down and a minute later, up came Gwenn.

Looking very pleased with herself, Gwenn came up to stand in front of Tara. "I found it. It was super easy. Well, sort of super easy. Still took me almost 20 minutes. Let me go to the bathroom and get a drink, and I'll show you where it is."

Tara went downstairs to look around and wait for Gwenn, who appeared about five minutes later with two sodas. "Hope you don't mind, but I was thirsty and figured you hadn't left while I was down here."

"Thanks. No, I don't mind at all. Make yourself at home. Really. Okay, where is the secret lever?"

After taking a drink from her soda, Gwenn walked over to the couch. "It's over here, on the table, beside the couch. It's an exact match to the one upstairs."

Tara growled at the release mechanism being the same as above.

"I know, right? I didn't think it would be that obvious, so I went around, pulling on books and pressing on spots. Then, bam. Saw the same vase as upstairs and easy peasy."

"Good. Now I won't be worried being down here by

myself. Thank you so much for this. It's really nice to have someone on the inside of this mystery with me. I sort of feel like Nancy Drew. You up to looking around for a bit more? Maybe you'll understand or see something that I didn't."

"Yeah, but let me show you the pictures I took down here first," Gwenn said while pulling the pictures up. "See here? This is the place where the desk goes into the floor down here. It was rather neat to see the desk go up and the opening down here cover up. The steps move back first, then the desk goes up and then the floor down here closes up. It's fucking cool. I even took a video."

"Oh, wow. That really is rather brilliant. So, then when it's open, it's all reversed? The floor down here opens, the desk descends into the open space, and then the steps move to be on top of the marble desktop?"

"Yes, exactly! Sort of reminds me of the moving staircases in Harry Potter, but these stairs don't go sideways."

Tara shook her head. "Wow, Dr. Roxbury was an odd bird, that's for sure. But at least she made the weird stuff cool as hell to find. Okay, let's look around for a bit."

"Sounds good." Walking over to one of the shelves, Gwenn looked sideways at the titles of the books. "I can give you a brief rundown of the history of this area, but I need to brush up on it first. It's been a while since I studied it. I didn't go to school after high school, but I love history, and when I was a kid, I would pretend to be an archaeologist." She glanced over at Tara and saw Tara looking at her. "And before you ask why I didn't tell you that before, you were on a roll, and I didn't want to get you to stop telling me about yourself with my information. I've read tons of books on history. American. Greek. Roman. Egyptian. Viking. I just love history. All history so I can help with that part. And what I don't know or remember, I have plenty of books you can research in."

Gwenn was looking at one of the corkboards. Turning her head from side to side.

"There's something about this, but I can't put my finger on it. Something is tickling my brain. I've seen this before, but I just don't know where. It looks familiar, but I can't figure out why it does."

Tara came over to stand beside Gwenn and looked at the drawing that Gwenn was talking about. "It does look like something I've seen also, and like you, I can't place it." Rubbing her hands over her face, Tara looked at Gwenn. "You know what, it's been a long day, and maybe we're too tired to see what it is. Let's give it a rest for right now. Maybe it will come to us when we aren't staring at it."

As if on cue, Connal and Gizmo started voicing their opinions that Tara was late with their dinner.

"Let's go on up. I need to feed these two monsters before they eat us alive. I also want to give you a key and the codes." On Gwenn's look of concern, "No, I really want to. I'm not doing it because I feel like I should. You know about this, so it makes sense for you to have access to the house. Never know, I might get stuck down there, and you'll have to come rescue me from my own Batcave."

They had come up from the secret room, closed it up, locked the main office door and had made it into the kitchen by this time. While Tara fed Connal and Gizmo, Gwenn made herself at home and got a glass of water.

"This has been a great day. I'm really glad I came out to visit," Gwenn said while leaning against the counter. "I'm going to have to dust off some old books. I know I've seen that one symbol somewhere.

"Tomorrow's Tuesday, so I'm back to making pizzas. Being the owner, I can be in and out, so if you want to meet up tomorrow or in the next couple of days, I can be available. Just not for long amounts of time. Or, if you want, come on in. Have a slice or two, and we can chat. Bring the babies because I have a surprise for them."

Tapping Tara on the shoulder, she made Tara look her in the eye. "This is all on your time. No pressure at all. If you need a bit of time to recover from today, I understand. No harm, no foul. I mean it," she added when she saw the doubt in Tara's eyes.

"Just text or call me, okay? That way I'll know you're heading in and I can let you know if it's a busy time or not. Now, I need to get home and get myself ready for the work week. Thanks for inviting me out. It really was a great day and thank you for trusting me enough to show me the Batcave. I'm excited to explore it with you!" Kneeling, Gwenn loved on the pups then stood up and on impulse, hugged Tara. She was pleasantly surprised when Tara hugged her back.

CHAPTER FOUR

"It's a freaking Viking rune!" Tara said at the same time Gwenn was saying, "It's a fucking Viking rune!" They both stopped and looked at each other, then started laughing.

Holding her side from laughing so hard, Tara looked at Gwenn. "So apparently, we've come to the same conclusion that the drawing is a Viking rune."

They were standing outside at Tara's SUV since Gwenn had come out to wait after Tara had called to see if now would be a good time for a visit.

Still chuckling, Gwenn smiled. "Yeah, I guess so. Come on in. No, bring Connal and Gizmo with you. I have a surprise for them and you," Gwenn said as she opened the car door and helped to undo the seat belts on the dogs. "Seriously, it's fine. It's all legit and fine with the health department. Which is me, by the way," Gwenn added after she saw Tara hesitate.

"Of course you are. But, okay. If you say so. Come on you two, let's see what your Auntie Gwenn has up her sleeve." Tara took Gizmo's leash and would have taken Connal's, but Gwenn was already heading into the restaurant with Connal walking beside her.

Gwenn and Connal led the way to the right of the door and

into the corner, directly by the front window.

Tara laughed and shook her head when she saw that Gwenn had taken white picket fencing and fenced off the booth. There were two dog beds, water dishes, and food bowls in the area with the dogs' names on each item.

"Wow. VIP treatment you two. I don't know what to say, Gwenn. This is just amazing. Are you sure this is okay?"

"Yes, it's fine. I promise. This area is away from the kitchen, and it's in a corner, so it's sort of isolated. Plus, it has a window. I've never had a line waiting at the door, so this is your designated spot from now on. No one else can use this booth or area. Well, that is unless I become a world-famous pizza place, then, I'll need the booth back. So, it's all good. Sit down and let me get us a couple of slices of pizza, drinks, and pizza bones." Gwenn led Connal through the little picket gate and took off his leash.

Tara chuckled again and led Gizmo into the area, then removed her leash. "Okay, you two. Behave. No poops or pees in here and no barking. We don't want to get Auntie Gwenn in trouble. Best house manners, okay? Between you and me, I think she really likes you two." But the pups were sitting on their beds, looking out the window, and ignoring Tara.

Gwenn came back with four slices of pizza, two beers, and half a dozen pizza bones for the dogs.

"So, a Viking rune?" Gwenn started while chewing her pizza. "I knew it looked familiar. So, I started looking at my books. And there it was, in a book about Vikings. I don't know what it means, but it's Viking! Wow!"

"I know. It would explain why Dr. Roxbury was so secretive. There is no known, significant evidence of Vikings in the United States. Oh, there are rumors and odd things have been found, some of them in Maine but not definitive proof. We have to find out where she saw this." Tara took a break to bite into her pizza. "God, you make the best pizza."

Gwenn smiled at the compliment. "Right, I remember reading something at one time about a penny that was found in

Maine. And it had something to do with the Vikings. I don't remember the specifics, though."

Nodding, Tara talked around the bite of pizza she had just taken. "The Maine Penny. It supposedly dated back to the reign of Olaf, a Norwegian King. That's about all I remember. Looks like we might need to add researching the Vikings to our studies."

"I'm not off until Sunday and Monday, but I can come out then, and we can hit this hard. Sound good to you?"

"Yeah, I like it. You can spend the night if you want. That way you don't have to worry about leaving too late and driving in the dark."

"Love it. I'll bring a bag. And no cheating and researching the rune before I'm there. I've purposely not looked it up to see what it means, so you can't either! Okay?" Waiting for Tara to nod her agreement, Gwenn then got up. "I'd love to discuss this more, but I need to make sure the new guy doesn't burn down my place. Stay as long as you want. I'll see you Sunday, say 10ish?" Tara mumbled a yes around another bite of pizza.

She and the dogs sat there and watched the going ons of the place after Gwenn left and the pizza and pizza bones were gone. It was busy, but not crazy busy. Muffled sounds and conversations lulled Tara into a sense of peace. She loved to people watch. If said people didn't want to have conversations with her. Which the ones she was watching didn't seem to want.

What she didn't notice were the two men a couple of booths away that had been paying close attention to Gwenn and Tara. They were too far away to hear what Gwenn and Tara had been talking about. At least normally, but the older one that was seated facing their booth was happy, for once, that he was deaf. He could read lips and what he read on Tara's lips during her conversation with Gwenn had him signing to the younger man across from him. That in turn, made the younger man scribble a note on one of the napkins on the table. After letting the older man read, it, they both stood up and walked past Tara.

Connal, then Gizmo both started growling low in their throats with Connal adding to it by baring his teeth at the men.

"Connal, no teeth. Both of you be quiet. Now!" Tara glanced up at the two men walking past the booth. "I'm sorry. They just aren't used to being in here." She smiled, trying to defuse any trouble that they might cause Gwenn.

Gwenn chose that moment to walk over. "Hi, Logan," she said this while looking directly at the older one. Turning her attention to the other after Logan smiled at her. "Jake. It's good to see you. I'd like to introduce you two to the newest resident of Eriksport. Tara McDowell, this is Logan and Jake Jensen. They're brothers and run a lobster boat. They sometimes do tours in the summer."

While Gwenn was talking, Tara had a chance to look at the two men. The older one, Logan was about 5'10" and a solid 210, if Tara had to guess. He wore his blond hair shoulder length and parted on the left. With his blue eyes and crooked nose, Tara thought he looked like a pirate.

Jake, the younger brother, was pretty much just a smaller version of his brother with his height about two inches shorter and without the crooked nose. But he shared his brother's hair color and style, along with the blue eyes.

Gwenn clearing her throat brought Tara back to the conversation. Seeing that Jake had his hand out, she took it and returned the handshake.

Jake smiled at her. "Nice to meet you, Tara. Sorry to upset your dogs. Corgis, right?"

"Yes, they are corgis. I'm sorry they growled at you." Turning to Logan, Tara held out her hand but put it back down after Logan made no move to shake it. She could still hear the low growls coming from behind her.

"Logan has a hearing disability, but that doesn't affect his manners, which I know he has. I know his mother, and she didn't raise him to be an ass," Gwenn said while looking at Logan and after a brief staring contest, Logan looked down and held out his hand. Tara gave it a halfhearted shake, then ended the contact.

"Anyway, we were just on our way out. The pizza was great, as always, Gwenn. Tara, nice to meet you." Jake took Logan by the arm and led him out of the restaurant.

"Well, Logan's not a real friendly guy, is he? No biggie because I didn't like him either," Tara said to Gwenn before going back and sitting down at the booth.

"He's a bit of a hot head, but he's usually not that much of an asshole. Sorry about that. I need to get back to the kitchen. You okay?"

"Yeah, no worries. We're going to get out of here, though. We'll see you Sunday."

Tara took Connal and Gizmo for a quick pee break, then after getting the pups into the back seat and hooked up to their seat belts, she came around the back of the SUV and hopped in. Then hopped right back out to get a note that was under her windshield wiper.

Looking left then right, Tara didn't see anyone hanging around. "Weird. I didn't see anyone around the car. And you two didn't. Otherwise, there would have been barking and howling going on."

Opening the note, she read it. And immediately went from confused to pissed. "What the hell? Seriously? Nice welcome to town, assholes." This last part she said louder, just to let anyone listening know she was pissed. Balling up the note, she threw it into the passenger seat. Then after buckling up and pulling out, she flipped off whoever put the note there. "Just in case the assholes are watching."

Heading back to her place, muttering and cussing to the dogs about asshole people, she didn't see the truck that slowly followed her out of town. Just before she got to her driveway, the truck stopped and watched her pull off the road and to her gate. It waited until the gate opened, then closed before doing a three-point turn and heading back in the direction of Eriksport.

"So, where do you want to start?" Gwenn asked. She had

shown up on Sunday at 10 AM on the dot.

After putting her overnight bag in the room across the living room from Tara's, they had made their way down to the Batcave. It wasn't a cave, and there were no bats, but they both giggled when one of them would say 'to the Batcave,' so it had stuck. Now, standing in the middle of the Batcave, they looked at each other.

"Hm, okay. Where to start? Let's start with what we know. I got another wipeboard for us to list known stuff on." Tara wheeled out a new board and a set of new dry markers.

"We know that Dr. Roxbury was a pro and had found something that made her want to hide what she had found." As Tara said this, Gwenn wrote it as point 1 on the board.

"We're pretty damn positive that this drawing is a Viking rune." Tara had taken a snapshot of the rune in question and had then printed it out as she didn't want to use the original drawing. She handed the printed copy of the drawing to Gwenn, who in turn taped it to the board beside point 2.

"We know that me being here is bugging someone, so that leads me to believe that there is something that someone doesn't want me to see/find." This made Gwenn turn around and look at Tara.

"What do you mean?"

"Oh, wait a minute. I have to show you something. I'll be right back."

Tara returned with the crumpled-up note. "Look at what some asshole put under my windshield wiper Friday. I found it as I was leaving your place," she said as she handed the note to Gwenn.

Gwenn took the note and uncrumpling it, read it then looked at Tara. "Why the hell didn't you come back in and tell me about this? What the hell, Tara? This is serious. How did you know that they hadn't dicked with your car? Or followed you?" Gwenn stood there with the note in her hand and the other hand on her hip.

Connal, sensing Gwenn's anger at Tara came to lean against Tara's leg while Gizmo chose to sit down between Tara and

Gwenn.

After the initial head jerk of shock, Tara shrugged her shoulders. "I didn't think that it was that big of a deal. Really. Just some asshole having some fun. Do you really think this is a genuine threat?" Tara quietly questioned Gwenn.

"OH, I don't know. A note put on your car that says, and I quote 'Quit looking for what Roxbury was looking for. Or you'll end up like her' sounds like a FUCKING THREAT!" Gwenn took a deep breath, then leaned down to pet Gizmo, who had come over to her. Standing back up and pinning Tara with a stare. "Did you even notice that it was written, badly I might add, on one of the napkins from my restaurant? That means that whoever did this was in there when you were and when we were talking. They overheard something that they didn't like, so grabbed a napkin, wrote this nasty assed little note and put it on your car. You don't find any of that concerning? Seriously, I'm calling Fred. He needs to see this."

Gwenn was on her phone and dialing before she even finished the last part. "He'll be here in 20 minutes. We need to go upstairs so that you can let him in when he gets to the gate," Gwenn stated as she left the Batcave. "Are you coming up or am I locking you in there?" she asked, standing in the office with her hands on her hips.

Tara glanced down at the dogs and whispered, "Damn, she's really pissed guys. Let's go before she locks us in here. You two go first. She's not mad at you." Tara let Connal and Gizmo go up first and she was barely off the top step before Gwenn lifted the sea glass vase and the desk slid back into its place.

While Tara headed for the kitchen, Gwenn veered off and went into her room and closed the door. Tara stood there for a minute, shaking her head. "Wow, I thought I had a temper. Note to self. Don't piss off Gwenn. Come on you two, let's go find some snackies. Maybe if we feed the savage Gwenn beast, she won't bite us."

Tara spent the time waiting for Fred to buzz the gate sitting on the kitchen floor and playing with Connal and Gizmo. She wouldn't admit it out loud, but having Gwenn upset with her, hurt her feelings. Yes, she had just become friends with Gwenn, but Tara hated having anyone upset with her, much less a friend. So, she opted for some corgi loves to make her feel a little bit better.

When Fred did finally buzz the gate, Tara went out to meet him.

While Fred was getting out of the cruiser and walking over to her, Tara had a chance to evaluate him. She guessed him to be mid-50s, starting to bald but had some blond hair still at the back of his head and over his ears. He was clean shaven, as was expected from a law enforcement officer. His nose was flat and wide which made his face appear even pudgier than it was. Tara could see red blotches on his cheeks and forehead and now that he had removed his sunglasses she saw that he had blue eyes that were bloodshot and red-rimmed. Fred came over to Tara and shook her hand.

"Hi. I'm Fred Toft, the Sheriff for Eriksport. Gwenn called me and said you needed to talk to me."

"Hi, I'm Tara McDowell. It's nice to meet you. Come on in." Tara returned the handshake then turned to lead him into the house, where Connal and Gizmo were waiting.

Fred stepped in behind Tara, and immediately Connal started barking and growling and advancing toward Fred. Gizmo, picking up on Connal's distress added her barks and growls to the mix, though she didn't try to move toward Fred. Grabbing Connal by his collar to stop his forward movement toward Fred, Tara ended up having to physically pick him up to get him under control.

"I'm so sorry. He's not usually like this. Must be all the excitement with the move and all."

Still holding a growling and snarling Connal and standing between Gizmo and Fred, Tara led the way into the house, then into the kitchen.

"Just give me a minute to put them in my bedroom. Please have a seat," Tara said as she walked toward her room.

Once inside, she put Connal on the bed and sat down

beside him and Gizmo, petting both to get them to stop shaking. "What's wrong, you two?"

Looking at Connal now, "You've never acted like this with a human. You were standoffish with Barb, but you really wanted to eat Fred, didn't you?" She could still feel low, little growls coming from Connal and the occasional shiver. "Calm down now. It's okay. I'm only going to be a few minutes, then you can come back out. After he's gone."

Leaning down to kiss him on the head, Tara held him close then turned to Gizmo and kissed her on the head as well. "You didn't like Fred, either, did you? That's like the third person you two haven't liked since we got here. At least you didn't try to get at Fred. You were a very good girl. Stay here and calm down, okay? I won't be long." Tara got up and headed back to the bedroom door, but had to stop when Connal jumped off the bed and ran to the door, followed closely by Gizmo.

"Guys, stay. It's okay. I'll be right back."

As soon as she closed the door, Connal started barking and scratching on the bedroom door.

Reopening the door, "Connal. Quiet. Go lay down. Now!" Connal hesitated, then laid down at the door. This time when Tara closed the door, there was no barking or scratching, but she could hear the low growls and the sniffing under the door.

Heading back to the kitchen, Tara didn't waste any time with pleasantries. She was concerned about why the dogs had reacted like that, and she wanted to get back to them as soon as she could.

"Hi. I'm sorry about that. They're usually friendly. So yeah, I got a note put on my car Friday night, and Gwenn said you needed to see it. Would you like a cup of coffee?" Tara glanced over to her bedroom door, where she could still hear an occasional growl or scratch at the door.

"Sure, sounds good. Black, please. I thought Gwenn was here with you," Fred said as he took a seat at the island.

"She is, but she's pissed at me about the note and is taking a time out," Tara muttered while putting a cup of coffee down in front of Fred.

"Ah, the Gwenn temper. And you're still standing. Congrats." Fred toasted Tara with the cup of coffee.

"Kiss my ass, Fred," Gwenn said as she came into the kitchen. Getting herself a cup of coffee, she came to stand beside Tara. Bumping her hip into Tara's, she gestured with her head. "This stupid-assed woman gets a threatening note on her car and thinks nothing of it." She leaned over the island to hand the note to Fred.

Fred took out his reading glasses, read the note, turned it over and then reread it. "Well, Tara, I'm on Gwenn's side about this. This is a bonafide threat. We don't much like threats of this nature up here. I want every detail of that evening. What you were doing? Where you were? Who you were with? If anything odd has been going on since you got here. Everything. And Gwenn, stop smirking. I vaguely remember you doing some stupid things a time or two."

Tara sat down, and for the next half hour she detailed out her Friday afternoon at the pizza place, finding the note on the car, the drive home. For whatever reason, though Tara chose not to fill Fred in on the fact that it was a napkin from Gwenn's place and that someone probably overheard them talking.

Gwen added bits and pieces to the details as needed, but she also chose not to mention the napkin being from her place.

Finally, Fred stopped writing and looked at Tara intently. "Okay, that's all important information and gives me a good background of what was going on. Now, I need to get personal with you, I need to know about you. So, I have to ask you some personal stuff." Fred stopped and looked directly at Gwenn.

"I can take the pups for a walk," Gwenn said as she started to get up, but Tara shook her head.

"I have nothing to hide. So, fire away." She sat back, crossed her arms and waited for the questions.

"Okay, good. Let's start with the basics. Full name, age, place of birth, where did you grow up. Married? Parents."

"Tara Elizabeth McDowell. 45 years old. Born and raised in Cincinnati, Ohio. Went to college in Dayton and Cincinnati. Married for 20 years but I've been divorced for about eight months. My parents are both dead. No siblings. No kids."

Fred finished writing, then looked up. "So, no family. What did you study in college? What do you do for work? Why did you move here?"

"I have a master's in archaeology. Did the digging until my back said enough, then moved onto the museum side of anthropology. Eventually, I followed my ex into working as a contractor for the government.

"I don't know why I moved here. I've never been to Maine, so no idea why it appealed to me that night on the internet. Couldn't sleep, so was browsing real estate websites and this place popped up. Before I knew it, I was buying it with a 'Buy It Now' button. Seriously," she added at the look of disbelief on both Fred's and Gwenn's faces. "No idea why, but I'm writing it off as fate. I needed something different and new, and this fit the bill."

Fred recovered quickly from the quick jerk he made when Tara had mentioned being an archaeologist. "Any enemies? Any reason for anyone to want to harm you from your previous jobs? What did you do for the government?"

"No enemies. No one has ever threatened me, so no to any harm being done to me. I was a contracted archaeologist for the government. My team and I would go to various places and recover human remains and cultural artifacts."

Fred nodded and wrote a couple more notes, then looked up. "That sounds interesting. I thought you said your back kept you from digging?"

"I was the team lead, so I didn't do the digging. I did the reports and the interpretation of what was found. The paper and management side of it."

"I'm going to have to run you through the system and see if you have any tickets or warrants on you."

"You do realize that you running me in the system is going to ping the government on my clearance, right? I really would rather not have that kind of attention. So, if you would take my word—Yeah. That's what I thought." Tara looked at him for a minute then sighed and rattled off her social security number. "Well, enjoy the phone calls your query is going to cause. Are we done?" Tara was suddenly drained and wanted to be alone.

"Yup, I'm good. I'm going to keep the note if that's okay with you. I doubt there's any fingerprints on it, but you never know." Fred stopped and turned around as he got to the front door. "One more question. Do you know how to handle a gun?"

Still sitting at the island, with her arms crossed, Tara looked Fred in the eye. "Yes, I know how to handle a gun, and I have several. All legally purchased. You'll see that when you run me."

"Alright, good. Well, you ladies try to have a good day and let me know immediately if there are any more threats or concerns."

"I'll walk you out Fred," Gwenn offered. She was a little shaken by the questions and answers and needed a moment or two to process what she had heard.

After Fred had left, Gwenn stood outside for a bit. What a strange turn of events. Tara had worked for the government and had a clearance of some sort. She also had guns. None of that really bothered her. What was bugging her was the way Tara had answered all the questions. She had gone into auto mode, answering the questions, but with no emotion. Those damn walls had gone back up. "Guess I'll just have to knock those damn things down again."

Walking back into the house, Tara and the dogs weren't where Gwenn expected them. So, she headed towards Tara's room, and there she found Tara standing outside on the porch. She was leaning against the rail, arms crossed and staring at the cove. And she was nowhere in there. She was so far into her head, Tara never heard Gwenn come out on the porch.

Gwenn leaned back against the rail and looked at Tara and waited.

Tara closed her eyes, drew in a deep breath, let it out, opened her eyes and returned Gwenn's look. "You still mad at me?"

Gwenn leaned over and hugged her as her answer. Tara resisted the hug for a second or two, then relaxed into it.

"I'm sorry. I didn't think. At all. And I know better. Or, I did. I let my temper take over and didn't assess the situation for what it was."

"Forgiven. Now, I'm hungry, so let's find some food and try to forget about this for a while," Gwenn said, as she headed back into the house.

Waiting for Tara to close and lock the French doors, they went back into the kitchen, where they worked together to make a tray of snack-sized meats, cheeses, and crackers. Since they had lost time with the interview, they took their snack tray and drinks to the Batcave.

Now, Tara stood in the middle of the room and slowly turned. Stopping, she looked at Gwenn. "I know we both want to attack the Viking rune possibility, but I think that we need to use our limited time together to organize the stuff down here into groups first. We can research that rune separately if we have to. I think we need to organize so that way we know what we have. There is a ton of information down here, books, photos, notes, etc. So, I think we should put the books in one pile. Photos in another pile. Handwritten notes in another. That way we can see what we really have. We might have more information about the rune in here, and we don't know it. Does that make sense to you?"

Nodding, Gwenn agreed. "Damn it, but it does. If we go off half-cocked, we won't find anything. Let's see what batty old Dr. Roxbury had down here."

"The artifacts that she collected can stay on the shelves. The books, we will have to read or at least look through to see if there are any notes written in them. Maybe divide them up, and the reader can do a cliff notes version of what they read? Mark the information that might be of use?" Tara suggested while petting Connal's ears.

He had not left her side since she went into the bedroom after Fred had left. Petting his ears now, Tara wondered what about Fred had caused him, in particular, to react so strongly. She had never seen Connal advance on someone. Tara was positive that if she hadn't grabbed him, Connal would have attacked Fred. That worried her. A lot. She didn't like Fred, at all. But she hadn't come to that conclusion until half way through the visit. Connal and Gizmo had reacted badly on immediate introduction to Fred. Her father's words came back to her that if a dog didn't like someone, there was a reason and she had learned to trust that. Connal and Gizmo didn't trust or like Fred, therefore Tara would be wary of the man.

"Yeah, good idea. A little light bedtime reading." Gwenn walked over to the shelves that held the artifacts. "What are these, anyway?"

Tara went to stand by Gwenn. "Well, most of these are lithics. Stone tools and the debris from making the stone tools," she added when Gwenn glanced over at her with a confused look. "Arrowheads, points, knives, and blades mainly. Dr. Roxbury also found some animal bones that had been modified for use as well. I've not seen anything that would be earth shattering in the archaeology world. She found prehistoric artifacts, which I would be surprised if she hadn't, given the location of this property. Still, it's a nice little personal collection she had going on. I have a good book on lithics if you are interested in learning more."

"Yes, please. I would love to read it. Archaeology has always fascinated me, and now I have a friend that digs. Perfect. Anyway, back to the piles, huh?" Gwenn turned away from the shelf and looked at the rest of the stuff that was to be their homework.

"I think that some of these photos don't have anything to do with the real subject." Tara handed Gwenn a couple of photos. "See. These don't have anything to do with the rest of the pictures. These are photos of plants. They have no significance in the artifacts she's been collecting."

Gwenn studied the three pictures, then looked at the other

dozen or so photos, then back to the three. "I think you're right. There are no plants in any of the other photos she's taken. She did take photos of scenery, but these are of a plant, with nothing else in the photo. So, why add three photos of one plant to the mix?"

When Gwenn said plant instead of plants, Tara looked closer and realized that Gwenn was right. There were three pictures of a single plant. Not three photos of three different plants.

Gwenn continued with her thought. "And, this plant isn't even local, I'd bet money on that. Granted she could have bought it and planted it somewhere here, but I agree, it has nothing to do with everything she has collected down here."

After adding the three photos of the plant to her pile, Gwenn started to really look at the others that were her assignment. There were scenery shots. Turning her head, she laid the photos down on the floor and stood up, then bent over and readjusted the positions of them. "Holy shit, I know where this is!"

Tara got to her feet and came to stand by Gwenn. "When you're done with your victory dance, can you clue in the person not from around here."

"Yeah, sorry about that. This is a small area, not too far from here and it might even be on your property. I don't know. But my high school boyfriend and I used to go parking here. Do you have a map of your property? If you do, I can show you where this is, and we can see if it's on your land."

"Yeah, I have the survey on my computer. Let's head back upstairs, and I'll pull it up."

Gathering up their various piles of research and following the dogs, they went back up to the main office. Closing up the Batcave entrance, Tara sat down on the couch and booted up the computer.

"Yes, I know I have a perfectly great desk over there, but I also know that it falls into the Batcave. Freaks me out," Tara answered Gwenn's questioning look. "Okay, here is my property survey. Where was your high school necking place?"

"Ha ha. Okay, it's here. Damn, it is on your property! Have you been over that way?" Gwenn did another victory dance.

Tara shook her head and chuckled. "No, not yet. I don't think we can get there by car, can we?" When Gwenn shook her head, Tara smiled. "Well, then, let's go to the equipment barn and see what toys we have that can get us over there."

After a quick bathroom break, grabbing their jackets and a couple of bottles of water, they headed to the equipment barn, where they decided on a four-seater Gator, with a cargo bed.

Gwenn was driving since she knew where she was going and Tara soon learned that was a terrible idea. The woman drove like a maniac, only using the brake to keep from hitting trees. Between Gwenn's driving and her freaking out that Connal and Gizmo weren't seat-belted in the back seat of the Gator, Tara didn't know whether to cry or throw up.

Connal and Gizmo didn't seem to care at all, though. In fact, they were sitting side by side, tongues flapping in the wind and huge smiles on their furry little faces.

"They're loving this so quit helicoptering them, Mom," Gwenn said, after a side glance at Tara. "Chill and enjoy the scenery of your place."

"What scenery? I can't see shit with you driving like a banshee." Tara had her eyes closed and a death grip on the grab bar.

Gwenn chuckled but took her foot off the gas. "Wimp. Apparently, I need to teach you how to off road. It's a thing up here. You'll love it."

"Yeah, no thanks. But thanks for slowing down. Now I might be able to actually see the scenery."

Gwenn's only response was sticking out her tongue.

The oaks, maples, and birch trees were all in full bloom, and various bushes and flowers were showing all their beauty. There were reds, blues, and yellows flying by. It was gorgeous and she could just make out the smell of honeysuckle in bloom. Tara sat back, calm enough to enjoy the ride and the scenery. This was all hers, she wasn't sure she would ever get used to that. The route that Gwenn was taking wasn't overly rough, and she thought she would make a trail out here. It would be a great walking trail for her and the dogs.

The stopping of the vehicle prompted Connal and Gizmo to start barking and dancing. They wanted out so that they could explore this new area. Laughing, Tara obliged. Clipping on a 20-foot leash, she put Gizmo on the ground, while Gwenn did the same with Connal. It struck Tara as funny that Connal abandoned her for Gwenn whenever Gwenn was around. Taking a moment to analyze it, she found that it didn't hurt her feelings. It endeared Connal, and Gwenn, to her all that much more.

"Yes, I know. I'm evil, but I don't trust either of you not to go running after bears or bigfoots. So, just quit it and enjoy the freedom you have with the long leashes," Tara added the last because Connal, then Gizmo went belly up in protest of being on leash. She did a slow 360. "Okay, this is amazing."

Gwenn came over and agreed. "Yeah, it is and it's so peaceful. Let's see if we can find where these photos were taken." She handed one of the photos to Tara.

"Geez, get me out here, after trying to kill me, and won't even give me a minute to enjoy it," Tara teased Gwenn.

They separated, and each took a section. Walking slowly, Tara and Gwenn compared the photos to what they were looking at. It was quiet, except for the occasional sharp bark of one of the dogs.

"Hey, over here."

Tara headed towards Gwenn's voice. "Did you find the place?"

"Yeah, look." They both looked at the landscape photos, then at the area that Gwenn had found.

"Damn, if it's not the same place. Good eye, Gwenn. Let's get some photos of this. Just to be able to verify that we're in the right place."

"Sounds good. Let me go get the Gator. Be right back."

Tara looked around while she waited for Gwenn to return with the Gator and the equipment they had brought. It really was perfect. She could make out the ocean through the trees, as well as hear the waves crashing on the shore. The land here didn't have a cove to calm down the waves, so it received the full brunt of the ocean.

Looking down at Connal and Gizmo, Tara smiled. "It's pretty, isn't it? I think we lucked out you two. We have our own little heaven," Tara murmured to the pups as she leaned down to pet them both.

That's how Gwenn saw them when she came back with the Gator. "A girl and her dogs." She sat there enjoying the sight then grinning, she beeped the horn and called out. "We going to work here or are we going to just stand around and enjoy the view?"

"I guess we'll work for a bit. After all, we brought all this equipment. Would be a waste not to." Following Connal and Gizmo, Tara walked over to the Gator and reached into the back of the Gator for her camera.

"Where do you want me to start?"

Tara handed the camera to Gwenn. "We'll use the photo scale to show what direction north is and the size of the object you are taking a picture of. Once we get back, we can make the photos black and white, or leave them in color. I think that we should get shots of the various plants around here. Since we aren't sure of when she took her photos, we can't be certain which plant she was photographing."

Gwenn nodded her understanding and went to work, taking pictures of the landscape and various plants.

While Gwenn took the photos, Tara looked at the area to see if anything was obvious to her eye. Seeing nothing from a quick scan, she called Gwenn over. "Okay, that should be enough on the photographing. Let's work on looking around. Not really disturbing anything. Let's see if there is anything that is out of place. Something that is man made in here. Something that doesn't fit. If she found artifacts up here, there might be flagging tape or marking pins somewhere. Or, we should see disturbed ground."

After walking for just a few moments, Gwenn called Tara

over. "Is this flagging tape?" She pointed to a piece of blue plastic sticking out of the ground.

"Yep, that would be flagging tape. Good catch. So, this is where she was finding some of the artifacts. Yes, see here on the tape? She wrote on it so she would be able to see what artifacts she found here and read the corresponding notes for this site. Go ahead and take a photo of it, would you?"

Tara and Gwenn continued to look and found several other areas with flagging tape for the next hour before they finally stopped finding anything new.

"Okay, let's take a break." Tara handed a bottle of water to Gwenn, then got the water dish for the pups out of the Gator. After sitting down beside Gwenn, she leaned her head back and closed her eyes.

"What's up?" Gwenn shouldered Tara.

Tara shrugged and sighed. "Just tired all of a sudden."

"Well, it's been a long and weird day. Let's call it and go back and relax." Not waiting for Tara's response, Gwenn stood up and started putting the equipment back into the Gator.

Tara peeked over with one eye, then got to her feet and helped with the last few things and the dogs. "Thanks."

"No problem. I want to get my room organized anyway. That is if I'm still spending the night?" Gwenn looked over a Tara to see her reaction.

Smiling, Tara nodded. "Yeah, you're staying."

Back at the house, Gwenn went to her room to put away the stuff she had brought with her and Tara took the pups outside to run and play at the cove.

She took that time to rest and relax. She was on edge and wasn't sure why, but she was. Something was just outside her range of mind, and it was bugging her. Knowing that something was there, but not being able to figure it out was bugging her. Today was bugging her and she couldn't put a finger on it. And that bugged her. "God, I'm just bugged today, aren't I? I hate when I feel like this," she grumbled out loud.

"What's bugging you?" Gwenn had walked up during Tara's little conversation with herself.

"Holy God, don't do that!" Tara sat with her hand on her chest, "Are you trying to kill me?"

Gwenn chuckled and sat down beside her. "Not at the moment. Sorry. I had called to you before I came down. But you were having quite a conversation with yourself. You didn't hear me. So, what's up?" Gwenn looked at Tara and waited.

Tara sighed and shrugged her shoulders. "I don't know. Something's bugging me. I just can't figure out what it is. No, it's not you," she added when she saw that Gwenn was going to say something about her staying there. "There's something about the rune and where we were today. Something doesn't feel right about it. I can't put my finger on it, and it's bugging the hell out of me."

Connal and Gizmo had come up when Gwenn sat down. Tara reached over to pet them. Their fur was soft and warm to the touch, almost like velvet. Somehow, petting a dog had always calmed Tara down. It helped her to let go of the anxious feeling that she had in her belly. Just as she turned to ask Gwenn her thoughts on dinner, Gwenn's cell rang.

"Hello? Hey, what's up? Yeah, I know the place. There is? Ah, are they open now? Is it on their website? Okay, let me go look, and I'll see what I can do." This last part, Gwenn said while looking at Tara. "Okay, thanks. I'll let you know what happens. Bye."

Gwenn disconnected the call, then turned to Tara so that she was looking at her fully. "So, that was my friend Mike who just called. There seems to be a corgi-like dog in a local shelter. Thought I might mention it to my friend that likes those corgi dogs and lives at Corgi Cove." She chuckled because Tara looked at her, confused. She smiled now. "Yes, he called your property that. Most of the locals call your place Corgi Cove now that you live here and have two corgis. I think it's cute."

"I had no idea, but I love it," Tara said, with a smile.

"Anyway, he said that the dog is on the shelter's webpage—

" Gwenn stopped because Tara had gotten up and was heading into the house.

After taking several steps, Tara stopped and turned around. "Well, are you coming in to show me this corgi dog?" Then laughed when Gwenn squealed and came running after her.

Googling the shelter, they saw that it was indeed still open and less than an hour south, so after calling to express her interest in the corgi, they all hopped into the SUV.

"I can't believe that we're here. I know he's going to be your dog, but I feel like I'm getting him," Gwenn said practically dancing in her seat.

They were seated in a private room at the dog shelter, with Connal and Gizmo, waiting to be introduced to the corgi that was supposed to be there.

Tara nodded and smiled. "I know what you mean. There's something so exciting and scary about adopting a pet. Almost like Christmas. He looked so sad in the picture. We had to come."

Looking at Connal and Gizmo, Tara tried her strongest *I mean it* voice, while rubbing their ears. "You two be nice to him."

All eyes, human and corgi, turned to the door as the shelter staff member carried in the corgi that Tara had already fallen in love with.

"Hi, my name's Samantha, and this is Peanut." After putting Peanut on the floor, Samantha sat on the floor behind him. Tara and Gwenn followed suit, but sat down in front of him and waited. Peanut looked similar to Connal and Gizmo with the white chest, undercarriage and white socks on his feet. He had a little white star between his ears and a white blaze that started between his eyes and merged into the white on his muzzle. Tara could also see that he was a sable instead of the red and white like Connal.

Rubbing his ears, Samantha continued. "We've renamed him Peanut because he's small, he's just a peanut. Figured he needed a new name since his old owners didn't want him anymore. New start, new name. He has trouble with his back legs, but it seems to be mostly weakness versus an injury. We did x-rays, and there are no obvious reasons for the weakness. The legs work, but not well on these floors, so we've taken to carrying him, which he loves. He's great on carpet, grass, and dirt, though. His owners surrendered him because they didn't want to take care of him anymore. They say he is 10 years old and that the leg issues have just started. He's neutered and is clear on heartworms. He's in pretty good health, all in all. We've had him here for just over a week. He's a sweetie, and we've all fallen in love with him."

Peanut sat there and looked around. He seemed interested in the new humans in the room and the other dogs but didn't move toward any of them.

Connal was the first one to make a move when he got up and went to Peanut. After the cursory smelling of each other, Connal laid down beside Peanut and looked at Tara.

"Oh, bud. Do you want him as a brother?" Tara had tears in her eyes at the immediate acceptance.

Not to be outdone, Gizmo went over to Peanut, sat in front of him and looked into his eyes. She then leaned forward and licked Peanut's face. Peanut returned the favor then slowly scooted forward to lay his head in Tara's lap. Placing her hand on his head, Tara leaned down to kiss his head. "We'll take him if we can."

"He's yours," Samantha said quietly. "Let me get the paperwork done, and we'll get you all out of here so you can get home and get acquainted."

CHAPTER FIVE

"I'm going to run into town and get us a pizza, or maybe lasagna for dinner," Gwenn told Tara after they got home with the three dogs. It had been a quick process to adopt Peanut, and now that they were home, Gwenn was starving. "That way we can focus on getting Peanut settled and relaxed and not have to figure out what to eat. I'm also going to swing by my place and get a couple more things since I'm going to be hanging out here for a bit."

Tara and Gwenn had discussed Gwenn staying at the house with Tara and the dogs on the trip home. They had come to the conclusion that Gwenn spending a couple of nights out at the house would be a good idea. Tara didn't want to admit it, but the note had rattled her and having someone else around for a couple of nights made sense. Just until she got her balance back. Plus, with Peanut just coming into the house, Gwenn really wanted to hang around to love on him.

"Pizza sounds great. Once you get back, I'll change the codes to the gate."

"Sounds good. I'll be back in a bit. Maybe an hour and a half."

Tara took the time to get Peanut settled. "This is our bedroom, Peanut. This is the ramp that you three use to get up and down off my bed."

Connal and Gizmo ran up the ramp as soon as Tara walked over to the bed. Peanut sat and looked up at them, but made no move to follow them. "I'll teach you how to go up it later, sweetie. They're just showing off." Tara stroked his head, then because Connal and Gizmo had come to the edge of the bed, Tara scratched their ears as well. "No reason to be jumping off and on. Gotta save those long backs. Connal likes to sleep on my left, with his head on my pillow. Gizmo prefers the bottom left of the bed. So, you have the whole right side to yourself. If you don't want to sleep with us, there are beds on the floor for you. You can sleep where ever you want to, baby."

Tara kept the running dialog during the tour of the rest of the house. "Okay, this is the kitchen. And from the looks I'm getting from Connal and Gizmo, it's dinnertime. See? Told you," Tara remarked after Connal and Gizmo started doing their food dance.

"You all get a quarter cup of kibble. Then I add some green beans, pumpkin and a bit of warm water to it. Connal gets his dish over here by the fridge. See how he sits and waits? Good boy! Gizmo gets her bowl in front of the stove. She's still learning her manners, but she's getting better. And you, my Peanut. You'll have your dish spot over here by the pantry door. Now sit."

Peanut promptly plopped his butt on the ground.

"Good boy! Wait." Tara held her hand in front of Peanut's nose. "Go ahead," as she removed her hand.

Peanut nosed the food around and looked up.

"Go ahead, baby. Eat your dinner. Oh, you're a slow eater. That's okay. The two sharks won't get your food. Take your time."

Connal and Gizmo were done with their dinners and were watching Peanut as he slowly ate one piece of food at a time.

"You two, go on. Leave him alone. He has manners and doesn't inhale his food like you two." Tara leaned against the counter and made sure that there were no food issues with the three dogs.

When Peanut was finally done, the game of check the other dishes began. Each dog went to the two dishes that weren't theirs, just to be sure that the other two had the same thing for dinner.

"Want to go out?" That got all three of the pups coming to her, barking and running in circles around her. "Boy, you fit right in Peanut."

Opening the door, the three dogs were out and running and barking before she got the door shut. She followed the frapping dogs while they did their business and investigated.

Sitting on one of the steps of the porch outside her room, she watched the dogs. Her three dogs. If someone had told her three months ago that she would be sitting on the porch steps of her house in Maine, watching her three dogs frapping by the ocean, she would have had them admitted to a mental hospital. None of the last few months was her norm. At all. But somehow, it was working for her. Now, she watched her three dogs play, already best buddies, even though they had only been together for three hours. They were so accepting and loving with no ulterior motives.

Life was weird sometimes, and she was just going to have to learn to go with it. She could plan and overthink everything down to the last tack, but in the end, life would do what life wanted, and she was just along for the ride. She sat there and let the pups play and snoot and snort until it got to be too cool to be outside for her, then called them in for the evening.

"Okay, let's see what we can do for some area rugs in here for you, Peanut." Tara got onto her favorite online shopping site, and 20 minutes later had a variety of area rugs and throws ordered. "They should be here in the next couple of days. That will make it so much easier for you. Until then, we'll have to make due. I can make a sling for your belly with a towel, so when you are trying to get up, I can help you not slide around so much. But you don't seem to be doing too bad in here."

Sitting there, looking at the three dogs sleeping on the sofa, she should have been content. But she wasn't. Something was off. "God, this seems to be the theme for the day for me. What the hell is bugging me now?"

Getting up, Tara went to make a cup of coffee. Waiting for the Keurig to finish, she looked at the clock. "What time did Gwenn leave?"

Going back to her computer, she logged into her security system. "Okay, the outside gate was opened at 3:30 PM. That would have been Gwenn leaving. It's now 6 PM. She said an hour and a half, right?" Tara looked at the three dogs and tried to ignore the panic in her gut. "Maybe she texted or called." But after finding her phone, there were no calls or texts.

She dialed Gwenn's phone. "No answer. Okay, relax. She doesn't carry her cell around all the time either. Maybe she's laid it down."

But Tara didn't like that Gwenn was over an hour late. Heading back to the kitchen, she found the card that Fred had given her that morning. She stood there for a minute, going back and forth on whether to call Fred. "I'll call Gwenn one more time. No answer, I'm calling Fred."

Dialing Gwenn's number again, she listened to it ring and ring. On the fourth ring, just as she was getting ready to hang up, it was answered. "Oh, thank God! You had me worried!" Tara collapsed against the counter.

"Ran into a bit of an issue here, Tara. Someone broke into my damn house. Tore my place up. Doesn't look like anything was taken, just wanted to do some damage and they did. They also left me a note similar to yours. Fred's here, and I'm just finishing up with him. He's going to be following me out to your place. Tara, I'm fucking freaked. Can I stay with you until this is figured out?" Gwenn's voice cracked and Tara could hear the tears threatening to start.

"Holy shit! Yes, you can stay here. Bring anything and everything you'll need. I'm so sorry, Gwenn. This is bullshit, and the little assholes that are doing this will be found and caught. Do what you need and get back here. You can stay here as long as you want to."

After Gwenn had hung up the phone with the promise to

94

be there soon, Tara went to the closet in her bedroom.

Standing in front of the gun safe that she had put into the back corner of the closet, Tara sighed, then placed her hand on the biometric reader. Once the safe was open, she looked at the gun collection. Making up her mind, she picked up the 9 mm. It was a Smith and Wesson MP 9. Reaching down, she took the 15-round magazine for it. Methodically, she loaded the clip into the grip of the weapon, slapping the clip to make sure it was seated. Pulling the slide back then pushing the button to release the slide, the gun was now loaded, with one in the chamber. Sliding the gun into a holster, she walked into her bedroom and opening the nightstand drawer on the left side of her bed, she placed the gun in the drawer. Tara stood there for a moment and grieved for the loss of her feeling of safety without a gun close by.

Shaking herself, she went back to the closet and chose her next weapon. This time a Beretta 12-gauge shotgun. This one she loaded with three shells, then taking a box of extra shells with her, she headed to the front door. After making sure the safety was on, she placed the shotgun and the shells in the entryway coat closet.

Once again, she went to the closet. Taking another Smith and Wesson MP 9, she repeated the process of loading it and went to the kitchen. This one was placed on top of the refrigerator.

Tara went back and forth to the closet two more times. She put another 12-gauge shotgun in the mudroom and the last 9 mm in the end table, beside the couch in the living room.

Locking the safe, Tara turned off the closet light and left her bedroom. She was ready for whatever was coming.

Tara had just finished taking the pups out for their last out of the night when Gwenn got back to the house.

Gwenn was greeted at the breezeway door by three wiggly, barking dogs and she needed it. She sat down on the floor and let the pups love on her which brought on the tears. "I fucking hate crying," she told the dogs and Tara, who had been watching her quietly during the whole welcome home.

"I do too, but sometimes it's needed. When you're done with your love fest with the dogs, I'm going to make some grilled cheese sandwiches and tomato soup. The ultimate feel good food. Why don't you pop us a couple of beers and sit? I don't expect you to go over what happened right now. We'll do it at your speed. You're here now, and safe. So, we can go over it when you want."

Gwenn smiled in appreciation that she didn't have to go right into the mess that her house was in. Grabbing the two beers, she handed Tara hers, then leaned against the counter beside the stove and watched Tara put the sandwiches in the cast iron skillet. They worked in silence, plating the food, then sitting across from each other at the island, they looked at their dinner, then each other and started laughing.

"Well, aren't we just the fun of the party?" Gwenn quipped and put her head in her hands.

"Yep, the thrill of the party here. We need to at least attempt to eat something. We haven't had anything to eat since lunchtime," Tara reminded Gwenn and made a show of eating her sandwich.

After they had eaten and the kitchen had been cleaned up, Tara looked at Gwenn. "Let's get your stuff in the house, then we can be done for the night. Maybe we can watch some TV and try to relax a bit before bed. You look beat up."

"I am. I feel like someone sucker punched me." Rubbing her face, Gwenn shrugged. "I really don't have that much to bring in. More clothes, my pillows, some books, toiletries, just the basics. I'm going to have to get to the house tomorrow and start cleaning up the mess."

"We'll go with you. Two people can clean up a mess faster than one."

It only took two trips to get all of Gwenn's stuff into the house and into her room. Now Gwenn stood there. She wanted to show Tara something, but she wasn't sure how she would take it. "Um, I brought a couple of things that I hope you won't be upset with. I don't think you will be, but it's your home, and I'm not sure how you will feel about it. If it bugs you, I'll put them back in the car, but I've brought two guns with me." Gwenn had taken the handguns out of a bag as she spoke. "I know you have guns in the house, but they're yours. These are mine. Actually, they were my daddy's, but they're mine now."

Tara looked at the guns, then at Gwenn. "You know how to use them?"

Gwenn nodded.

"Okay, I'm fine with them. Now I want to show you something."

Tara walked to the entryway closet and opened the door, then stepped back so that Gwenn could look in.

Gwenn turned to look at Tara. "Loaded?"

"Yeah. The safety is on, though. Do you know how to use a shotgun?"

"Yeah, I do."

Tara took Gwenn around to all the places she had put the guns. "I hate having to have guns all over the place, but I'd rather be prepared." Tara felt like she needed to explain.

"No need to explain it to me. After your threat letter and my house being broke into, and my threat letter, it's smart to be prepared. We aren't two weak women, and we aren't nutjobs. If someone wants to fuck with us, then by God, let them try. We're loaded for bear."

Gwenn sat down, hard, on the couch. "Someone tore up my house, Tara. I stopped by the house on the way to the restaurant to get us dinner and found the back door open. I knew I had locked it, but I had that moment of doubt that maybe I hadn't. As soon as I walked in, though, I knew. They emptied all the drawers in the kitchen, threw everything on the floor. Silverware, plates, glasses, food. It's a mess. I'm going to have to go in there with a trash can and a shovel, there's nothing left to save in there.

"The rest of the house is a mess, but it's all worth saving. All the furniture was flipped over, and my dresser drawers and closets were pulled apart. But most of that just needs to be straightened up. They didn't take the TV, stereo or any jewelry from the quick inventory I did. I'm so glad I had my laptop with me out here. I guess I can use this as an excuse to spring clean, huh?" Gwenn tried to smile but ended up with a half sob.

Tara sat down beside Gwenn and put her arm around her shoulder. "What did the note say?"

"Oh, they were real original in it. It was verbatim to your note. So, apparently, they aren't the sharpest tool in the shed. I don't know why I keep saying they. We don't know how many did this, but if it was one person, he was very busy, that's for sure. I really need to head over there tomorrow and clean up that kitchen before it starts smelling."

"We'll go with you. Make a day of it. Two adults and three dogs should have everything cleaned up in no time. You aren't alone in this."

Gwenn smiled her appreciation. She felt better now that she was in a house with another person. Three dogs around added to the comfort level. And knowing the house was alarmed and they had weapons around, she was starting to move from scared to pissed.

The next morning, Tara sat down at her computer and changed the passcode for the main gate, since last night had turned into a mess. She then changed the passcode to the garage and the house. And while she was at it, Tara paid for the software update for the security cameras. She hadn't been using them, but now, they were all functional and active. Tara downloaded the app to her cell phone and made sure that she could see the various cameras and that the notifications came in correctly. Then she had Gwenn do the same thing. Nothing and nobody was going to sneak up on them.

Since today was a cleaning day for Barb, Tara had decided today would be the day to discuss access and Barb's schedule with her. She had been putting it off for too long. But with the break in at Gwenn's and her note, it was time to tighten up her security.

"I'm not going to tell her all the gory details," Tara said an hour later while sitting on the porch with Gwenn.

"I agree. Bill and Barb don't need to know what's been going on. They just need to know that you have amped up the security some and that you have changed your codes and that you want to change their access. That's an entirely normal thing for a new owner to do." Gwenn had her feet up and her eyes closed. She could tell that Tara was nervous to confront Barb with changing the access to the house.

"Agreed. I just hope that I don't upset them when I tell them that they'll have to call for me to open the gate from now on. I'm not going to give them the code because I'm not sure how much I trust them. I mean they're a sweet couple, but Barb's become all school teachery to me when she's over here. Oh, she's polite but doesn't really talk. Granted, I'm not a chatterbox myself, but I do notice when a chatty Kathy stops chatting when I ask a question they don't like. Just seems odd. And odd puts me on the defensive."

Tara glanced sideways at Gwenn when there was no response and found her sleeping. Smiling, Tara got up and went back into the house to refill her coffee, then dropped the coffee cup and grabbed the gun on top of the fridge when the house alarm went off. At the same time, her phone started buzzing to show where the signal was coming from.

Gwenn came running into the house and grabbed the handgun from the end table beside the couch and then looked at her phone to see where the alarm was. While all of this was going on the dogs were adding their voices to the noise.

Heading to the front door, Tara and Gwenn both saw a petrified Barb standing there, hand still on the doorknob and mouth hanging open in shock.

Cursing, Tara opened the app and turned off the alarm.

"I'm so sorry. I don't know what I did wrong. Oh, my goodness that is a loud alarm. I'm not sure I've ever heard it go off. I don't think it's ever been used," Barb said, holding her chest.

Tara quickly hid her gun in the waistband of her pants, then stepped to Barb and laid her hand on Barb's arm. "No, I'm sorry Barb. I changed all the codes and hadn't had a chance to let you know. This is my fault."

"Come in and sit down. Let me get you a glass of iced tea." Gwenn took Barb over so that Tara could focus on the dogs and get them to calm down since all three of them were still doing an occasional bark or growl. Peanut was following Connal's and Gizmo's reactions and staying away from Barb.

Barb looked down at the dogs with a mild look of distrust and dislike, only then noticing Peanut. "Oh, you have another one. It's becoming quite a dog house here." She smiled, thin-lipped and slightly disapproving. "So, tell me about this new one."

Tara sat down across the island from Barb. "His name is Peanut, and he's 10 years old. We just got him from the shelter last night. He has some rear weakness, so I've ordered several area rugs, so he won't slip on the floors in here. He's a lover. He slept on my pillow last night. So, now I have a corgi on each side of my head at night." Tara obliged Barb with the information on Peanut. "He's also what is called a sable color. See, look at the base of his hair." She slid off the stool to push Peanut's fur up so that Barb could see the hair at the base of Peanut's back. "It's black. If you look at Connal's hair base, it's the same color as the tips of his hair. Connal is a red and white."

Standing up, Tara took a drink of her iced tea and braced herself. "I really am sorry Barb. I feel horrible for the scare that you got. I've changed the codes to the main gate and the house, but I'm not going to give you or Bill the codes. I would prefer that you and Bill call to gain access to the property from now on."

At Barb's shocked look, Tara continued. "I've been here for almost two months. Figured it was time to make the codes my codes and to use the system that is installed. I'm a very private person, and you two are great, but I prefer my privacy. I would love for you to continue to do the grocery shopping for me, but I would like to cook and clean my own house. I hope you understand."

Barb sat ramrod straight, lips pursed and nodded. "As you wish, my dear. It's your house after all. As I'm sure you are aware, Bill and I have a contract that is good until October. The previous owner had prepaid the year of our contract just before she passed on, so that's why we're here. It's entirely up to you on how you wish to continue with the contract since it's really no money out of your pocket."

Tara nodded and tried to remember she was an adult and not a 10-year-old, being talked down to by a school teacher. "Yes, I read that in the house paperwork a couple of weeks ago. I'm very sorry if this hurts your feelings, but I need to make this place mine. And to do that, I need to take care of it for myself. If you don't want to grocery shop for me, I understand. I won't ask you to move out of your house until the contract ends, and since I didn't pay anything extra in the buying of the house for your services, you are free to not continue any services that were outlined in the contract. The same goes for Bill. The manuals are very detailed on how to run all the equipment, so if he chooses to not continue on as handyman, I understand."

"I'm sure he'll still want to do his duties, and I don't mind doing your grocery shopping. Just email me your list and when you would like the groceries delivered. I think that would work well."

"That will be fine. Oh, one more question, Barb. When did you come through the gate today?"

"A little over an hour ago. I brought Bill some coffee and a sandwich. We sat and had an early lunch together. If that's all now, I think I'll go." Barb turned stiffly on her heel and after nodding to Gwenn left the house.

Gwenn grimaced. "Well, that wasn't painful to watch, at all. She's pissed. No. You were right, and you have every right to decide who has access to your house," she added when Tara started to interrupt.

"I didn't come off as mean then?" Tara was already second guessing and replaying the conversation in her head.

"No, definitely not. Barb just isn't used to anyone standing up for themselves. She'll get over it and if not, it's her problem. Why the question about coming onto the property this morning?"

"Just wanted to see how she got on the property after I changed the code. She had to have come on before I changed it, then stopped for lunch with Bill. And in the meantime, I changed the code and the security system so when Barb came to the house, the alarm went off," Tara explained.

"Oh, that makes sense, and I didn't even think about the time gap." Walking over to Tara, she shoulder bumped her. "You did the right thing so stop replaying it in your head."

Taking a drink of her iced tea to hide the smile from Tara's look of shock, Gwenn turned to lean against the island and look at Tara. "I think I'm going to head over to the house and start cleaning it up. I want to take my time and make sure nothing is missing. Nothing appeared to be missing last night, but that was just a quick walk through. Plus, I need to inventory and take pictures of all the things that are broken. That's what my insurance agent said to do. And, I figured since I have to clean everything up, I might as well spring clean and see what I don't want anymore. I've decided to make a positive out of a negative. See this as an opportunity to downsize and reorganize my crap."

"We'll come with you. Just let me get the dogs ready," Tara said, standing up and putting her glass in the sink.

Shaking her head, Gwenn held up her hand. "No, I'm good. Really. I need to do this myself. But thanks."

Swimming was usually relaxing for Tara, but not when she was attempting to do laps, all the while being paced and barked at by Connal, Gizmo, and Peanut. "I swear to God, if you three don't stop, I'm going to throw you in here."

Then, after thinking about it, she went to the shallow end and coaxed them down the steps. Before she knew it, they were all doggie paddling around her.

"This is great exercise for all of you. Especially you, Peanut. This will help with your back legs. As for you two brats, it's good exercise for you as well, since I think you've both gained weight." She played with the pups in the shallow end for a little bit more, then when she saw that they were getting tired, she taught them how to get out of the pool.

After taking a quick shower, Tara purposely sat down at the desk. She tried not to think about the fact the desk was part of the secret entrance to the room below. With a cup of coffee, Tara fired up her laptop and after doing a quick check on Facebook, set to work on making notes of what all they found and did yesterday.

She uploaded the photos that Gwenn had taken of the site and inserted them into her own field notes. It might seem like a waste of time to duplicate what Dr. Roxbury had already documented, but for Tara, it helped to make everything hers.

Now, sitting there, she looked at the photos. The landscape photos looked the same in both sets, the ones that Gwenn had taken yesterday and Dr. Roxbury's. So, they were in the right spot, that was evident. And according to Dr. Roxbury's notes, she had found artifacts in that place, which coincided with the flagging tape that they had found at various locations yesterday. Looking at the notes again, it seemed like the majority of the lithics had been found on the surface, so there would really be no units to dig or document.

"So basically, she went for a walk and saw artifacts on the ground at this one spot. She documented what she found, flagged the placement of each artifact and brought them home. Okay, I get that. I would've done the same thing. Why wouldn't she have dug though, to see if she had found a hot spot? Would I have dug if I found lithics on the surface? I don't know. Maybe. Maybe she was planning to dig later, then died. She marked the area, so maybe that was the plan. Nothing in her notes to indicate one way or the other. Maybe we'll go out there and do a test pit. See if there is anything there."

Rubbing her hands over her face, Tara glanced over to the other side of the office, where the pups were sprawled in various positions, and saw that the three dogs weren't listening to her ramble, as they were all asleep. "Geez guys, no thoughts on this at all? Fine, I didn't want to hear your opinions anyway. I really don't see anything from yesterday's out and about to warrant Dr. Roxbury's secrecy. Maybe she was just a batty old woman."

Saving and closing the field notes on her computer, she turned to the drawing of the rune that they had found in the Batcave. "Now you. You make no sense at all. I looked around yesterday to see if I saw anything in that area that looked like a rune and nothing. So, why would she draw this? Why not take a photo of the rune? If I found a rune, I would take a photo of it. Hell, I'd take multiple photos of it and maybe a selfie or two. After all, it's a freaking rune. And the photo would be to scale and with orientation marked. Any decent archaeologist would, which from what I've been seeing, Dr. Roxbury was. She was a professor for God's sake. This is lazy work. Why draw it if you found it?"

Tara continued to look at the pictures and drawing. "She documented every other object she found, but with the rune, she made a drawing. There are no field notes, nothing. Just one drawing. This is all wrong. The only reason to have a drawing is if you haven't actually seen the object. Otherwise, there would be a digital photo, she's proven that." Leaning back in her chair, Tara ran her hands through her hair. "Frig me. She didn't find a rune out here, that's why it's a drawing. Maybe she had a theory that she was working on, but there's no rune. Damn it to hell. Now I have to tell Gwenn that this is a dead end."

CHAPTER SIX

After Gwenn's break in, the next couple of days went by uneventful. Gwenn went to her pizza place early and came back late, and Tara spent the time getting acquainted with Peanut. Things were almost normal. That normal when you are just waiting for the next thing to happen.

Since it was a sunny day, Tara and the dogs were outside at the cove. While Tara walked the beach, looking for sea treasures, Connal, Gizmo, and Peanut were running and playing with seaweed and driftwood. At least until Gwenn drove in, which resulted in barking and a wet, mad dash to see her. Laughing, she met all the little wiggle butts as best as she could then walking down to the cove, she flopped on the beach.

"Oh, thank God, it's the weekend. As the owner, I've given myself the entire weekend off. I need it. I'm wiped out. There has been a crazy run on pizza this week. I think about half of it is folks being nosy and wanting to know about the break in." Gwenn paused for a minute and took a drink from the water bottle she had. "Mind you, I love the business. Business means money and Gwenn likes money. But damn, they don't all have to come in at the same time."

"So, you have the weekend off, huh? Think you're up for

an honest to goodness brainstorming session on what's been going on? I have some thoughts and would love to discuss them in detail with you." Tara looked over at Gwenn.

"Yeah, let's do that. I've been dying to get into researching that rune. We haven't had a chance to do that. I'm tired of pizza, so how about some good old-fashioned steak and potatoes on the grill? Salad on the side? Working food. Then we can pick this son of a bitch open and start working on solving it." Gwenn had her eyes closed, and Tara noticed that the last few words had slurred just a bit.

Smiling, Tara leaned back on her elbows. "That sounds great, and by coincidence, I have two steaks thawing in the kitchen, and I'm pretty sure there are bakers in the pantry. And salad? That's that green stuff, right?"

"Wow, rabbit food isn't all that bad, and neither was the real food. Need to do that more often." Gwenn was busy putting the dishes in the dishwasher, and Tara was in the process of feeding the dogs.

"It was rather tasty, and I almost feel healthy. I'm going to take the pups out for their bathroom time, then if you're ready, let's pow-wow in the living room?"

"Sounds good. I'm going to get a pot of coffee going and just so we don't feel overly healthy, I brought home a cheesecake to go with the coffee. Then I'll get the books and photos and our laptops, okay?" Gwenn was feeling at home, but she didn't want to overstep by going into Tara's room and office without her permission.

Tara closed her eyes and smacked her lips. "Mm, coffee and cheesecake. My two favorite things. Are you sure you aren't my long-lost sister? I've uploaded those photos from the other day, and I have notes, so if you get my laptop, that would be great. Actually, grab all the stuff on the desk, please. I'll be right back."

Tara came back in with the dogs 15 minutes later and found the living room had been redecorated to resemble a full-blown base of operations.

Gwenn had moved two of the corkboards from the Batcave up, and they were situated in front of the French doors in the living room. The coffee table had been moved to the side, and the laptops were on either arm of the couch, which had also been moved. The couch now faced the corkboards. Gwenn had also moved the end tables on either side of the couch, and those were now set with mugs of coffee and slices of cheesecake. Not to leave the dogs out, there were three dog beds and a toy bin off to the side of the board, closer to Gwenn's door to her room, Tara noticed.

"Damn, I leave for a bit, and you rearrange the whole place. I love it, I'm just teasing," Tara hurried to add to ease the look of worry on Gwenn's face.

Gwenn shrugged one shoulder. "I just got on a roll, and before I knew it, bam. I'll move it all back after we're done for the day."

"We'll see. Maybe I'll leave it this way. The view really is amazing." She stood and took in the view of the cove behind the boards. "Okay, let's get this party started, shall we?"

Sitting down at her assigned end of the couch, Tara booted up her laptop. Gwenn followed suit and did the same.

"I did some field notes from the other day. I also attached the photos that you took to the notes." Tara moved closer to Gwenn so that she could read the notes.

Gwenn leaned over Connal so that she could read Tara's screen. "I agree with all of that. I also took it upon myself to write out my thoughts of the day."

Now it was Tara's turn to lean over Connal and read. "Well, damn if we don't seem to be on the same page with note taking. Something has been bugging me about all of this. I want your honest thoughts. So, why don't you look at everything you brought up on the corkboard. See if something seems off to you. Take your time. If it's okay with you, now that we're together, I want to research that rune while you look at all we have."

"Yeah, go ahead. See what it is and means. Let me see what we have here." Gwenn stood up and started looking at the items pinned to the corkboard.

Tara let her do her thing and brought up Google to search rune images. It didn't take long for the rune that was hanging on the board to appear. After reading several websites on the rune, Tara copied and pasted the information into the field notes. She would share with Gwenn after she had gotten to the same place as she had.

Gwenn was talking quietly to herself. Mumbling would be a more appropriate word. Tara stood up and went over to her.

"Want to talk it out?"

Gwenn nodded. "Yeah. I don't know your field of study that well at all, so I'm just going to wing it. But here," she pointed to the three pictures of the plant, "Dr. Roxbury has multiple photos of a plant. But then over here," now she pointed to the drawing of the rune, "here, she draws a rune. Doesn't take a photo. She draws it. Now, me, if I had found an amazing Viking rune in BFE Maine, I would have taken a shit ton of photos of it, including several selfies. I wouldn't have drawn it. But she draws the rune. And takes photos of a plant. That doesn't make any sense. Right? We know she was detailed oriented because of the documenting she did for the artifacts that she found, so why would she become super lazy if she had found the find of a lifetime? It just doesn't fit with what we know about her." Gwenn turned to Tara and was rewarded with a huge smile and nodding.

"Exactly my thought. I would have photos of the rune. With scale and direction. I might have drawn it later, to include it in the field notes, but there would have been digital photos. Did you notice that the plant photos are set to scale? Why? What is the big deal with it? It's just a plant, but she's giving it the same amount of attention as she did the artifacts that she found."

Tara got her laptop and brought up the image of the rune she had found. "I think that Dr. Roxbury researched this rune for some reason. It sort of looks like a pitchfork, doesn't it? Or a capital Y laid over a little l. Sorry, squirrel moment there. Anyway, it's called Algiz, and it's the Z rune of the Elder

Futhark runic alphabet. Then when the Younger Futhark runic alphabet was adopted, Algiz was flipped upside down so that the pitchfork part was on the bottom, and took the name of Yr and the R sound. That looks like it happened about the 7th century. Following me so far?" Tara glanced over at Gwenn.

"Um, yeah. Elder is older than Younger. Ha ha. They took the rune, flipped it and changed its meaning from Z to R. Right?" Gwenn shook her head a little.

"Yeah, that's basically what I'm getting from all of this. Anyway, the Yr rune translates into Yew. Since we don't know which side is up on the drawing, we don't know if it's the Algiz, which means Elk, or the Yr rune. I don't know why she drew this, but my gut says she didn't find this. I think it just interested her for whatever reason." Sighing, Tara looked over at Gwenn.

Gwenn stood there and looked at the board while she digested what Tara had just said. Slowly nodding her head and sighing. "Damn it, but that makes sense. So, it's not about a rune or Vikings or anything super cool like that.

"But she was still doing something weird and sneaky. She had a Batcave built, and that's not a normal thing to do. But I agree, the drawing of the rune is nothing. So, now what?

"We've ruled out the artifacts she found as the reason for all the secrecy. You said that what she had found was interesting but not earth shattering in the world of archaeology." Gwenn took the photos of the artifacts, along with the note cards and field notes off the board as she said this.

"And we've just ruled out the rune as something she was interested in since there are no photos or notes. Just a hand drawing of it." Gwenn removed the drawing from the board.

"So, that leaves us with three photos of a plant? Really? That's what we have left? What's the big deal over a stupid plant?" Gwenn flopped on the couch and picked up her coffee.

"I have no idea, but I think we need to research it.

Granted, Dr. Roxbury might have just been a crazy old woman, but something is telling me there is more to this. Even crazy people do stuff for a reason. Usually. I mean, why would she have several photos of a plant? Why would she have the photos to scale? That's just not a normal thing to do with a plant unless she was a serious landscaper or gardener and I'm not getting that vibe from her at all. I mean, she hired Bill to maintain the property, so her interest in landscaping seems nil. That plant must mean something. So, let's see if we can find this plant and what it is."

"Geez, this is going to be easy. Google green plant. Only 539 million results," Gwenn retorted dryly.

"Yeah, this is going to be a challenge. Why don't you work on the green plant googling and I'm going to try something different. I'm going to see what I can find on Dr. Roxbury. Maybe the plant was at one of her dig locations. What was her first name?" Tara paused in her typing and looked at Gwenn.

"Oh, nice. Leave me to 539 million results while you get to research one person. That doesn't seem fair at all. Give me a minute on the first name, I know it, I just can't remember it at the moment." Gwenn was quiet long enough for Tara to think she was being ignored, so she started googling using Dr. Roxbury and got two million results.

"Seriously? Two million hits on Dr. Roxbury. That's just crazy," Tara grumbled to Connal who was leaning against her side, then jumped when Gwenn shouted.

"Edna! Edna Roxbury was her name." Proud of herself, Gwenn returned to her plant googling.

"Awesome." Adjusting the search with the first name and adding professor of archaeology, Tara turned her laptop so that Gwenn could see an image of a lady, mid-50s, short gray hair and horn-rimmed glasses. "Is this her?"

"Yep, that's her. See. You got the easy research. No fair," Gwenn grumbled while scrubbing Gizmo's ear and rubbing Peanut with her foot.

"Suck it up, buttercup. Okay, Dr. Edna Jean Roxbury. BA in archaeology from the University of Texas, MA in archaeology, also from the University of Texas. Then she got her Ph.D. from the University of Illinois, Carbondale. She did her fieldwork for her dissertation in Peru. Actually, she did a ton of work in Peru. She retired from a university in Peru as the archaeology department head six years ago. Then, we know that she moved up here. Okay, so maybe research green plants in Peru."

Gwenn adjusted her search. "That's a little better, only six million, three hundred thousand hits now. Where in Peru?"

"Hold on, I'm looking at her studies. I know she worked for a university in Ica, but that doesn't mean that's where she dug or where her focus was."

Several minutes with nothing from Tara, Gwenn got up and went to the kitchen to put away the dishes, then gave the dogs some treats and freshened their water. With nothing still from Tara, she headed into her room and made sure her outside doors were locked, and the curtains were drawn. She repeated the process in Tara's room and in the other two bedrooms of the house. When Gwenn walked back into the living room and noticed that Tara was completely into the article she was reading, she headed to the front door and made sure it was locked.

"Try the Ica region of Peru. It looks like that area was her specialty after all," Tara yelled out.

Gwenn came back into the living room and picked up the search for the plants. "Well, that brought us down to one million, nine hundred thousand results. Should be easy now, right?" Gwenn sighed as she started her newest search.

Now, it was Tara's turn to get up and move around. "I'm taking the pups to the riding arena for final outs and to make sure everything is locked up out there." Gwenn answered with a distracted wave that looked more like a go away gesture.

Tara opened the mudroom door, and the three dogs sprinted to the riding arena door and waited, impatiently, for Tara to open the door. While the dogs ran and rolled and did their business, Tara went to each of the doors in the arena to make sure they were all locked up. She knew they were, but it had become a habit to check. And by checking to make sure everything was locked up, it helped to ease the concern that had set in on her since the notes and Gwenn's break in. She knew that the property was fenced and alarmed, but having locked doors added to her sense of peace. Coming back to the dirt arena, she watched the dogs run off some energy, then cleaned up after them before leading them out of the arena and back to the house. She locked the door to the breezeway and turned around to a smiling, proud of herself, Gwenn.

"I found it, I think." She led the way back to her laptop and sat down. "So, the plant is called psycho something. I'll send you the link so you can see what its official name is. Anyway, it's a perennial shrub from South America. When the leaves are boiled with the vines of another word that I can't pronounce, but that starts with a B, it becomes yet another word that I can't say, but it means a tea that gets the drinker high. Tara, those photos we have are of a plant that can be used to make a drug. It's a tropical plant so it wouldn't be able to grow here in Maine, at least not outside. So, that eliminates the possibility that it's just a pretty plant that Dr. Roxbury liked and wanted to try to grow here. Why would she have photos of a plant she can't grow here?"

"Holy shit. If this is true, this just got really big and really ugly, Gwenn." Tara was pacing, occasionally stopping to look at the photos of the plant that Dr. Roxbury had taken and then looking at the pictures on the Internet that Gwenn had found. "This is beyond us, you know that, right? We need legal and professional help if this is true. But who? I don't know any of the law enforcement up here. Should we call Fred? I don't like Fred. I know he's your friend, but I don't like him. And would he just blow us off? Son of a bitch! Thoughts anytime, Gwenn."

Gwenn had been sitting and following Tara's pacing back and forth, and quietly chuckling because Connal, Gizmo, and Peanut were pacing behind Tara in some sort of weird, little train. She shook her head to come out of her silly thoughts. "First, let's calm down. I think we should print out a copy of this plant from the Internet, blow both the photos up and see if they're the same plant. I could be wrong. It might not be the same plant once we actually look at the leaves and such. We know that the plant wouldn't be able to grow up here, so that's something else to consider. If it is here, where is it being grown? We know it's not outside and I haven't seen a greenhouse anywhere around here, have you?"

Tara stopped so quickly that Connal ran into the back of her legs, which caused Gizmo to run into Connal and Peanut to run into Gizmo. Tara didn't seem to notice, but Gwenn thought she should win an Academy Award for not falling off the couch laughing.

Nodding now, Tara looked over a Gwenn. "Okay, those are all good points. And you're right. We need to calm down and think about this methodically. Let's blow up the photos and see if they're the same plant."

Twenty minutes later with the photos blown up to show the leaves and detail of the plants, Tara flipped back and forth between them and tried to see a difference.

"You can look as hard as you want, Tara. It's the same fucking plant," Gwenn mumbled from the couch. She had her head back on the couch and her eyes closed. "It's a fucking plant that can be used to make a drug tea."

Tara joined Gwenn on the couch and assumed the same position Gwenn was in. "Son of a bitch. Why couldn't it have been Viking runes? Why does everything always come back to drugs? Now, what do we do? Call the cops? But why? For a photo of a plant that when mixed with another plant makes a drug tea? There is no evidence that the plant was here. Just some photos, that's it. So, we really have nothing. For all we know, Dr. Roxbury could have taken these pictures when she was still in Peru. She was a professor of archaeology. Maybe she was trying to learn about the drug to better understand the culture. This could be absolutely nothing. We could be jumping to conclusions here."

Tara got up and went to the kitchen to put the tea kettle on to boil. Getting two mugs out, she put in green tea bags and honey to wait for the water to boil. "We have a batty-assed old lady that had a secret Batcave built and photos of a plant. That doesn't mean anything."

"Good points. We really don't have anything—What?" Gwenn had joined Tara in the kitchen and was dunking her teabag in her cup, but stopped when Tara turned white. "What? Are you okay? Here, sit down."

Instead of sitting down, Tara grabbed Gwenn's arm and pulled her to the office in her bedroom.

"What the hell, Tara? You're scaring me."

"Sorry, but when I first started looking for the Batcave, I did a thorough search of this office. During that time, I looked in all the cabinets and in this one," she opened the cabinet above the Keurig coffee pot, "I found this container. I didn't think anything of it, other than the tea leaves stunk." Tara handed the container to Gwenn, and Gwenn slowly pulled the lid off.

"You don't think that this is the leaves of that plant in the photos, do you? Please tell me you don't. Son of a bitch! Tara, if this is the leaf of that plant, then where did she get them from? She left Peru six fucking years ago!"

"I don't know. Let's see if we can Google what the dried leaves of that plant smells and looks like. Maybe it's just a stinky-assed tea leaf. But first, what do they look like to you? And what do they smell like? That way we have our reference before we read anything."

"Okay. To me, the leaves are reddish brown, and it smells—Wait, we can't get high smelling them, right?" Gwenn stopped just before putting the container to her nose.

"Shit, good question. We'll hold off on the smelling portion until we know more. But I agree on the reddish brown. Let's go up and see what we can find on the dried leaves."

It didn't take long for Tara and Gwenn to resume their previous positions on the couch. This time, Connal had decided to lay on Tara's feet, and Gwenn had both Gizmo and Peanut at her elbows. Their research had proven what they knew before they had left the office. The dried tea leaves were from the plant. With their heads back and their eyes closed, Tara felt like crying.

"Dammit to hell. I'm going with my gut here, Gwenn. This stinks all over. All of this is odd and weird, and on top of all of this, Dr. Roxbury died here. My gut says she didn't just die. I think she was killed. Now, we find out that she has photos of a Peruvian plant that can be used to make a drug and she had a container of the plant leaves? That makes my gut sit up and take notice." Turning her head, she glanced over at Gwenn.

Gwenn sighed, then turned her head to look at Tara. "Yeah, I agree with you. This is all pointing to Dr. Roxbury being into something illegal, and it got her killed. But the big question now is where would you grow a plant from Peru in Maine?"

Tara sat up and sipped on her tea. "That's a damn good question. Well, we know that the plant is a tropical plant, so outside is out of the question. As you've pointed out, there are no greenhouses or hothouses on the property and I've not seen anything that looks like a plant in the riding arena or the equipment barn."

Pulling her knee up in front of her, Tara turned to face Gwenn. "This is going to be out there, but she had a freaking Batcave built under her house. Why couldn't she have had a hothouse built underground too? The Batcave is climate controlled so it would be possible to have another climate controlled room underground here too."

Gwenn slowly nodded her head and turned to face Tara. "She could have. She already has one secret room down there."

"I know you want to look tonight, and so do I, but it's getting late, and we're both tired. I think we need to knock this off for the evening. Let's try to relax a bit, then tomorrow, we go to the Batcave and see if there is a secret lever to another room. What do you think?"

"Yeah, that sounds good, even though I really want to go

and look. But, you're right, it's late, and I'm drained. We would probably miss something that would be easy to find normally. So, let's try to put this on the back burner for the night and hit it again tomorrow morning. Maybe it won't seem so bad in the morning."

Early the next morning, Tara and Gwenn, along with Connal, Gizmo, and Peanut were standing in the middle of the Batcave.

"Let's divide up the room right down the middle, okay? You look for anything on the couch side, and I'll take the kitchenette and bathroom side. If there is another secret room down here, it would make sense to have it connected to this room," Tara said to Gwenn. "At least, that's what I would do. If I was a batty-assed old lady that built a Batcave and grew drug plants."

"I think after all of this we'll both be batty-assed old ladies that once thought a Batcave was a cool thing. Okay, so let's see. Where would I put a secret lever to an underground hot house?" Gwenn started feeling along the walls and bookshelves on her side for anything that felt different and knocked on things along the way.

Tara was doing the same thing on her side. It was silent except for the knocking, which resulted in a sporadic little boof or growl from the dogs and the occasional grunt or mumbled curse word from the humans.

"This is stupid," Tara growled out after over two hours of fruitless searching. "Stop. Just stop. We aren't going to find shit this way. No. Wait. Before you start arguing, I have an idea. And it will be a faster, and I think, a more productive search then this."

Sitting down on the couch, Tara reached down to pet whichever dog head appeared in front of her. "I'm going to have to make some calls later, but I'm going to get a ground penetrating radar. That way we can search for another secret room but from the outside. We won't have to touch, tap, push, and pull every freaking thing in this room, or maybe the house, for that matter. For all we know, the other room might not even be connected to the office. With the radar, we can see where it is, then we can continue looking for the entrance."

Sitting down beside Tara, Gwenn took over the head petting of Connal. "That's a fucking brilliant idea. So, since we're basically stuck on looking for the plants, I think we've worked enough. I'm going for a swim. How about you?"

"Nah, but if you could take the pups with you, they need the exercise since they've been useless during all of this and slept. That is if you're up to water wrestling three dogs. I'm going to figure out something for lunch since we really didn't have anything before we started searching. Something easy. I'm tired, and I think comfort food will help. Lunch in about an hour, okay?"

Gwenn gave a thumbs up as she headed up to her room to change, followed by the three dogs. Tara chuckled, then closed the office door and headed to the kitchen to figure out lunch.

While Tara, Gwenn, and the dogs spent the rest of the day relaxing, they didn't know that just outside the mouth of the cove, there was a small lobster boat. But it wasn't setting lobster pots. The man on board didn't care about catching dinner. He was more concerned about the two women in the house that his now dead girlfriend had owned. Had those two bitches found the plants? And if so, where? He had been all over that damn property and had never found the plants.

He was still pissed about the notes and the break in. He knew who was responsible, and he had chewed their asses for it. The idiots were messing up his chances of finding the plants since it had caused Gwenn to move out here.

He noticed that the tremors were starting again, so he unscrewed the lid of the thermos he had beside him. Pouring out some of the tea, he drank it down like you would a shot of liquor, instead of sipping it. He preferred it cold and sweet. That way he could drink it faster and not have to linger over the taste of it. Even cold, the taste was horrible.

"I really hope they figure out how to get this in pill form

soon. This stuff tastes like shit." He took a drink from the water bottle that he had with him, then spit overboard. As he turned the boat away from the cove and north toward Eriksport, he could feel the tea starting to work.

Tara spent most of the next morning on the phone calling old friends and acquaintances. It was Sunday morning, and Gwenn typically didn't work on Sunday, but she had decided to go to work, even though she said she was taking the whole weekend off. Tara knew that she was nervous and going to work would take her mind off what they had learned.

"Finally!" Tara leaned back in her chair. "Looks like it's time for a road trip guys."

All three furry heads popped up on those words. "No, not at this moment," Tara told the pups. This reply prompted the sighing and the laying down of all three furry heads. "But tomorrow. Now, since we're caught up with what we can do, why don't we have some swim time?"

The three dogs took off for the door to the breezeway, which led to the swimming pool.

"Nope, today we play at the cove. It's a beautiful day, so let's go enjoy it. Let's go get some sun and fresh air, you stinky little fur-balls."

After changing into a lighter shirt and shorts, grabbing a couple of towels, a bottle of water and her cell, the four of them headed out the door toward the cove. Just as Tara got settled down into the lounge chair, her phone alerted to someone at the gate.

"Great. Well hopefully, she won't be in teacher mode today," Tara mumbled to herself after she opened the gate for Barb, who had the groceries for the week.

"Perfect day to relax and enjoy the water," Barb commented twenty minutes later, as she took a seat on the grass beside the lounge chair that Tara was in.

"I thought so. They seem to be loving it. Too cold for humans, but furry little dogs don't appear to have an issue with it." Tara motioned towards the three dogs, who were lying in the sand at the edge of the water, almost asleep.

"The new one, Peanut, what's wrong with his back legs? He seems to drag them some."

Tara nodded and after glancing over at Barb to gauge her attitude, decided to give her a full answer, instead of the snarky yes she had been prepared to give. "Yeah, he does. I'm not 100% sure, but I'd bet he has DM. Degenerative Myelopathy. There is a test that I can order to verify the DM and I probably will, but right now, I'm guessing that's what it is. It's a disease of the spinal cord. Sort of like ALS in humans," Tara explained to Barb. "I'm a member of a group of folks on Facebook who all have, or have had or will probably have dogs with this disease. I'm going to ask about getting a wheeled cart for him. Not to use all the time, but it will help to get him used to it before he needs it all the time." Tara finished and waited to see where this conversation would head with Barb. It was sort of like playing Russian Roulette. Which statement would trigger the snippy Barb?

But, today, Barb seemed to be chatty and friendly. "Isn't that cruel for him? I mean, doesn't it hurt him? The disease. Isn't he sad that he can't move?"

"No, it's not cruel. Is it cruel to put humans in wheelchairs when they can't walk? Or to use crutches when you hurt a leg? It's the same concept. And since it's a disease of the spinal cord, the nerves basically die. That causes weakness and the loss of use. Like being paralyzed. Dogs are resilient creatures in that they live in the moment. He isn't sad or upset. He's a happy boy, and he'll be a happy boy with wheels." Tara had turned to look at Barb during the conversation.

Barb turned back toward Tara and smiled. "I like that. We'll have to get him knobbies for the sand and a racing flag so we can see where he is."

Tara chuckled. "Yeah, bigger tires would be good for the sand and the rocks. And the flag wouldn't be a bad idea either. I'll talk to the owner of the group tonight and work on getting the measurements for the cart. The sooner Peanut has the wheels, the sooner he can learn to use them."

"I could stay like this forever, but I have stuff to do. I made you girls a lasagna and a big pot of beef stew. I know you said you didn't need me to cook for you, but I wanted to. Sort of a peace offering. I thought over our last conversation, and you have every right to want your house to be yours." Getting up, Barb patted Tara on the shoulder before heading to her car. "Now you make sure you eat them. I outdid myself on the lasagna if I must say so."

"We will. Thank you, Barb. For the dinners and for understanding."

Barb waved as she left.

"Twenty more minutes, then we need to get up and do something," Tara told the pups, then closed her eyes.

"Well, that was a long twenty minutes," Tara grumbled, as she was getting dressed after a quick shower. The twenty minutes had turned into an hour-long nap in the sun.

Looking in the mirror, she realized that she had needed both. The nap and the sun. The dark rings under her eyes weren't as prominent now and the fresh bronze the sun had kissed her with helped to dull the paleness of her face. After another critical look in the mirror, she turned and went into the living room.

"Hm, what to do, what to do?" Tara stood in the middle of the living room and slowly turned, tapping her fingers on her thigh. "We could clean the house." She looked down at the three dogs that were sprawled out in the rays of sunlight. "Yeah, that doesn't sound like fun."

Walking over to the French doors, she stood and looked out past the cove. Usually, that view held nothing man-made, but today, there was a small boat anchored outside of the mouth of the cove. Not close, but it was still there. Tara absently rubbed her arms.

"It's just a lobster boat. Even though we haven't seen a boat anchored anywhere near here the entire time we've been here." Squinting her eyes, she tried to get a better look at the boat, but it was too far away to really see clearly. "Damn. I wonder who that is." Frustrated, Tara stood there, watching the boat. What she didn't know was that the man on the boat was watching her and he had the benefit of binoculars so he could see that she was looking in his direction.

"Oh, so you see me, do ya? That's okay, I'm just a lobsterman." He splashed a lobster pot over the side of the boat, closest to the house. "There you go, sweetheart. Nothing to see here," he chuckled to himself.

"See, he just placed a pot. Nothing to worry about," Tara told the dogs and the empty house. But she still had that weird little feeling in her gut that something wasn't right. "I think it's time to do some shopping for binoculars and maybe a telescope."

CHAPTER SEVEN

Tara left the property early the next morning, and despite the disapproval of the dogs, she went by herself on this adventure. The drive just to get the ground penetrating radar was about two hours there, then another two hours back plus add to that she had lunch plans with the friend that had gotten her the unit. She didn't want to leave the three dogs in the car during lunch, which she knew would be a long lunch, so she had left the house to three disapproving Corgi faces.

But the dogs were in good hands. When had Gwenn become good hands? Tara wasn't a trusting person, so the fact that she was trusting Gwenn with her dogs confused her. It also scared her because she wasn't used to having someone be there to support her. Now, giving kudos to Wyatt, he did the best he could, but she had always needed to ask. He had never just done the support on his own. With Gwenn, she just stepped in and did it. There was no asking, and that was weird. When Tara had told Gwenn about the road trip to get the ground penetrating radar, Gwenn had answered with what she and the pups would do while Tara was gone. Just that simple. It was a weird and wonderful feeling to have someone there, and Tara could get used to that. Gwenn really was a great person, and somehow, she had gotten deeper than pretty much anyone else in her life. That was perplexing and odd for someone that had always been on her own, even when there were people in her life that wanted to help.

Shaking her head to clear the internal dialog, Tara put a P!nk CD into the player. Road trips deserved good music. And good music required it to be blasted at ear bleeding levels and sung, horribly, at the top of her lungs. That's how the next hour and a half passed, but as Tara got closer to her destination, the level of music and singing came down in volume.

Twenty minutes later she pulled into the parking lot and turned off the car, then just sat there for a moment. It had been a long time since she had seen her friend, and Tara had some mixed feelings. On the one hand, she had good memories of Teresa and their time working together in the field. On the other hand, were the not so good memories of where they had been friends at. When she had called Teresa yesterday, it had brought back the last time she had seen her.

And, of course, those thoughts turned to Charles, the jerk that had gotten her fired. No, not fired. They had given her the option to quit first. And she had. It wasn't that she had been in the wrong, it was more the fact that they were calling her integrity into question. So, with pride in her heart, she told her bosses to shove the job up their asses and left. It still burned her that Charles had told her supervisor that she had falsified a report when in reality he had. But he was one of the boys, and she was a greenhorn, so bye-bye to Tara. Karma had bitten him, though, and he was still at the same place, job, and title that he had 15 years ago.

She had moved up and had gained the reputation of a no-holds barred archaeologist. Her work was beyond any question, and she had been sought out for her expertise. A little bit of her hoped that jackass Charles had heard her name as she climbed the ladder.

Smiling at that thought, Tara got out of the car and headed to the front door of the cultural resource company that Teresa worked at now. Since it was not the same place that Tara had worked with Teresa, there was no chance of seeing Charles. She wasn't sure she wouldn't have still walked up and kicked him in the balls if she ever saw him again. Yes, she knew being the bigger person was the way to go, but the image of him doubled over on the ground, with his tiny, little balls in his throat, put just a bit too much of a gleam in her eye. Walking in, she headed to the receptionist but was grabbed in a bone crushing hug.

"Tara! Honey! It's awesome to see you again," Teresa exclaimed. "God, I've missed you! It's been too long." She held Tara out at arm's length and looked her up and down. "Damn girl, you've lost some weight! And you've been in the sun. You look great."

Tara reciprocated the greeting. "It's really good to see you too. I've missed you, and I've been a horrible friend for not keeping in touch with you. Tell me what you've been up to. You look amazing, by the way. But then again, you always looked more like a model on a photo shoot than an archaeologist digging in the dirt."

Teresa answered by wrapping her arm around Tara's waist and walking down the hallway, leading away from the receptionist. "Let's get the equipment first, then we'll do lunch to get you all caught up on the life of Teresa. It's going to take a bit, and it will require margaritas. And I want to know all about the life of Tara too. I think I might have to take the afternoon off for this lunch."

Stopping in front of the equipment cage, Teresa glanced at Tara. "So, you need a GPR? What are you up to girl? Where are you digging? What are you digging? I must admit that you calling me yesterday got me to wondering what you've been up to. I've seen and heard your name throughout the years, so I know you have been busy and doing damn well for yourself. Unlike Charles. Sorry. That was rude and snarky, but he deserves it for the shit he pulled on you."

Teresa was silent while she worked the lock on the grated door to the equipment cage. "I think I'm going to sign you out with this one. It's a good and easy GPR to use, and it's one of the four-wheeled models, so it's not evil to push around all day. Do you need the instruction book?"

Tara nodded after walking around the unit. "Yeah, I most definitely need the book. It's been a little too long since I've played with one of these, so having the manual would be a good idea. And thanks for thinking of my old body and giving me the four-wheeled model," Tara teased. "As for the digging, I'm not really digging anywhere. I just bought a new property and want to see what's in the ground. You know how it is. Fresh ground and you want to make sure you aren't sitting on a buried pyramid or the Ark."

"Uh huh. Fine, keep it to yourself. For now. But you know I'll get it out of you eventually. And you know I'm always up for some rogue digging." Teresa knew that Tara was evading the question and she would work on getting the answer out of her over lunch. "Come on then. Let's get this to your car, then you can follow me to lunch. I know just the place. You'll love it. Should bring back memories of that time we were digging in Virginia and got lost in that little town. Remember? The one with the clothing optional bar? Wow, that was a wild dig. I miss those days."

Five hours later, Tara pulled into the garage and turned off the car. Talking to Teresa and reminiscing had gotten her thinking about where she had started and where she was now. She was a landowner. She had three corgis. She had a friend. A real friend. She would even say a best friend if you could have a best friend in less than a month of knowing someone. Who would have thought? Strange how life does a 90-degree turn and you start heading in an entirely different direction than what you had planned. She was about as far away from her plan that she had made at 18 years old as she could have been. There had been some bumps and hairpin turns, along with one or two roadblocks, but she was very happy with the overall trip so far.

Shaking her head, Tara got out of the car and headed into the house. There was immediate barking and toenails scratching as her herd of corgis came to greet her. Yeah, this was the good life. Smiling and laughing she got down on the floor and had a love session with the pups.

"When you're done loving on your evil herd, I've made dinner. They missed you if you haven't figured that out by their display. It was rather sad really. They slept at the door most of the day. Of course, I had to try to cheer them up with a swim or two, some outside play time and lots and lots of treats." On the word treats, the three dogs abandoned Tara and rushed toward Gwenn.

"And the true love of their lives has been revealed. Treats." Smiling, Tara got off the floor and walked to Gwenn. "Thanks for staying with them today. It made the trip easier, and I didn't worry about them. So, I got the GPR. Ground Penetrating Radar," she explained when Gwenn looked at her questioningly. "I want to start working with it tomorrow morning. It makes the most sense to start above the Batcave. That way we can see what the signal will look like if we find something else."

They moved into the living room and sat munching on a pizza that Gwenn had made. Of course, all three dogs were sitting between the two of them to remind them that pizza bones were appreciated and expected. Tara didn't disappoint and tore the crust of her pizza into three pieces and gave equal portions to each of the pups.

"That makes sense. Do you really think there are more rooms down there?" Gwenn was not to be outdone and gave the three dogs equal amounts of her pizza crust as well. "I'm going to have to start making pizza bones as a side item at the restaurant. I'm betting that it's a rather common thing for dog owners." Laughing, she rubbed all three heads after giving out the last of her pizza bones.

Tara chuckled, then snapped her fingers, which brought Connal, Gizmo, and Peanut to her. "Okay, that's enough you three. Go lay down now."

After some grumbling and backtalk from Connal, the dogs laid down, within eyesight of the pizza.

"That's a good idea, and I'm sure they would be a big seller. I don't know if there are other underground rooms, but Dr. Roxbury put in the Batcave, so maybe she put in a growing room for the plants. With the equipment, it will be easier and faster to find anything that isn't natural. Might as well verify or negate the theory, then we'll know for sure." Standing up, Tara took Gwenn's plate.

This action had Connal, Gizmo, and Peanut on their feet and beside Tara, waiting to see where they were going next and hoping for more pizza bones.

"Since you made dinner, I'll clean up. Then I want to get the equipment out of the car and get a feel for it. I don't really want to spend the morning figuring out the equipment. Would rather use the time to see what might be down there. It's been several years since I used equipment like this and I'm sort of excited."

"I am too. I'm starting to feel the need to order a fedora online. Maybe the whip, too." Gwenn came to sit at the island, watching Tara clean up.

"I have those websites bookmarked if you want to order the fedora and whip. It's a requirement to buy them when you graduate with the degree." Tara glanced over to see Gwenn staring at her, mouth open. Tara chuckled. "I'm joking. Close your mouth. It's not a requirement, but I do have a fedora. Graduation gift from my parents."

Gwenn pointed her finger at Tara. "You'll pay for that one. Anyway, I've read about remote sensing but have never seen it used. Are you going to let me play too?"

"Maybe. Depends on how much fun I'm having," Tara said while putting a plate in the dishwasher.

"You suck, you know that? You're lucky you have cute dogs because that's all you have going for you," Gwenn retorted back. "Finish cleaning up the kitchen, funny lady. I'm going to take my cute pups for a walk outside. Yes, my dogs. They've abandoned you for their fun-loving and treat giving auntie." She stuck her tongue out as she left the house through the living room French doors.

"So, you ready to see what might be in the ground here?" Tara asked Gwenn early the next morning.

They had made a quick fix of coffee and donuts for breakfast and were now standing at the corner of Tara's porch off her bedroom, closest to the cove.

"Yep. Let's see what else that crazy old woman did out here." Gwenn stood on the porch, holding her cup of coffee between her hands and watched a bird fly over the cove.

Tara led the way off the porch to the GPR, which caused Connal, Gizmo, and Peanut to renew their barking from inside the house.

"I'm sorry guys, but we really don't need you three trying to trip us or play with the GPR. Now shush," Tara told the dogs through the screen door. "I'm glad they don't realize it's just a screen keeping them inside."

Gwenn walked over to Tara and the unit. "Let's hope they don't figure it out."

"Okay, let's see what we can find." Tara started pushing the machine at a steady pace alongside the porch that faced the tree line from her room. She looked like she was mowing grass, except there were no noise or grass clippings flying.

The GPR had four wheels, two in the back and two in the front. Between the wheels, hung the transceiver or radar that would bounce signals to the receiver unit on the handlebar, where all of Tara's attention was focused at the moment.

After walking for just a few minutes, Tara called out. "Okay, so this looks like the edge of the Batcave. See how the read out bumps up here? That's most likely a wall. We'll be able to verify that as we get more passes done. But, this is really good, and it looks like it's going to be pretty evident if we find other rooms. Does that make sense?"

Gwenn walked over and looked at the screen and nodded.

"So, what we're going to do is basically walk back and forth, and whenever there is a bump up on the screen, we'll place a red flag to show that we have an anomaly. Go ahead and put a flag here. We're going to be a little lazy and not mark each path before scanning because this ground is rather flat and I think we can keep it pretty straight. If we start veering, we can always stop and mark scanning lanes. Just watch me, and if you see me starting to veer out of the line I'm in, let me know, okay?"

"Roger dodger, boss." Gwenn leaned over and pushed a red flag into the ground where the bump showed on the receiver of the GPR.

After the next pass, Tara stopped and looked at Gwenn. "You know what? I think we need to mark where we're ending the passes too, so if you could grab the blue flags and whenever we turn around, put a blue flag there? That way we see where we've been and it's just another reference to keep the lanes straight."

Gwenn nodded but remained silent as she went to the porch to retrieve the blue flags.

Tara wasn't sure why, but she was getting that uneasy feeling that maybe Gwenn was upset about something. But pushing it away to deal with later, Tara continued pushing the equipment, and when she stopped and turned the machine 180 degrees, Gwenn put another blue flag at the corner.

"Awesome, this is great. I want to map this later. That way we know where everything is that we find." They were sitting on the porch outside Tara's room, and having a coffee break. "I think we'll continue the same track until we get to the tree line. See if there is anything over that way. We'll continue with the same color flags, red for an anomaly, blue for the turns. That way we know where we have been and we don't get ourselves confused with several different colors." Tara was in full discovery mode now and talking more to herself than to Gwenn. Looking up, she saw Gwenn staring at her.

"What? Do I have a bug on me?" Tara looked at her shirt and shoulders to see if there was something on her.

"No. No bug. Just watching that brain of yours spinning. It's rather amazing to watch."

"Oh, um. Thanks. I just love this stuff. You never know when you're going to have a hit and find something. Do you want to try the next section?"

"Hell yes!" Gwenn jumped up and headed for the GPR.

"I guess break time is over," Tara chuckled as she got up to follow Gwenn.

"Since we don't know if there is anything here, walk back and forth until something interesting shows up on the screen. Like I was doing. Not too fast, not too slow. Just a good steady pace. I'm going to put blue flags at the end of each pass, so we know where we have been. Ready when you are."

Rubbing her hands together, Gwenn slowly started pushing the GPR. "Let's find the secret plant room."

It took everything that Tara had not to check the monitor to see if Gwenn was missing something. Again, there was very little talking between them. Gwenn pushed the GPR and watched the screen all the while with her tongue sticking out of her mouth and a furrow between her eyes.

Tara followed and placed blue flags at each turn, but since there had not been an indication from Gwenn to place a red flag, that was the only thing Tara did.

Gwenn was a fast learner and was keeping the passes even so that the area covered was a square, then soon became a rectangle, with nice straight lines.

Finally, after almost an hour, Gwenn stopped. "Okay, I need a break."

"Sounds like a good idea. Let's take a break, get some food and something cold to drink. You did great. You kept the edges straight and even. You're a natural," Tara said to Gwenn as they walked into the house.

"Thanks, I wanted to find something, though. But that little screen never bumped up."

"I know, but part of archaeology is not finding anything. It just makes the finding even more exciting."

They spent the rest of the afternoon following the same routine. Tara and Gwenn took turns walking and looking at the screen and pinning turns with the blue flags. In between taking turns, they sat on the porch, chatted and let the pups out so that they could snoot and snort on the new flags in the ground, and have a peeing contest on the flags.

"I'm wiped. Let's call it a day," Tara said after the last section on her side of the yard was over. "Tomorrow, we can map this. Take a break from the walking. I don't know about you, but I'm tired and sore."

"Sounds like a good idea. I'm rather tired too. It's hard work pushing that thing around all day. I'm going to go in and put together a quick dinner. Nothing fancy," she added when Tara started to protest. "Thinking some cheese, crackers, meats, and olives. More of a finger food plate."

"That sounds great. I'm going to put this away and walk the pups around for a bit. I'll be right in."

"So, I printed up the survey of the property. Figured we can get the scale figured out and then we can draw in the places we scanned yesterday. I know it's rather anal, but I want a decent representation of what we did yesterday." Tara handed the survey to Gwenn, who looked at it, then back at Tara.

They were outside on Tara's bedroom porch again, but today Connal, Gizmo, and Peanut were outside as well. Since they would be mapping, the pups wouldn't be in the way. They were both equipped with a cup of coffee and instead of the GPR, the equipment for the day was a tri scale, an open reel tape and two walkie talkies on the table.

"I think it would be easiest for one of us to measure and radio the measurements to the other that will be here at the table. That person will transfer the measurements to the property survey. I'm okay with either job. So, why don't you pick what you want to do." Tara leaned back and sipped her coffee.

She had spent a sleepless night, over-thinking and over-analyzing the prior day. Had she been over demanding? Had she hurt Gwenn's feelings with making all the decisions? She had noticed that Gwenn had grown quiet as the day progressed yesterday, and Tara was afraid that she might have upset Gwenn with basically telling her what to do. She wasn't going to ask, but somewhere around 3 AM she had told herself that she would be more open with the jobs and see what Gwenn wanted to do or try. That's how you learn after all, and Gwenn had an interest in archaeology. In addition, she had a great head on her shoulders, so she learned stupid-fast. So Tara was trying to let go of some of the controlling tendencies she had. Making that decision, she had finally gotten a couple of hours of sleep before her furry herd of corgis decided it was time to get up and start the day.

Now sitting there, looking at Gwenn, she knew she made the right decision. Gwenn's eyes had initially hooded over when she had started talking but then opened wide when Tara had given her a choice of what she wanted to do.

Gwenn leaned forward and looked Tara in the eyes. "What happened? Yesterday, you talked at me. Basically, told me what to do. Oh, you let me work the GPR, but you were definitely in control mode. Granted, I really don't know what we were doing, but I sort of felt like a worker bee yesterday. Now today, you're including me. So, what happened?"

Tara sighed because she had been right. She had been a control freak yesterday. "Well, I replayed the day over in my head last night, and I saw what I did, and I didn't like it. I figured if I didn't like it, you probably hadn't enjoyed it either. You are my friend. Strangely enough, considering we just met, my best friend. And the way I took over yesterday wasn't the way you treat a friend. I'm sorry. I'm not great at this friend thing."

Gwenn nodded her head once, then smiled. "I think I'd like to draw. Will you show me how to do that?"

"Sure. Since we did mainly squares and rectangles, it will be rather straight forward. You'll be able to see where I'm measuring, so you'll be able to keep where we are in relation to the survey easy enough. Thinking we can use the radios, so we aren't yelling at each other." Tara stopped to give Gwenn a chance to agree with using the radios, which she did with a head nod.

"I'll radio you the distance, then you will use the tri scale. Its official name is an engineer scale, but it's called a tri scale by archaeologists. We use it to convert the distance to the drawing. Looking at the property survey, we can see the scale they used for the drawing, so you'll use the same to keep everything the same size. Looks like they used the 1:20 scale." Tara picked up the scale and handed it to Gwenn. "Do you see how each of the six sides has a different measurement scale? 10, 20, 30 and so forth to 60. Since the property survey is 1:20, you'll use the 20 side."

"What does that mean? 1:20?" Gwenn asked while looking at the scale.

"It means that for every twenty feet I measure, you'll draw one whole number. For example, if I say the measurement is 40, you'll draw a line from 0 to 2. That's 40 feet on this scale. Does that make sense?"

Gwenn nodded. "Well, that seems simple. Let's get this party started."

Tara took another drink of her coffee then grabbed the reel tape and one of the radios. Taking a marking pin with her, she pushed it into the ground beside the first blue flag that was at the corner of the porch where they had started yesterday, and after securing the end of the measuring tape on it, she walked along the length of the porch to the first red flag that they had placed yesterday. "Okay, the first measurement is 30 feet," she radioed to Gwenn. And waited. She would not walk over there. She would not walk over there. She would not walk over there. Tara repeated over and over. She watched Gwenn as she looked up to see where she was standing, then to the survey. Tara watched Gwenn drew the line, mutter to herself, shake her head and erase the line.

To keep from offering to help, Tara mentally made a shopping list of all the things she wanted to buy for the house and the dogs.

After what seemed like an eternity, Gwenn radioed back. "Okay. Ready for the next one."

Tara walked back to the corner of the porch and removed the pin and wound the reel tape up as she walked back to the first red flag and as she had done before, she pushed the marking pin into the ground right beside the red flag. Then she secured the tape to the pin and walked toward the tree line to the second red flag. "Okay, this measurement is also 30 feet." This time while she waited for Gwenn to draw the measurement, she unhooked the tape from the pin at the second flag and walked back to the first flag at the corner of the porch. After placing the marking pin and the tape, she again walked toward the tree line and to the next red flag.

This time, Gwenn radioed back in less time. "Got it. Next."

Tara smiled. She could hear the confidence in Gwenn's voice. She was getting the process. "Okay, this measurement for the Batcave is also 30 feet."

Following her process from before, Tara set up the measurement between the one red flag they had just measured and the second red flag. Between these two pins, there were several additional red flags that Tara knew showed a wall underground. She waited for Gwenn to ask for the last measurement. She knew that the last measurement placement was probably confusing Gwenn, but there were no questions about it on the radio. She also knew that Gwenn saw where she had measured because she had looked up to verify Tara's placement in reference to the survey.

"Okay, I'm betting the next measurement is going to be 30 feet too," Gwenn radioed.

"Good guess. Yep, 30 feet."

Tara pulled the pin, wound up the tape and came back to the deck to sit and drink her now cold coffee.

She watched Gwenn draw the last line, then lean back and also take a drink of her coffee. Silently Gwenn pushed the survey over to Tara.

Tara looked it over and saw that Gwenn had indeed drawn the walls of the Batcave to scale. "You got it. Perfect. You even figured out how to triangulate the last point to make sure it was 30 feet from the second and third flags. You're a natural."

Gwenn leaned back with her coffee and smiled. "Thanks. You had me confused for a minute there when you went back to the first flag at porch for the third measurement, but then when you gave me the fourth measurement, I made a little mark, then extended the line from the second and third points up a bit and the same for the second and fourth points. And where they met became the fourth corner."

"Exactly right. I'll make you an archaeologist before you know it."

"Does that mean you'll buy me a fedora?" Gwenn asked, glancing over her cup coffee at Tara.

Tara laughed. "Sure. First fedora is on me."

They spent the rest of the day measuring and drawing the plots that they had scanned the day before. Gwenn had added to the drawing using colored pencils to mark the turning points with blue, and the anomalies with red. By the time they finished for the day, Tara's side of the house had been scanned with the GPR and drawn to scale on the survey map.

"Looks like we're scanning again tomorrow. My thought would be to start on your side of the house, closest to the cove. Sort of like a mirror of what we did over here. After that, it will get a little trickier since we will be scanning around the garage, riding arena, equipment garage and the pool building. We have a lot of scanning still to do. What do you think?" Tara asked while putting the lasagna that Barb had made into the oven.

Gwenn nodded as she prepared the garlic bread. "Yeah, that makes sense. That way we don't miss a spot. Systematic. Work our way around the house. But can you do that by yourself? I have to go to work tomorrow."

"Oh, no problem. You have a business. I've got to remember that. I'll make you a deal. I'll scan the next couple of days. Then on your next day off, maybe you can help me get it mapped."

"I like that, and I like mapping. Sounds like a plan."

For the rest of the week, Tara spent the days scanning and flagging plots, and Gwenn took care of her pizza business. In the evenings, they would eat and catch up and discuss thoughts and ideas about the plants. Where they might be if Dr. Roxbury was growing them for the drug side of it? And if so, who had she been selling them to? If she had been murdered and if she had been, who killed her? How did they get on the property that was so secure and kill her?

It wasn't all deep and dark, though. There was also plenty of dog time. Tara and Gwenn had gotten into the routine of taking the dogs to the pool in the evenings after dinner. The swimming was great for everyone, human and dog.

During one of the evenings Tara, with Gwenn's help, had measured Peanut for a cart. After the cart had arrived and they got it set up, Peanut had really livened up inside with the wheels. He was all over the place, running and playing. And crashing into the corners of walls, furniture, and the occasional human leg. But the cart had been a great idea, and Peanut seemed to love being put into it. Connal and Gizmo didn't appear to notice any difference with him in the cart and played and roughhoused with him like they did before.

Now, sitting out on the porch after another afternoon of solo scanning, Tara enjoyed the sunset. She was happy. Truly. She wasn't sure that had ever been the case before. Oh, she had been content with her life, most of the time. But she wouldn't have called it happy. But now, sitting on her porch, overlooking her cove and the sunset, with her dogs as company she was happy. It was nice and somewhat scary. She was afraid to say it out loud. Murphy's Law said that if you bragged, it would bite you in the ass. What she didn't know was her thought was closer to the truth than she would have liked.

Because just out of the sight of her cove, the lobster boat sat. And on the lobster boat, the man watched Tara through his binoculars. Cursing at himself, he moved his view from her to the many flags of two colors that dotted the yard around the house.

"What the hell are you doing now? What are all the flags for? What do the red flags and the blue flags mean? God, I fucking hate this woman," he said to himself.

It was about time to get her ass off that property and he needed to find those plants. According to his contact who was wanting—no demanding the plants—they should be getting close to harvesting. And the asshole was getting tired of the excuses. Yes, it was time to get the bitches and those three dogs out of the way so he could find the plants. Otherwise, well he wasn't stupid, the people that he was dealing with would get rid of him.

CHAPTER EIGHT

"Well, that was a bust," Gwenn said and slouched down into the chair on the porch.

Tara and Gwenn had finally finished scanning and mapping the last section of the compound and now looking at the yard, it looked like they had planted a yard full of blue flags. Minus the four red flags.

"I thought we would find something. I don't understand this at all. I really thought that Dr. Roxbury had built another room down there for the plants. But now we know she didn't. At least not around the house. So, what now? Do we scan the entire 40 fucking acres to see if there's a secret plant room? If this is archaeology, it sucks." Gwenn slouched even farther down into her chair and stuck her lower lip up in pure adolescent pouting mode.

Tara chuckled and patted Gwenn's arm. "Yes, this is part of digging, and it does suck, but then you find something and all the sucking doesn't matter. I'm not too surprised we didn't find anything. I was hoping to have more hits, but that would have been too easy, and after all, if this were easy, everyone would be Indiana Jones. We have to remember that the Batcave is under my office—Well, son of a bitch!" Tara jumped up and walked over to the red flags. "Frig me!"

Gwenn watched Tara walk, actually it was more like stomping around and cussing. After a moment, she joined Tara at the red flags, but she really couldn't see the reason for Tara's meltdown. Gwenn stood beside her once Tara stopped stomping and cussing for a second.

"Is this an archaeology thing or is there something you want to share with me?"

Tara stopped in front of Gwenn, took a deep breath and closed her eyes. Releasing the breath and opening her eyes, she took Gwenn by her shoulders. "The Batcave is below my office." When that only received a head nod and a shoulder lift from Gwenn, Tara growled in her throat. "The Batcave is directly *below* my office, Gwenn." This time she emphasized below and then waited for that comment to hit Gwenn.

Gwenn looked at Tara for a moment, then turned her head to look at the flags then she looked at the house. Back to the flags. Back to the house. "Well, fuck me!" Now it was Gwenn's turn to mumble and walk around and have a hissy fit. "We already found the goddamn thing! First try! We thought we were scanning and mapping the Batcave, but we couldn't have. The fucking Batcave is *under* your fucking office, not beside it. We couldn't have seen it on the equipment. Son of a goddamn bitch!" Gwenn flopped on the ground and stared at the flags.

"Okay, we had a really, REALLY dumb moment, but we would have had to check the entire area anyway, to rule out any other anomalies. So yes, we had some serious brain farting going on, but now we can focus on the room we did find." Tara sat down beside Gwenn and shoulder bumped her. "This is good. We found it."

Gwenn mumbled and kicked at one of the flags, returned the shoulder bump and smiled. "We found it."

"So, you ready to go to the Batcave and see how we get into that new room? We know it's there now, so there has to be a way in there."

"Well, fuck me. Apparently, that's my phrase for the day.

139

Anyway, how can this be so hard? We know there is a damn room over there. Why can't we find the way in?" Gwenn was sprawled out on the couch in the Batcave with a dog on each side and one on her feet. They had been looking for the entrance to the new room for over an hour, with no luck.

Tara was standing with her hands on her hips, staring at the wall where the newest secret room was located. "We could just say screw it and break a hole in the damn wall. I'm sure there is a sledgehammer in the equipment barn. It would be a great way to take out some of our frustrations on this whole damnable mess."

Gwenn rose and joined Tara looking at the wall. "Hm, that would get our frustrations out for sure, but I'm not sure beating down a wall is the smartest thing. The office is up there and with the way our luck is running, we would bring it crashing in on us. Maybe we're thinking too hard about this. After all, the way to open and close this room is in plain sight. Maybe this one is too."

Gwenn started walking around and looking at the obvious things in the room. "If I were Dr. Roxbury, I would make it easy. She's already done that with the Batcave. It would be something simple, and I would have it close to the other trigger. Maybe something else on the end table."

Tara joined her at the end table and looked. "Okay, I see how you're thinking. So, we know the sea glass vase down here is the trigger to open and close the Batcave. Same as upstairs. The lamp would be obvious, so I don't think that's the trigger. What about the ashtray? Was she a smoker?"

"I really don't know, but the house doesn't smell like she smoked. And now that I think about it, I haven't seen an ashtray anywhere else in the house. Have you?"

Tara shook her head, then tried to pick up the ashtray, but she couldn't lift it. "I think we have something here. I can't lift it up."

"Try sliding it. I think we've found it!" Gwenn was now bouncing on her toes, with her hands to her mouth.

Tara followed Gwenn's suggestion and slid the ashtray, first front to back. "Nope, not that way. Let's try side to side." As Tara pushed the ashtray to the side, the wall behind where the desk slid into the floor swung out.

"Yes!" Tara and Gwenn both shouted in unison and fist bumped. On impulse, Gwenn grabbed Tara up in a hug which Tara returned with the same enthusiasm.

Side by side, they walked over to the opening, followed by Connal, Gizmo, and Peanut. After a brief pause to peek in, Tara led the way into the new room, then moved to the side so that Gwenn could come in. Inside the partially-lit room were eight rows of waist-high tables, running the entire 30-foot length of the room. And on those tables, were pots of plants.

"Well, son of a bitch. I guess that answers the question on whether Dr. Roxbury was growing the psycho plant." Gwenn had forwarded Tara the information on the plant and after seeing its official name, had adopted Gwenn's version for it. "Looks like a freaking rain forest in here. Feels like one too with the high humidity and the low lighting." Tara walked over to one of the tables of plants. "Look at this setup. She has a trickle system going to each plant, and each table has its own bank of lights to make sure the plants get the best light to grow. Holy shit."

"It looks like the trickle system and the lights are on a timer. Look at this." Gwenn nodded toward a control box on the wall just inside the opening. "She definitely knew what she was doing."

"Brilliant actually. Roxbury didn't have to come in here all the time to take care of the plants. She just set the control box, and it took care of all the work. You can't even tell that these plants haven't had anyone looking over them for several months. I hate to say it, but I'm impressed. We're going to have to—" Tara's thought was interrupted by the buzzer of the front gate and the corresponding barking of the three dogs. "Worst timing ever," Tara mumbled as she used her cell phone to see who was at the front gate. "Crap, it's Fred. I'll go up and meet him. Can you close this up if you come up? I think that we need to leave most of the humidity in this room." At

Gwenn's head nod, Tara headed up and into the kitchen.

Tara put the three dogs into her room then went outside to wait for Fred to pull up. She was hesitant on asking him into the house because if Connal and Gizmo heard his voice, it would upset them. But then she thought that not inviting him in would look odd, so after the handshakes outside, she led him into the kitchen.

"Can I offer you a cup of coffee?" On Fred's headshake, Tara busied herself prepping herself a cup of coffee. She needed some time to get herself back to level. She didn't have an issue with law enforcement, but something about Fred made her tummy funky. No idea why, but there was something there. As she turned back to Fred, Gwenn walked into the kitchen and gave him a hug and kiss on the cheek.

"Hi, what brings you out here?" Gwenn had felt Tara's uneasiness as soon as she came into the kitchen so figured running interference would be a good idea.

Tara smiled at Gwenn to let her know she knew what Gwenn was doing and it was appreciated. Leaning back on the kitchen counter and holding her coffee in both hands, she let Gwenn deal with Fred.

Fred smiled at Gwenn and patted her hand on his arm. "Just wanting to check on you ladies. Haven't seen you that much in town and wanted to touch base to make sure there hadn't been any more issues out here. Also, wanted to see if you had a chance to go through your house and make a list of anything missing. There hasn't been anything new on the break in. And the notes, both of them, didn't have any fingerprints on them. So, I hate to say it, we're just going to have to wait until someone messes up and brags about what they did. I'm real sorry."

"That's sweet of you, coming out here to check on us. Yeah, I spent a couple of days cleaning up and looking for anything missing, and the asshole didn't take anything. Just made a mess out of the kitchen, and that's where most of the loss was. I had to make a list of the stuff that had been destroyed and needed to be replaced for the insurance company. Let me tell you, that was a pain. But, everything is back where it should be in the house. Had Stan come over and install new doors and lock sets too. Figured it made sense. It's been quiet out here, just getting Tara settled in here and helping her with some upgrades to the house. You know new owner, new ideas." Gwenn smiled and winked at Fred.

Fred blushed and smiled back. "Yeah, there's nothing more fun than making a new place, your place." Turning to Tara now, he smiled, but it didn't reach his eyes. "Noticed all the flags around the place. You planning on adding to the house?"

Tara fake smiled back. "Nah, those are just flags to mark where I'm thinking of putting new flower beds. I love flowers."

"You must really like flowers." He was digging for information, and Tara knew it, so she decided she would play the game for a bit.

"Oh, they all won't be flower beds. Some will be plants, I'm sure. I'm more of a visual person, so I like to use props to see what it might look like. I'll slowly remove the ones I don't like over the next few days." Tara held Fred's gaze over the edge of her coffee cup as she took a sip. It was probably just her imagination, but she could have sworn that Fred had twitched when she said plants.

"Noticed a lot of blue flags, but only a couple of red flags. I'm guessing that the different colors mean something?" Fred wasn't hiding the fact he was digging for information now.

Tara shook her head. "Nope, not really. Started out with the blue flags, but ran out near the end, so went to a different color."

"Odd that the red flags are in the middle of all the blue flags. But then, I'm not you, so I guess it wouldn't make sense to me. Anyway, betting Bill is hating having to try to mow around all those flags."

Tara was feeling the funky tummy big time, and she had grown tired of the game. "Well, since it's my property, I don't really care if Bill is put out with having to deal with what I do on it." Crossing her arms, she looked Fred in the eye and let him see that she wasn't playing any longer.

"Fred, how have you been? Have you been out on the water? You look like you've been getting some sun," Gwenn asked, trying to ease some of the tension between Tara and Fred.

Fred looked at Tara for a moment longer, then turned his attention to Gwenn. "I've been good, and yeah, I've been out fishing a couple of times. I don't get to go out as much as I'd like but I love being out on the boats this time of year. Not too hot, not too cold. Just about as perfect as it can be. It's always relaxed me." Standing up, he hitched his holster belt up.

"Anyway, I got to be getting back into town. Make sure you call me if you have any trouble out here." Fred shook Tara's hand and held it and her gaze for a second longer than necessary.

Tara returned and held the gaze and handshake until Fred broke the contact first.

Fred then turned to Gwenn and gave her a hug and kiss on the cheek. "Gwenn, always a pleasure. I'll show myself out."

Gwenn waited until Fred had gone through the main gate before she turned to look at Tara. "Why do I feel that you and Fred were having a little dance of wills there? There was enough tension in here, you could cut it with a knife."

"Hold on a minute, let me do this before I forget to. Can you let the pups out of my room for me?" Tara walked over to her laptop and opened up the program that controlled all the security for the property. She pushed some buttons and then turned to sit down on the floor.

Connal immediately came over and placing his front feet on her crossed knees, barked into her face.

"I'm sorry, buddy. I know you don't like Fred and you could hear him. I had to let him in, though, and since you wanted to eat him the last time, you had to go to the bedroom." Tara rubbed Connal's ears. That only lasted a second before two more corgi heads were in her face. "Okay,

I'm sorry you guys." Tara laughed, then stood up and faced Gwenn.

"I changed the main gate code again. It's 646872. I also turned on all the cameras, not just the ones I turned on after your break in. The entire system is now active. I don't like him. I know he's a friend of yours, and I'm sorry, but there is something there that I just don't like. I can't place it, but I get funky tummy when he's around. I know he's a cop and he's meant to be nosy, but his nosy seems to go beyond the average cop nosy."

Gwenn slowly nodded then bent down to give the three dogs some ear scratches. "Okay, you get a funky tummy when Fred is around. Got it. I've known Fred my entire life but I also trust gut instincts. Maybe you're getting a vibe I'm not because I've known him forever."

"Thanks for not negating my funky tummy. Most people do."

"I'm not most people and you need to remember that. Now, what are we going to call this new room? We already have the Batcave, so we have a theme going on here. I think it needs to be something with Batman." Standing up, Gwenn leaned on the island.

"Well, it's a room of plants that can be made into drugs, so not sure a superhero lair name would be appropriate." This received a head nod from Gwenn. "So, how about we call it The Lab? I know it's not imaginative, but it's sort of a lab."

"I can work with that. The Lab it is. To the Batcave!" Gwenn said while opening and lifting her arms like she was wearing a cape.

Connal, Gizmo, and Peanut barked, and Tara laughed. "That looked more like Dracula, but I'll let you have it. After you, sidekick." Tara bent and made a sweeping motion with her arm, while the other was behind her back.

Gwenn put her hands on her hips. "Hey, why am I the sidekick? I'm actually taller than you, and everyone knows that the sidekick is the short one."

"Yeah, I don't think so. It's my place, therefore I'm the

superhero and you, by default, are the sidekick. You should be happy, I could make the corgis my sidekicks."

"They can't be sidekicks. They barely have any legs at all."

"Oh, did you hear that, guys? She's making fun of your little legs. Attack the sidekick." This resulted in the three dogs barking and jumping up on Tara and Gwenn.

Laughing, the five of them made their way back to the Batcave and The Lab. Once in The Lab, the magnitude of what they had found became evident again.

"What are we going to do with all of this?" Gwenn quietly asked, looking at the tables of plants.

"I don't know. I really don't. I'm not sure if we should call the authorities. And if we do, who? It feels bigger than local law enforcement, and as you know, I don't like Fred. Therefore, I don't trust him. Do we just destroy all the plants and ignore everything we've learned?" Tara touched one of the leaves of a plant, then turned to look at Gwenn.

Gwenn shook her head. "No, that doesn't feel right at all. I feel like this is all tied to Dr. Roxbury's death. I think she was killed because of this and if we just destroy the plants, then someone gets away with what they did."

"Agreed. Okay, so we won't destroy the plants. Let me reach out to some of my old contacts. Maybe one of them will have an idea on who we should call about this.

"I think I'm done with all of this for the day. Between finding a room full of plants and Fred's drop-in visit, I'm really just not into trying to figure out what to do next with this whole mess. So, how about we take the rest of the day off and veg and enjoy the cove and the pups? Recharge some. Then, maybe, all of this will be a little bit clearer and won't seem so huge and dirty." Tara walked over to the door, then back at Gwenn. "At least it looks like getting out of this room is simple enough. Look, there is door handle on this side, so no need to play 'find the secret lever' when we're in this room."

"You know what, that sounds great to me. I'm wiped out from thinking of all the different things this could all mean. Maybe I'll try out one of those kayaks in the boat shed and see if I can keep it upright."

After spending the day outside swimming, kayaking and sunbathing, Tara and Gwenn made a quick dinner and went to bed before midnight.

That was unusual for them as they both seemed to be night owls. Tara, because she had issues with sleep. She slept, just not well or often.

Gwenn, because she was usually doing pizza restaurant business in the evenings. Invoices, bills, schedules, orders and the website didn't take care of themselves after all.

But tonight, they were in bed early, so when the security system started going off a little past 2 AM, they were both startled awake by the alarms and the dogs alerting to something being wrong.

Tara jumped out of her bed, grabbed the gun that was in her nightstand and made her way to the living room, just in time to see Gwenn coming out of her room with her gun. They both stopped and looked at each other, nodded that they were both okay, then walked over to the kitchen counter where Tara's laptop was serving as a monitor for the security system on the property.

Pushing a button, Tara muted the alarms so that the pups would calm down, then looked at the screen. "I don't see anything. Do you?"

"No, it could have just been a moose or another animal that set it off." Setting her gun down, Gwenn got closer to look at the screen.

"Yeah maybe, but let me playback the camera recording, just to see."

When the playback started, at first they saw nothing unusual, then both of them gasped. There was movement on the camera.

"That's not a moose," Gwenn whispered.

"No, moose don't walk upright. So, unless there is a bigfoot that knows how to use a flashlight, we had an intruder," Tara growled. "He didn't get past the main gate, but he tried. Look, he has a ski mask on. So, it's not an accident, and he knows we have cameras. So, we can rule out someone that just wanted to see what was on the other side of the gate. Let me save this recording for later." Tara made quick work of saving the file to a flash drive.

"You have to work today, so you should try to get some more rest. I'll stay up, just in case he thinks about having another go at it. I'm done sleeping for the night anyway."

Gwenn shook her head. "Nope, I'm fucking wide awake now, so it's not worth the tossing and turning of going back to bed. So, let's go watch some stupid TV shows and wait for the sun to come up. I bet you haven't seen a sunrise here yet. Betting it will be a gorgeous one."

"I'm going to go make us some hot chocolate."

With no words needed, they left several lights on in the house, and they both kept the handguns within reach. Tara sat facing the living room area while Gwenn sat facing the cove.

"I love Gibbs," Gwenn stated after the third episode of NCIS. She was laying down on the couch, with Connal curled up in front of her and Gizmo curled up behind her knees.

"Me too. And McGee. Tony is cool, but he tries too hard. McGee is a teddy bear. With a gun. It took me quite a while to like Ziva after they killed off Kate the way they did. But now I really like Ziva, too. She's such a badass. Hey, it's almost daybreak, so I'm going to go make a pot of coffee," Tara said getting up and heading to the kitchen.

"I'm going to let the pups into the riding arena after I get this going. I don't want to let them outside until it's full light outside. But when we get back in, I think we should sit outside and watch the sun come up."

"That sounds like a very good idea. Hold on, and I'll go with you all to the riding arena."

"I can call in and have Joyce take my shift at the pizza parlor today," Gwenn told Tara several hours later as she was preparing to go to work.

"One last time, no. Thanks, but no. Go to work. We'll be

okay here. If you want, we can drive you into town, then come get you tonight."

Gwenn shook her head. "No, I'm fine driving myself and I think it would look really odd if we did that. I really believe that someone in town is doing this shit. So, if you drive me in, they will see that they're rattling us. Can't give the dickhead that impression. But I'll call you as I leave and I'll stay on the phone with you until I walk into this house. Okay?"

"Good point. Need to keep like nothing is going on or bugging us. That will piss off the jerk. I like the idea of the phone call. Do the same thing going into town. On the phone when you walk out of here and hang up when you get to the restaurant. Deal?"

"Deal. I don't like this feeling. I'm going to start carrying my gun with me. And I think we should both have a gun within reach at all times." To make her point, Gwenn made sure her gun was secure in the holster, then put it in her purse.

"Yeah, I was thinking the same thing. This place is huge, so carrying makes sense. Not only for assholes that try to get on the property, but for bigfoots and bears and mooses."

Gwenn laughed at the last part. "It's moose. Not mooses or moosies. I think you just like to say mooses or moosies. As for bigfoots, well they're nice, so don't shoot them. Bears, fire away. I have to go get ready for work, or I'm going to be late."

Tara grabbed Gwenn's arm to stop her from leaving. "You're just screwing with me about bigfoots, right? You haven't actually seen one. Have you?"

Gwenn chuckled. "Yes, bigfoots and yes, they're around here. Most everyone in town has seen one or more in their lifetime. The local favorite is named Max." Patting Tara's arm before she turned to go to her room, she added, "They don't usually hurt humans. Most of the time, anyway."

"She's messing with me, right?" Tara looked down at Connal, who looked back at her, then at the retreating back of Gwenn. "Yeah, she's screwing with me. I think I need to do some research, though, just for the fun of it."

After Gwenn had arrived at the restaurant safely, Tara sat in the living room for a bit, staring at the TV and thinking. She didn't like that someone had tried to get on the property. She didn't like that Dr. Roxbury might have been killed because of the plants that were hidden in The Lab. She didn't like that she now felt the need to carry a gun with her in her own house. She didn't like that there were regular sightings of Bigfoot in the area. And it was past time to take control of the situation instead of reacting to the circumstances.

Getting her laptop, she deliberately went out on the porch off of the living room. She was not going to be a prisoner in her own house.

"You three keep an eye out for an eight foot, furry-assed ape, okay?"

Connal, Gizmo, and Peanut each found a spot, facing different directions and Tara could have sworn they were on look out.

"Time to network. Who do I know, that I trust enough, to help with this mess?" Talking to herself, Tara went through her contacts until she came upon Wyatt's name.

"Dammit. I knew it would be him. Of course, it would be. Who else would it be? After all, I trust him, and he knows a ton of people that know how to keep their mouths shut. Okay, I just need to keep this basic so that he doesn't get all manly and decide to come up here to help. I think an email would be best. That way I can get all the information in there, without interruptions or him being able to read my emotions in a phone call." Tara glanced over at the three dogs to see if they were listening to her and saw that they were all asleep.

She smiled at the sight. "Geez, great bigfoot guard dogs you three are. I guess I'll just do the networking and the ape watching." Doing a quick scan of the area, Tara cursed Gwenn for planting the bigfoot information in her head. "She'll pay for that. I don't know how, but she will."

Opening up an email to Wyatt, Tara started with the precursor how are yous/I'm fine/loving Maine/new dogs added to the family, then she started typing the real reason for the email. Thirty minutes later, she put the laptop on the table and leaned back to let her eyes rest. And that's when she saw the boat.

Getting up, she went into the living room and came back out with the binoculars that had been delivered earlier in the week.

To make a point, she walked to the edge of the cove, followed by the dogs and stood where the man on the boat could see her. She made a show of putting the binoculars up to her eyes. "See that asshole, I'm looking at you," Tara mumbled. She didn't know if the person on the boat was just someone fishing or sightseeing, but her gut was telling her that the person on it was up to no good and was there to watch her.

To prove her right, the boat's engine immediately came to life, and it turned out to sea. But not before Tara got a look at some of the registration numbers on the bow of the boat. Repeating the numbers to herself, she went into the house to write down 11 N.

"Bam, two points to me! I know this isn't the full registration, but it's a start."

Later that evening, Tara told Gwenn about the boat and the registration numbers she had gotten off the boat.

"Damn, girl, you've got balls. Walking down to the cove, and basically flipping the guy off. I love it, but I need to be the worried friend for a minute. That was really rather stupid. What if the asshole had a gun and shot you? Or decided to call your bluff and come into the cove? Now," holding up her hand to stop Tara's rebuttal, "I know why you did it, and I would have probably done the same thing, but don't do that again. Please. We need to be smarter than this jerk. Okay, friend lecture done.

"Let me see the registration numbers. I have a friend that might be able to figure out who owns the boat." At Tara's raised eyebrow. "Fine. I dated the guy, and he owes me. And no, I'm not telling you why he owes me. It's old history, but he's a good guy, and he'll be discrete. Granted, I might have to go out on a date with him." Gwenn waggled her eyebrows at

Tara.

Tara chuckled and handed Gwenn the paper with the two numbers and letter she had seen on the boat. "It's really not much, but maybe your friend can get something from it. And you're right. That was dumb walking to the cove and essentially showing my hand to the jerk. I let my emotions get ahead of the brain. Again. Believe it or not, I usually do think things through before I do something stupid."

Gwenn looked at the paper and whistled. "Wow, that really isn't much. Looks like you got the end of it, so that doesn't help to narrow down the state. The beginning of the registration shows the abbreviations of the state the boat is registered in and without that, I think it will be like looking for a needle in a haystack. But, I'll see what he can find out for us. Might have to go on two dates with him, though. Did I mention that he is smokin' hot?"

Laughing, Tara sat down on the couch. "I'm thinking you're just looking for an excuse to have to go out with this old boyfriend. But whatever works for you. Speaking of old flames, I wrote an email to Wyatt, my ex."

"Oh!" Gwenn clapped her hands and came to sit down beside Tara. "Do tell!"

"Geez. Get your mind out of the sex gutter. I couldn't think of any of my other contacts that I trusted enough not to leak any of this and who would give me good advice. I haven't sent the email yet. I wanted you to read it to make sure that it was basic enough and that it won't cause him to come riding to our rescue."

"Oh, now who's looking for excuses. Sex gutter? Gross." She laughed when Tara tossed a pillow at her. "Okay, let me see if you're sending out the Bat-Signal that you need a big, strong ex-husband to come rescue you." Gwenn tossed the pillow back.

"I really do hate you, you know that right?" Tara teased and put the pillow back in its place on the couch. "You can edit as you read if you see anything I missed or if something sounds dire."

Instead of sitting there watching Gwenn read the email, Tara went into the kitchen to get the pups a treat. "Sit," she told Connal, Gizmo, and Peanut, then laughed when all three wiggly butts promptly hit the floor. "Take it nice," she said as she gave each dog their treat. She had got the dogs to *down, roll over* and was starting on *stay* when Gwenn called from the living room.

"Okay, I'm done. It was well written, so I didn't need to edit much. Just needed to add a line or two in there that you were in a hot, torrid love affair with a local lobsterman and were getting married next weekend."

Tara started to laugh but then stopped because of the expression on Gwenn's face. "You're joking, right?" When Gwenn didn't say anything and just looked at Tara, Tara started to sweat. "Please tell me you're just screwing with me and that I don't have to kill you now and bury you somewhere."

Gwenn couldn't hold the straight face any longer and fell onto her side on the couch, laughing so hard she couldn't breathe. "Oh my God! I got you, and I got you good! You should have seen the look on your face. No, I didn't do anything of the sort. I would never do that. Even though you deserved that after saying you hated me." Sitting back up and holding her ribs, she reached over to pet Gizmo.

"Anyway, all joking aside, I don't think the email will cause him to come up here. So, sit and try to get your breathing back under control. You look like you're going to throw up."

Sitting down beside Gwenn, Tara looked at her. "You're evil. Remind me to always be your friend. You would be a wicked enemy. Thanks for looking it over. I'm going to send it then."

Gwenn watched Tara send the email, then looked at Tara. "It's getting late so what's the plan for sleeping? I mean, we could both go to bed and trust the alarms to warn us, but I don't know. After last night, it feels wrong just to go to sleep and not keep watch. Granted, I'm not sure what we would watch for. It just feels weird. Does that make sense at all?"

"Yeah, it does, and I agree. After last night, maybe having someone awake at all times would be a good idea. Not necessarily watching the cameras all night, but just up. I think shifts. Since you work tomorrow, why don't you do the first couple of hours, then wake me up and I'll take the rest of the night? That way you can still have a fair amount of sleep before you have to go in?"

"I like the idea of shifts. Why don't you get some rest and since it's almost midnight I'll wake you up at 3. That way you only have a couple of hours until sunrise, and I can sleep until I have to get up and go to work. Will that work for you?" Gwenn asked.

"Yep, that sounds great. Now get. I'm going to make sure all the alarms and doors and such are on and locked."

Closing the blinds on the French doors caused the man on the boat to cuss. Now he couldn't see what was going on in the house.

Last night had been a bust. He knew that the place had alarms and cameras, but Roxbury had never used them. But this one had the place alarmed and there were cameras everywhere, so getting onto the property would be harder than he thought. He had known that the main gate was alarmed and had cameras, that's why he had tried to go over the fence away from the gate. But that hadn't worked because he had seen the red light come on a camera just as he put his foot on the bottom rail of the white fencing. Apparently, the entire fence had sensors on it, which turned on the cameras when something set them off. So, instead of continuing to climb the fence, he had turned around and left.

Now he had to figure out another way onto the property so that he could look for his plants. He had started seeing them as his plants after Roxbury had died and since he was now on the hook to produce them for the buyer. But how? Unless... what about the cove? Maybe that was the weak area.

Tomorrow, he would have to look at that area harder. If there were no cameras there, that might be where he could get on the property and look around. Or hell, maybe he could just take the boat into the cove and see if he could convince the bitch and her friend and dogs to go away. Or maybe it was time for a terrible accident to happen out here that would scare them all away.

CHAPTER NINE

Tara spent the better part of three hours the next morning confirming that the mapping of the scanned areas was complete and that everything made sense. It might have seemed silly but it was still information, and if it was information, it needed to be correct.

After she was happy that the mapping was solid, she went around and pulled all the flags out of the ground, then turned and looked at the cove. "I need to put a camera pointing toward the cove. It's not an easy route onto the property, but it's still a route. I wonder if I can get some flood lights installed that would light up the area too?"

Pulling out her phone, she made a note to check on installing the floodlights and the camera to cover the cove.

Just as she was finishing with the note, she saw an alert on her security app that someone was at the front gate of the property.

"Hello. Can I help you?" she asked, after pressing the microphone button on the phone.

"Tara, open up. It's Wyatt."

"Shit! Damn it! Frig me!" She swore and stomped her feet, but pressed the button to open the front gate. "Damn it to hell! I knew emailing him was a stupid idea. Shit. Shit.

SHIT!" The last one was yelled to the wind.

Tara had just enough time to put the flags down on her table outside her bedroom and to come around the side of the house before Wyatt pulled up in front of the garage in his truck. Tara stood her ground. It was her property so he could walk to her. And he did, slowly and with a swagger.

"Damn him to hell," she muttered under her breath as Wyatt came to stand directly in front of her. He then stopped and just looked into her eyes. She hated when he did that, he had the most intense blue eyes, and she always thought that they could read her mind and soul.

Finally, he smiled, which made his eyes even more intense and just a bit dangerous. "Hi. You look great Tara," he said as he stepped into her space and gave her a hug.

She resisted for just a moment, then returned hug. "It's good to see you. Even though you didn't need to come up here. And how did you get here so fast anyway? I just sent you that email last night." Tara stepped out of the hug and crossed her arms.

"I've been working in upper New York for the last couple of weeks, so after I read your email, I grabbed some stuff and hopped in the truck and 10 hours later, here I am."

"Well, come on in. I'm sure you're ready for a beer." Tara led Wyatt into the house and introduced him to the newest members of the family. Connal barked at him at first, then realizing that he knew this human, he wiggled and aarrroooed his hello to Wyatt.

"Well, hello to you too, Connal. Have you missed me?" Wyatt asked the wiggly corgi as he gave him belly rubs. Not to be let out of the belly rubs, Gizmo and Peanut presented their bellies to Wyatt, and he obliged their request.

Tara grabbed two beers from the fridge and motioned with them to the porch.

Wyatt walked out to join Tara on the porch, then stopped to look around. "This place is gorgeous. The pictures you've been sending me don't do it justice. You did good. I have to admit that I thought you had lost your damn mind when you bought this place. But now. Well, home run for you, Tar." Toasting her with his beer, he used her nickname that only he got away with.

Returning the toast, Tara smiled at him. "Thanks. It really is amazing. I got lucky on buying it. I had my doubts and thought I had finally lost my mind too, but it was meant to be. I truly believe that. I'm happy here."

Wyatt studied her, then nodded. "Yeah, you are. I can see it, and it looks good on you. So, tell me what you've been up to since the last time we really talked." He took her hand as they sat there and caught up while enjoying the view.

That's how Gwenn found them 30 minutes later. She came out of the house, carrying a pizza box and came to a sudden stop at the sight of Tara holding hands with some guy. Some damn good-looking guy with brown hair that hung just a little too long and framed a square face, with a nose that had been broken at one time. Add to that a set of full lips and intensely blue eyes and Gwenn wasn't too far from drooling.

"Oh, um hi. Didn't mean to interrupt," Gwenn said, as she walked farther out to the table and set down the pizza. "Decided to cut out early from work and brought home dinner."

Gwenn extended her hand for a handshake while looking between Tara and whoever this was. "Hi, I'm Gwenn, Tara's newest best friend. Who are you?"

Tara chuckled and shook her head. "Gwenn, this is Wyatt. My ex-husband. Wyatt, this is Gwenn, my newest best friend."

"Oh! Well hello, Wyatt. Why are you here?" Gwenn now had her arms crossed and was actually tapping her foot while trying to stare down Wyatt.

Wyatt smiled. Standing up, he offered his hand. "Hello, Gwenn. I think it's nice to meet you. I'm here because of Tara's super carefully worded email. I could tell by the lack of real information in the email that she was into something a little more than she was saying. So, I took a week off work, jumped in my truck, and I'm here. Problem with that?" Wyatt countered Gwenn.

Gwenn stared at Wyatt for another minute then unfolded her arms, smiled and shook his hand. "Nope. Glad to have you here. I'm going to get plates for the pizza. And maybe a salad. Another beer, Wyatt?" At Wyatt's negative nod, Gwenn disappeared into the house.

"Wow, she's a little intense. I got the impression that if I had answered her question the wrong way, she would've kicked my ass."

"I think she would've tried. She's just protecting me. Somehow, she's become my best friend. Don't look at me like that, I'm serious. She's actually staying out here since her house was broken in to."

Wyatt turned to look at Tara directly now. "You didn't say anything about a break-in in your email."

"No, I didn't. And yes, I think it's all tied to some of the other odd things going on, and I should have. I guess I didn't tell you because I knew if I did, you would do exactly what you've done. Drop everything and come up here to protect me. Don't look at me that way, you've just proven me right." Tara pointed a finger at Wyatt.

Thin-lipped, Wyatt grabbed her finger, then just palmed her hand. "I didn't come up to protect you. You're more than capable of doing that yourself. I came up here to help you with whatever is going on. So, from now on, full disclosure. I can't help if I don't know what's going on. This isn't me trying to be the big man and saving the women. This is a friend wanting to help another friend." Wyatt leaned back and waited for Tara to process this.

Tara slowly nodded her head. "Okay. Full disclosure from now on. At least pertaining to what's been going on up here. But if it's okay with you, we'll tell you what's going on after dinner, okay? Until then, can we just relax?"

"Yeah, we can do that. Want to screw with Gwenn some more and hold hands again?"

At Tara's laugh, Wyatt took her hand and waited for Gwenn to come back out before kissing the back of Tara's hand. At the look of shock and surprise on Gwenn's face, he knew that there would be some girl talk going on later and laughed. Tara hated girl talk, and with the daggers that Tara was throwing at him right now, he knew that she knew he was having some fun at her expense.

Wyatt rewarded her daggers with a huge smile, and getting up to go into the house, he leaned down and brushed a kiss on her cheek, then roared with laughter at Gwenn's expression. This was going to be fun.

After dinner and letting the dogs out for their evening playtime Tara, Gwenn, and Wyatt sat down in the living room. Since it was getting dark, and after all the recent activity, Tara took the time to close all the blinds and made sure all the doors and windows were locked. Lastly, she checked the security program on her laptop to make sure the alarms and cameras were working.

Wyatt had sat and watched this process quietly. This wasn't his Tar. Something had spooked her. And if he wasn't mistaken, she was carrying. He could just make out the outline of a handgun at the small of her back. Gwenn was carrying too. Why would two ladies be carrying at home, where you're supposed to be safe? And what had Tar spooked enough to close blinds, and check security in her own house? It was time for some answers because he wasn't liking the vibe he was getting.

"Dinner's over. Dogs are taken care of, and you've secured the house. So, why the hell don't you tell me what has you freaked out, Tar? And don't say it's nothing. Don't insult my intelligence with that lie," Wyatt added when Tara opened her mouth.

"I wasn't going to deny it. I just don't know where to start with it," Tara snapped.

"Beginning is best," Gwenn helped.

"Actually, seeing is better, I think. Let's show him what we've found in my office. That's the biggest part of this mess, then we can fill in the blanks."

"Well, fuck me! You have a goddamned secret room in your house, and you didn't tell me? I'm just a little bit jealous. This is just too cool!" Wyatt stood in the middle of the room below Tara's office, hands on his hips while he turned and looked.

"Well, it was very cool. At first. But it's not so cool now," Tara replied. "This is where the story gets ugly. So, Gwenn and I found this room, and at first, we thought the previous owner had it built because she was hiding a secret archaeological find. See?" Standing in front of the boards, Tara gestured. "The drawings and photos and notes on the corkboards had us looking for something she had found and was wanting to hide from the world, at least until she was ready to reveal her discovery. But then we decided that the artifacts she had been finding weren't anything earth shattering.

"Through the process of elimination, we were left with these three photos of a plant." Tara handed the photos to Wyatt. "Gwenn figured out from the photo that the plants weren't native to Maine and after some Internet research, discovered that the plant in these photos is native to Peru. More research and we now know the plant is one half of the formula to make a tea that makes the drinker high. Just let me finish!" Tara held up her hand to stop Wyatt when he started to speak.

"So, we knew that the plant was from South America. Therefore it couldn't grow outside, but since Dr. Roxbury had built this room, why couldn't she have built another room? With the use of ground penetrating radar equipment, we found another room underground." Tara moved over to the couch and end table, and with Wyatt watching her intently slid the ashtray to open the hidden bookshelf door.

Silently, Gwenn led the way into the room full of plants. "We call this The Lab."

Wyatt followed Gwenn in. Quietly, he walked farther into the room and slowly turned in a circle, then stopped to look at Tara. "What the hell, Tar? If these are really the plants that are a part of a drug, this isn't something to be fucking with.

What the hell were you thinking? We need to call the authorities and have this shit removed. I'm now seeing that your email didn't tell me shit about what was going on up here. Why didn't you say anything about this in your email?"

He walked over to her and put his hands on her shoulders. "I'm still your friend, goddammit." He looked at her and then to the side at Gwenn. "Is this why you're both carrying, and you're running security on your own house? Tell me the rest."

Tara leaned her head onto Wyatt's chest and sighed. "Let's finish this upstairs, I could use something to drink."

Back in the living room, Tara told Wyatt about the threatening note on her car, and the one that Gwenn had received, along with the fact that Gwenn's house had been broken into. She told him about the failed attempt of an intruder two nights prior and that since then, they were carrying at all times. Then, she told him about the boat that she had seen several times outside of the cove and of the couple of registration numbers she had been able to get off the boat the day prior.

Gwenn had let Tara dump all of the information on Wyatt, with the occasional comment or remark added.

Finally, Tara leaned back and sighed.

"Is that everything, Tar?"

"Yes, that's it. Everything."

"Okay. Damn it to hell! This is dangerous and scary. First thing in the morning, I'm doing a full security check of this place. Inside and out. Don't give me shit, Tar!" Wyatt added when Tara went to interrupt.

"Will you stop thinking I'm going to argue with you every time I interrupt! I'm not going to give you shit. I was just going to say that the cove isn't covered well. I noticed today that I need to add cameras and flood lights out there. And maybe a motion detector."

Wyatt got up to get his cell phone and made a note on it. "Okay, I have that down. I want to see how this place runs and where the vulnerabilities are. After we're secure, we'll figure out who we know that can help with those damn plants.

They have to have been left by the old owner, but why would she just leave them here? I have a feeling I'm going to be upset with this answer, but what happened to the lady that lived here before?" At Gwenn's and Tara's glance at each other, Wyatt sighed and sat down. "Okay, spill."

This time Gwenn told the story of Dr. Roxbury. She told Wyatt about the information that Tara had found out about her. That she was a retired professor of archaeology that had specialized in Peru. How she had moved to Maine and built this house and that the current security was what she had installed.

"That's all nice backstory, but it's not telling me why she left those plants downstairs. Why did she move, Gwenn?" Wyatt was growing tired from both the long drive and from the information overload that had been happening. Now he just wanted straight answers, without the flowers.

"Well, she sort of died. She was found in the cove about six months ago," Gwenn quietly replied. She knew that this information would truly show Wyatt how big of a mess this all was.

"Fuck me to hell! This just keeps getting worse by the minute." Wyatt rubbed his face with his hands. "Continue Gwenn. I know there is more than that so finish it."

"So, Dr. Roxbury was found in the cove by Bill, he's the handyman out here. Bill said he had come up to talk to Dr. Roxbury about something and couldn't find her in the house, so he went through all the buildings. When he couldn't find her anywhere inside, he walked around and started to look outside. That's when he found her floating in the cove. Of course, he went out and pulled her in, so he was the first one to see her.

"From what his wife, Barb, Bill told her, Dr. Roxbury had a horrible wound to the back of her head. Well, Barb called Fred, our local sheriff, who came out and he said it looked like an accident. That basically ended any investigation from what I understand. It's a small town, and if the sheriff didn't suspect foul play, then there was no reason to have an investigation.

"There wasn't a funeral or anything for her here. I guess she had all her funeral arrangements premade, so the local funeral home took care of getting her to wherever she wanted to be. We all just accepted that she probably slipped and hit her head, then fell into the cove and drowned. Of course, some folks think she killed herself. She was a very odd woman, so suicide was an easy sell.

"But now, with all this new information, Tara and I think that maybe the accident wasn't an accident or suicide. We think she was murdered because of those plants." Gwenn finished and clamped her hands between her knees to stop the shaking that telling Wyatt had caused.

"Fuck me sideways. Well, that's just the topping to this whole fucking mess. Security is definitely a top priority now. If you two are right, and I agree with you, that Dr. Roxbury was murdered because of those plants, we need to make sure that this place is airtight. Then we need to figure out who to call about all of this. I'll be right back, I need to go to my truck." Wyatt stood up and started heading for the front door.

Tara rubbed her face and looked at Gwenn. "Well, that was painful. He's pissed. And concerned. I can't say I would be feeling any different if the situation was different. I mean, we just tossed a ton of information at him."

"You think? I didn't get that vibe at all. Yeah, he's pissed. And he's concerned, for sure. But I'm going to say, I'm glad there is someone else here with us. Three people are harder to get rid of then just one or two. Safety in numbers, right? And it doesn't hurt that he's all big and muscly and shit. I'm going to go get one of the other rooms set up for him. Unless—" Gwenn stopped and smirked at Tara.

"Shut up, Gwenn. There's nothing between us anymore. Just friends. That's it. I think while you get a room set up for him, I'm going to let the pups out into the riding arena for their last trip out. I'll be back in soon."

When Wyatt came back in, carrying several bags, the living room and kitchen were empty. "Hello? Where'd everybody go?"

Gwenn popped her head out of the hallway just off the kitchen and on the same side as Tara's. "Hey, I'm in here. Come on in, this will be your room. I'm just finishing up getting it set up for you."

Wyatt walked into the room and stopped. "Wow, this is nice. Thanks for getting this ready for me, but it wasn't necessary. I could have done it myself." He set down his bag and the large hard case that he was carrying.

"Gwenn, I know you are Tar's friend, but you do know that I'm going to have to check you out, right? I mean in light of all the information you two gave me tonight, I need to make sure you really are one of the good guys. I'm sorry if that upsets or pisses you off. But I'm being straight with you."

Gwenn stopped smoothing out the quilt on the bed and looked him in the eye. "I'd be pissed and worried if you didn't. You don't know me, and I only know you from the little bit Tara has told me. Tara is my friend. I'm not sure how it happened, but somehow she has become very important to me. We need to make sure she stays safe. So, check me out. You'll be bored with the lack of background on me. Oh, and as a side note, you hurt her any more than has already happened, I'll hand you your balls as I kick you out of here."

Wyatt tucked his hands into his back pockets and rocked on his feet. "Wow. Ouch. But okay. We seem to be on the same page about protecting Tar. I like you. Where's she at anyway?"

Gwenn finished putting a pillow case on the last pillow. "Out in the riding arena, letting the dogs have their last trip out before bed."

"Show me?" Wyatt asked as he pulled the Beretta 9 mm handgun out of the hard case. Checking to make sure it was loaded, he put it in the holster at the small of his back.

As they walked out of his room and into the kitchen, they heard Tara and the dogs in the breezeway. Coming into the kitchen, Tara closed and locked the door.

"What?" she questioned when she saw Gwenn and Wyatt standing there.

"Nothing now. We were just coming to check on you," Gwenn replied.

"I really can't wait to see the rest of this place tomorrow. But, listen, it's getting late, and I'm tired, so how have you two been handling sleeping? Are you doing shifts?" Wyatt asked while leaning over to scratch Connal's ears.

"Yeah, we have been. Why don't you both get some sleep? It's getting late, and you both need your sleep more than I do. If I really feel the need to, I'll wake Gwenn for the last shift. This way, you can get a good night's sleep from working all day yesterday, then driving today. Gwenn, you okay with that plan?" When Gwenn nodded her agreement, Wyatt stood up and looked at the two of them.

"I can do a shift, but a full night's sleep does sound great. Make sure to wake me up if you need to, though. After tomorrow, we won't have to do shifts. Good night ladies."

"Damn, he's fiiinnnneee. We're going to have to have a girl conversation about him soon, Tara." Gwenn smirked and walked toward her room before Tara could reply.

"Well, it's just you and me now guys. Might as well get comfortable," Tara told the three dogs as they all settled into the living room to watch TV and the security cameras on her laptop.

Wyatt was just finishing up making his first cup of coffee when Tara and the pups came back into the house from morning outs. Taking out another mug, he poured a cup for Tara and handed it to her as she got to the island.

"Thanks. I start a pot before I take the dogs out. That way I don't have to stand here and stare at the coffee while it drips. How did you sleep?" Tara sipped on her coffee while getting the pups' breakfasts ready.

"Slept like the dead, thanks. Since you didn't wake me up, I'm assuming it was a quiet night?"

"Yep, nothing moving out there last night." Putting the dog dishes in their respective places, Tara held her hand up, then after making sure all the furry butts were sitting and waiting, she lowered her hand to release the dogs to eat.

"That's impressive as hell," Wyatt commented as he watched Connal, then Gizmo and lastly Peanut finish their meals in under two minutes.

Gwenn chose that moment to come stumbling into the kitchen. "Please, God, tell me there's coffee." Wyatt answered that by handing her a cup of coffee.

"I might love you," Gwenn mumbled to him in thanks while inhaling the steam from the cup.

Wyatt laughed. "That was easy. I'm going to start my walk around. No need to hurry up and catch up with me. I'm a big boy, I can see what I need without you. I'll make a list of things I find and any questions I might have. Maybe we can go over what I find at lunch?"

"That sounds like a good plan." Tara grabbed his arm and then handed him a piece of paper. "You might need this. It's the code to get into the main gate."

"Writing codes down is bad form, Tar," Wyatt said, as he headed to the entryway door.

"So, memorize it, then eat the paper."

Wyatt did just that, which got a laugh out of both Tara and Gwenn.

Glancing at Gwenn, Tara knew that Gwenn was going to try to start questioning her about Wyatt. "Don't start with your questions until at least my third cup of coffee. I mean it. I need more coffee than normal to discuss Wyatt. Actually, I might need a couple of beers, too."

Gwenn wisely closed her mouth and just nodded that she valued her life and that she would not poke the Tara bear. At least not for a bit.

Wyatt spent the majority of the day scoping out the layout of the land and where all the cameras were. After a quick lunch in which they discussed what he had found and wanted to do, he installed a couple of new cameras pointing toward the cove. He also installed three flood lights above the cove cameras.

Tara didn't question where these new cameras or flood

lights came from. She hadn't ordered them, and the little hardware store in town didn't carry them. Wyatt had come prepared to make her safe, assuming that she would need it. That pissed her off a bit. She was perfectly capable of making herself safe. She didn't need an ex-husband to come riding in on his big-assed truck and protect her. She hated to admit it, but she was glad to have the cove cameras up. And it did save her the time of researching and buying said cameras.

For the most part, Tara had stayed out of Wyatt's way. Since Gwenn was at work, Tara spent the time with the pups, which they all needed. She brushed all three of the dogs and clipped and dremeled their nails. Then taking them outside, they played fetch and ran around and just spent time together.

When Connal and Gizmo had been sufficiently tired out, she worked with Peanut on his cart. He was getting along very well in it, but Tara had noticed that it needed a few adjustments. So, after a Skype meeting with a Facebook friend who was an expert on DM and the use of carts for dogs, Tara was able to tweak the cart to better meet Peanut's needs. He didn't need the wheels all the time, but it was good to get him used to the wheels before he had to use them. Plus, using the wheels had Peanut out and about and more active, which made for a happy dog.

Now lying back in the grass, facing the cove, Tara closed her eyes and enjoyed the feel of the sun on her face. She could hear all three of the pups beside her, snoring at varying levels. That made her smile. Listening past the sleeping dogs, she could hear birds chirping and the breeze rustling in the leaves of the trees. She could smell the ocean and hear the waves. She let herself focus on the sounds, smells and feel of the outside and she did something she rarely did during the day. She fell asleep. In broad daylight, lying in the grass with her dogs.

That's how Wyatt found her when he walked around the side of the house to see where she was. He stopped and watched her. She looked healthy and happy and content. Those weren't things his Tar had ever been. And she wasn't his Tar anymore. The divorce had ended that. Surprisingly, that made him sad.

"About time you woke up," Wyatt teased Tara 30 minutes later. He had gone into the house and gotten a couple of glasses and a pitcher of lemonade and was now sitting beside her in the grass. "Don't scowl at me or I won't let you have any lemonade."

Tara finished brushing the grass off her shoulders and getting most of it out of her hair. "It's my lemonade, so hand it over. I fell asleep."

"Way to state the obvious," Wyatt remarked back and handed her a glass of lemonade. "After you wake up, want to show me your program for the cameras? And if you have some steaks, I'm available to be the grill master for the evening meal."

"That sounds amazing. Gwenn is already half in love with you. A steak, off a grill, will most likely seal the deal. I'll text her and see if she can get a couple of lobsters on the way home to add to the steak. You haven't been properly welcomed to Maine yet."

Tara finished off the text to Gwenn, then walked into the house and pulled three ribeyes from the freezer. "Gwenn says sure. Anything else we need?"

"We square on beer? And I wouldn't mind something sweet."

"Oh, good thought! Okay, she said it's slow at the restaurant, so she's heading home in about an hour with the lobsters and beer. Now let me show you the security program."

"I think I'm going to have to marry you and have your babies now," Gwenn groaned from her slouched position on the porch. "My God, that was a fantastic dinner, Wyatt. Thanks for grilling."

"Thank you for the lobster. I've never had lobster that fresh before. And the beer. Nice and smooth. Maine's not that bad at all." Wyatt leaned back in his chair and took another long pull from his beer.

"I'm stuffed. So stuffed. But I want more." Tara laughed, then held her stomach because it hurt to laugh with her belly so full.

"What's for dessert?" Wyatt joked.

Heading back in, Tara went around and closed blinds and doors and made sure the house was locked up. While Tara did that, Gwenn and Wyatt cleaned up the kitchen.

Since Tara finished locking up the house before Gwenn and Wyatt had finished in the kitchen, she changed into her bathing suit and took the pups for a swim.

Gwenn and Wyatt joined her and the dogs a while later, and they took turns watching and playing with the dogs as they swam around. When the dogs let themselves out of the pool, they knew that swimming was over and it was time to head in for the night. Wyatt went to the new monitor for the security system that he had mounted to the wall.

"I'd like to show you both what I did today." Touching the monitor, Wyatt brought up the cameras. "I've installed three cameras on the cove side. One on each corner of the house and one in the middle. This way, you have a full view of the entire cove area. No blind spots. Also, there are now three spotlights above the cameras, and they're motion detected, so if anything taller than a corgi comes around, the lights will automatically come on, and you will have an alert sound on this monitor and on your phones. It will start recording automatically as well.

"The rest of the security was great. I tweaked the software a bit and added more spotlights over all the cameras. They're all wired the same way as the cove. There are no blind spots."

Tara nodded and smiled. "I like it. Thank you."

"I tweaked the front gate a bit, too. Again, mostly software tweaks. I did the same with the doors and windows of the house, in the garage, riding arena, gym and the equipment barn. Everything is wired into this monitor. I hope that you don't mind that I installed it on the wall here, but it needs to be in a central location and out of the way. So, I figured the best place was close to the island, on the wall beside your counters. I can move it if you don't like it."

"No, this is a good place. No need to move it."

"Good. You can scroll through all the cameras by swiping your finger to the left. You can also zoom in and out like you do on your cell phones and tablets. It's very quick and easy to use. And I've already installed the software on your phones and laptops."

"How did you do that? You didn't ask to see my phone or laptop," Gwenn questioned.

Wyatt just smiled, and Tara laughed. "He's a computer engineer, he has skills."

"Oh, well thanks. I think. That's actually creepy, in a way. You just installed the software, right? You didn't look around on my phone or laptop? Like at pictures or texts or anything?"

"Sorry, but it saved time, and I wanted us all on the same page ASAP. No, I didn't snoop. I promise." Wyatt stepped back from the monitor now and let Tara and Gwenn play with the program.

They took turns scrolling through the views and zooming in and out on various feeds. They also figured out how to manually turn on the spotlights in one area or the entire system of spotlights. While they were experimenting with the program, Wyatt walked away and into his room.

He wanted them to hear what the alarm to a door being opened would sound like, so he went to the French door that led out to the porch and opened the door.

Immediately, the alarm went off on the monitor in the kitchen as well as on all three of their cell phones. In a matter of seconds both women were in his room, guns out, followed by three howling and barking dogs.

"Just testing. Good, you saw where the threat was on the monitor," Wyatt said and showed them how to turn off the alarm from his cell then closed and locked the door.

Bending over, he took over getting Peanut to calm down,

while Tara soothed Connal and Gwenn took Gizmo. "So, now that this place is officially Fort Knox, no more shifts. Time for you to live normally again. Now, take those three stinky little dogs and get out of my room. I've got some work to do, then I'm going to bed. Have a good night, ladies."

Gwenn led the way back to the living room and sat down on the couch and was joined by both Connal and Gizmo. Petting their ears, she looked over at Tara as she sat on the floor to give Peanut some attention. "I'm glad he showed up. I know you are a little put out that the man came riding in like the knight on a freaking white horse, but I'm glad he did. It's good to have another set of eyes looking at the place and making it super-duper secure."

Since Peanut had laid down, Tara now transferred the petting to his chest. "I'm glad he's here too. And I agree, he's so much more up to date with security than I am, so it's good to have him here and covering areas I missed. We're still friends, and I really do trust him with knowing all of this. He knows more people that can help with the ugliness of all of this.

"And yes, I love him." On Gwenn's squeal and fist pump, Tara added, "But I'm not in love with him any longer."

Gwenn growled under her breath and scrunched up her mouth.

"I don't. He'll always be my family. We have been in each other's life for more than half of our lives, but we aren't in love anymore. We respect each other, would kill for each other but that's it. Like family. Not lovers. Does that make sense?"

"Yeah, it does. He's so damn hot, though! And he looks mighty tasty in jeans."

Tara laughed and agreed. "Yeah, he is. And if you are interested, I'll try to be okay with that."

Gwenn shook her head. "No, that's just too weird. And I think it breaks a best friend rule somewhere. So, I'll see him as a friend, anything else is just bordering on icky. But damn. Okay, I'm done."

"So now that that is settled, I'm going to take my three

monsters for last outs, then I'm going to bed. Maybe read for a bit."

"I'll wait until you get back in, then I'm heading to bed too."

CHAPTER TEN

The rest of Wyatt's weeklong visit went quickly and quietly. Since the Fourth of July snuck up on them, they celebrated with an honest to goodness New England clambake, prepared mostly by Gwenn.

Following the clambake, they had a bonfire on the beach to celebrate, and Wyatt fixed the lack of fireworks by bringing out one of the TVs, so they watched and listened to the Boston Pops Celebration while enjoying s'mores and mountain pies. Connal, Gizmo, and Peanut spent the evening chasing each other along the beach and begging for bits of the human snacks.

After the holiday, they spent time lying in the sun or playing in the cove. And the boat shed got a thorough clean up, thanks to Wyatt.

"Everything had its own spot on the walls now: the kayaks, paddleboards, and life jackets—or PFDs. Wyatt had even installed shelves to store the variety of snorkeling gear." The canoe and the sea doos were out of the water but could be placed in quickly now that the dry dock hoist had been fixed. Again, thanks to Wyatt.

It wasn't just the inside that had been cleaned up. The outside of the boat shed had a new coat of paint on it as well.

Nothing splashy, but a nice nautical blue, with white trim. Wyatt then outdid himself and made sure that the boat dock got a new coat of stain.

Wyatt had also decided to add a couple of cameras and spotlights on the boat shed and dock.

Tara decided that since Wyatt had done so much work on the boat shed, that she would have to use it, and the equipment in it, more often. After all, it would be a waste not to now.

"I'm going to have to measure the pups for PFDs. If I'm going to go kayaking and canoeing, they have to learn to like it too. I just have to convince them of that." Tara made a mental note as she walked out to the garage where Wyatt was putting the rest of his stuff in the back. "All packed?"

"Yep, that's it. I'm heading back to upper New York, but I would like to head back here next weekend. I know you can take care of yourself, but humor me, okay?" Wyatt stopped her argument before she could get going. "I'm going to reach out to some of my contacts about the plants. Hopefully, I'll have some information for you and Gwenn when I get back here."

"Thank you for all you did and are doing. It means a lot to me. Safe driving and let me know when you get in, okay?" Tara stepped to him and gave him a hug.

Wyatt returned the hug, then jumped into the truck. "See ya soon Tar. Be safe."

Tara watched Wyatt drive away, then walked into the house. She was by herself, and it felt weird.

Gwenn was at her house in town. She had spent the last two days there, and Tara was sure it was because Wyatt had made sure that her house and restaurant were secure too. More cameras and spotlights had been installed, and those two places were now tied into her monitor in the kitchen, as well as to all three of their cell phones and laptops. There was no privacy now. Tara chuckled at that.

"Feels like the Big Brother house guys. So, it's just us. What shall we do with our quiet time?" Tara glanced down at the dogs. They, in turn, were looking at her, waiting for her to decide what they were going to do for the day. "Nothing?

Really? I have to do all the planning here? Fine. I say we play in the cove for the day." At the excited barks, bouncing and running in circles, Tara laughed and went to change into water clothes.

"Just a gal and her three little noisy dogs. What could be better?" Tara said as she sat down on the lounge chair and picked up the ball that Connal had brought to her. "What? You want to play ball?"

Connal bounced on his front legs and barked.

"Are you sure?"

He barked and spun in circles.

"Ready?"

Now he jumped up and tried to snatch the ball out of her hand.

"Okay, go!" she said as she tossed the ball out into the water and watched all three dogs body check each other to get to it first. That process went on until first Peanut, then Gizmo and finally Connal came to lay down beside Tara and bake in the sun.

"I'm hungry. Are you guys hungry?" Tara asked the pups several hours later. They were still sitting outside but had moved to the porch off the living room. Those words brought about a chorus of barking and dancing. "Of course you're hungry. You're corgis. Let's go in and scrounge for food."

"It's not dinner time yet, so just snackies." Grabbing a banana and a yogurt for her snack, Tara opened up the cookie jar that was the dogs' and gave each pup a doggie cookie. Still munching the banana, Tara got her laptop and decided to shop for the PFDs for the dogs, which required measuring three wiggly dogs.

As she finished ordering the PFDs, she got a text from Gwenn that she was going to stay at her house for the evening. She replied okay and to enjoy her quiet, and that she would chat with her in a little bit. "So, it's just us for the evening, too. It's been a long time since we've been by ourselves for the night. Let's see what's for dinner."

Tara had a quiet dinner and then spent the evening playing on Facebook. When that got boring, she caught up on the DVRed shows she hadn't had a chance to watch.

As she came in from letting the dogs out to the arena for their last outs, Wyatt called to let her know he was in New York and to make sure everything was okay.

"Well, you have this place wired for sound, so you know I'm perfectly fine. All locked in and up for the night. Gwenn stayed at her place, but you know that too, don't you?" Tara teased.

"I will not confirm nor deny that I have checked the cameras a couple of times to make sure all is secure there. Looks like you got some sun there, Tar."

"What? How the hell—Did you install cameras in the house too?" Tara said, looking around the living room.

"Maybe one or two. But nothing too invasive and they're only in the living room and kitchen area. And I added a couple more in the arena, pool, garage, equipment barn and the boat shed to cover some blind spots. They're all on the scroll of cameras, so it's not like I didn't tell you. You just didn't look at all the camera folders," Wyatt hurried to add when Tara didn't comment.

Tara sighed heavily. "I'm not sure I like that, Wyatt."

"You already had cameras all over the place, so it's not like I crossed a line. I just added more and adjusted the fields of vision on them. No blind spots now. I didn't set them up to peep at you or Gwenn. Yes, I have some at Gwenn's house too. I just want to see that you're okay when you're both alone. Once all this is over, they can be turned off or removed. But until then, they make me feel better." Wyatt knew that appealing to his feeling better would stop any continuing argument about the cameras.

"Okay, but I'm going to have to call Gwenn and tell her you're a perv."

Wyatt laughed at that. "Better you than me. Just make sure she remembers I'm a concerned perv."

Tara and Wyatt talked for a bit longer, then hung up with

the promise to keep in touch during the week and that Wyatt would do some networking about the plants.

Sitting back down after getting a beer, Tara dialed Gwenn's cell. "Hey, what are you up to?" Tara said after Gwenn answered her phone.

"Sitting here, reading and watching stupid TV. You?"

"Playing on the computer and watching stupid TV. Just talked to Wyatt. You need to wave at him. He was a perv and installed a couple of cameras in your house."

Gwenn jerked up from reclining on her couch and looked around. "Wait. What? Where? I'm glad I haven't been running around here bare-assed naked."

"Yeah, I know, I'm not pleased either, but I get why he did it. Just in the living room and kitchen." Tara wasn't sure why she felt she had to defend Wyatt, but she was. She knew it, and so did Gwenn.

"What if I cooked naked? Did he think about that? I'm just teasing. I get why he did it, but it doesn't mean I'm not going to bust his balls about it next weekend."

After they had talked about their days, Tara hung up. "I'm bored. What the hell. I used to love my quiet, alone time. I miss having Gwenn here," Tara grumbled to the pups. Connal came up to stand on her lap and gave her a lick on the chin. Rubbing and scratching Connal's sides, Tara leaned her cheek on his shoulder. "You miss her too, don't ya?"

Tara reached over to smack at the alarm but didn't connect. Cracking one eye open, she found herself on the couch in the living room. And the alarm wasn't her alarm clock, but her cell phone and the monitor in the kitchen.

"What the hell!" Tara shouted as she jumped up, grabbing the gun as she went. Looking at the monitor on the wall, she saw that the alarm wasn't for anything on the property. The alarm was alerting to a fire at Gwenn's house.

"Shit!" she yelled as she dialed Gwenn's cell.

"I'm okay, I'm outside. My fucking house is burning, Tara!" Gwenn said in the way of hello. "I've called the fire department. Oh my God, Tara, my house."

"I'll be there in a few minutes," Tara replied, then hung up before Gwenn could argue. She rushed to get dressed and to get the pups in the SUV. She made sure to put the handgun in the holster at her back and pulled out of the garage. Closing the garage, she ran the code that Wyatt had shown her to use when she was leaving the house for any amount of time. As she pulled through the main gate and made sure it closed, her cell rang.

"Is she okay?" Wyatt immediately demanded.

"Hey. Yeah, she says she's okay and that she's out of the house, but she's upset. The dogs and I are heading that way right now. Why don't you talk to me until I get there?" Tara knew that this would end any argument about her leaving the property, plus it made her feel safer.

"I can do that. I got the alarm and saw the smoke in the house. It's going to be a complete loss, Tar."

"Damn it to hell, Wyatt. This isn't an accident. You know that right? This needs to end and soon. I know you replayed the video. Did anyone show up on it?"

"Yeah, I replayed the video, but it doesn't show a fucking thing. I'm going to scrub all the video in a bit and see if I missed something. I know this wasn't an accident. Someone is trying to scare you two. I'm getting with my contact tomorrow. It's time for this to end and to find out who is doing this."

"I agree this needs to stop. Okay, I'm here. My God, Wyatt, there's nothing left of her house. I'll call you when we head back to the property."

Getting out of the SUV, Tara did the only thing she could. She hugged and cried with her best friend.

As they mourned the loss, a man stood back and quietly cheered. He had hurt at least one of them. No, not physically like he would have preferred, but emotionally and sometimes that was worse than a broken bone or bruise. And by hurting Gwenn, he had hurt the bitch that didn't belong here. He was careful to not smile, this wasn't a happy occasion, but inside, he was dancing with happiness.

They spent the next several days going through what was left of Gwenn's house, sifting through the rubble, saving a picture here or a piece of clothing there. But, in the end, there really wasn't much left to save.

Now sitting at the table overlooking the cove, Gwenn covered her face and cussed and cried. Tara didn't try to comfort her. Gwenn didn't need or want that, at least not right now. Now she needed to purge the anger and loss out without comfort or back pats.

"I'm going to fucking kill the asshole that did this. I swear to God, I am. I didn't have a lot, but dammit, it was mine."

Tara let Gwenn cuss and cry until nothing was left, other than the occasional sniffle. Clearing her throat, she waited until Gwenn looked at her.

"I've been thinking, and I'm sure my timing sucks, but maybe it will help you to focus on something new and different. And hopefully exciting. I'm not negating your loss at all, so please don't take this that way. But I would like you to move out here with me permanently. Just stop and let me finish. Not to live in this house," she added when Gwenn started to shake her head and interrupt.

Gwenn furrowed her brow.

"Shit. Let me try that again. I want to you live out here with me, but I would like you to have your own house. For you to live in. It would be your house, and if you didn't like the fact that it was on my property, maybe I could sell you a piece of the land," Tara sputtered to an ending. Shaking her head and mentally kicking herself, she knew that she was royally screwing this up.

Gwenn reached over and touched Tara's hand, but Tara could see that Gwenn had misunderstood her and was a little upset. "Tara, you don't have to feel bad for me. I'll land on my feet. There's no need for charity."

Sighing, Tara shook her head. "This isn't charity, it really isn't. And I've really screwed up the offer. But I was thinking the night this happened, before the fire, how I missed you and having you out here with me. The dogs have been missing you too.

"So, I got to thinking, wouldn't it be cool to have you living out here? Like in your own place. And that with 40 acres, we wouldn't be up each other's ass all the time. I'm alone and so are you, so it just seems to make sense. We would be close enough if we needed or wanted it, but still have our own space.

"Plus, I've thought about it, and I know what I want to do out here, and I would love for you to help me with it. Having you on the property would be best for my plan." Leaning back Tara fought the urge to cross her arms and close herself up. She had said what was on her mind, so now she needed to be open enough to let Gwenn see she meant it all.

Gwenn leaned forward, over the table and looked Tara dead in the eye. "What do you want to do, Tara?"

Tara took a deep breath, then leaned forward and returned the eye contact. "No laughing or I'll have to kick you out, but you know I love corgis. All animals really, but corgis are my weakness. I want to start a place for elderly corgis to live out their last days or years. So many senior dogs are just thrown away. I want to help them. I want to give them somewhere to come that they will be loved and warm and safe."

"That's fucking beautiful and so perfect," Gwenn said, with tears in her eyes. "I'm in. On one condition. I get to have some of the pups stay with me when I'm home."

Tara let out the breath she didn't realize she had been holding. "Deal. Of course, you will have full input on your house, but I would love it if you were close. Maybe clear some of the land off on my side of the house. That way you would have a view of the cove too. And easy access to the equipment barn, pool and the riding arena." Now that Gwenn liked the idea, Tara was excited about the plan.

"Three bedrooms, two baths. Open floor plan, one story and wrap around porches. Something that mirrors this house," Gwenn added, getting into the excitement of the moment.

"Yes, exactly. This is going to be great!"

They spent the rest of the afternoon discussing the new house and the senior rescue. Then after dinner, Tara showed Gwenn how to groom the dogs. Gwenn wanted to know everything, now that she would be helping Tara with the rescue. So, Tara showed Gwenn how to brush and comb the pups. How to clean ears and brush teeth, which had Gwenn in stitches because Connal loved to try to eat the toothbrush and if he got it loose from you, he would play keep away with it.

Later, as they turned in for the evening, Tara smiled and ruffled Connal's fur. "Did you see the smile on Gwenn's face? I put that there. She's going to move out here with us. Permanently. You'll love that, won't you? Just remember, that you are my boy, not hers." Tara leaned over to kiss Connal's head, which had him leaning up to lick her chin. "Yeah, you're my boy. And you are my boy too, Peanut." Tara turned to Peanut who had made his way up on the bed and petted his ears. Gizmo, not to be denied, muscled Connal out of the way so that Tara could give her belly rubs with her other hand. "And you are my baby girl. All my babies," Tara said, as she laid back on her bed, petting and smiling.

Wyatt arrived back at the house late Friday night, and he thought he was going to sneak into the house, but the three barking alarms said otherwise. Tara had been on the couch with her laptop and had seen the alerts when the main gate opened and closed, then the spotlights come on, so she knew he was arriving. She was at the door when he came in and attempted to quiet the dogs before they woke up Gwenn.

But that wasn't the case since Gwenn walked into the living room to see what the barking was about.

Wyatt walked over to her and pulled her into a hard hug to convey his feelings about the loss of her house. "We'll make the bastards pay for this, Gwenn. I promise."

Since all three were wide awake, they spent some time catching up on the week and small talk, until first Gwenn, then Wyatt and finally Tara went to their respective rooms for the night.

The man in the boat outside of the cove watched the dually pull up to the house and into the garage.

"Now, who the hell is that? Maybe it's just a bootie call. But whoever it is, is making themselves at home. Just pulling their big truck into the garage like they live there. Fuck, now there are three people in that damn house. And those yappy-assed little dogs.

"This is getting out of hand. I need to get this under control again. I need to find out where Edna has those goddamn plants. If they're still alive, and she was smart, so I bet they are, they have to be getting ready for harvesting. I need to find them, not only for that dickhead of a buyer, but I'm fucking running low on my supply. I can't lose that crop. I won't."

Turning the boat away from the cove, he kept the motor on low until he was farther out to sea, then he gunned the engine, just as the first raindrops hit the boat.

"My friend couldn't find out much about the numbers that you got off the boat. Without the beginning of the registration, it could be registered in any of the 50 states, or Canada for that matter," Gwenn informed Tara and Wyatt the next morning. They had finished breakfast and were sitting outside, watching the dogs run and play.

"I was afraid that would be the case. It was a good try, though. Maybe the asshole will show up again and give us a better view of the registration." Tara whistled to the dogs, and when all three heads turned her way, she threw the ball that she had snuck out of the house. The result was a mad dash of legs and wheels to see who would get to the ball first.

"Well, I had some success on finding a contact while I was in New York last week. Tara, I called Bob. He's with the DEA and based in DC now. Had lunch with him midweek since he was in my area and we discussed some of what is going on up here. He's interested in seeing the plants, so I'd like to go back into the room and take some detailed pictures and video for him. I have to be in DC on Tuesday, so instead of emailing, I'll show him the pictures and video in person.

"But, he said if you two are correct, there's only one guy that specializes in that plant in New England. Bob's going to dig up some more information on this guy. If those plants are the real deal, he would like for you to work with him to take down the operation up here. I told him I would talk to you about it. Hear your thoughts on it." Wyatt picked up the ball that Gizmo had got to first on the last throw and launched it, then winced when Peanut body checked Connal with his wheels and got to it first.

"I haven't seen Bob in a couple of years, but he's a good guy, and I trust him. So, yeah, let's do this. It's most likely what got Dr. Roxbury killed, and it's sitting in a secret hideaway under my house. So, yeah. Let's use the plants to draw out the assholes that are using it to make money and hurt people." Tara looked over at Gwenn, who had been quiet, "Gwenn, if this is too much—"

"Don't you even start that shit with me, Tara. I'm in. The bastards burnt down my house. So, hell yeah, I'm in. Let's catch these assholes." To seal the deal, the three of them clinked coffee cups.

Wyatt spent most of the morning walking around the property and making sure that all the cameras were clean and there were no issues with them. He checked bulbs on the flood lights, and after all of that, he walked farther into the tree line surrounding the house. He wasn't just casually walking. He was looking. Looking for anything that might have said that something other than an animal had been traipsing around. He didn't find anything and sighed a breath of relief.

That eased his mind. It didn't stop him from installing some wireless field cameras, though. Better safe than sorry he told himself. If those plants were really drug plants, this was very dangerous, and he wanted to make sure all avenues had been covered. He stepped out of the tree line in time to see a middle-aged woman walk into the house.

"Who the hell is that?" As he went to investigate, he checked the handgun and re-holstered it before walking into the house.

The middle-aged lady turned with a smile on her face, which turned to shock and surprise and a little squeal escaped her.

"Can I help you?" they said to each other at the same time.

Tara walked out of the mud room at the same time to see and hear the confusion on both Wyatt and Barb's faces. She hurried over and smiled.

"Oh, Barb this is Wyatt, my friend. Wyatt, this is Barb. She and her husband live in the house before the main gate. She helps with household things when I need them. I called her a bit ago and asked her to come over."

Wyatt smiled and held out his hand to Barb. "Hi, Barb. Sorry for the fright. It's nice to meet you."

Thin-lipped, Barb barely touched Wyatt's hand before she released it. "Likewise." Turning, she held up a bag. "I brought the powder that I use to remove grass stains out of clothing. I also brought over some chowder and a beef stew for you, dear. I'll put it in the freezer, and then I'll be on my way."

Glancing at Wyatt out of the corner of her eye, she hurried into the kitchen to put the containers in the freezer. Then, throwing one more quick look over her shoulder, Barb left.

"She's different," Wyatt commented after Barb had left.

"Yeah, she runs hot and cold. Sometimes she's almost nice, then she flips a switch and turns into evil school teacher. She did seem like she was almost mad you were here, though."

Wyatt had taken out his phone. "What's her full name, Tar?"

"Barb Ohlson." She went ahead and added, "she lives with her husband, Bill, up the lane on the left, before you get to the gate. They came with the property. At least until October. That's when their prepaid contract expires.

"She is technically the housekeeper and cook, but I limited her time at the house. Felt weird having her in to clean and cook for me. Plus, I didn't really like them having the gate code to come and go.

"Bill is the handyman. Makes sure the equipment and house are all up and running. I don't see him much at all, and I don't think I've ever actually talked to him. Anything I need from either of them is set up by email or text."

Wyatt made a few more notes. "Okay. You know it's just standard, but I want to check on them. Anyone else been out here that just seems odd?"

"No. Wait. Yes. The local law enforcement. Fred Toft. He gives me funky tummy," she supplied, quietly.

Wyatt glanced up from typing in Fred's name. "Funky tummy? Okay, he's definitely being looked at, too. I'm not making light of your funky tummy so don't get all defensive on me. It's a thing, and I trust it."

Tara smiled at that. She always felt self-conscious about her gut feelings.

"One more thing I want to check out. What were the numbers off that boat you saw? Maybe I can get some more information that Gwenn did."

"I just got the last bit of it. 11 N. Now, I think that's enough work for the day. It's a gorgeous day, and I want to spend it outside."

Wyatt took Connal out on the paddleboard, but only after Tara put his PFD on him. This made Connal, and Wyatt, moan with indignation.

"He's a dog, Tar, not a kid. Look at him, he's embarrassed," Wyatt actually whined to Tara.

"I don't care. He's my kid, and he wears a PFD. And shut up before I make you put one on."

Glancing down at Connal, who was looking up at him, Wyatt shook his head sadly. "Sorry buddy, but you're on your own. I don't want to have to wear one of those damn things."

Connal gave the most pitiful look to Wyatt, but they both knew Tara was going to win. Connal soon forgot the horror of the vest when Wyatt started paddling around, and he could see the fish below him. He barked and ran back and forth on the board, which caused Wyatt to lose his footing and fall into the water.

"Thanks a hell of a lot buddy! Fuck me, that water is cold." Wyatt tipped the board, causing Connal to fall into the water beside him. "Serves you right, little dog."

Turning toward shore, he called out, "Just testing out the PFD Mom, no need to worry."

"They're silly, aren't they? Out there, being all manly and they're both soaked. While we sit on the beach, getting our tan on." She reached over to either side and rubbed Gizmo's and Peanut's ears.

As Tara sat there and watched and laughed at Wyatt and Connal, she saw movement out of the corner of her eye. Turning her head slightly, she saw the boat just outside the cove. "Son of a bitch," she muttered.

Picking up her camera, she took photos of Wyatt and Connal in the cove. "Just taking pictures of the fun day. Nothing to do with you, you asshole." Tara made sure to zoom in and get some good photos of the boat too. It was too far out to see if it might be the same boat as before, but a couple of photos wouldn't hurt. She would tell Wyatt about it later.

CHAPTER ELEVEN

It was around 11 PM when all three were able to sit in the living room around Tara's laptop. Tara had downloaded the pictures she had taken from earlier after dinner while Wyatt had been showering. After some tinkering, she had been able to zoom in on the boat that had been outside the cove earlier that day and was now ready to show the other two what she had discovered.

Now, she had to share the photos with Wyatt and Gwenn. "Hey, now that you two are both here, I have something to tell you."

Gwenn and Wyatt turned in unison and looked at Tara, waiting.

"When Wyatt and Connal were playing around in the cove today, I noticed the boat just outside of the cove."

This got Wyatt's attention. "And you didn't mention it to me, why? What the fuck, Tar? You said no more holding information back."

"No, I didn't mention it to you at the moment. I didn't see a reason for it, and I didn't want to spook the guy."

Wyatt was on his feet and pacing by now. "Fuck spooking him, I would have shot at him."

"And that's exactly why I didn't say anything. If you would

sit down and shut up for a minute so I could finish, that would be great. I'm not stupid, Wyatt. You seem to forget that. I took pictures of the boat. And while you were showering, I uploaded the pictures and played with the resolution and zoom. It's the same boat as before."

Since both Gwenn and Wyatt were now sitting on either side of her, she opened the pictures and slowly scrolled through to show them photos of the boat. There, in the last photo, the boat registration number was clear. "ME 0711 N. We can find out who this is now."

"You still should have told me," Wyatt mumbled.

"Why? So that the person watching would have run away when you got all Neanderthal out there? This way, I got pictures of the boat without the person thinking anything of it. We have good information because I didn't tell you," Tara said, leaning back on the couch and folding her arms.

Gwenn snorted at the Neanderthal bit and nodded her head to agree with Tara. "You know you would have, Wyatt."

"Shut up, both of you." But Wyatt was smiling. "This is good information, Tar. You did good."

"A person could get used to this life," Gwenn mumbled as she and Tara were lying out in the sun, almost asleep. Wyatt was again on the water, this time in a kayak. And instead of Connal, he had Peanut with him. After the cursory argument with Tara, Peanut was wearing his PFD. Wyatt teased Tara about it, but silently agreed it was a good thing for the dog to have a PFD on.

"Just in case you try to drown us and all," he whispered to the dog.

Peanut was loving the kayak. He was sitting up straight, his head on a swivel and he had a very large smile on his face. Wyatt paddled slowly around the cove, enjoying the quiet and the slow wave action. He was also looking to see if there were any areas that he might have missed in his security plan.

"Your mom doesn't need to know what we're doing, okay? We're just enjoying the day on the water so don't tell on me," he said as he reached up to pet the dog.

"You do know he's doing a security kayak about, don't you?" Gwenn cracked one eye open and glanced over at Tara.

Tara nodded her head. "Yep. I do. And he's making it look like he's just enjoying the time with Peanut. He seems to forget that I know him. He's not a dog person. At all. Yesterday, he paddleboarded with Connal. Today, kayaking with Peanut. Gizmo's going to feel left out if he doesn't take her out on a sea doo or in the canoe later. I'm going to make sure to point that out to him."

"You have some evil in you, you know that?"

"And I'm thinking steaks for dinner. On the grill. That way Wyatt can feel manly and all, cooking for the women. After all, it's the least we can do for him, showing he does have Neanderthal DNA in him."

"Oh, that's good. 'Mmm. I'm man. Must make food for woman. Mmm.'" Gwenn tried to imitate her best caveman. "Okay, now shush. I fully intend to fall asleep in the sun for the day."

Tara must have napped too, because the next thing she knew, she was being rained on. But it wasn't raining. It was ocean water, and it was coming from Wyatt who was holding a very wet Peanut over her so that the water would drip off the dog onto her.

"Look, Mom. I fell in," Wyatt said in one of the most pitiful attempts to sound like a dog talking.

"I hate you," Tara grumbled when she opened one eye to see Wyatt's smile. "Do it to Gwenn."

"Damn woman. She knew what I was doing. I'm not going to be able to move my arms for the rest of the week." After rowing back to the boat dock, Wyatt had helped the dog onto the dock, removed the PFD and stored the canoe and the oars. Heading to the house, all he wanted was a shower, or maybe that hot tub in the pool house and a beer. But he had been drawn over to the two sleeping women and figured he might as well wake them up. Which had somehow backfired, because the girls had *convinced* him to be manly and grill steaks for them tonight. He, of course, obliged.

Now, just as he was coming into the house, the front gate alerted to a visitor. He changed his course of movement to the monitor to look over the shoulders of the girls, who had come into the house before him. "Who's that?"

"That's Fred, the local law enforcement," Tara grumbled and after pressing the button to open the gate, turned to head to her bedroom. "I need to put the dogs in my bedroom. They don't like Fred."

"Really? That's interesting because Connal loves everyone." Wyatt considered, then followed Gwenn outside to meet Fred. Gwenn walked over to greet Fred, while Wyatt waited in front of the garage.

He glanced over at Tara as she joined him. "Gwenn seems friendly with him."

"She is, she's known Fred forever. Small town, so everyone seems to have known everyone forever." That was all Tara could say before Gwenn led Fred over.

"Fred Toft, I would like you to meet Wyatt Perry. Wyatt is a friend of Tara's from Ohio. Wyatt, this is Fred. He's Eriksport's sheriff."

"It's nice to meet you, Fred," Wyatt said while holding out his hand.

"Nice to meet you. Long way from Ohio. You two must be good friends," Fred replied, taking Wyatt's hand to return the handshake and glancing over at Tara.

"Yeah, we're more like family." Wyatt placed his arm over Tara's shoulders to send a silent peeing on his territory message to Fred. Fred acknowledged the message with a smile and a single nod.

"So, what brings you out, Fred? Do you have news on the assholes that burned down my house?" Gwenn asked, sitting on the retaining wall between the garage and the walkway to the house.

Seeing that he wasn't going to be invited inside, Fred shifted the gun on his hip and sat down beside her. Sitting like this made him breathy and the red blotches on his face more pronounced. "Just checking in on you all. I'm real sorry Gwenn, the county fire marshal is looking into it, but it's looking like an electrical issue. It was an old house, so it sort of makes sense. He said he should have the final report in the next week or so. That way you can start your insurance claims and stuff."

Gwenn nodded, but she knew that this was crap. She had spent over eight grand over three years ago, replacing all of the wiring. "Well, that's good news, I guess. At least it's not some little dick running around, getting his jollies off torching houses. Thanks for keeping me informed. Just drop off the report by the restaurant when it's ready, okay? That way I can make copies of it in town."

"I sure will." Standing back up to get his breath, Fred made a point of looking at the flag-free yard. "Oh, looks like you decided not to plant any of those flower beds after all."

"Actually, I did. I planted bulbs. Used one of those bulb tools, that way it didn't destroy the grass," Tara answered. "Thinking it should be a gorgeous view next spring. I really hate to be curt Fred, but we're all starving from working all day, and we need to get the grill going."

"Oh sure. I understand. I plan on doing a steak on the grill myself tonight. Nothing like a good steak on the grill, after working all day. Wyatt, nice to meet you." Fred shook Wyatt's hand again. "Gwenn, take care. I'll get in touch with you if anything new comes up on the house and I'll drop off the report as soon as I get it." Giving her a hug and a kiss on the cheek, he nodded and smiled at Tara before getting into his truck and leaving.

As they turned to head back into the house, Wyatt whispered to Tara, "I'll run him first thing Tuesday. I don't like him at all."

Wyatt left early the next morning to head to D.C. and to meet up with Bob. He didn't say when he would be back, but Tara knew it would be over the weekend. She knew that this would be the routine until all this drug business was over.

"It doesn't bother you that he will be back this weekend, does it? Not like before?" Gwenn had a knack for reading Tara's mind.

"No, I'm okay with it. Truthfully, with all the odd things going on, it's a comfort to have another person involved. I think I'm going to veg for the day. Haven't had a chance to really be online and waste time for a bit, so I see some of that going on. I need to do my bills too. What do you have planned?"

Gwenn was quiet for a minute. "I have no idea. It's Monday, so I'm off. I'll veg too. Maybe we can find an old movie on the TV?"

"I like it. I'm making more coffee. It feels like a coffee all day sort of day."

The day of vegging lasted until the end of the third movie. Then it was just too much for both ladies.

"I'm going to go to the pool," Tara announced, which caused all three of the dogs to scramble up and to the kitchen door. "Geez, want to go with me?" she teased them.

"Yeah, enough vegging for me too. Enjoy your swim with the vermin. I think I'm going to go to town. I'm hungry for cake and ice cream. I don't suppose I could interest you in some junk?" Gwenn laughed because of the look of pure bliss that crossed Tara's face. "I'll take that as a yes. I'll do a quick inventory to see if there is anything else we can't live without. I won't be more than an hour, hour and a half at most."

The man on the boat outside of the cove watched as the second vehicle left. "Three people were there, two have left. That leaves one person and three shitty, little dogs. Look at me, doing math and shit."

He steered the boat down shore and to a small landing area that only the real locals knew about. As his feet hit the ground, his pulse quickened. This was dangerous, he could be caught. But that was some of the fun, wasn't it?

Wyatt was almost to New York when his phone starting

pinging. Glancing over at it, he saw it was an alert from Tara's house. "Shit!"

Pulling over to the shoulder of the road and putting on the blinkers, he grabbed his phone to see what was alerting. It was one of the trail cams he had just installed. The ones he hadn't told Tara about. Yet. Now, looking at the live feed, he saw a figure sneaking through the tree line of the house. "Fuck!" He touched Tara's face, and the phone immediately started ringing.

On the third ring, Tara answered, "You have afterburners on that truck?"

"Tar, there's someone in the woods on Gwenn's side of the house. He's sneaking around between the boat shed and Gwenn's room."

Tara was out of the pool and getting the dogs into the house before Wyatt finished the statement. "You're going to tell me how you know this later, but right now, lead me to the asshole."

"No! Stay in that goddamn house. He's being recorded. Maybe he'll be dumb enough for us to get his face on camera. Just make sure the house is locked and alarmed and get you, Gwenn and the dogs into the Batcave until he's gone." Wyatt had Tara on speaker now so that he could watch the figure on the live feed.

"Gwenn's in town. I bet he's been watching us! Saw you leave, then Gwenn and grew some balls to come sniffing around. Oh, I really want to put a round in his ass."

But she did what Wyatt had said. She got the pups and herself into the Batcave. "I frigging hate hiding like a little girl when some dickhead is on my property, Wyatt."

"I know you do, but this is the smartest way. We're getting him on record." Wyatt slammed his hand into the steering wheel. "Fuck! I have the cameras angled too low, I can't see his face, but I see his body. Maybe he'll fuck up and bend over, and we'll get his face on camera. I'll let you have first crack at him. I promise."

"Actually, Gwenn gets the first knee to the balls of this

asshole. Don't hang up but I need to text Gwenn to stay away until he's gone." She came back on the line a minute later. "Okay, she's going to go to her restaurant for a bit. Do you still see him, Wyatt?"

Tara was pacing back and forth, and the three dogs were following her. When she would turn around, they would scatter to get out the way.

Instead of yelling at them, she took a breath and sat down on the floor to comfort them and herself. She didn't tell Wyatt, but she had left all her guns upstairs. That would be remedied as soon as this latest incident was over.

"Yeah, the fucker's just nosing around. He's over behind the boat shed now. He's smart, he's staying in the tree line. He must know that there are cameras on the house. Now he's walking the tree line, I can't tell what he's really doing, but it just looks like he's checking out the house. Maybe trying to see if there's a weak spot. There isn't, asshole, so move on. Tar, if he comes to the house, don't destroy him. Big picture here, remember what Bob wants to do. I'm not saying you can't hurt him, but we need him to get the big dealer of those plants."

Tara blew out a breath. "Goddammit. Yeah, big picture."

"I have an idea, Tar. Go crack open the door closest to the tree line in Gwenn's room. Not the whole way, just enough for the sound to get out then get the dogs barking. This has been going on too damn long. It's time to take back the control."

"Good idea. I'm sick of cowering down here anyway." Tara's first stop was for the gun in her nightstand. Making sure it was locked and loaded, she and the dogs went into Gwenn's room and cracked opened the French door facing the trees.

Tara said the one thing that she knew would cause her dogs to bark and raise holy hell. "You want a cookie?" Connal, Gizmo, and Peanut let everyone within hearing distance, that yes, cookies were wanted. "Well?" Tara came back on the phone.

"What the hell? He's a ballsy dick, that's for sure. He's not moving away. Doesn't seem to faze him at all. He's just walking inside of the tree line, looking at the house. Dammit, bend over you bastard. Let me see your damn face."

"That makes no sense, Wyatt. The barking should have scared him off. Why wouldn't it?" Tara made shushing noises to quiet the dogs, who were having none of it. They wanted their cookies. "Quiet, you three! In a minute, I promise."

"I don't know, but I don't like it. Okay, new plan. Turn on the spotlights on that side of the house and the boatshed. Maybe he just thinks the dogs are barking to bark, but if the lights come on, that will let him know someone's there."

"Okay. I'm going to the kitchen to do that." Tara pulled up the app on the monitor in the kitchen and manually turned on the spotlights. "Okay, did that work?" She grabbed three cookies from the dog's treat jar to fulfill her cookie promise to the dogs.

"Yeah, that fucking got his attention. He turned tail and ran into the woods, away from the house. Tell Gwenn to come home, then lock that place up and keep the spotlights on tonight. I'm going to get the rest of the way to New York, and I'll call in a couple of hours. Be safe and be smart, Tar."

"Well, hell. I leave, and you have all the fun," Gwenn said, trying to make light of the fact that whoever was doing this, had intruded on home turf. She was pissed. And scared. "So, Wyatt put up field cameras without telling you, and that's how he saw this asshat?" Tara nodded. "Not sure whether to be happy about that or mad."

"I'm alternating between both of those feelings. On the one side, I'm glad he did because he saw the asshole and we have video of the guy. On the other, he's been all up my ass about telling him everything, and this is the second sneaky thing he's done. First his perv cameras in your house and mine. And now the field cameras. I'm not sure what to feel because both have been useful. But I do know one thing for sure."

"What's that? That you're going to hand him his ass?"

"Well, that too. But, I really want that damn ice cream and cake that you got. Dish it up, woman."

Since the day had taken a turn for the scary, it was decided to indulge and make their dinner the ice cream and cake. Tara even gave Connal, Gizmo, and Peanut a scoop of frozen vanilla yogurt that Gwenn had brought home. Gwenn had said she wasn't sure if Tara had issues with milk, so had gotten the yogurt just in case. But Tara knew that was just a ruse when Gwenn mentioned that she had read that yogurt was safe for dogs.

They each made excuses to get up and check on the security monitor, or to look out of a window throughout the rest of the day. They were nervous and anxious, and they both knew it, but they chose to try to hide it from the other.

"Those things make it daytime out there," Gwenn said when dusk had fallen, and Tara turned on the rest of the spotlights.

"That's a good thing. Hard for someone to sneak around with that much light outside." Standing up from the couch, Tara looked over at Gwenn. "I know it's early, but I think I'm going to go and read for a while. See if I can't get myself calmed down to sleep. I need some me time, I hope you understand."

Gwenn smiled and nodded. "Completely. I could use some grounding time by myself too. If it doesn't bother you, I'd like to stay up and watch some TV and read out here."

"Won't bother me at all. Good night, Gwenn."

Tara led the pups into her room and partially closed the door, so the dogs could go out of the room if they wanted a drink or to go visit Gwenn.

But instead of reading, Tara went into the office and worked. She journaled everything that had been happening, adding notes and photos to the journal. She got everything out of her and into the journal.

Feeling better and a bit more clear-headed, Tara pulled up Google Earth and zoomed into her property than to the side where the intruder was. Slowly moving toward the ocean, she looked for a place to land a boat or to park a vehicle. Where someone could walk onto her land and snoop. Zooming in closer and closer, a small beach appeared. It wasn't big, and it was just down the coast a bit from her cove.

Pulling up her property survey, Tara put it up side by side with Google Earth. After looking back and forth for several minutes, she finally had to admit that the beach the intruder probably used was on her side of the property line. The perimeter cameras and sensors wouldn't have caught whoever this was because he was inside the fence. He had found a weak spot.

"Damn it to hell," she grumbled, scrubbing her hands back and forth in her hair and flopping back in her chair. "That bastard knows my property better than I do. That will change and fast."

Pulling up an email, she shared this new information with Wyatt, along with the link to the little beach she had found and attached the property survey to the email. Making a note to tell Gwenn about the beach tomorrow, she shut down her laptop and headed to her bed only to toss and turn for the night.

Gwenn was greeted the next morning by a very cranky and grumpy Tara, who had also had way too much coffee. And was presently in the mudroom, cleaning.

"Um, good morning?" Gwenn stood at the entrance of the mudroom, unsure of what this was. It looked like Tara had been cleaning for a while. "In a cleaning mode?"

"Stating the obvious," Tara quipped back while wiping down the walls.

"Ooookaaaay. I'll just leave you to your whatever this is." Gwenn circled her hand in the air, then backed out of the room slowly. "Wow, your mama has the grumpies today. What happened last night after you all went to bed? One of you pee on her head or something? I think I'm going to play it safe and stay clear of Ms. Cranky Ass," Gwenn told the three dogs.

Getting her coffee, she went toward her room, followed by the dogs. "Oh, you guys too? Okay, come on in. We'll be safe in here."

Gwenn's room was the safe haven for the dogs until it was time for her to go to work for the day. "Sorry guys but I'm going to escape and go to work. You all are on your own."

Cautiously peeking into the mudroom, Gwenn saw that Tara was now on her hands and knees, scrubbing the perfectly clean floor. "I'm off to work. See ya later." Shaking her head, Gwenn ducked back out before Tara had a chance to respond or grumble.

Tara continued her cleaning and organizing until it was dinnertime for the dogs. Then she stopped and realized that she hadn't eaten and that her back was screaming at her. This just made her angrier. She hated when she was like this. Angry at everything and nothing. She didn't even like to be around herself when she was in this mood.

After feeding the dogs and letting them in the arena to run and play for a while, she settled on Advil and a sandwich. Then she talked herself into the hot tub. That would ease the back. To help with the constant commentary in her head, she made sure she had music playing when she got into the hot tub.

With her head back on the edge of the hot tub, Tara turned her head to look at the three dogs that were lying beside the hot tub, watching her. "I'm sorry guys. Mama's been an ass today. I'll make it up to you in a bit."

Connal stood up and stretched, then walked over to Tara's head and snooted her ear before licking it. Lying down, he kept his head close to hers. Tara reached up and scratched his ears. "Thanks, buddy."

Gizmo and Peanut, seeing that Connal was getting loves, both walked over and after sniffing Tara's head, laid down so that Tara had a dog on either side of her head and one behind her. Alternating petting heads, Tara smiled and closed her eyes and finally relaxed.

When Gwenn got home after work, Tara met her in the

kitchen with cake and ice cream in hand. "I'm an ass. I'm sorry."

Taking the peace offering, Gwenn sat down at the island. "Got that bug that was up your ass, out? You were rather cranky, but it's okay. This is starting to get to you. It's starting to get to both of us. And I'd bet my piece of cake, you didn't sleep last night."

"Yeah, I think yesterday got to me more than I expected. Until yesterday, the jerk hadn't been on my property. Oh, he had tried, but he hadn't succeeded. Yesterday, he did, and it freaked me out." Tara talked around a bite of cake. "And no, I didn't sleep last night. I want to show you something." Putting down her bowl, she pulled up Google Earth on her laptop and showed Gwenn the beach.

Gwenn leaned over and looked, then shrugged. "Okay, not sure what I'm supposed to be seeing here, Tara."

"Hold on." Tara brought up the property survey and put it side by side with Google Earth. She turned the laptop back to Gwenn. "What do you see now?"

Gwenn glanced at Tara, then looked at the Google Earth map and then to the property survey. Pulling the laptop closer and taking over the mouse, she zoomed in, looking back and forth between the two. "Son of a fucking bitch!"

"Yep, that's what I said last night. That bastard found a weak spot, and he used it. I emailed this to Wyatt last night, and his response was just about the same as both of ours. That will be fixed and soon. He's coming back Thursday, and he's bringing Bob. Let's go into the living room, my back is not pleased with me, and these chairs are killing me." Tara led the way to the living room. Groaning, she slowly sat down.

"Wow, you're really hurting. That's what you get for cleaning like a crazy-assed woman. I've lived here my entire life, and I didn't know that there a little beach there. Whoever this jerk is, he's local. That's for sure."

"Thanks for the sympathy there, friend. Yeah, he's a local. Has to be." Picking up the remote, Tara glanced over at Gwenn. "I DVRed NCIS. Want to watch?" At Gwenn's nod,

Tara started the show and sat back to enjoy the hour of make-believe and the company of her friend.

The next two days went by quietly. On all accounts. Gwenn went to work each day, and Tara spent most of the time lounging around. Her back was hurting quite a bit, and she had learned to listen to it. So, she spent time on the deck or lying in the sun. Sometimes reading, sometimes staring off into space. By Thursday afternoon, she finally felt good enough to get into the pool. She didn't swim, just walked in the water and did some light stretching. That was followed with the hot tub and finally a shower.

Barb had called to be let into the gate to drop off the groceries while Tara had been in the pool. Even though Tara had told her that she didn't need to bring meals, Barb always seemed to bring something homemade each week when she dropped off the groceries.

Going to the freezer, she looked to see what Barb had made them. Wyatt and Bob would be in some time that evening, and having something hot to eat would be a plus for both the men. She decided on the beef stew. Pulling it out to defrost, she saw that Barb had also bought a loaf of French bread. Taking that out as well, she would start warming up the stew in a couple of hours.

Sitting down at the kitchen island, she brought up her journal and notes and photos to refresh her memory and to make sure she had everything down. Bob wouldn't be here long, so she wanted to make sure that he had all the information at once. Making an occasional note here or there, she finally sighed and saved her work.

"Time to feed my hungry, hungry hippos," she told the three dogs that were sleeping under and around her stool. She felt the need to spoil them, so they each got a bit of hard-boiled egg mixed in with the kibble and green beans. Of course, the hard-boiled egg was inhaled first, followed by the green beans and lastly, the boring kibble.

After they were done, she let them out the living room

doors to enjoy some outside time. Sitting on the porch, she let them do their own thing, with the occasional whistle from her to keep them somewhat close. As she sat there and enjoyed the view, she got a text from Wyatt that said that they would be in around 8 PM. She texted back, then looked at the time.

"6 PM now, so about two hours. Okay, you rotten dogs, time to go in. Need to start heating up that stew for when Wyatt and Bob get here." As she closed the door behind the dogs, she caught sight of the boat outside of the cove. "Oh asshole, this will be ending very soon." She flipped him off just because she could.

Tara spent the last few hours of solitude slowly heating the stew up and making up the fourth bedroom for Bob. "For a loner and introvert, I now have a four-bedroom house full of people. How did that happen? I thought this place would be too big for me when we first got here. Now, I have all four bedrooms full. Who would have ever thought that huh?" She said, looking at the dogs that were watching her. It was shocking to her to see how much her life had changed in such a short amount of time. She wouldn't change any of it. "Come on you three, let's stop furring up Bob's room before he's even here."

Following the dogs into the kitchen, she was alerted that the main gate had opened. Walking over to the monitor, she saw that it was Wyatt. "Well, our quiet time is over, guys. You haven't met Bob before, but he's a good guy, so be nice to him," Tara said while she did a quick stir of the stew then when the monitor alerted to the garage door opening, she turned and waited.

Wyatt came in from the breezeway first, followed by Bob. Of course, the dogs were there waiting, initially wagging their nubs for Wyatt, then barking when Bob came in.

Leaning down, Bob put his hand out for the dogs to smell him, then took turns scrubbing each doggie head.

Tara watched and silently breathed a sigh of relief that the dogs hadn't gone into defense mode with Bob. She had secretly been concerned that Connal in particular, had become unfriendly. Oh, he was friendly with Gwenn right off the bat, but then had tried to eat Fred and reacted badly to Logan and Jake. Tara figured that Gizmo and Peanut were basing their reactions on him, so if Connal was unfriendly, they would be too. At least until they got more comfortable in their new home. But seeing Connal's reaction and in turn, Gizmo's and Peanut's, to Bob, those fears subsided.

"Hi, you two." Tara walked over to Bob and gave him a tight hug and kiss on the cheek, then did the same to Wyatt.

It had been some time since she had seen Bob, but he hadn't changed much at all. Still lean and muscular at 5'8", he reminded her of a swimmer. Unlike Wyatt and his overgrown hairstyle, Bob's was a military cut. Add the blond hair and hazel eyes to that chiseled jaw and Bob was a damn fine-looking man.

Tara grabbed a couple of beers, then led the men into the living room, where Connal, Gizmo, and Peanut promptly abandoned Tara for the men.

Bob sat back on the couch, petting Connal and took a long drink of his beer. "Thanks. This place is fantastic, Tara. And, I think I'm already in love with your dogs. They're beyond cute."

"Yeah, it really is. I still have moments that I have to remind myself that it's mine. The pups seem to love you completely. Remember how cute they are when they're herding you where they want to you go. I just need to heat up the bread when you're ready to eat."

"I could eat," Wyatt and Bob said at the same time.

Laughing, Tara went and put the bread in. "It's going to be about 10 minutes for the bread if you want to wash up first. Bob, your room is over here." Tara led the way to the room, and after showing Bob the basics, she left him to get cleaned up for dinner.

Just as they got ready to sit down to eat, the alerts for the main gate, went off.

"That'll be Gwenn," Tara said, getting up to get another bowl of stew. "Hey, Gwenn. The guys just got here, and we're just sitting down to eat." She walked over to Gwenn and put the bowl down. "Gwenn Flanery, I would like to you meet Bob Cammon. Bob, this is my friend, Gwenn."

But instead of shaking hands, Gwenn and Bob just stood there, looking at each other. Tara and Wyatt looked back and forth between the two of them, then Wyatt looked at Tara and winked. Tara returned the wink with a smirk. *Well, well, well. This would be interesting*, she thought to herself.

CHAPTER TWELVE

Tara was the first up the next morning. She really couldn't have slept in if she wanted to with three little dogs that insisted on getting up with the chickens for out time and food. Since they had all gone to bed late last night, Tara kept the pups outside and down towards the cove. She was working on another rousing game of get the stick out of the water when Wyatt came out of the house. He stood on the deck and watched Tara and her dogs for a few minutes, before walking down to the cove.

"Morning," he said, handing Tara a fresh cup of coffee.

"Thanks. Morning back at ya. Did we wake you?" Tara picked up the soggy stick and tossed it.

Wyatt shook his head and sipped on his coffee. "Nope, not at all. So, it seems like Bob and Gwenn are getting along well," he added with a smirk.

Tara quickly took a sip of coffee and nodded. "Oh my God, I know! I wasn't expecting to feel that much electricity. It was almost painful. But I'm glad. They're both great people so it would be nice if they do get together. They're both gorgeous. I wonder if the babies would be redheads or blondes."

Peanut came over and sat on her foot, so she tossed the

stick for just Connal and Gizmo, she glanced toward the house in time to see Bob allow Gwenn through the door first. "Well, speak of the devil. Look, they're even coming out together. This is going to be fun to watch happen, and I have something to tease Gwenn about now."

After a quick breakfast, Wyatt and Bob went to look at the beach where the intruder had gotten onto the property. They took several wireless field cameras with them, along with a couple of wireless flood lights.

"Just so the asshole knows we figured it out if he wants to try it again," Wyatt told them.

The door hadn't closed behind the guys before Gwenn turned to Tara and started the questions. "How old is Bob? Single, I know, but is he divorced? Does he have any kids? What does he do at the DEA? Why didn't you mention him before? Did you have a thing with him? Oh my God, doesn't his butt look good enough to bite?" Gwenn said, putting her head in her hands and dreaming of doing just that.

Tara shook her head and laughed. "Damn. Slow down speedy. Bob's 42. Never married, no kids. He's straight, so he's available as far as I know. Not sure what he does at the DEA, but we were all contractors with the same company back about five years ago. No, I'm not going to tell you what he did. That's his story to tell. And I've not mentioned him before because it wasn't relevant and I've only known you for three months. Now that I know you are looking, I'll do a PowerPoint of all the eligible men that I know, or have known in my life. And yes, his ass is biteable perfect." Tara chuckled at the death look that Gwenn threw at her for the last response. "Not that I've had the opportunity, nor do I wish to bite it."

"Smart ass. Well, he's very purrdy. I might have to see if he thinks I'm purrdy," Gwenn drawled, sipping on her coffee.

"Yes, he is. If you are into that kind of guy. You know, swimmer's body, blond hair, hazel eyes. I always figured he was what Adonis looked like."

"Damn, I didn't think of that, but I like it. So, he's purrdy, and he looks like a God. We would make purrdy babies."

Tara's response was choking on the drink of coffee she had just taken.

"I'm going to run into town and get some man food. You know, steaks and lobsters. Just in case the guys want to grill," she told Tara.

"Sounds like a great idea and man food sounds good enough for us women folk, too. I'm going to be a lazy butt and chill while you all are doing important stuff. Be gone! Fetch man food." Tara waved her hand, shooing Gwenn out of the house.

Going into the living room and sitting on the couch, Tara opened up her laptop. "It's amazing really, I'm technically retired, and I'm busier now than I ever was. I don't even get to check my email or Facebook regularly anymore. Retirement is hard work, guys," she told the three dogs that had taken up the rest of the couch beside her. Scrolling quickly through the majority of the emails, she was getting ready to close out of email when a new one arrived. It was from Teresa about returning the GPR.

"Crap! I completely forgot about that." Tara relayed this lapse of memory to Teresa and set up a time next week to bring it back to the office. Pulling up her calendar, she made the appointment on it and then made sure that the meeting showed up on her cell as well.

She was finishing up when Wyatt and Bob came back from the beach and was followed by Gwenn a while later.

Once they all had another cup of coffee and the donuts that Gwenn had brought back, Tara led the group into her office, then down into the Batcave and finally in The Lab.

"Well, this is one hell of a setup, I have to say. You have more secret rooms than some of the buildings in D.C."

Bob walked farther into The Lab and slowly walked up and down the rows of tables. "From what I've researched, they're almost ready to harvest, so whoever was working with Dr. Roxbury, will have to move them soon, or lose the crop. That works in our favor."

"So, they are the psycho plant?" Tara questioned, using Gwenn's version of the scientific name.

Confused, Bob turned to look at Tara. "The what? Oh, I get it now," he added and chuckled. "Yeah, they're the *Psychotria viridis* plant. At least most of them are."

"Wait? Most of them?" Gwenn stepped closer to Bob. "What do you mean, most of them?"

Bob motioned with his hand for the others to follow him. "These are the Psychotria viridis, or commonly known as the psycho plant." Bob tipped his head to Gwenn and smiled.

Turning and walking farther into the room and to the left, he stopped at another table. "These," he gestured with his hand, "are *Banisteriopsis caapi* vines."

Tara and Gwenn stepped closer to look at the plant.

"Well, son of a bitch," Tara whispered. "I didn't look around in here after we found the plants. Didn't realize she had the entire makings of the tea in here."

"Holy shit," Gwenn muttered, shaking her head. "Well, it sort of makes sense that she would grow everything if she were using, as well as selling. But damn."

Bob nodded. "I agree. If she were using, she would want a constant supply."

Leading the way back to the door and the three dogs that were there, Bob turned back to Tara, Gwenn, and Wyatt. "This is a large crop. From what I've been learning about this drug, this crop is worth upwards of three million dollars. Dr. Roxbury wasn't playing in the little league here since a crop like this takes several years to get to this size.

"What they do is harvest the leaves of the psycho plant, then they boil the leaves, along with the crushed-up stems of the flowering *Banisteriopsis caapi* vine. Let me guess Gwenn, it's the B vine?" At Gwenn's smirk and nod, Bob smiled. "The resulting brew becomes ayahuasca," he hesitated and looked at Gwenn.

"Tea that gets you high or drug tea," she supplied.

"The resulting brew becomes a drug tea, which contains Dimethyltryptamine or DMT. It can cause hallucinations, along with elation, fear, and paranoia. The effects don't last long, so it's usually used recreationally."

Tara and Gwenn both sighed and went into the Batcave to sit on the couch.

Bob knelt down in front of Tara and rested his hand on her knee. "Tara, if you aren't comfortable with a sting, I can have these plants removed by Tuesday. Just takes a phone call and they'll be gone, and you can get back to your quiet, retired life. No harm, no foul."

Tara looked at Bob, then Gwenn and finally at Wyatt. "No, that wouldn't end the asshole trying to get the plants because he wouldn't know they had been removed. And it wouldn't get the dealer of this drug off the street. Plus, even though I didn't know Dr. Roxbury, I can't let her death be for nothing. So, let's do the sting."

Bob smiled, patted her knee and got up. "That's my Tara. Knew you would say that. Now, why don't we go upstairs and Wyatt can show me the full security of this place? I should be getting some feedback on the searches I did on Dr. Roxbury and the boat ID you got."

"One more thing." Tara went up the stairs to the office and waited for the others to join her, then she went over to the kitchenette counter. "When I was first looking around here, I found this canister of tea leaves. I thought they smelled horrible and was going to toss them, but then I found the secret Batcave door and forgot about it. Later, Gwenn and I researched what the leaves look dried up, and we think this is some of the leaves."

Taking the canister, Bob opened it and smelled it. "Well, I'm not sure, but I'll bag and tag it and send it to the lab guys so that they can run it. Is there anything else that you think has to do with the plants?"

Tara shook her head. "No, you've seen everything that we've found. I don't know about you all, but I'm done with all of this for the moment. Let's head up and have something to eat."

While Wyatt spent time going over the security and the monitor with Bob, Gwenn and Tara made up a snack tray of meats, cheeses, crackers, pickles and olives.

"This is getting really scary." Gwenn finally broke the silence.

"Yeah, it is. I don't really want to do this, but then I don't want not to do this. It's the right thing to do. I know it is. But, it's big scary. I want to make sure that we're all safe and no one gets hurt. Human or dog. I know we won't let that happen and it's just my brain in overdrive thinking of everything that can go wrong and trying to figure out how nothing will go wrong."

Gwenn leaned over and shoulder bumped Tara. "Nothing is going to go wrong. It's not just one person in this. There's four of us, and it's harder to get rid of four people. Plus, this place is a fortress. Nothing's going to happen to you, the pups or the rest of us."

Smiling, Tara shoulder bumped Gwenn back. "Thanks for that. Why don't we sit outside and enjoy the day?"

Bob's cell beeped just as they were finishing up the finger foods outside. "Finally." He looked at his phone. "It's the information on the searches I—well, fuck me!"

Standing up, Bob stopped at the door and looked at the other three. "I need to log onto my laptop to review this information. Give me a few minutes then why don't you guys meet me at the dining room table and we can go over the info."

Walking inside as a unit, Gwenn and Wyatt went to their respective rooms while Tara sat on the living room floor and played with the pups. "Whatever Bob got in the reports must be big, he's not one to be shocked like that," Tara whispered to Connal. Connal sat down in front of Tara and nudged her hand until she automatically started petting his ears. "I have a feeling the shit is about to hit the fan, buddy." She turned to pet Gizmo and Peanut. "Yes, you two, too. My love hounds. You know when I need some comfort, don't ya?" After one last pet on each head, Tara stood up, dusted the fur off her butt and lap and went to join Gwenn and Wyatt at the dining table.

Tara had just sat down when Bob walked out of his room and setting down his laptop, sat down and sighed.

"Okay, I got some information back. There's quite a bit of it so let me try to get through most of this first before the questions start, okay?" After Tara, Gwenn, and Wyatt had nodded, he pulled his laptop closer.

"Wyatt gave me the names of Dr. Roxbury, along with your local cop, Fred. Also, Bill and Barb Ohlson. And you Gwenn," he added, waiting for Gwenn's angry response. When none came, he smiled. "Gwenn, you came back clean, which we all knew, but we still had to check."

Gwenn smiled back and polished her nails on her shirt which got a chuckle from Bob and a head shake and smirk from Tara and Wyatt.

"Tara, the backstory you got off the internet on Dr. Roxbury was right. She was a professor of archaeology. Specialized in Peru. Retired here. But a search with Interpol showed that she's been in trouble in South America for 30 plus years. Little stuff at first, but then the drug charges started. Possession, using and finally dealing. She was eventually released from her contract with the university she was associated with because they suspected she was smuggling drugs and plants out of Peru and to the States in the artifact containers." Sitting with her arms crossed, Tara growled and shook her head, but didn't interrupt. "She was essentially blackballed in her field of study. Unofficially, of course. None of it could be proven, but she was basically fired. That's when she bought this place and built the house and all the buildings." Bob stopped to grab beers for each of them. The next part was going to be more difficult.

"I can't say I'm too surprised, knowing that she has the plants downstairs. Obviously, she was into something illegal. Professors make decent money, but not the amount of money this place had to have cost to build. But to use the artifact containers? That pisses me off. She had no respect for her field. It's insulting. And unethical."

Taking a deep breath, Tara looked at Bob. "Tell us what you else you found, Bob."

Taking a drink of his beer, Bob looked at his laptop. "Bill Ohlson is the handyman, correct?" Tara nodded. "Well, his full name is William Rohon Ohlson. And he's 60 years old. He has an interesting story as well. Gwenn, I know his backstory from what you told Tara and what she said to me, but it's not correct. You said he's not from this area and that he moved here to work on the boats." Bob looked at Gwenn for verification.

Gwenn leaned forward on the table and nodded. "Yeah, that's what he was telling folks when he showed up in town. That he was from down south somewhere. I think Texas or Florida."

"Well, that's all a lie. He was born in Eriksport," Bob held up his hand to stop Gwenn's outburst. "I know, Gwenn. Let me finish first."

Gwenn nodded once, and thin-lipped, folded her arms across her chest.

"Soon after he was born, his mother took him and moved to Texas. Bill's mom had his last name legally changed to her maiden name, Ohlson.

"He has a long record of drug charges. The norm: possession, using and dealing. He also spent time in jail for it. It was after his last stint in prison for possession and robbery that he moved up here. Now, that's all fine. Folks move around all the time. And maybe he was trying to get a clean slate and start over somewhere new. But, he came up here because he has family here that could help him get reestablished in society.

"The probation officer in Texas was a real nice guy and told my guys that have been doing the searches that a cousin of Bill's called down there and offered to take Bill under his wing. Make sure he abided by the law and cleaned up. Now, usually that wouldn't make a difference to a parole officer, but the cousin was in law enforcement, so it was a done deal." Bob took a quick sip of his beer to wet his throat.

"His cousin is Fred. Bill's dad and Fred's dad are brothers. Bill's birth name is William Rohon Toft. You didn't know that, did you, Gwenn?"

Gwenn shook her head, still in shock. "Holy shit. No, I didn't. How is that possible? I've lived here my entire life. How did I not hear about this? I don't understand this at all. There are folks in town that had to have known Bill when he was just born. Why would he, and they, lie about all of this? Does Barb know?"

"All good questions, Gwenn. But I don't have the answers. Let's get back to the story. So, Bill moves up here, gets a new lease on life because of his cousin vouching for him. That's innocent enough even though they were sneaky about letting folks know that Bill was born here. But whatever. He meets and marries Barb, then Dr. Roxbury hires them to work here. Sounds like Bill is becoming a first-class citizen. And from what I've been able to find, he's been clean since he moved up here. He really could be just a guy starting over in life and doing good at it." Bob leaned back in his chair and looked at Tara, waiting.

"What did you find out about Barb?" Tara asked quietly.

Bob glanced at his notes on the laptop. "Barbara Ann Junge Ohlson, age 60. Has no criminal record. She was born and raised here, just as she claims. Looks like her people have been here for quite some time.

"I don't know if she knows about Bill's past and his lies. I would like to think he snowed her, but she was born here, and they're about the same age, so I find it hard to believe that something didn't click in her memory about him. Or that someone in town wouldn't have mentioned it to her. I just don't know."

Tara released the breath she had been holding. She hated thinking that she had been letting a criminal in her house. It was bad enough to know that her handyman had prison time under his belt, but Bill never came into the house. Unlike Barb.

"Let's talk about that boat that you've seen outside of your cove. I had the registration ID run, and the results show that the boat belongs to Bill." Bob stopped and waited for the explosion, and wasn't disappointed.

"Son of a bitch! So, it's been Bill doing the snooping outside of the cove? He's the bastard that I keep seeing? That doesn't make sense. He has full access to the entire property. Why would he be using his boat to spy?" Tara said as she stood up to pace the kitchen floor.

"Tara, I don't know, but it's on a list that is getting longer by the minute of questions that I have. I'm in the process of finding out where the boat is docked and will have it put under surveillance." Bob stood up and walked to Tara. "I promise these questions will be answered."

Wyatt had been quiet through all of this, but now he stood up and sat at the island. "What did you find on Fred?"

Taking a drink of his beer, Bob sat down at the island beside Wyatt and faced the dining table. "Frederick Rohon Toft, age 53. He's been the sheriff in Eriksport since his father retired 30 years ago. Seems to be a family thing from what the research shows. His grandfather was the law before, and it goes back that way for many generations.

"Fred's dirty. He's beyond dirty. Oh, he's smart enough not to shit where he eats, so to speak, but he's had multiple out-of-state warnings and arrests for alcohol and drugs. Along with some assaults and batteries. Just an all-around piece of shit. His most recent run-in with other law enforcement was last year. He went to Florida last year on vacation." Bob looked at Gwenn to verify.

Gwenn nodded. "Yeah, he did. He was gone about three weeks and came back looking sick as a dog. Said he had gotten a terrible cold on vacation. Bitched and moaned for another month about how shitty of a time he had on vacation, being sick and all."

"Well, it wasn't a cold or the flu or whatever he told the folks in town. According to my information, he was hospitalized for a drug overdose." Holding up his hand, Bob continued. "He had DMT in his system. Knowing what we know now about the plants downstairs, I'm betting he was getting high drinking ayahuasca. The drug tea." Bob glanced at Gwenn and winked. "Of course, he tried to deny it. Used the fact that he was a cop and wouldn't do something like that. That someone had to have drugged him without his knowledge. But the local cops didn't buy it. And according to the police down in Florida, it's the 'new' drug of choice down there, and they've been seeing an increase in overdoses involving it." Bob stopped to take a drink of the beer and to give everyone a chance to process this new information before he told them the next part.

"My sources also tell me that he and his lady friend fought a lot down there. There were several domestic violence calls to the hotel that they were staying in. Along with a call to a restaurant they were eating at. Some of the calls were from him calling for help, and some were from her."

Gwenn interrupted now. "Wait. What? Fred had a woman with him last year? I didn't know he had a girlfriend. I don't think anyone knew Fred had a girlfriend. News like that would have spread. We would have known if Fred had a girlfriend. Maybe it was just someone he hooked up with in Florida."

Bob looked at Gwenn, then shook his head. "No, she wasn't someone he just hooked up with in Florida. The evidence shows Fred and this woman arriving in Florida together as well as leaving Florida together. My guys were able to pull airport video along with the hotel videos and the police records and got a name and picture of the girlfriend." Bob turned the laptop for them all to see.

Gwenn was the only one to gasp and cover her mouth. "Oh, my God that's Dr. Roxbury!"

Tara and Wyatt looked at Gwenn, then at Bob for verification.

"Yes, it's Dr. Edna Roxbury, according to the reports." Bob stopped and waited for them to get to where he was in his thinking.

They all seemed to get to the same thought at the same time, but Tara was the one to put it into words.

"So, Dr. Roxbury was fired because of her involvement with smuggling drugs, I'm tired of calling them plants, into the States. Moves here and somehow hooks up with the dirty sheriff of Eriksport. We don't know if Fred was already using drugs, but she got him hooked on the drug that was her specialty.

"About the same time Bill, his loser-assed cousin from Texas, moves up here to start over. Bill meets Barb, and they get married. Then somehow, and I would bet money that it was Fred's doing, Bill and Barb just happen to get hired on out here to help Dr. Roxbury with the property. Roxbury and probably Fred and maybe Bill go into the plant growing business, because why not? By now Roxbury has to be so hooked on the shit, why shouldn't she start growing and producing the crap?" Tara was up and pacing, talking more to herself than to the others, while the dogs followed her.

"But I don't think Roxbury told Fred and Bill about the secret rooms. If she had, the plants wouldn't still be down there. I think that they got into an argument with her about the plants and one, or both, killed her.

"Bill has full access to the property, so why would he use his boat to snoop? He can snoop as much as he wants, right under my damn nose. I think Fred has been using the boat to see if he can find the plants. Which seems stupid considering Bill is all over this place and he can look, and it wouldn't look suspicious. Something just doesn't make any sense to me." Tara stopped pacing, leaned back on the island and crossed her arms.

Now it was Gwenn's turn to pace, with Connal and Gizmo following her. Peanut had given up and was sitting on Tara's foot. "I've lived here my entire life, and I didn't know anything you have told us, Bob. I don't understand that. Yes, Fred and Bill are older than I am, but I would have thought someone would have mentioned that Bill was from Eriksport and that Fred was his cousin. Why would you hide something like that? And how did Barb not know? They're all the same age. I don't get it. Maybe it's because my parents weren't born here. They moved here after they were married and dad got a job on one of the boats. But I was born here. I'm a local!" Gwenn sagged against the counter with Tara, dejected that she didn't know her townspeople as well as she thought she did.

Bob came over to lean against the counter between Tara and Gwenn. "I don't know the answers to your questions, but I do know that all of this stinks. Big time. And we'll find the answer to the questions about the plants, at least. As far as Barb not knowing about Bill, that's something that will have to be asked of her. Fred has a shit ton of questions to answer, as far as I'm concerned.

"We all need time to process this information, then we can readdress it. I'm going to print up the information and leave it on the table so that we all can look at it when we need to."

Putting his empty beer bottle in the trash can, Bob turned to look at Tara, Gwenn, and Wyatt. "But now, I think we need to let this go for a bit. Just for a bit," he added when Tara started to interrupt. "Let's have dinner and try to relax. An hour or two of normal. Then we can come at the information again from a different angle."

While Wyatt and Bob got the grill ready for the steaks and lobsters, and Gwenn made the salad, Tara took Connal, Gizmo, and Peanut outside. She sat on the grass while the dogs ran around and did their thing.

"How in the hell did this happen? Buy a house on the internet. It's a nice house. Gorgeous location. On the ocean. Perfect. At least it seemed to be. Should have known that karma would bite me in the ass," Tara grumbled to Connal, who had come over to sit beside her.

Putting her arm over his shoulder and petting his chest, she laid her forehead on his head. "I'm sorry, buddy. This has turned into a bit of a cluster, hasn't it? But we're all going to fix this mess. Then we'll get back to relaxing and being lazy. You've been a good little dog, putting up with not getting as much attention as you are used to."

Connal turned his head and gave her a lick on the cheek, then stood up, shook and took off after Gizmo and Peanut, barking the whole way.

Later, after the kitchen and grill were cleaned up and the house was locked up and secure, Tara, Gwenn, Wyatt, and Bob were back at the dining room table. Connal had taken up his place between Tara's feet. Gwenn had Gizmo in the same position, and Peanut had commandeered Wyatt.

This time they had come prepared. They each had pads of paper and pens or pencils and laptops were up and active. They all seemed to defer to Bob to run the discussion and now sat and waited for him to start.

"So, we've all had a chance to digest the information that I shared with you. I think we're in agreement that Fred is the focus of the drug investigation now that Dr. Roxbury is no longer around." At the nods of agreement, he continued. "I think we need to call Fred out on this. Point blank. Tell him we know of his involvement and that the only option he has is to help us nab the dealer. I mean, we could wait until he sneaks on the property again and catch him red-handed, but I would rather control as much as we can."

Wyatt nodded on this. "I agree. Less business on the property if he's working with us. We can get the plants out of The Lab and supply them to him for the bust. No one needs to know about those rooms down there."

It was Tara's turn to nod. "Yes, I like that. Getting those plants out of here seems the safest bet. No one needs to know what has been growing here or where. This way, I can get back to feeling safe in my own house. Less chance of any of us getting hurt or my home becoming more of a crime scene than it already is."

"I agree. Let's get those damn plants out of here. And I agree on confronting Fred upfront. So, what do we do? How do we catch Fred? Won't he just deny it all?" Gwenn was the last to speak.

"He could and probably will, at first. But we have the videos, photos and police reports from Florida," Bob answered.

"I'm sure he'll give himself away when he sees the plants. And, I'm going to let him know that I'm having Dr. Roxbury exhumed and that the ME in D.C. is going to take another look at the cause of death. I'm betting that Fred buried the cause of death since he's the sheriff and the body would have been sent to the county coroner. When the coroner sent Fred the report, Fred just buried it. After all, he's the sheriff, so it was easy to do. Small town and Dr. Roxbury was an outsider. Fred just told the folks that were asking that the death was ruled accidental or suicide or whatever. I'm sure when I drop that I'm having Dr. Roxbury's cause of death looked at, he'll start sweating bullets. He can deny all he wants, but we have the proof that he's dirty."

Bob turned to look at Tara. "Tara, can you send me those photos of the boat outside of the cove? All of them. I want my computer guys to see if they can pull in closer and make out the face. It would just be another nail in the coffin for Fred."

Tara nodded, then worked on getting the photos attached to an email to Bob. "On the way to you."

"And on the way to my computer guys. They work magic. Let's see what else they find."

"When do you want to confront Fred with this information, Bob? And where?" Wyatt asked.

"I'm thinking this weekend. I mean, why wait? Let's give it until Sunday to give my guys some time to work on the photos and for me to get all of this tight in my head. Then, I think it's time for Fred to meet a DEA agent. I think it would be best to call him and have him come out here. No, wait. Just hear me out." He held up his hand when Tara, Gwenn, and Wyatt all started to protest. "We don't know who else in town is working with him. If a DEA agent comes walking into his office to chat with him, it might send up the alarm. Have Fred come out here, where we're in control. Sit him down at the table and tell him what we know. That way it looks like he's here on police business. He's been out here a couple of times because of the problems at Gwenn's house, so it won't send up any red flags in town."

"That makes sense, but what if he doesn't cooperate, or he runs?" Gwenn asked.

Bob smiled. "He won't have a choice but to cooperate after we're done. And if he runs? I have some neat toys in mind so that we will know what Fred's doing and where he is."

Wyatt, Bob, and Tara spent the majority of the next morning in The Lab, documenting and cataloging each plant before removing the potted plants to the riding arena. They had decided last night to show Fred the evidence of Dr. Roxbury's growing business, but they had all agreed that Fred would never know about The Lab.

When the last plant was finally moved out of The Lab, Tara made sure that the trickle system and lights were turned off. Walking out of the room and closing the secret entrance, she didn't know what she would do with that room, if anything. But for now, it was empty.

Gwenn had spent the time the others were working, playing with the pups outside. Now, she stopped by the riding arena on the way to work to see if they needed anything from her and to offer to call in sick again. She had called in sick yesterday, and she was willing to do it again today if she was needed. Tara thanked her but told her the three of them had it under control and to go to work. To act normal.

"Yeah, right. Act normal. It's a regular, everyday thing for us to be setting up an interrogation of Fred. We do that all the time here in BFE Maine," she mumbled as she left.

There was nothing left to do now but wait. So, while Bob and Wyatt played on the sea doos, Tara passed the time grooming the dogs. After baths, brushing and clipping toenails, she sat on the porch with the dogs and watched Wyatt and Bob.

She was tired. She hadn't been sleeping well at all. Not for a while. She just wanted all of this to be over. It did make her feel better to know that the plants were no longer in the house, per se. They were still on the property, but they weren't under her feet. And soon, they would be off the property, and all of this nasty business would be over. Then she would be bored. Laughing to herself, she picked up the book that she had been trying to read for the last month, but after reading the same line six times, she gave up and put the book down.

Heading into the house, Tara grabbed three glasses and the pitcher of iced tea, then walked out to the deck just as Wyatt and Bob came up from the boat shed. Sitting down, they tried to relax and enjoy the day. Other than the occasional comment about the dogs or the weather, there were no real conversations. Each was inside their own head, preparing for the next day.

Tara was the first to go back into the house. Grabbing a Pop-Tart, she watched as Wyatt opened the fridge and after debating got a couple slices of the ever-present pizza. Not bothering to heat it up, he came to stand by Tara and ate the slices. Bob, being the civilized one, opted to reheat the beef stew.

"Shit! I need to let Barb know that I don't need groceries delivered tomorrow. Don't need her to come in while Fred is here," Tara mumbled around the bite of Pop-Tart in her mouth and reaching for her phone to send a text.

"Good thinking and it reminds me that I need to call off next week," Wyatt said, pulling out his phone and heading to his room, still chewing on the last slice of pizza.

"I need to call in too. I'm not leaving until this deal is done. And I need to update my bosses of the status and the plan." Bob followed Wyatt's idea and headed toward his room.

"Son of a bitch! I'm losing my mind. I need to cancel on Teresa." Leading Connal, Gizmo, and Peanut to her room, then into the office, Tara got on the laptop and apologized to Teresa that she would have to cancel on Tuesday. And that she would contact her soon and tell her what was going on. She looked at the calendar, just to be sure she wasn't missing something else. "Good, all clear. Well, might as well fart around for a bit. Let's see what's going happening on Facebook."

As soon as she logged on, she saw that she had a series of messages from a corgi friend. The messages were about a pair of bonded corgis that needed a new home. Their owner had passed on, and no one in the family wanted to take on the two senior corgis. Sitting there, looking at the pictures of the two, she knew she had to have them.

Tara replied to her friend, saying that she would take them, but that they would have to be fostered for a week or so because she wasn't able to get them until then. She wouldn't bring any more dogs into the house until after the drug business was finished. Looking over to the sofa where the dogs were lounging and watching her, she turned to face them.

"Looks like you three are getting a new brother and sister soon. Cute names too. Indy and Annapolis. We're getting to be a herd out here. Five corgis, I must be nuts."

Smiling, Tara logged off and heading back into the living room, she found it had been overrun by guy stuff. Amazed at how fast Wyatt and Bob had made the room their own with beer, chips and salsa and a baseball game on her TV, she shook her head and went to straighten up the kitchen.

"I'm taking the dogs to the arena for some run time and last outs," Tara called to the men in the living room. Receiving dual hand waves as a response, she opened the door to the breezeway, which the dogs now saw as a race track.

Connal, Gizmo, and Peanut took off, barking and body checking each other to get to the arena door first. Chuckling, Tara opened the arena door, and the three dogs ran in, then came to an abrupt halt and started barking at the new addition.

"It's okay, guys. It's just pots of plants. Drug plants, but plants none the less. They won't attack you." Connal was the first to approach one of the pots, then after the cursory sniff, lifted his leg and peed. Peanut seeing that Connal was marking the plant had to come over and do the same, which resulted in a peeing contest. "Good boys. Pee on the drug plants."

While the dogs investigated the plants, then any new smells

that the arena might have got since the last time they were out there, Tara walked the outside perimeter of the arena.

She knew that the doors were locked, and it was secure, but she still did a slow walk, turning on the bank of lights to look into each stall. She was nervous about tomorrow. She didn't want Fred in the house, but they needed him there, so she would just have to suck it up. She hated that she would have to put the dogs in her room and that they would be upset because Fred was in the house.

"Maybe I'll put on the radio in there so that you won't be able to hear him." Since she was back in the arena and talking to the dogs, Tara made sure not to say Fred's name. "That way, you won't be so stressed out Connal, which won't stress out Gizmo and Peanut." She nodded her head. "I like that plan. All about controlling the situation."

Coming back into the kitchen, Tara gave the dogs their after last out treat, then grabbed a glass of water, said goodnight to the guys, who acknowledged with another hand wave, and went into her room.

Since she was still feeling the nervous energy, Tara opted for a long bubble bath, which turned into a laugh fest because the dogs loved to *attack* the bubbles she blew at them.

Finally, crawling into bed and waiting for Connal, Gizmo, and Peanut to settle into their places, she turned on her TV and looked for something to watch. She switched the TV off when she didn't find anything that looked interesting after the third time through the channels, Tara tried the book again but soon threw that onto the bed.

"Nope. Dammit. Fine. Let's try sleeping." Turning off the lights, she laid there, watching the clock until thirty minutes had passed.

"Screw this." She flung the covers off and headed back out to the living room to watch the ballgame with the guys, just as Gwenn came in with a fresh pizza.

Tara was the first to wake up. Sitting up, she groaned and rotated her neck. "Too old to fall asleep on the couch."

Looking around, she saw that they had all fallen asleep in the living room. She had shared her couch with Connal and Gizmo, who were watching her with their heads on their front paws. Wyatt was snuggled up to Peanut on the floor, using one of the dog beds as a pillow. She chuckled. That was so going on Facebook. Then she saw Gwenn and Bob, spooning on the other couch and her heart mushed. Finding her phone, she took a picture of Wyatt and Peanut, then one of Gwenn and Bob.

Getting up as quietly as the dogs would allow, she went to the kitchen to take them to the arena.

When Tara let the pups back into the house 10 minutes later, Wyatt had just finished starting the coffee.

"Morning. How'd you sleep?" Tara asked.

"I'm too old to sleep on the floor," Wyatt grumbled and watched the coffee drip. "Why are these machines so damn slow?"

Tara laughed. "Where's Gwenn and Bob?"

"They went to freshen up. I think it was more that they were embarrassed that we saw them all snuggly on the couch." Wyatt glanced over at Tara and smiled.

Pulling her cell out of her pocket, Tara pulled up the picture and handed it to him. "How much do you think this is worth to them?"

"Oh, at least their first born. This is a really good picture of them." Wyatt handed the phone back.

Tara then brought up the other picture and showed him. "What about this one?"

Wyatt glanced over, then missed his coffee cup with the sugar he had been pouring. "I'll kill you and bury you in the arena if that shows up anywhere."

Laughing, Tara put the phone back into her pocket. "I'm not going to share it. It's just a cute picture of the non-dog person cuddly with a dog. On a dog bed. Now quit bogarting the coffee," she said as she bumped Wyatt aside with her hip.

When Bob, then Gwenn came into the kitchen, Tara and Wyatt chose to not bring out the cuddle session. At least, for now. Now that they were all together again, the weight of the day sobered the mood.

"You ready for this?" Wyatt looked over at Tara.

"Yeah, I want this dirty business done so I can feel safe and feel like this is really my place. Not just a scene in a movie. I love the property and want to make it mine, but I'm worried to get too attached or to do too much until all this is over.

"I have two more dogs that will be coming to me as soon as it's safe for them. I'm actually very concerned about the safety of these three as it is. We can protect ourselves, but they rely on me to protect them. I can't let anything happen to them." Tara turned to lean her back against the island and look at Connal, Gizmo, and Peanut, who were lying in the middle of the kitchen floor.

"They'll be safe. We'll protect them, us and the property." Wyatt tapped Tara's shoulder to get her to look at him. "I promise."

"I agree. We'll all make sure that the dogs, the four of us and your place will not be harmed," Bob added, walking to stand in front of Tara. Then he turned to Gwenn, who had joined them at the island. "Gwenn, since you have a reason for Fred to come out, would you be up to making the call to get him out here?"

Rubbing her arms, Gwenn nodded. "Yeah, I can do that. I want to know where the report is on the fire at my place anyway, and with it being Sunday morning, Fred has never turned down an invitation to Sunday breakfast. Let me get some coffee into me, then I'll call him."

CHAPTER THIRTEEN

Gwenn had made the call, and now the four of them were waiting for Fred to arrive. Wyatt and Bob were talking quietly at the kitchen island, while Gwenn paced back and forth between the monitor and the front door.

Tara took the dogs into her bedroom, and after making sure the music was loud enough to hopefully drown out Fred's voice, sat on the bed with them. "I'm sorry guys, but this is almost over. Soon, I won't have to lock you in here because soon, he won't be around. You guys stay in here and listen to the music and nap. I promise when this is over, there will be serious playtime." Leaning down to kiss each dog on the head, Tara got up and left the room.

Joining Wyatt and Bob at the island, she rubbed her hands through her hair. "I hope that the music works to drown out his voice. I don't want them anymore stressed than they already are from reading our emotions."

"They'll be okay. This will be over soon." Wyatt reached over and took Tara's hand and gave it a squeeze. "We're in control of this Tara. All of it."

"I know we are. Doesn't mean I won't worry." Tara smiled and returned the hand squeeze before releasing his hand and looking at Bob.

Bob stopped Gwenn on her next trip from the monitor to the front door. "You're all armed, right?" When all three of them nodded that they were, Bob smiled. "Okay, good. The only portion of this I'm concerned about is the fact that Fred is armed. If he tries to pull his weapon, we need to disarm him quickly. We don't want a firefight out here. So, I think you ladies should lead the way out to the arena when the time comes. Wyatt and I will stay behind him. If he's going to do anything stupid, it's going to be when he sees the plants. That's when he's going to realize he's screwed. Seeing the plants will surprise him, and that's when I'll take his weapon. With me being a DEA agent, I essentially outrank him, so he can't get too pissy with me about it. Are you all okay with that?"

Gwenn nodded then continued her pacing.

After Wyatt had nodded, he went to the coffee maker for another cup of coffee.

"Yeah, that makes sense," Tara said going to check on the dogs one last time, but she veered to the monitor when it alerted to someone at the front gate. Verifying that it was Fred and opening and closing the gate, Tara turned to the others. "It's show time."

As was the plan, Gwenn went out to meet Fred, while Tara made a fresh pot of coffee and Wyatt and Bob went into their respective bedrooms to wait for Fred to come into the house and sit down.

Tara was nervous, and she knew it was showing. "Get ahold of yourself, dammit. Fred's going to be able to tell something's off if you don't get yourself under control. There are four of us, and we're all armed. He doesn't stand a chance against those odds. So, just calm your ass down." Closing her eyes, Tara took several deep, slow breaths and let each one out slowly. Focusing on the breathing technique calmed down the panic attack that she felt trying to take hold. She opened her eyes after the last breath and watched Gwenn lead Fred into the house.

"Come on in, Fred. I'm really glad you could come out and

see us this morning," Gwenn said, ushering Fred into the kitchen, then sitting down at the kitchen table. As they expected, Fred sat down across from her.

Smiling, Tara turned. "Hello, Fred. Can I get you a cup of coffee?" Tara noticed that Fred didn't look well today.

His red-rimmed, bloodshot eyes were even redder if that was possible. He also appeared to have a fever since he had that sheen you often got when you're sick. He was also fidgety and seemed nervous. She wasn't positive, but she was guessing that Fred was jonesing for his tea.

"Sure. I've never been one to turn down a good cup of coffee. Just black, thanks."

Tara sat his cup down in front of him, and after heating up Gwenn's cup, she sat down beside Gwenn.

"Gwenn, like I told you on the phone, there really isn't much more to tell you. The fire is still looking like it was an electrical fire. And I'm real sorry for how slow the fire marshal is being with the report. I'm going to have to call and bug him about it again. You had insurance, right? That should be a decent settlement." Fred smiled while sipping his coffee.

Gwenn mirrored Fred's actions, sipping her coffee. "Yeah, I have insurance, but it doesn't replace all the furniture that my parents left me or the pictures or the family heirlooms. Plus, it was my family home. So, money isn't going to replace that." Gwenn looked down at her coffee and sighed. Her parents hadn't left her any heirlooms, and all the family pictures had been scanned and saved years ago. But she wanted Fred to maybe feel a little bit sorry for his actions. If Fred didn't set her place on fire, he knew who did. She was almost positive about that now.

Fred put his coffee cup down and linking his fingers, he did indeed look a little upset with this newest information. "Oh, wow. I didn't think about that. I would be mighty upset and sad if I lost all my family stuff in a fire. After all, family is everything. I'm really sorry for that loss—" Fred jumped a little when Wyatt came out of his room.

Wyatt walked into the kitchen, taking his time refilling his coffee cup. Coming over to the table, he sat down beside Tara. Only then did he address Fred. "Morning Fred. Good to see you again." He put his arm on the back of Tara's chair while crossing his legs at the ankles.

Fred recovered quickly and smiled. "Wyatt, right? Nice to see you again. Didn't know you were back in the area. You going to become a local?"

Wyatt smiled back, but the smile didn't make it to his eyes. "I don't know. It's a nice enough area."

Bob chose that moment to come into the kitchen.

Glancing over at Bob, Wyatt looked back at Fred. "Let me introduce you to a good friend of Tara and mine. Fred, this is Bob Cammon. Bob, meet Fred Toft, the local sheriff."

"Nice to meet you, Fred. Refill?" Bob offered since he was the only one standing up. They had decided on this strategy, everyone sitting, except Bob. It showed that Bob was in charge of this conversation. It was also the reason he had purposely not gone to shake Fred's hand. It was all part of the dance to keep the suspect off balance. At Fred's shake of his head, Bob came over and leaned on the island.

"Well, it's real nice of you to come up here to visit with Tara. How do you know Tara and Wyatt?" Fred asked, trying to get back under control. He wasn't sure what had him nervous, but he was.

"Oh, well Tara, Wyatt and I all worked together as contractors for the government years ago. We've all since moved in different directions, but we've stayed in touch and see each other regularly," Bob answered, sipping his coffee and looking Fred in the eye.

Fred tried to maintain the eye contact but broke it off when he realized he wouldn't win that contest with Bob. "Never have asked Tara, or Wyatt for that matter, what they do for a living. It's real interesting that you all worked for the government as contractors. What'd you all do?" He played with his empty coffee cup now to have something to do with his hands and as a way to calm his nerves. He could feel his heart pounding, and he really wished he would have taken just a small drink of his tea that morning. He was running out and was trying to make it last, but he really needed it right now.

Tara leaned forward on the table and cupped her coffee cup. "I don't work for the government anymore. Quit that job to become a property owner here. Yeah, I worked as a contractor with Wyatt and Bob, but as Bob said, we all went different paths awhile back," she answered the question, without answering the question.

Fred's mouth hardened just a bit, but he gave a half smile.

"I'm just as boring as Tara, sorry. I was a contractor for a time then I moved onto another agency. Now, I spend most of my time traveling to various government facilities. Rather boring stuff really." Wyatt, like Tara, answered the question without giving any information at all. Fred didn't try to hide the frustration this time, and without so much as a nod, he looked at Bob.

"These two have always been shy about talking about what they do. But, I'm not. I'm an agent for the DEA." Bob leaned against the island, drinking his coffee, all the while, holding eye contact with Fred.

After his initial jerk of surprise, Fred got control of himself. "That's a cool job," he said as he spun his coffee cup in his hands faster.

"Oh, it is and I love it. Getting drugs and dealers off the streets. It's my passion. My visit up here isn't all leisure, though, Fred. And now that you know that I'm DEA, we need to show you something. Tara, if you wouldn't mind leading the way to the riding arena."

Tara nodded, got up and went to the door to the breezeway. Gwenn and Wyatt joined her there, but Fred stayed sitting.

"Fred, I really need you to see this. It worries me," Tara said, playing to the male ego, and it worked.

Fred pushed up from the table and after standing there for a second to get his balance, followed Tara and Gwenn into the breezeway.

Once they got to the door of the riding arena, Tara paused

to make sure that Fred was still close. Now turning to look at him, she opened the door and turned on the light. "I found these on the property recently. I've been bringing them in here because I didn't know what else to do with them."

Tara stood back and let Fred walk through the door first, followed closely by Bob and Wyatt with Gwenn and Tara coming in last and closing the door.

Fred's eyes grew accustomed to the lighting, and he took a sharp intake of air. That sealed it for Bob who reached up and removed Fred's service weapon before Fred could react.

"Give me my goddamn gun!" Fred recovered quickly and started to advance on Bob, but Wyatt grabbed Fred's arms and twisted them behind his back.

"Fred, just stop. You don't need to get hurt, and I'll hurt you if you continue with your struggling," Wyatt whispered in Fred's ear.

"Fucking let me go. I'm a goddamn cop, I'll have your asses for this. I swear it." But Fred slowed on the struggling because Wyatt had the upper hand.

Bob came over and looked at Fred, then bent down to check for a clutch piece. Not finding one, Bob stood back up. "Your reaction to the plants told us what we needed to know. Wyatt, would you please take Fred back into the kitchen."

Once they were back in the kitchen, Bob did a more thorough search to make sure there were no more weapons on Fred. Then, taking Fred by the arm, he walked him over to the table.

"I'll fucking press charges on you. I'll own your badge by the end of the day," Fred ranted while rubbing his shoulder.

Bob smiled at Fred. "Go for it, Fred. But you might want to hear what I have to say first. Sit down." When Fred didn't, Bob added, "I wasn't asking Fred. Sit. Down."

After hesitating for just a second, Fred sat down at the table and glared at the four of them.

Bob let Fred sit there at the table while he went and refilled his coffee. Taking his time, he added the cream and sugar and then taste tested it. Wyatt and Tara were smiling behind their coffee cups, but Gwenn seemed confused, until she looked at Wyatt, who winked at her. Ah, so Bob was playing with Fred. Good! Gwenn had decided to watch this part from the kitchen island. She wasn't sure why, but this felt like something that Tara, Wyatt, and Bob had done before, and she didn't feel like part of it. She would stay back and watch. She wasn't sure what she was getting ready to watch, but screen grabs of Gibbs in the interrogation room made her smirk.

Tara saw the smirk and turning her back so that Fred couldn't see her, she mouthed 'Gibbs' to Gwenn.

Gwenn covered the outright smile with her coffee and nodded.

Now that Bob had his coffee just right, he grabbed the file folder and his laptop that were on the island. Taking the seat between Wyatt and Tara, they all were quiet, looking at Fred. Finally, Bob opened the file folder, and Fred let out a shuddering sigh. It was beginning. He wasn't sure if he was happy that the suspense was ending, or scared. Both, he thought.

"Before we get into the guts of this, I need to read you your rights. Got to do this all legal and such." After confirming that Fred did indeed understand his rights, Bob began. "Frederick Rohon Toft, 53 years old. Born and raised in Eriksport, Maine. Graduated from high school, no other education. Became the sheriff here after your father retired. Looks like being the sheriff in Eriksport runs in the family. Nice little monopoly you have going on there. Single, no kids, no dependents." Bob stopped and glanced up at Fred. When Fred didn't react, Bob continued.

"That's the general information that a standard background check got me. Just the basic stuff, rather boring actually. I'm glad I decided to run an in-depth background check, though. That's where the reading gets interesting." Bob stopped to drink his coffee and read some of the file before continuing.

"I'm not telling you a fucking thing. So, you can sit there and read your goddamn file. I haven't done anything wrong. I'll have all of your asses for this." Fred leaned back in the chair and smirked. But the beads of sweat that were appearing on Fred's upper lip ruined the look of confidence that Fred was trying to portray.

"That's your right, Fred. You have the right to remain silent, remember? I'm just sharing what I found on you. That's all. Okay, so let's see what else I found. You have a cousin, but so does pretty much everyone. But you have one cousin that interests me. I'm talking about your cousin that has an extensive record and convictions for drugs. Your proverbial black sheep in the family. It was really nice of you to help get him out of his last jail sentence and move up here. But then, he's family, right? His probation officer in Texas just gushed about the conversation you two had about your cousin."

Fred's head had jerked like he had been punched when Bob started talking about Bill and he started bouncing his left leg and stared at the table in front of him.

Bob flipped a couple of sheets in the folder. "We'll come back to Bill Ohlson in a bit, though. I'm really interested in the information I have about Dr. Roxbury."

Fred looked up, surprised, and now the sweat was starting to appear on his forehead, and he was feeling sick to his stomach.

"Oh, that got your attention, didn't it?" Bob made a note on the pad of paper in front of him.

"Dr. Edna Jean Roxbury, 55 years old. She had a Ph.D. in archaeology, specializing in Peru. She moves here, after being requested to retire from her job. She buys this property and builds all these fancy buildings. So, at what point did you two start dating? Before or after your cousin and his new wife moved out here to care take for her? I'm a little blurry on that fact. I know that you helped Bill and Barb get the job out here, but I don't know if you were dating Roxbury at that point."

"Now hold on one goddamn minute! I wasn't dating that woman. I only saw her maybe a dozen times. So what if I helped Bill and Barb get a fucking job out here? That's not against the goddamn law," Fred yelled, standing up and placing his hands on the table to attempt to tower over Bob.

"Really? Okay, hold on. And sit down," Bob said without looking up. Opening up his laptop, he looked at Fred. "I'm not going to keep repeating myself, Fred. I said sit down." Fred huffed and flopped down in his chair, crossing his arms again. "Ah, here they are. So, you didn't know her? Didn't date her? Only saw her maybe a dozen times? That's your story? Are you sure, Fred? You don't want to retract that statement?"

Fred sneered at Bob. "No, I don't want to retract my fucking statement. I didn't know her or date her. She wasn't my type. She was too into her books and her head."

Bob nodded, then turned the laptop so that Fred could see the picture of himself and Roxbury going through security at the airport in Florida. Fred turned white and slouched in his chair. "Then Dr. Roxbury must have a twin. This sure looks like various pictures of you two in Florida last year. And these," he brought the hospital photos forward, "these, look like she pissed you off, royally."

Fred slammed his hands onto the table and jumped up again. "I didn't do that! I don't know what the hell happened to her. You have no right! I'll fucking sue you for this."

Bob stared at Fred until he sat back down again. "That's not what the police report says."

Fred, breathing heavy from his last outburst and with red splotches evident on his cheeks, sat down, crossed his arms over his chest and putting his chin on his chest, glared at Bob.

"But, okay, you didn't know her, didn't date her, didn't beat the shit out of her. And I'm sure you're going to deny your admittance and treatment for an overdose on that same vacation, right? Not you. You don't do drugs. It was food poisoning. The fish was bad."

Fred sat there and glared at Bob, but it didn't seem to faze Bob at all. Fred knew he was screwed and he couldn't seem to come up with anything to counter this DEA agent's questioning. The fucker was going too fast for Fred to try to come up with a good story. Maybe a bit of a stall would get his head back into the game. "I need to use the bathroom."

Bob nodded. "Sure. Wyatt and I'll take you to the bathroom, and maybe the ladies can get us something cold to drink. I don't know about you, but I'm rather thirsty."

While Wyatt and Bob escorted Fred to the bathroom in Bob's room, Tara and Gwenn pulled out the lemonade and some glasses.

"Plastic, no glass. Glass breaks and can become a weapon," Tara added when she saw Gwenn's look of confusion.

"Oh, I didn't think about that. I'm not sure I'm impressed or scared that you would think of that. You and I need to have a talk about how you know all this stuff after all of this shit is over." Gwenn glanced out of the corner of her eye in time to see Tara hesitate then continue with putting the lemonade on the table.

Tara's only response was a single head nod. That just made Gwenn more determined to find out the secrets of her best friend. Any further conversation would have to wait because Bob and Wyatt had just returned and sat Fred back down at the table.

"Okay, break time's over Fred. Let's get to brass tacks, shall we? I've grown tired of playing with you. Plus, you aren't looking good. You jonesing for your tea?" When Fred flipped him off, Bob chuckled. "Okay, it's time for upfront and in your face, Fred. Are you ready? It's going to get ugly." Bob straddled the kitchen chair, his arms crossed on the top of the chair. "You went to Florida. Shut up." Bob pointed his finger at Fred when Fred started to protest. "This is where you sit and shut up and listen. I'll let you know when I want to hear your bullshit." After pausing to make sure that Fred understood he meant it, Bob started again. "You went to Florida last year with Dr. Roxbury, your girlfriend. You had some fun, some not fun, you overdosed, and they saved your sorry ass.

"Then you came back here, and something happened between you and Dr. Roxbury. Something bad. I'm betting it's because she got you hooked on the drugs that those plants in the arena produce and she wouldn't tell you where the plants she was growing were. I'm sure that you weren't innocent of using illegal drugs before Roxbury introduced you to her choice of drugs," Bob said and watched Fred's eyes jerked up then back down when he had mentioned the plants.

"I figure Dr. Roxbury got addicted to the drug from the plant in Peru and as with most addictions, it got worse and worse. Bigger and bigger. First, she used, then sold small amounts, and it continued until she was requested to leave her job because she was using the shipping containers for artifacts to smuggle the drug to the States. She told you all of that since you were lovers. I don't know which one of you decided to start growing and trafficking it up here. I don't really care because I'm going to nail you for all of it now that she's dead.

"You two set up a grow operation, but she wouldn't show you where she is growing them. That had to have pissed you off. She didn't trust you enough to show you where the plants were. You were just her little boy toy. She probably even gave you an allowance of the stuff, just to control you completely. Is that what she did? Each week or month, she gave her good little peon his drug tea? But she needed you, didn't she? With you being in law enforcement, you were the one that found the contact to sell the junk, right? Did Bill help you with that? She had you by the short hairs, didn't she?

"So, you confronted her, and in the heat of the moment, you hit her. Not sure with what, but you hit her in the head and threw her into the cove. And since you're the sheriff, you buried the county coroner's report. But guess what, Fred? I'm going to have the DEA coroner exhume Dr. Roxbury and take a look at it. And I've already requested a copy of the report from the county coroner's office.

"But, even with Roxbury out of the picture, you still can't find the plants, and you know that they're going to die and you won't be able to supply your contact. And probably even worse, your supply is dwindling. I figure you have to be getting pretty low on it considering you're starting to show classic signs of withdrawal."

Fred had stopped reacting to Bob and just sat there, arms crossed and leg jumping.

"That puts more pressure on you. Then to make things even worse for you, Tara buys this place, so you can't just snoop around. Was Bill helping you with that? So, you decide to scare Tara." Bob laughed now. "Oh, you really fucked up when you put the note on her car. It didn't frighten her, it put her into defense mode.

"So, you borrow Bill's boat, yeah we know about the boat, and snoop. You stop by, on official business, to snoop. But you can't find anything. That's pissing you off, so you grow brave and beach the boat on the little beach just south of here. It's on the property, so no fences. That was good thinking on your part. I'll give your kudos for that one. You found a weak spot. But, we fixed that. Anyway, you sneak up to the house and look around. Oh, how do I know about that? Field cameras, courtesy of Wyatt." Bob jerked his chin toward Wyatt and smiled.

Bob tapped the table to get Fred's attention. "One thing I don't understand, is if you were trying to get in here and on the property, why would you screw with Gwenn? First, the break in and the note. Then the fire? That's just stupid. I mean, you don't do something that will cause more people to stay at the place you are trying to get into."

Bob put his chin on his folded arms on the back of the chair and looked at Fred. Fred wasn't looking well at all. He had quit trying to interrupt or argue with him, and now he just sat there, looking down at the table. He was jittery and sweating and very pale. Taking a drink of his lemonade, Bob glanced to the right at Tara. She was stony-faced as she always had been during interrogations. Looking at Wyatt, he looked bored, as was his usual interrogation face. He missed this part of working with the two of them.

"Okay, so that concludes the tell part of this discussion. It's time for the show portion." Bob placed the laptop at the end of the table so they could all see. "Gwenn, come on over and have a seat beside Tara. This is the fun part."

"So, we've all seen the vacation pictures from last year, so no need to see them again. Unless you want to see them again, Fred?" Bob glanced over at Fred, and when there was no reaction at all from Fred, Bob continued. "Okay, let's move onto some of the boat snooping pictures." Bob clicked the mouse and the first photo came up. "Fred, can you see well enough? I don't want you to miss any of the damning evidence we have on you." When Fred didn't reply but just stared at the laptop, Bob shrugged.

"In this picture, you can just make out half of the boat registration numbers, 11 N." Another click of the mouse. "But then you came back and gave Tara another chance to get the full registration number, ME 0711 N. Which she did. Thanks for that, by the way. Made my job so much easier. So, that's how we know that the boat is Bill's boat."

Bob glanced over at Fred and saw no argument coming from him. "Let's move onto the trusty field cameras that Wyatt had installed. Nifty little toys. Wireless and direct live feed, so Wyatt knew the minute you hit that tree line. See, there you are, sneaking just inside the tree line. You hunt, don't you? Sorry, off topic there." Bob clicked through the next several pictures. "See, we have many, many photos of you sneaking around and snooping. At least your torso. Wyatt got lazy and didn't set the cameras high enough for a head shot, but let me zoom into a couple of the field cam photos. Bad day to be wearing a sleeveless T-shirt for you. There, see that? On the upper right arm? It's a tattoo."

Gwenn grabbed Tara's arm under the table and glanced over to her, but Tara did a quick headshake to let Gwenn know not to say anything.

"We don't need your face on the photos with that nice defining feature showing so prominent." Bob stopped and looked at Fred. "Fred, show us your upper right arm."

Fred thought about saying no. He really did, but he knew if he did, the asshole would just force the issue and he would have to show his entire arm. If he cooperated, then he could show just the upper arm where his tattoo was, and they would never know the truth. Sighing, he unbuttoned his uniform shirt just enough so that he could pull the shirt down to just above his elbow. Pulling up the T-shirt that he wore under the uniform shirt, he exposed his upper right arm. On it was a 3-inch black tattoo, and it matched the one that Bob had just shown them from the field camera.

"Well, well, well. That's a match. So, yeah that ends the picture portion of the Fred-is-fucked show-and-tell." Bob leaned back and stared at Fred.

Fred sat there, pulled his shirt down his arm and tried to think. Of anything. But he couldn't. They had him, dead to rights. Granted, some of the information wasn't right, but he would go to his grave before he would let them know that he hadn't been the one that the field camera had gotten pictures of. Or that he hadn't put the note on Tara's car, just like he didn't do the break in, note or fire at Gwenn's. He would take all of that to his grave. He protected his own, goddammit. If that little bastard Logan would have just listened to him. But it didn't matter anymore. Fred would pay the price to protect the families. That was the way it always had been, and it would always be that way. So, he would let them think it was all him. He would take the fall for the greater good.

Bob got up and got a bottle of water and placed it in front of Fred. "Drink some water. Slowly. It will help your stomach," Bob coached quietly. "I know your stomach is flipping and you want to throw up. This is all damning evidence, that is for sure. But, there is a way to help make this better."

At this, Fred looked up at Bob. Opening the water, he took a couple of sips, then fixed his shirt.

"With the plants that are here, you have to have a rather large dealer working with you. If you help me nail the dealer, it will look favorably at your trial. I'll vouch for you and having a DEA agent on your side goes a long way. Or don't do anything and you go to jail. Where the dealer will most likely have people. You're a cop, so jail would be pure hell for you.

Along with being rather short-lived, I'm afraid. You'd most likely be dead within two months."

Fred put his head in his hands and closed his eyes. If he went to jail, he was dead. He knew that. If his contact found out about the DEA knowing about the plants, he was dead. But, if he worked with the DEA and brought the bastard down, then maybe he could live. Maybe he would still have something left after he got out of jail. Maybe he could start over and put all of this behind him. Looking over at Bob, Fred asked, "What do you want me to do?"

"That's real smart, Fred. You're going to help in a sting to take the dealer out of business. But Fred, I can only help you on the drug part of this. You'll still be on the hook for your part in Roxbury's death. Whether you did it or not, you covered it up. You used your office and position and covered up a murder. That, you'll have to pay for."

"I didn't kill her. I loved her," Fred said, quietly.

Bob tapped on the table and when Fred looked up, looked Fred in the eyes. "Then who killed her, Fred? Who did you help to clean up the mess? I'm thinking it had to have been someone close to you. After all, I sure as hell wouldn't help the average Joe cover up a murder. It would have to be someone near and dear to me. Like family. Who killed Dr. Roxbury, Fred? Who killed the woman that you loved?"

Closing his eyes, Fred leaned back in his chair. Slowly shaking his head, he opened his eyes and looked at Bob. "I can't tell you. I just can't."

"Well, then I can't help you at all on the murder of Dr. Roxbury. I hope whoever you're protecting is worth it to you. That's a long prison sentence that you're going to get for him." Bob stood up and gathering up the laptop and folder, he put them on the island. Turning back around, he glanced at Tara, Gwenn, and Wyatt to see that they were paying attention.

"Fred, I know you're using the tea that the plants make. And I know you have to be getting low on it, I can help you with that."

Surprised, Fred looked at Bob.

"I can't give you the tea, but I can have a medication prescribed to you that will help with the withdrawal. Is that something you want?" Bob watched while Fred debated this.

Fred looked Bob in the eye and nodded. "Yeah."

Bob smiled and patted Fred on the shoulder. "Okay, I'll get it set up for you and have it ready for pick up in the next town south of here. You're okay to drive down there?"

Fred nodded.

"Good. Now, I'm going to give you your weapon back and let you go about your business like you always do. Don't do anything out of the ordinary. But know this, I'll know if you are trying to sneak out of the deal. I'll know everything you are doing. Everyone you are talking to. Don't be stupid and that will go a long way with me. Understood?" Bob waited for Fred to nod, then laid Fred's unloaded gun and clip on the table.

Standing up, Fred picked up the gun and put it in the holster, then put the clip in his pocket. With Bob and Wyatt accompanying him, he left the house.

Tara went and opened the door to her bedroom so that Connal, Gizmo, and Peanut could rejoin the humans. The three dogs ran and followed Fred's scent everywhere he had been, growling low in their throats the whole time.

"He's gone, guys. The bad guy is gone. Connal, you were a good boy alerting me to him. You didn't like him, and you were right about it. Good boy." Tara sat down on the floor to gather Connal on her lap and rub his head. Putting her face into his fur on his neck, she used the time to ground herself. At least until Connal had enough, then he grumbled and wiggled loose to restart the tracking of Fred. Gizmo and Peanut took that as an invitation to come over and replace Connal on Tara's lap. So, Tara obliged with tummy rubs and ear scratches until Wyatt and Bob came back in and Gwenn returned from her trip to the bathroom.

"How will we know what he's doing and who he's talking to?" Gwenn asked as soon as the four of them were back together in the kitchen.

"Spy toys," Bob said while opening up his laptop. "Wyatt attached a small GPS and listening device to the inside of his gun holster when he subdued him."

"But, he's not on duty all the time. What if he doesn't carry the gun all the time?" Gwenn questioned.

"He's a cop and a bad guy. He always carries his weapon. But just in case he doesn't, I sprayed him with a tracking substance when I was frisking him. See?" Bob pulled up a program on his laptop, and they could see a little dot named Fred heading toward town.

"Holy fuck. I thought that was just NCIS magic," Gwenn mumbled and sat down on one of the stools at the island to watch the Fred dot move.

"We can take turns listening and watching his moves, but I also have my team following him, so we're covered. He's not going to be able to blink twice without us being aware of it. There will be no double cross. And before you say anything about texting or calling, my guys have all his electronics covered. He's ours." Bob sat down beside Gwenn and leaned in closer so that he was touching Gwenn's shoulder with his own.

"We need to deal with Bill next. Fred isn't going to spill who killed Dr. Roxbury, but I'd lay odds that he's covering for Bill. I think he killed Roxbury, then called his law cousin to help fix it. I'm not sure how deep Bill is in the drug mess, but I highly doubt that he's just an innocent bystander. Wyatt, you up for a visit with him?"

Wyatt nodded. "Yep. Let's have a chat with him and see where he fits into this mess. I vote for the sooner, the better. You two want to come along?"

"No. I'm done with this ugly shit for the day, and I want to spend some time with the dogs. They need some mama time, and I need some serious doggie time after that. I'm sure you two can give us the cliff notes version of what goes down," Tara said.

Gwenn jerked her chin toward Tara. "I'm with her. I'm done for the day. Be careful. Bill's a quiet guy, but he's fucking strong as an ox."

"Holy shit! Fred has the fucking rune tattooed on his arm. That can't be a coincidence, right?" Gwenn questioned as soon as the front door closed.

Tara shrugged. "I don't know, Gwenn. It could be as innocent as Dr. Roxbury researching a cool rune for a tattoo for Fred. I just don't know. But it does have my Spidey sense tingling that maybe there is more to the rune than we thought before. Maybe Dr. Roxbury got a matching tattoo. Could have been a couple thing to do on vacation last year. People do it all the time, right?" Tara glanced over at Gwenn.

"Yeah, they do. Hell, I've done it, so that's not too far of a stretch. Maybe it was just a couple tattoo, nothing more, nothing less." But they both had the feeling that it wasn't just an innocent tattoo. There was more to it, they felt it.

CHAPTER FOURTEEN

"Well, that was interesting, to say the least," Bob said while getting a beer for himself. He and Wyatt had just returned to the house after confronting Bill about his possible involvement with Fred in the drug ring.

Wyatt followed suit, grabbing a beer and downing half of it in one take. "Yeah, that got ugly." Now, sitting down beside Bob at the island, they faced the girls and just stared.

"Well, what the hell happened? You can't say shit like that and not tell us what happened," Gwenn spoke for herself and Tara.

Tara tipped her chin toward Gwenn. "What she said. What happened?" Tara took Wyatt's beer and took a drink. "Talk."

Bob looked at Wyatt, and after Wyatt shook his head that he wasn't going to fill in the girls, Bob sighed. "Well, we went over there to see what Bill knew. At first, it was fine. He isn't much into talking so he mostly just glared at us and let Barb answer the questions about how he moved here and met her and whatnot.

"It was going okay until I started asking him about his time in Texas and his drug charges. Well, then he found his voice. Boy, did he. Got belligerent as hell about us out-of-towners nosing into business that wasn't ours to look into. Of course, Barb started questioning him about his time in Texas. I guess she had asked about his prior life before, but he always evaded her. Anyway, he started getting really defensive, and you know how I love when they do that. I started tossing some facts about his time down there, and he got more and more angry. Told me that was behind him and what did any of that matter?

"So, I told him about Dr. Roxbury growing the drug plants and that Fred was in on it. And since Fred was his cousin and had got him up here from Texas, with the premise that he would take charge of him to his probation officer, it seemed to suggest that Bill knew about the drug plants too. He actually seemed confused on that. I don't think he knows anything about Fred and Dr. Roxbury's side business." Bob looked over at Wyatt for his opinion.

Wyatt nodded. "Yeah, he was shocked. I don't think he had any idea about the plant business."

Taking a long drink of his beer, Bob continued. "Well, that's when all hell broke loose. Barb fixated on the cousin part and demanded to know about that. Bill didn't answer, so I told Barb what I had learned. Man, she has a wicked temper. Wyatt had to physically hold her back, she wanted Bill's blood that much. So, Barb was all wild about the lies but Bill, he'd gone all quiet. But he was smoldering, you could feel it." Bob leaned forward, getting into the storytelling.

"Next thing I know, he's launched himself at me, linebacker style. I have to say he looks like Popeye, and he's built like him too. Tried to hit me, but I got him under control. I had to pin him to the floor and handcuff him." Bob scrubbed his hands over his face.

"Boy, did he find his voice then. In between all the cussing, he said he didn't know anything about any drugs. Never did and he didn't help Fred with them either. Said he hadn't touched a drug since he got out of prison. He also said he didn't know that Fred had been using his boat. He did agree that Fred got him out of Texas and up here because they were family, but he maintained that he was off the drugs and didn't want anything to do with it. Bill also said that Fred got Barb and him the job out here, but again, nothing to do with the drugs. He was emphatic about that.

"Finally got him to calm down enough to sit up on the floor, still handcuffed and the bastard tried to bite me. Now, I'm fine with a headbutt or a sucker punch, but biting? That crosses the line. So, I called in a favor with a buddy of mine who based out of Bangor. Anyway, he ran Bill and come to find out the dick has several outstanding warrants out of Texas still. So, Bill's now sitting in a holding cell in Bangor on the outstanding warrants, assault and battery, and resisting arrest. Fucker shouldn't have tried to bite me.

"Wyatt and I took Bill halfway to Bangor, then passed him over to my buddy. Before we left Barb, we made sure she understood that she needed to keep quiet about the information that I had told them. That it was an ongoing investigation, and she said she would." Bob stopped and finished off his beer, then leaned his elbows on the island.

"Holy shit." Gwenn got another beer for Wyatt and Bob, taking a drink of Bob's before handing it to him. "That had to have been horrible for Barb. I feel bad for her." Sitting back down, she mirrored Bob and leaned her elbows on the island.

"Wow. Poor Barb. I'll have to check on her tomorrow and make sure she's doing okay." Tara stood up and came around the island to hug Bob where he sat. "I know you didn't go over there expecting to have him removed, he did that to himself when he attacked you."

Rubbing her face, Tara walked to the breezeway door. "I'm going to the pups out for their last out in the arena. I need to try to process everything that has happened today, and they need to have some play time before bed. Oh, Gwenn and I ate, but there's plenty of leftovers from dinner. She made lasagna."

"We're good. We got burgers on the way back here from meeting up with Bob's buddy. Thanks, though. Go spend time with your dogs. I'm going to go take a very long, hot shower, then find a ballgame to relax with." Wyatt got up and after a backward wave closed the door to his room.

Bob smiled. "Ditto what he said. Night ladies. Try to get some sleep."

Gwenn stood there and looked at Tara. "I know you want your quiet time with the dogs, so I'm not going to horn in on it. I've got restaurant shit to work on, so I'll say good night now."

Tara smiled her appreciation that Gwenn really did understand her need for her time. "Thank you, Gwenn. Good night."

The next morning Bob and Tara were the first ones up, and after topping off their cups of coffee, Bob sat down across from Tara at the island.

"There'll be a DEA team in tomorrow to remove the plants from the property. They're going to need to catalog it as evidence and to get them ready for the deal after Fred contacts the dealer. It shouldn't be too much longer before those plants are off your property." Tara smiled and raised her cup to toast that. "Oh, and the analysis of those leaves came back. You were right, Tara. Those are the leaves of the psycho plant mixed with the B vine." Bob chuckled and shook his head. "That cracks me up everytime I say it. Gwenn's a character, isn't she? Anyway, we're going to use that as evidence in the case as well." Bob cupped his hands around his coffee cup and looked at Tara. She hadn't slept, he could see that in the dark circles under her eyes.

"This will be over soon, I promise. Then you can truly enjoy your new place. Which is gorgeous, by the way."

Smiling, Tara took a sip. "That's great news that the plants will be gone tomorrow. Can your team go over that room and make sure that I won't have any surprise plants springing up later on? I want anything to do with those plants gone."

Bob nodded. "Yep, it's already on the list for them to do a complete scrub of the room. I'll add the Batcave in the scrub too if you want."

"Yeah, that probably wouldn't be a bad idea. Thanks. Oh,

one more thing, Bob. I was wondering if you had gotten a copy of the county coroner report yet?" Tara asked the question that had been on her mind all night.

"I requested a copy of it, but it hasn't been emailed to me yet. Why the interest in the report? Is there something else you think we should be looking for?" Bob who had been watching the dogs wrestle, turned to face Tara directly.

Tara purposely tried to avoid the eye contact, but it was a losing battle with Bob. Sighing, "No, not really. I'm just curious to see what the cause of death was, that's all," she said, glancing up at Bob quickly, then back to her coffee cup. "Also, if she had any tattoos."

"Tattoos? Why? What are you working on in that head of yours, Tara?" Bob knew Tara well enough to know that the question about the tattoos wasn't just a casual question. Something was bugging her, big time, and he wanted to know what it was.

"Ah, hell. Fred had a tattoo on his arm, so it got me to thinking that maybe Dr. Roxbury had tattoos also," Tara mumbled but knew it sounded as lame as it was for an excuse.

Bob stared at Tara, then sighed. "Uh huh. Sure, Tara. I know you won't tell me what the real reason is if I keep poking, so I'll wait until you have it figured out in your head."

Tara's answer was a nod and a smile.

Bob was true to his word because the next morning a team of DEA agents arrived at the property and started removing the plants. It was a small team of four agents, and they had come in a delivery truck so as to not draw attention to themselves. After all, she was new to the area, and surely, she would be buying new furniture or appliances that would need to be delivered.

Tara stood there for a while, watching them labeling, cataloging and photographing the plants, but before long, she lost interest in the process.

Going back to the house, she decided that she would make a salad for the four of them. They hadn't been eating very healthy, and she was actually craving vegetables.

Tara was just finishing making up the salad when Gwenn came into the kitchen from swimming in the pool, followed by three wet corgis.

"Mmmmm, salad. That looks great! Maybe grilled chicken to go with it for dinner? Something healthy and light."

"Chicken sounds good. You could have dried them off, you know?" Tara pointed her chin to Connal, Gizmo, and Peanut who had flopped in the middle of the kitchen floor and were oozing water. "I have to clean this place, remember?"

"Yeah, but what's the fun in that? They didn't want to be dry. And it's your own fault you're cleaning your house. You have a contracted housekeeper, so it's on you." Laughing when Tara stuck her tongue out at her, Gwenn sighed. "God, I feel so sorry for Barb. I don't know what I would have done if all that shit had been dumped on me at once. Bill should be thanking Bob for arresting him, because I bet Barb would have torn him limb from limb if they had left him there," Gwenn said and bumped Tara over with her hip so that she could help chop the vegetables.

"Oh, I know. I can't imagine the level of anger and betrayal that would be. After dinner, I want to go check on her, but not until those plants are out of here," Tara said while she was busy making up a marinade for the chicken.

"I'll go with you. More support in numbers. Maybe take her some food for once, since she's always feeding us. It'd be good to return the favor." Gwenn came up beside Tara and added a couple of her own spices to the marinade. "This will either be amazing, or I'm calling pre-dibs on the leftover pizza."

Wyatt and Bob walked into the house about an hour later, and after grabbing a couple of beers, Bob said, "They're all finished, and the plants are on the way to a warehouse to wait for the deal. We looked all through The Lab, and there is nothing left from the plants. It's just a huge hole in the ground now. Did a scan of the Batcave, too. It's all clear. Any evidence of those plants is now off your property, Tara."

Tara's answer was a smile and a hug. Kissing Bob on the cheek, she went to the fridge and got a beer for her and Gwenn, then clinked bottles with each of them in celebration.

"I think since there's still a decent amount of afternoon left, I'm going to go for a swim and play with the water toys." Wyatt looked at the others to see if anyone else would join him.

"Sounds like a damn good idea. Relaxing for a bit will be nice. You two coming?" Bob looked at Gwenn first, then glanced at Tara.

"No, I'm staying in here. But you three go and have fun," Tara answered, making it subtly clear she needed some alone time.

Gwenn acknowledged Tara's need with a single nod of her head, and as the three of them headed out to the cove, Gwenn turned around and whistled for the dogs, who about knocked her over in their rush to go play. "I'll make sure they wear their life jackets, Mom. Go and veg now, we'll keep them safe."

Smiling, Tara went to the kitchen for a glass of water. She would sit outside and work on her computer for a bit. Part of the fun, but not in the middle of the fun. She needed some recharging time. She loved the three of them, but with the Fred interrogation yesterday, then the DEA team here today, she needed her quiet time. So, she logged into Facebook and browsed her newsfeed, taking her time to read and like her online friend's posts. She did the same thing on Twitter and Pinterest, liking and saving various items that interested her. Then spent time doing some emails, catching up with the few friends that she had an interest in actually staying in contact with.

Finally, she opened her journal, and she spent the rest of the time journaling her feelings, what was going on, what was bugging her, what scared her. What she wanted to do with the senior dog rescue and her worries that she wouldn't be able to handle the heartache that the rescue would bring. After she had finished dumping everything into her journal, she reread it and then deleted the entry. She never saved the entries; that wasn't the purpose of this journal. The purpose was to get it all out. Then burn the thoughts, metaphorically speaking. It helped to get it out of her head, and most times, it made things clearer and not so scary.

Gwenn was up early and getting ready for her day at her restaurant the next morning. She was in the middle of ordering supplies and bills when Bob came into the kitchen. Getting a cup of coffee for himself, he walked over and topped off Gwenn's.

Gwenn glanced up and smiled. "Thanks and good morning."

Bob nodded and asked, "What are you working on?"

"Ordering supplies and doing bills for the restaurant. All the fun parts of owning a business," Gwenn mumbled around the pencil she had between her teeth.

"Oh, okay. I'll leave you to it then. I don't want to be responsible for you ordering 30 extra bags of flour or something," Bob said as he turned to walk away.

"No, don't leave. I need a break." Gwenn closed the laptop and turned to him as he sat down beside her.

"Okay. So, why a pizza place?" Bob asked.

"Well, that's easy. I love pizza. And I love to cook. Always have so it just made sense. And, who doesn't like pizza? Just seemed like a no-brainer. And since Eriksport has only one place to eat out and it's a fancy seafood place, it made sense to open a more casual place. With amazing pizza. So, now my turn. Why a DEA agent?" Gwenn asked while holding her coffee and sipping on it.

Bob chuckled at Gwenn's quick change of topic to him. "Well, it just sort of happened. It wasn't something that I had planned. I joined the Air Force after high school, did eight years of active duty. Just enough time to get a couple of overseas deployments in. Then realized I didn't want to do that anymore. So, didn't re-enlist when the time came. Did a few odd jobs and then a contractor position opened up that interested me. I applied and got the job as a contractor for the Air Force, working in the reconnaissance area. Found out I liked it and was good at it, so stuck with it. Made some good connections—it's all about networking—so when a couple of folks noticed me and offered me this job, I took it. Seems the way of things. Once military, there is always some sort of tie back to it. It's a big family, and everyone gets the mission." Bob took a drink of his coffee and watched Gwenn.

Gwenn had sat, sipping her coffee and watched him while he talked. "Okay, nice standard answer, but you didn't really tell me anything. I've noticed that Tara, Wyatt and you are all very good at nice, standard answers without actually answering."

After the initial shock of being called out on it, Bob laughed. He looked down at his coffee and smiled. "Damn, you're good. It's just what we do. Sorry. It's not that we don't trust you, it's just that it's been ingrained in us to evade. It becomes a way of life, so I don't think we even realize we do it anymore. At least until someone calls us out on it. After this is over, maybe we'll sit down and chat."

"And another evasion technique. The 'we'll talk about it later.' But we both know that won't happen. No. It's okay, I sort of get it. I'm just being nosy," Gwenn added when Bob started to interrupt. Opening her laptop, she effectively stopped any further discussion.

"I'm going for a run, want to join me?" Bob offered. He knew she was frustrated and a little upset with all of them right now.

Gwenn glanced over. "Why? Is someone going to be chasing us? Hell no! I'm going to finish ordering 30 extra bags of flour."

Wyatt was just finishing up his run when Bob met him at the riding arena.

"Hey, great morning for a run," Wyatt gasped while leaning with his hands on his knees and catching his breath.

Bob slowly started his stretching exercises. "I hope so. Need to get some exercise. I'm feeling antsy."

"Yeah, me too. Just an FYI, stay on the road, there are all sorts of dangers if you go into the tree line. Squirrels and little vermin that like to try to trip you up."

Chuckling, Bob moved to side stretches. "Good to know. So, Gwenn was asking why I became a DEA agent. Gave her the standard answer and damn if she didn't call me on it. That woman is smart. Damn smart." Bob moved to jumping jacks.

"Yeah, she is. She knows that the three of us were contractors for the government, so the curiosity is flowing. I have a feeling she's going to be like a little bug until one of us gives her something to satisfy that curiosity." Wyatt jerked his chin toward Bob. "So, why don't you?"

Bob stopped mid jumping jack and actually whined. "Why me?"

Snorting, Wyatt rolled his eyes. "Dude, seriously? You two are all hot for each other so it would make sense that her *lover* would tell her. Hell, you two already slept together the other night."

"We have not!" Bob shouted, then lowering his voice. "We haven't."

"Yeah, you did. On the couch the other night. Tar has proof of it. She took a picture."

Bob opened and closed his mouth before he found the right words. "We fell asleep! It was innocent. And I'll have to kill Tara now. I'm sorry, I know she means a lot to you, but she must die now."

Still laughing and holding his side, Wyatt clucked his tongue. "Innocent, my ass. You want more and I'm telling Tara."

Bob punched Wyatt in the chest, hard. "Fuck you, Wyatt. Maybe I do like her. Maybe she likes me. But, it can't go anywhere. We're way too far apart in our lives. We have absolutely nothing in common."

He shook his head slowly, and rubbed his chest where Bob had hit him. "Wow, way to shoot it out of the air before it even takes off. Go for your run, lover boy. Maybe that will help you clear your head," Wyatt said turning to walk to the house.

"So, where's Gwenn's restaurant?" Bob asked after returning from his run and a shower. "I thought it would be nice to go in and see the town and get something to eat." Bob knew that sounded lame, but any other way he had said it in his head sounded just as bad.

"It's very easy to get to. Turn right off my road and drive about 15 miles. You will literally run right into it." Tara provided the information all the while attempting to keep a straight face. "It's a little town. Not much to see. Grocery store, drug store, hardware store, pizza place and some little mom and pop shops."

Nodding, Bob asked, "You two up for a ride?"

"Nope, I'm good. Staying close to the house for the pups," Tara immediately answered and turned to Wyatt. "Wyatt? What about you? You want to go into the town and watch Bob moon over Gwenn?"

Wyatt laughed. "Nope, I'm good too. You're on your own with the mooning, Bob. Have fun," he said, waving and smiling.

"Fuck you both. I hate you, and you both suck," Bob replied, but with a smile on his face. "I shouldn't be long. I do want to do a recon of the area, though. See if anything feels weird."

Bob drove directly to Gwenn's, and it was as easy as Tara had said. Turning around, he drove to the middle of town and parked, then he got out and walked. He took his time noting the businesses and their hours. He walked into the grocery store and shopped while looking around and getting the feel of the locals. "Can never have enough toilet paper."

He went to the drugstore for Tylenol and to the hardware store for a couple of nuts and bolts. After putting his purchases in the car, he turned in time to see Fred coming out of the police station.

Fred jerked to a stop and looked at Bob, but Bob gave him a cursory glance, then turned to walk to Gwenn's.

"Don't make a show of looking at me dammit," he mumbled to himself. Turning around on the presumption of making sure his car was locked, he saw that Fred had moved on to his cruiser. "Good boy. Time for pizza."

While Bob was in town, Wyatt decided to walk the property and make sure everything was secure and working. On Tara's insistence, he had three corgis with him. "How did that happen? I don't even like dogs, and now I'm doing a security check with three short-assed ones." Connal, who had been walking beside Wyatt, looked up and barked at him. "Sorry, little dog. But hate to break it to you, you're short. And don't you dare think about pissing on my foot. Why don't you go and bug your brother and sister? Great, now I sound like a dad. And I'm fucking talking to dogs." But he was smiling and chuckling at the antics of the three dogs.

Every time he stopped to check a camera, the three congregated around him to see why they had stopped. Finding that boring, Connal and Peanut would pee on everything and Gizmo would just lay down and watch him or find something interesting to roll on. The sight of a short-legged dog, rolling on her back with her little legs moving reminded him of a roly-poly bug and that just made him laugh. "Keep that up, you'll be up for a bath when your mom gets a look at you."

With Wyatt and the dogs out and walking security, Tara was alone in the house, and just as she was sitting down to enjoy another cup of coffee, the front gate alerted. "Of course." Looking at the monitor, she whimpered. "Well, frig me." She pushed the button to open the gate for Barb, then closing her eyes and taking a couple of deep breaths, she waited for Barb.

Tara got up to meet Barb, and after waiting for her to put the bags on the counter, she did something very uncommon for herself. She enfolded Barb in a hug and held her while Barb had another crying fit.

"Here, drink this. It will help." Tara offered after she got Barb calmed down and sitting at the table.

Barb finished blowing her nose and looked at the glass that

Tara had sat in front of her. "Thank you. What is it?"

"It's a shot of whiskey," Tara responded, taking Barb's hands and wrapping them around the glass. "Thinking you need it today. Now, sip on that and relax. Have you eaten?"

At Barb's head shake, Tara opened the fridge and pulled out the salad. "How about some salad? No comfort food or anything heavy. Healthy and light and fresh are what you need. And we'll eat it on the porch. Some fresh air will help as well. Why don't you head on out and I'll be there in a minute? No. Take that drink with you and sip on it. I'll bring iced tea out to have with lunch."

Tara took some time getting the salads ready. She wanted to get her thoughts together, and she wanted to give Barb a few minutes to get herself under control. She was a feeling person. Sometimes too feeling. That was one of the reasons she didn't like being around people all the time. She seemed to pick up and feel their feelings and it was tiring and emotionally hard. It wasn't that she didn't like people. She did! She actually loved people. Her career choice was anthropology after all, which is the study of man. How could she not love people? She just loved them in small doses. Then she needed her cave time, as her mom used to call it. Time for her to hide away and regroup and recharge. That's why this place was the perfect fit for her. She had her space that she could open or close to the outside world as she wanted and needed. But now, Barb needed her, so she would be there for her, and she would deal with the emotions she took from Barb later.

Walking out to the porch, Tara set the salad, plates, silverware and the three bottles of dressing on the table. "I didn't know what type of salad dressing you would like, so you have a choice." Tara then went back in for the iced tea and the glasses.

Finally taking the seat across from Barb, she waited. She had learned, the hard way, not to push. Pushing caused people to leave. So, she waited for Barb to start talking.

Barb looked at her, then smiled sadly. "The salad looks great. I'm sorry about earlier. It just comes on me, and I can't control it." She busied herself with putting some salad on a plate, then passed it to Tara. Then she fixed her own plate and poured the iced tea. She sighed heavily. "I'm so sad and mad and angry and betrayed. I'm just all sorts of things, and I'm not sure which one will show up." Choosing a salad dressing, she took a bite of the salad.

"I understand. No. Really, I do, I'm not just saying that. The only advice I have is to let the feelings come. If not, it will make you sick, and it will be worse. So, let it happen. Have you talked to Bill?" Tara asked while taking a bite of her salad.

"No, and right now, I don't want to. He's called a couple of times, but I won't accept the collect calls. You know that your friend Bob got him locked up, right? After they got him to the jail, they found outstanding warrants on him from Texas." Barb stopped eating and leaned back in the chair, cradling the glass of whiskey.

Tara nodded her head. "Yeah. He didn't want to do that, but Bill left him no choice when he attacked him. Plus, Bob didn't like the amount of anger that he saw last night, and after knowing Bill's past history, he didn't want anything bad to happen."

Sipping on the whiskey, Barb sniffed. "Yes. When Wyatt and Bob showed up at the house and started talking to us, I couldn't believe what they were saying. I wouldn't believe what they were saying. Until I looked at Bill. His face said it all. Everything they were saying, it was all true. Bill just looked at me and said sorry. That's it. No explanation. Just sorry. I've been married to him for two years. And I didn't know him at all. It hurts. I mean, how did I not know he was a local? I feel betrayed by him, and the whole town. No one told me. Why?" Barb stabbed at a tomato and ate it.

"I don't know why the folks in town didn't tell you. That's very odd to me. Maybe they didn't know? I know this all sucks and hurts so much, but it will get better eventually. It will take time, but it will get better." Tara reached over and held Barb's hand. "We'll get through this. I'll be right back. I need to use the bathroom. Try to relax now. I'll be right back."

As Tara stepped into the house, she pulled out her cell phone and opened up the security program. Glancing back to make sure Barb was still on the porch, Tara went into her bedroom, then into the bathroom. But she didn't use the facilities. She pulled up the camera just above the door of the living room. Zooming in and making sure that the camera was recording, she had a moment of guilt while she watched Barb.

Then the guilt switched to anger because after Barb looked in to see that Tara wasn't in eyesight, Barb leaned back in her chair. Her shoulders relaxed and sipping her whiskey, she smiled and laughed. "I should have been an actress. She bought that hook, line, and sinker. Poor Barb. Didn't know anything about Bill being a local," she scoffed. "I know everything about this town. I'm one of the families, after all. We know all. Stupid little twit."

"I knew she was a fake," Tara ground out. Keeping the camera active, she calmed herself and decided she would keep this to herself for the time being. Now to go get Barb out of there as soon as she could, without making her suspicious.

Gwenn knew the second that Bob walked into her restaurant. Glancing up, their eyes locked and she almost smiled. But then she remembered they were in town, and she wouldn't know who he was, so she walked over instead and played hostess. Seating him in the booth that she had formally set up for Tara and the dogs, but after Tara's insistence had turned back into an everyday booth, she went to get him the soda that he ordered. And to give herself a minute to calm down. There was something about Bob that just made her body all quivery.

"Knock it off. You're not a horny teenager for God's sake," she told herself while waiting for the glass to fill up at the drink machine.

Walking back out, she set down the soda and recommended the lasagna, which he promptly ordered. To an outsider, they looked like a waitress and a customer, making the small talk that usually resulted in a decent tip. Which was exactly what Bob wanted. He wanted to see how she would react to his impromptu appearance.

"She's quick on her feet. No giving away she knows me. She's good," Bob mumbled to himself, with pride. He wasn't sure why he felt the need to test her, but he was, and she had passed the test. Bob stayed as long as was normal for a customer, then he got up and went to the register to pay. Gwenn was very professional, taking the cash and making change with just enough chitchat to be friendly.

Heading back to the car, he took his time. The sidewalks were a little busier now, so he had a chance to people watch. Nobody really interested him, but still, he watched. Finally, with no other excuses to stay in town, he got into his car and went back to Tara's.

Bob got back to the house just as Barb was leaving and they came face to face in the kitchen, with Barb gasping when she saw him. Preparing himself for the possibility that Barb was going to yell or hit him, he stood there and waited.

Barb stood there and looked at Bob for a minute, then took a deep breath and relaxed her posture. "Hello again, Bob. I'm not mad at you, you're only doing your job. And Bill didn't make things any better for himself with attacking you. I won't tell anyone that you're here at Tara's or what is going on. It's none of their business, and since they kept Bill's family connections secret, I don't owe any of them anything. But please, tell me, that I'm safe out here."

Bob looked Barb square in the eye. "Barb, you're safer here than you would be anywhere else. If you want, Wyatt and I can come over and add some cameras and flood lights outside of your place."

Barb gave a little smile but shook her head. "That's not necessary. But thank you."

"Okay, if you're sure. But if you change your mind we're just a phone call away. Call anytime. I mean it." Bob opened the door for Barb, then turned to Tara, and saw the anger on her face.

"Whoa, why so angry?" He walked over to Tara and took

her hand.

Tara debated whether to share with Bob, then remembering Wyatt's words of not hiding anything, blew out a hard breath. "She's playing us, Bob."

"Wait? What? How?" Bob led Tara to the island, and sitting down beside her, turned to look at her.

"Let me show you." Tara got up, walking over to the monitor on the wall, then called up the video recording of Barb on the porch. "Watch. Tell me what you see."

As Bob watched the video of Barb, his face hardened, and his mouth thinned. "So, she did know about Bill. Okay, so she's a liar and a player. We know that now. We need to show Wyatt and Gwenn."

"Yeah, we do. I know what she's done isn't illegal, but it's deceitful and mean."

"That bitch!" Gwenn growled after Tara and Bob showed her the video later that afternoon. "That fucking bitch. I've never liked her, but I thought it was because she was a bitch of a school teacher. But now, I really hate her." Gwenn flung herself down on the couch beside Wyatt, who had been silent since seeing the video.

Wyatt reached over and rubbed Gwenn's shoulder. "She's shown her true colors, but she doesn't know that we're aware, so that's one up for us."

Still sulking, Gwenn muttered, "Still hate her." That earned a smile from Gwenn, Wyatt, and Bob. "Fuck her, I'm going swimming to work off some of this anger. Anyone else?"

Wyatt and Bob nodded, but Tara shook her head. She needed to be alone.

Tara spent the time with Connal, Gizmo, and Peanut. She took her time brushing each dog and giving them the attention that they hadn't been getting the last couple of days. They went outside and played fetch and walked the beach. It was healing and relaxing for all of them.

Once they were back inside, Tara contacted her friend on Facebook about the two new babies that would be coming to her as soon as it was safe. Her friend had sent some pictures of the two, and she was in love. Of course, she had to show the pictures to Connal, Gizmo, and Peanut, who were lying on the bed with her.

"Look at your new brother and sister. The boy is Indy, and he's 12 years old. He's a pretty sable boy. And look, he's a pirate. Says he lost his eye because of a cornea ulcer. The girl is Annapolis, and she's 11 years old. Gorgeous red and white, like you Connal. Has some kidney issues, so she'll have to have special food. And no, you three won't be stealing her food. So, don't get any ideas. They've been together their whole life. Their mama died, so they'll be coming to live with us soon.

"I think we need to get some ramps built on the decks. That way Mr. Wheelie," Tara looked at Peanut, "and the seniors won't have to fight the steps. And I'm thinking a better ramp in the bedroom and some smaller ones in the living for the furniture would be a good idea. Jumping on and off furniture is bad for your long bodies."

After researching and asking several corgi friends, she decided on the ramps and in no time, had them ordered. Along with new dog dishes, beds, collars and PFDs for the newest furry family members. "Wow, I should have bought stock in pet supplies. I'd be rich. I really need to find a good vet for all of you too."

More researching online and she found a prospective vet that did house calls, in the next town just south of her. Putting the number in her phone for later reference, she would call once all the drug business was over. Then closing up the laptop, Tara laid back, petting Gizmo's ear and Connal's butt while rubbing Peanut with her foot.

It was after dark when Gwenn, Wyatt, and Bob came back into the house from the pool, and since Barb had brought groceries and meals, it was decided dinner would be a grab and growl. They were just finishing their various meals when there was an alert on the front gate.

Since Wyatt was the closest, he checked the monitor. "It's

Fred."

Bob automatically checked to make sure he had his gun, then walked outside to wait with Wyatt.

"Dammit, I want this over," Tara said while she coaxed the dogs into her bedroom and after turning on the radio came back out to wait with Gwenn.

Wyatt, Bob, and Fred walked in a minute later. Tara wasn't feeling overly courteous, but after seeing how bad Fred looked, she exhaled loudly. "We're just finishing dinner. Are you hungry, Fred? Something to drink?" On Fred's negative head shake to both offers, she sat down at the island with Gwenn.

Fred looked at each of them, then scrubbed his hands over his face. "So, my contact called me today. He wanted to know what the status was on the plants. He knows that they're almost ready to harvest and he wanted me to know that he knew. I told him that I would have to get back to him. He didn't like that, but I didn't know what else to say." Fred finished and looked at Bob. "What should I tell him?"

Bob smiled at Fred. He didn't like the guy, but he felt for the guy, in his own way. Fred was screwed, and he knew it, but he was trying to help take the dealer down. "I'm glad you came to tell me. You and I are going to work all the conversations out so that it's like a script for you. That way you'll be more comfortable, and nothing will be a surprise. Just you and me. We'll do it until you are comfortable with it. Okay?" Bob glanced at Wyatt and Tara, and they got the hint. Heading into their respective rooms, they gave Bob and Fred the privacy to work. "Now, why don't you eat some stew? I know you're sick from coming off the tea, but you need food in your belly."

"He's scared and nervous, but he's good. As much as he's a bad guy, he's been a cop for as long, and he has the skills to pull this off," Bob told Tara, Wyatt, and Gwenn later. "We went over every direction the conversation could go. He took notes. He's either playing me, which I don't think he's smart enough to, or he wants this to work. He also gave me the dealer's name, so now I can research him and know exactly who we're dealing with." Tara, Gwenn, and Wyatt all looked at Bob, waiting.

"I can't give you his name, but he's the main guy up here, and he's connected to a very large cartel that runs in Texas and over the Mexican border. This is going to be a massive bust. I need to go call my bosses and let them know what I've found out. We're probably going to need more agents here for the bust too.

"But before I do that, I got Dr. Roxbury's coroner's report. I just got the email a few minutes ago, so let me log onto my laptop so we can see what it says. I haven't read it yet either since I only saw it come in on my cell."

It took Bob a couple of minutes to power up the laptop and open his email. "Okay, so here goes. Edna Jean Roxbury, aged 55 years old, Caucasian female. Gray hair and green eyes. Five feet tall and weighed 100 pounds. Tiny, little lady. Ah, here we go. Cause of death. It's being ruled as drowning, with blunt force trauma to the back of the head and neck contributing." Bob looked up at the three others, huddled around his laptop.

"What caused the blunt force trauma?" Tara asked, squinting her eyes to see the report.

Bob skimmed the report. "According to the report, it appears to have been a hard, curved object, about five inches wide. Length can't be determined because the injury didn't show the ends of the impact."

"Curved object? What the hell would that be?" Gwenn questioned and looked at each of them in turn.

"The coroner states that a drain spade fits the injury pattern," Bob supplied then watched the reactions.

"A shovel," Tara added to Bob's reply after seeing Gwenn's look of confusion.

"Holy fuck! Oh my God, this is just horrible. I was still sort of hoping that maybe she had killed herself and all of this drug plant business was just a terrible coincidence. But now. Just wow. I feel so sad for her. Someone killed her. Someone hit her in the head, with a fucking shovel, then dumped her into the cove to drown. Fuck me." Gwenn slumped onto the nearest stool and stared at the laptop screen.

Wyatt reached over and rubbed Gwenn's back. "What else does the report say, Bob?"

"Well, according to the coroner, she suffered from a closed skull fracture from the blunt force trauma, and that the injury severed her spinal cord at her C3 vertebrae. Says that she would have lost all movement in her arms and legs and that with the extent of the injury, she most likely appeared catatonic. But she was alive. Until she was put into the cove to drown." Bob leaned back and scrubbed his hands over his face, then let them drop to his lap while he looked at the others. No one said anything while they tried to process this information.

Bob leaned forward to continue to read the report. "She had a tattoo, Tara. On her upper right arm. Same place as Bob's. And," he pulled up the picture of Fred's tattoo on the other half of the screen, "it looks like the same tattoo to me."

"Well, son of a bitch," was the response from both Tara and Gwenn.

Wyatt had been quiet during this last part turned to Tara. "What am I missing? Why are we all interested in tattoos all of a sudden?"

Bob looked at Wyatt, then at Tara and Gwenn. "I don't know, Wyatt. But I think it's time for these two ladies to enlighten us on the sudden interest in body art."

"Hold on a minute, I need to get something that we need to show you," Tara said, leaving the kitchen. Coming back in a few moments later, she headed toward the living room. "Why don't we sit down in the living room? This might take a bit."

Once everyone was settled in the living room, which included the dogs, Tara started. "Just to get this out of the way, we weren't withholding anything from you guys. Well, at least not until we saw the tattoo on Fred's arm. We really didn't think that this had anything to do with the plants at all and it still might not." Tara handed the drawing to Bob who looked at it then turned it so that it resembled an upside down pitchfork. He gave it to Wyatt, who glanced at it and stared at Tara.

"Why do you have a drawing of the tattoo that Fred has and that we now know Dr. Roxbury had?" Wyatt asked quietly, rubbing Gizmo's ears.

"I found it in the Batcave the same day I finally got the stupid thing open. Just be quiet and let me explain, then you can yell and interrogate me," she added when both Wyatt and Bob started opening their mouths. "I found it in the Batcave and, at first, Gwenn and I thought that it was the reason that Dr. Roxbury was so secluded and secretive. That she had found a Viking rune in Maine. In the archaeology world, that would be a huge find and something you would hide so that no one could take credit for it. But then, after we went through her field notes and photos, we ruled it out as any great find. See, she had meticulous notes and photos on all the artifacts she had found on the property, but with the rune, she had a drawing. That was it. Just one hand drawing of a Viking rune. Now, if you had found a find of a lifetime, would you just draw a picture of it? No. So, Gwenn and I ruled the rune out as something she liked. That was until we saw the tattoo on Fred's arm the other day. That's why I asked to see if Dr. Roxbury had a tattoo. It could just be a tattoo that they got together in Florida, while they were on vacation. But, it's a rather odd one to get, in my opinion." Tara finished and after taking a gulp of her beer waited for the questions.

"Why?" Bob was the first to talk. "Why does that tattoo seem odd to you?"

"Well, Dr. Roxbury's field of study was in Peru. It would make more sense to me for her to get a tattoo with a Peruvian influence. In addition, of all the books and articles downstairs, there is not one thing having to do with Viking runes. It just seems off to me." Tara shrugged her shoulders and looked at Wyatt and Bob, hoping they didn't think she was crazy.

Bob, who had been petting Connal's belly, returned Tara's look. "I'm going to ask Fred when and where he got that tattoo and if Dr. Roxbury got hers at the same time. It could be as simple as a vacation tattoo, but we need to rule it out as anything else. I wish you would have told me about this when you saw it on Fred's arm, but I get why you didn't. Is that everything?" After Tara and Gwenn had nodded that that was indeed everything, Bob pushed up from his couch and brushed the fur off his pants. "Okay then. I really need to go call in and discuss the latest details with my bosses. I have a feeling it's going to take some time, so I'll say good night now."

CHAPTER FIFTEEN

After Bob's phone call to his supervisors, it was decided that this bust would indeed be a large one and that more agents on the ground would be needed. Bob had asked, and Tara had agreed, to allow her place to be the base camp for the DEA agents.

So, now there were over 40 extra people on the property and it bugged her. She tried not to let it, but it did. Bob had been sure to tell the agents to respect her privacy, and they were. She could only see them if she went looking for them. But it didn't matter. She knew they were there.

Tara hadn't seen much of Bob or Wyatt, for that matter, since the agents had arrived. She knew they were with the other agents, preparing for the drug raid.

During a quick stop in, Bob let her and Gwenn know that Fred had contacted the dealer and told him that the plants were almost ready for harvesting, but that this time he would be bringing the entire plant, not just the leaves. That with Dr. Roxbury being dead, he didn't know how to harvest the leaves without destroying the plant. And that Fred was waiting for a call back on the meetup time. As bad as Fred was, he had always made sure that the dealing was not done in his area. In the past, he would travel outside of town, south about an hour, and do the exchange. With this information, Bob had staged more agents south.

So, they were waiting again. Which was wearing on all of them. Tara had taken to eating her Pop-Tarts or anything sweet and Gwenn was overworking herself. She was at the restaurant from opening to closing, then up most of the night doing bills, ordering supplies or designing new menus.

Connal, Gizmo, and Peanut were cranky, snapping and snarling at each other at different times. It was all for show, but it concerned Tara that all the stress in the house was taking a toll on her pups.

Finally, Friday morning, as they were all sitting around the kitchen table, Fred called Bob.

"It's set for tomorrow night at midnight, in Windcliff."

"Okay, good. You'll need a van to transport the plants. You do this, just in case they're watching you. I doubt they are, but do what you normally did for the exchange. When you have a van, call me back, and I'll tell you where the warehouse is so that you can load up the plants. You'll have to do it yourself. Again, just in case they are watching. Is it the same place as you've done the deal before? How many men are usually involved?" Bob took notes, asked more questions, answered a few questions and just as he was about to hang up, Tara tapped on her right shoulder.

Nodding, Bob asked, "Oh, hey Fred one more question. When did you get your tattoo? Okay, thanks. What is it anyway? It looks Celtic or ancient. What about Dr. Roxbury? She had the same tattoo on her arm. Ah. Okay, thanks, Fred. Try to get some sleep and eat. This will all be over real soon." After ending the call, Bob turned to the others.

"He said he got his tattoo when he was 18 years old, after getting drunk. That Dr. Roxbury liked the tattoo and decided to get a matching one when they were on vacation in Florida. It's a rune or Celtic symbol or something that he liked, and he picked it out of a book at the tattoo place. So, it looks like it was just a cool tattoo that Dr. Roxbury liked and drew a picture so that she could get one too." He stood up and headed for the door. "I need to go talk to the team and let them know the latest info. I'll see you all later."

After Gwenn had left for work, Tara and Wyatt went into preparation mode.

Wyatt did a slow walk about and checked all the cameras and flood lights around the house. Then did the same thing for all the security devices inside the house and its buildings. He trimmed the bushes around the house and did anything and everything he could to stay busy.

Tara went into The Lab and cleaned it. When she was done, it was spotless. She had all the tables broke down and stacked neatly in one of the corners of the room. Tara hadn't tried to tackle removing the trickle system, but she had taken all the thin hoses and wound them up as high as she could. She'd have to get help to have them removed, but that would be later. While cleaning up the room, she had decided to make it a panic room, of sorts.

This would be where she would keep the dogs tomorrow night. So, she spent time setting up some air mattresses and bringing down pillows and blankets. Tara took down water and food for the dogs along with bowls, dishes and leashes. Then she took down human snacks and drinks.

"Getting your exercise today, aren't you?" Tara said to the three dogs, after the tenth trip down the steps.

"Need to see about having access to the outside installed in here. One way in, one way out is a bad thing. But that will have to do for now."

The last things she brought down, she took out of the safe she had hidden in her closet. "Just in case," she told herself. Standing with her hands on her hips, she looked at The Lab. Nodding, it was as safe and secure and comfy as she could make it.

As she was closing up the floor to the Batcave and The Lab, Wyatt came looking for her. So, she reopened the rooms and showed him her preparation.

Wyatt opened the mini fridge to look in and nodded. "This

is good. Nice and comfortable for when we're all down here tomorrow night."

"Oh, I thought you'd be with Bob."

"No, we talked. He's going to have 40 agents with him, so they don't need a non-agent in the way. I'm staying here with you, Gwenn, and the dogs. We'll hole up down here until he comes and gets us." Tara didn't want to admit it, but she felt a sense of relief knowing that Wyatt would be there tomorrow night too.

"Well, in that case, we need to add to the supplies. I only got for Gwenn and me," she said as she headed up to get another air mattress and bedding, along with more bottled water and snacks.

While Tara continued the prep of The Lab, Wyatt called, then texted Bob to make sure that they had cell coverage in the room when the doors were closed. Opening the door back up, he saw Tara stocking the bathroom in the Batcave with plenty of toilet paper and towels, etc. "Just in case we're down here for a bit. Can't have us running out of toilet paper."

"Good idea, but what about the pups? What if they have to go?" Wyatt asked while looking at the three dogs, who had each chosen an air mattress and were each busy furring up the sheets and blankets.

He saw that Peanut had picked his bed and was now lying on his pillow. Shaking his head, Wyatt chuckled. "They know I'm not fond of dogs, don't they? That's why he's on my pillow. Damn dog." But it was said in more of a loving manner than anger.

Looking at Peanut on Wyatt's pillow, Tara laughed. "Dogs are very smart. He knows you say you don't like dogs, but deep down, you do. After all, you cuddled with him." Then she laughed at the death look Wyatt threw her. "He's just trying to get you to realize it. I have puppy pee pads for them if they need to go. Hopefully, it won't come to that."

Later that evening, Tara and Wyatt showed Gwenn and Bob the set up in The Lab.

"Looks good and it's secure. This is all just a precaution and there really shouldn't be any problems here, but I'm leaving a couple of agents here, just in case. I don't see any reason why anyone would come here, but better safe than sorry. One night of being inconvenienced, then this is all done, and you can put it behind you. I have something to add to this. Give me a minute."

Bob returned a few minutes later and tried to hand each of them a flak jacket, but Wyatt and Tara declined and then pointed to their own jackets already in The Lab.

"Should have known you two would have your armor. Again, it's just a precaution, but Gwenn, let me show you how to put this on."

He led her off to the side and instructed on the easiest way to put on the flak jacket, then helped her take it off. After getting Gwenn into the jacket, then back out, Bob stated, "You'll have your guns down here as well." When Tara, Gwenn, and Wyatt all had nodded, Bob went back upstairs and this time reappeared with three AR-15s slung over his shoulder and an ammo box of magazines.

Tara immediately started shaking her head and put up her hand. "That's not necessary, Bob."

"Goddammit, Tara. Yes, it is. Don't argue with me." Bob cut her off, figuring that this would be the fight of the day with Tara. He knew she didn't like automatic rifles, but he had to make sure they were ready for anything, God forbid something went terribly wrong.

Tara sighed. "Why do you and Wyatt think that I'm always going to argue when I disagree?" Walking over to a closet along the inside wall of The Lab, she opened it then stepped aside so that they could look in. "I have it covered." Inside, were two AR-15s and several boxes of magazines, fully loaded. "Figured this would be the last stand area," Tara responded.

Bob slowly shook his head and put his arm around her shoulders. "I'm sorry. I really need to remember who I'm dealing with. I should have known you would have everything prepared. But there are three of you and only two rifles.

Wyatt—"

It was Wyatt's turn to shake his head. "I brought my own, so there is no need, Bob. Thanks, though. I'll bring mine down here later tonight and put it in here with the others."

Nodding his head, Bob looked at them. "Okay, well that's settled. Now we just wait until tomorrow."

Gwenn, who had been unusually quiet during all of this, decided it would be good to sit down on one of the air mattresses, then put her head in her hands. "Holy fuck. This just got really real."

Tara glanced at the men, then sat beside Gwenn and leaned into her. "Gwenn, I know this is a lot. We can get you out of here and safe, just say the word. No harm, no foul and we won't think any less of you. This is damn scary and possibly dangerous."

Gwenn shook her head and leaned back. "I'm not going anywhere. This is just a lot to take in. Give me a few minutes, okay? I just need to get used to the fact that this is really fucking happening and that there are real scary guns down here. I'm sorry, just freaked out there for a minute. This is all for show anyway. Nothing is going to happen here, except for lots of movies and popcorn."

Bob was gone when Tara, Wyatt, and Gwenn got up the next morning. They knew they wouldn't see him until this was over now. So, after a quick breakfast, they tried to keep themselves busy to keep their minds off what would be happening later that night.

Wyatt started working on the dog ramps for the decks, with Gwenn helping him. Tara could hear them bickering back and forth and the occasional laugh while she caught up on the laundry and house cleaning.

When that was done, she turned to the dogs, much to their chagrin. "Since we're all going to be stuck in here together, you three need baths. You smell like fish and seaweed."

Gwenn and Wyatt came in for lunch just as she finished Peanut. Coming over to sit at the island with them, she laid her head on the counter. "Damn dogs are going to kill me. It's like wrestling greased pigs when it comes to bath water." Sitting back up, Tara looked at the laptop with the ever-present Fred dot on it. It wasn't moving, but Tara couldn't look away from it.

Wyatt reached over to squeeze her hand. "This will all be over soon."

"I took a TV and DVD player down into The Lab, just in case we get bored." Gwenn had been watching the Fred dot as well, but now turned to focus on her friends. It calmed her to know that they would all be together while the drug deal was happening.

Tara turned away from the monitor and focused on Gwenn. "That's a great idea. And the Batcave has a microwave so some popcorn would be good too." She needed to remember that this was all new to Gwenn and she needed to focus on her friend and not on Fred. There were DEA agents to do that. Smiling now, she reached out and squeezed Gwenn's arm.

Wyatt, seeing that Tara was trying to lighten the mood for Gwenn mirrored Tara and reached over and grabbed Gwenn's hand. "We'll have a big-assed slumber party in the Batcave. Just the three of us. And the three mutts. Popcorn and movies sounds great."

Releasing Gwenn's hand, Wyatt pushed up from the island. "I'm going back outside to finish the ramps. You still up for helping me, Gwenn?" At Gwenn's smile and nod, they headed back outside to work.

A couple of hours later, Tara and Gwenn were sitting on the porch, while Wyatt ran to town to get some more screws for the ramps.

Tara took the ball that Connal, followed closely by Gizmo and Peanut, had brought back and chucked it down toward the cove. "This way they'll be tired tonight and not be overly obnoxious down there."

As the dogs took off after the ball, barking and body checking each other, Tara looked over at Gwenn. "How are you doing with this now that you've had a chance to process it? We can still get you somewhere safe."

Gwenn glanced over at Tara and was quiet for a minute. After considering it for a moment, she shook her head. "No, I'm not going anywhere. I'm as good as I can be about all of this. I'd rather be where I know and trust people, then in a room somewhere, by myself." Gwenn turned to face Tara fully. "Those guns in the closet, those are yours? Like you own them?"

Tara hesitated for a moment but then turned to face Gwenn and nodded. "Yeah, those are mine."

"And you have your own body armor?"

"Yeah, I do."

"Are you an agent? Or a spy?" Gwenn whispered now, after looking around to make sure no one was around to hear.

Tara smiled and chuckled. "No, I'm not an agent or a spy. Nothing exciting like that. I just had a job in the past that required that equipment, and when I left that job, I took it with me. That's it. Nothing James Bond or anything."

"That's all you're going to tell me, isn't it?" Gwenn asked, crossing her arms and leaning back in the chair.

Tara slowly nodded. "Yeah. For now. This just isn't the time for that conversation, but we'll talk about it later. Okay?"

"Yeah, okay. But, I've heard that before. That's the nice 'it's not going to happen, Gwenn. Mind your own damn business,' deflection," Gwenn grumbled.

"No, it's not. We'll talk. Just not now. Now we have to get ourselves mentally ready for tonight, and if we talk about why I have this equipment, it'll take away from our preparation. After this, I promise, we'll sit down, and I'll answer your questions." Tara looked at Gwenn, waiting to see if the promise would appease Gwenn for now.

Gwenn smiled and looked over at Tara. "Okay. Deal. We'll chat after all of this. I have your promise."

After spending the afternoon outside, either working on the dog ramps or tiring out the dogs, Tara, Gwenn, and Wyatt had decided on cheese, meats, and crackers for dinner. Wyatt supplemented it with chips and salsa. They weren't really hungry, but they went through the motions for the normalcy of the actions.

They were finishing up when there was a knock on the door, which caused pandemonium in the house. Connal, Gizmo, and Peanut tried to beat each other to the door, barking and slipping the entire time. By the time Tara got them to shut up and move, the agent on the other side of the door had to be coaxed to come in. He did so, but only two steps into the house.

"Just wanted to check in with you folks. Make sure you have everything you need?" he said, while cautiously looking at the three dogs now trying to get him to notice them.

Tara smiled and nodded her head toward the dogs. "You can pet them if you want. Put your hand down for them to smell it."

The agent slowly lowered his hand, and Connal as the leader sniffed the hand, then deeming the new person satisfactory, flopped over onto his side to demand belly rubs. The agent laughed and provided the belly rubs. This caused Gizmo and Peanut to do the same thing.

Wyatt cleared his throat and stepped forward. "Thanks, we're good here. We'll be heading down to the safe room in about an hour."

Standing back up from being on his knees and dusting off his pants, the agent nodded. "Roger that. Oh, Bob wanted me to give this to you," he said as he handed Wyatt a tablet. "It's a live feed to his camera. You should be able to see and hear the deal go down. He thought you all might be interested in seeing the bad guys lose tonight. Good luck and this should all be over very soon. If you need anything, or if something doesn't feel right, make sure to call over the radio, and we'll be here in a matter of seconds." Smiling and shaking each of their hands, he knelt down to pet the dogs one last time, then left.

Just before 9 PM, Tara let the pups into the riding arena for their final out before going into The Lab. Gwenn and Wyatt went with her. It was an unspoken rule now that they stayed together. Wyatt got the pups to run and play in the arena, to wear them out and to get rid of some of the nervous energy he was feeling.

After the pups had slowed down to just trotting around and smelling, he walked to each door of the arena and confirmed it was locked and alarmed. Tara and Gwenn had just done the exact same thing, but he still did his check. It wasn't that he didn't trust them. He did. It was more of having control of the situation. Verifying everything was locked and secure gave him control.

The three humans and three dogs then took the breezeway to the equipment barn and checked all those doors. Wyatt went a step further and unplugged the garage doors in there. Then he locked the door leading to the breezeway as they went back to the riding arena. In the main breezeway, Tara locked the riding arena door. They next went to the gym and pool building and secured it. Lastly, was the garage where Wyatt again unplugged all the garage doors.

Finally, they entered the kitchen, and Tara locked the door leading to the breezeway. Wyatt went to the monitor to make sure that all the inside and outside cameras were on in the arena, barn, pool, and garage. Then he turned on all the flood lights.

As a unit of six, they walked and checked all the doors and windows in every room of the house and that all the blinds were drawn. They left the lights on in the rooms so it would be easier to see on the camera and the harder for someone to sneak in.

After everything was locked up, Wyatt went back to the monitor and made sure all the main house doors and windows were alarmed and then turned on all the inside cameras.

Wyatt turned to Tara and Gwenn. "Okay, that's it. We're as secure as we're going to be so let's grab anything else you might have forgotten and let's get downstairs."

While Tara and Gwenn left to grab a few last-minute

things, Wyatt made sure that he had the current camera feed on his laptop and the charger and then followed the girls and the dogs downstairs.

After closing up the entrance to the Batcave, they each found a spot to make their own. Wyatt took the couch and opened up his laptop to watch the property cameras. He set the tablet that the DEA agent had given them beside the laptop on the end table. Plugging both in, he waited and watched. He could hear Bob talking to various people, but it was just basic conversation. They were all in wait mode.

Gwenn went into The Lab to lie on one of the air mattresses. Gizmo and Peanut had followed her, so she spent some time loving on them, seeking the comfort from them that she was needing. After a little bit, she worked on setting up the TV and DVD player. Putting in an NCIS DVD, Gwenn tried to relax and watch the show all the while petting Gizmo and Peanut.

Tara was on the other side of the Batcave, trying to play on her laptop, but Connal, who had stuck close to her all day, was now trying to sit on her lap, which was very out of the ordinary for him. He was not a cuddly dog or a lap dog by any stretch of the imagination. But he had wiggled into Tara's lap and was now upside down, getting belly rubs.

"You make it damn hard to play on my computer, you know that, right? You know I'm worried, don't ya? Thank you for being a lovey today and cuddling with me. This will all be over soon, and you can get back to being Mr. Aloof Corgi," Tara told him, all the while rubbing his belly. Anytime she slowed down the belly rubs, he would kick her hand with his foot, reminding her that he was giving up his space to make her feel better.

Twenty minutes later, Connal had enough and hopping off Tara's lap, he went over to lay on Wyatt's feet. Which resulted in more swats of his little paw to get the pets to continue whenever Wyatt stopped rubbing him with his foot.

Tara came over and joined Wyatt on the couch and watched the house cameras and Bob's feed. "I always hated this part. The waiting. Most times, it's worse than the actual mission." Leaning forward, Tara listened to Bob coaching the agents again on what was going to happen and how. "He's a good cheerleader."

Wyatt chuckled and leaned forward, elbows on his knees. "Yeah, he is. He's keeping everyone calm and on board. They can have nerves now, but not when it starts. He'll make sure they're ready. Once the mission starts, you're on autopilot, but before, everything that could go wrong is in your head. Gwenn ask you about your arsenal and armor?" Wyatt glanced over at Tara in time to see her grimace.

"Yeah, she did. Wanted to know if I was an agent or a spy."

Wyatt laughed. "Too much NCIS."

"Yeah. I'm going to have to sit down and tell her what we did before she makes up her mind that we're sleeper agents for the KGB or something."

"Yeah, you are. Enjoy that interrogation," Wyatt remarked and turned his attention back to the laptop and the tablet.

By 1030 PM, the anxiety had Gwenn pacing and mumbling to herself. Tara and Wyatt didn't know what she was mumbling, and they chose to ignore it. They knew it was her way of handling the tension.

The activity on Bob's camera was picking up and he was talking nonstop to Fred now. Building him up, telling him he would do fine, that he had just made bad choices, but tonight, he could redeem himself. There were conversations with the other agents too. Lots of last minute plans and rehashing orders.

At 1100 PM, Gwenn had stopped pacing. She came into The Batcave to join Tara and Wyatt, and after grabbing another chair, joined them in watching and listening to Bob on the tablet that Wyatt had moved to the desk so that they could all see the screen.

Sighing, Tara stood up and walked into The Lab and after petting the pups that had deserted them for the air mattresses, came back out wearing her flak jacket.

She handed Gwenn hers and helped her get into it. "It's just a precaution," Tara said, putting her hands on Gwenn's shoulders after making sure that it was secure and snug on Gwenn. Gwenn just nodded and tried to smile. Patting her shoulders, then giving her a quick hug, Tara went to Wyatt to make sure he was suited up.

Wyatt had donned his jacket but allowed Tara to verify it was snug and secure. He then returned the favor.

Touching her cheek, Wyatt turned to the bag on the floor and removed his AR-15 and magazines. Loading the magazine into the rifle and pulling the charging handle back, he pushed the release. He leaned the rifle against the wall beside where he was sitting on the couch. He didn't put the safety on because God forbid he needed it, he didn't want to have to try to remember to take the safety off.

Next, he took out his 9mm and checked to make sure it was locked and loaded. Placing the gun back into its holster at the small of his back, he turned to Gwenn.

"Gwenn," he said, holding out his hand. She put her gun in his hand for him to check it. "Do you want to wear it or have it close?" Wyatt asked as he made sure her handgun was also loaded and ready.

Gwenn crossed her arms or tried to. Now she understood why people that wore flak jackets always held the opening at the neck with their hands. Crossing your arms was next to impossible with the bulkiness of the jacket in the way. She shook her head to get rid of the silliness of that thought. "Close, I'm afraid I might shoot myself by mistake, I'm so nervous."

Wyatt nodded and put it on the desk in front of Gwenn. Patting Gwenn's cheek, he looked her in the eye, just to make sure she was listening to him. "Nothing to worry about. This is just us being over prepared."

Gwenn gave him a quick smile and patted his cheek back. "Rather over prepared than under. Thanks."

Tara had already checked her handgun, but now went to the closet and made sure each of the AR-15s were locked and loaded. Coming back out to the Batcave, she leaned hers against the wall much the same as Wyatt had done.

She took the third rifle over to Gwenn. "It's locked and loaded. It's just like any gun, Gwenn, just point and shoot. The safety is off."

Gwenn nodded and swallowed loudly. "Okay. So, if it gets to this stage, we grab these rifles and go into The Lab, to that back corner where all the extra bullets are?"

Tara nodded. "Yeah. That's our Alamo. But, it's not going to get to that point. There will be no problems here, other than the three of us being very uncomfortable in these jackets and having to smell corgi, and Wyatt, farts." Tara smiled and made gagging sounds.

Gwenn chuckled and smiled back. "The worst. Thanks for trying to lighten this up."

Wyatt looked up at them from his place on the couch. "I do not fart. It's always those dogs. They eat rabbit shit, after all."

By 1150 PM, Tara, Gwenn, and Wyatt were all leaned forward in their seats, watching the laptop monitor and Bob's feed. The pups had felt the increase in nervousness and by some unspoken dog rule, they had each come to one of the humans to provide support. Connal was lying on Tara's feet while Peanut sat up beside Wyatt for the continual head rubs he was providing. And somehow, Gizmo had gotten onto Gwenn's lap and was snuggled into her as tight as she could be getting ear scratches.

Bob and his team were all in their positions around the warehouse that had been set up for the deal. There was no talking now from Bob. They couldn't even hear Bob breathing. Everyone, the agents at the warehouse and the three of them in the Batcave, was waiting for Fred to arrive in the moving van with the plants.

At midnight on the dot, Fred arrived in the moving van. Stopping the van at the middle roll-up door of the warehouse, he honked three quick beeps and four long ones. Then he waited for the door to go up before driving the van into the warehouse. The door was immediately lowered.

Tara, Wyatt, and Gwenn were all on the edges of their seats watching Bob's feed with just the occasional glance at the house monitor.

"This is better than NCIS," Gwenn whispered, leaning closer to the screen and occasionally leaning left or right.

After the door had rolled down behind Fred's van, Bob instructed the agents to slowly and quietly move closer to the warehouse. They knew from watching the building all day that there were no outside sentries and they knew how many people were inside from watching them arrive, and from the thermal readers they had. Slowly and leapfrogging closer and closer to the warehouse they moved.

"It's almost like a ballet," Gwenn remarked. "They're so smooth and quiet. It's like they're dancing."

"I wish we had the feed from the inside," Wyatt grumbled, glancing at Tara.

"I know. It sucks just having the one feed. But I'm betting that we aren't getting all the feed because Bob doesn't want Gwenn to see if something goes wrong." Tara jerked her chin in Gwenn's direction.

Wyatt furrowed his brow and nodded. "Yeah, that's smart. She doesn't need to see all of it. Just enough to see that the bad guy gets caught and that Bob is okay."

Just as the agents got to where they could breach the warehouse with the smoke canisters and door rams, Bob called a halt to any further movement.

"I wonder what he's hearing," Wyatt questioned, leaning closer still to the tablet and squinting his eyes, hoping that he might see what had made Bob halt the team.

Tara was up on her feet and leaning on the desk, trying to hear anything that wasn't right. "He stopped forward movement. I really hope Fred isn't screwing this up."

Tara no sooner got the words out of her mouth, when they heard a gunshot come from inside the warehouse. "Son of a bitch!" Tara sat down heavily in her chair and put her head in her hands.

"Fuck." Wyatt put his hand on Tara's back and rubbed in circles. "Gwenn, come here," he added when he saw that it had finally hit Gwenn what had just happened. Standing up, he pulled her into a hug and held her head to his shoulder while she shook.

At the same time Tara, Gwenn, and Wyatt were reacting to the gunshot in the warehouse, so was Bob. "MOVE MOVE MOVE!" Bob bellowed to the agents. "Take that fucking building, now!"

The agents swarmed the warehouse from all sides. Using battering rams, they broke through the personnel doors, tossing in flash bangs to obscure their entry and to confuse the people inside. There were shouts of "Federal Agent! Don't move! Get down on the floor!" from all directions. But that didn't stop the men in the warehouse from shooting at them.

Bob led his group of ten agents through the main entrance, and they were immediately in a firefight. Taking cover, Bob peeked around the container he was behind. He couldn't see Fred. There had been a gunshot, and Bob figured Fred had been shot because the dealer didn't believe his story. But he couldn't see Fred anywhere so he couldn't be sure. It could all have been a setup, and Fred had turned the tables on him and the agents.

"Goddammit, let's finish this," he yelled into his mic. In a matter of moments, eight of the men inside were dead, with another three injured and handcuffed.

Bob stood up from behind the crates he had taken cover behind. "Fan out and search this place for the driver."

He walked over to one of the wounded men that was sitting up and with his hands cuffed behind his back. "Which one of you is Cortez? You?" Bob pointed to the other handcuffed man. "That one? One of the dead ones?" But the man on the ground wouldn't talk. He wouldn't even look at Bob. "Okay, that's fine. We'll play it your way," Bob said then ordered another agent to photograph each man, dead and alive and do a facial recognition scan. Bob had handed out photos of the main guy before the raid, but he had learned the hard way not to trust that sort of verification. Facial recognition was the best way to verify which one of the men was Cortez.

An agent on the far side of the building stood up and waved at Bob. "Over here. I found the driver."

Bob rushed over to where two agents were kneeling beside a prone body. It was Fred, lying in a pool of blood that was slowly getting bigger. "Fuck. Get me a first aid kit, pronto."

Bob knelt down beside Fred. "You did good, Fred. You did real good. No, don't try to move. Just stay calm. The EMTs will be here in just a minute."

Bob took the bandage that the agent behind him handed him and applied pressure to the chest wound, but it didn't slow the bleeding. Bob knew that with a wound like that, no pressure would stop the bleed out. But he still did it. He had to.

"I'm sorry. I tried," Fred gasped and grabbed Bob's arm. "I tried, but he knew. I don't know how he knew, but he did. He knew that I had set him up."

"I know you did. I heard you. I know you tried and you did good. Is there anyone that you want me to call? Anyone you want to talk to? I can call them for you. Let you talk to them now."

Fred closed his eyes and tears leaked out of the corners. "No, I don't have anyone to say anything to. Just make sure I get back home. I have to get back home. The town folks will take care of me."

Still applying pressure, Bob promised. "I'll make sure that you get home, Fred."

""I didn't kill Edna...Bill did...He...hit her in the head with a shovel." He took a shaky breath and gripped Bob's arm again, trying to pull himself up.

Bob put his hand on Fred's shoulder to keep him still. "You need to stay still, Fred. And try to calm down. I believe you. Can you tell me why Bill killed Edna? And do you know where the shovel is that he used? I'll make sure that Bill fries for her death, I promise. But I need you to tell me what you know. Do it for Edna."

Coughing up some blood, Fred loosened his grip on Bob's arm. "Bill was mad at something that she had done, and he snapped. He told me he picked up the closest thing and since they were in the equipment barn, it was a shovel. I don't know what he did with the shovel. He called me after and told me that he needed help, so I went over and helped put her in the cove. I got the canoe, and I rowed out to the middle of the cove, and I pushed her in. But I didn't kill her. Bill did. Bill hit her with the shovel. Not me. I didn't want to, but Bill is family. Family first. It's the code. I loved her," Fred gasped out.

"Okay, Fred, you did well. Try to calm down now and focus on me. I'm not leaving your side and the medics will be here real soon."

There were no more words. Just slower and slower breaths until…nothing. Bob sat beside Fred and kept his hand on his shoulder until the EMTs arrived.

Standing up, Bob looked down at Fred, then told the EMTs, "Make sure the local funeral home in Eriksport is notified."

Tara, Gwenn, and Wyatt had watched and heard the entire breach of the building, the shootout and the death of Fred from Bob's camera.

Gwenn sat, silently wiping tears from her eyes. "Oh my God, that really just happened? Fred is dead? Holy shit."

"Yeah, it did. I'm sorry, Gwenn. I know you were friends with Fred." Tara came over to hug Gwenn.

"Gwenn, I'm really sorry. And I'm sorry you had to see him die. It's a hard thing to witness." Wyatt walked over and wrapped his arms around both of them. They stayed that way for a bit, then Wyatt extracted himself to go watch the house cameras.

Tara went into The Lab for a little alone time and to be with the dogs. Lying down on the mattress and cuddling with her pups, Tara let her mind work on everything that had happened.

Yes, Fred was a bad guy, but seeing him die still affected Tara. He had been a drug dealer. And he had killed Dr. Roxbury, even though he had said Bill did it. But the coroner's report didn't lie. Yes, Dr. Roxbury had blunt force trauma to her head, but she had died from drowning. Fred admitted that he pushed her into the cove, so he had killed Dr. Roxbury. Did he know that he had? That was something that would go to his grave with him. He had tried to right the wrong of the drugs, though. So, maybe he didn't know she had been alive. But it was finally over. All the nastiness of the death and the drugs. She thought she would feel better, but she didn't. The shootout had sobered her excitement on getting the property to herself, without the underlying drug and death business. Eventually, she slept.

Gwenn came into The Lab, and after covering Tara with a blanket and petting the dogs, she laid down and fell asleep.

But Wyatt stayed awake and watched the cameras. "Just to be sure," he told himself.

He kept watch until he saw Bob and his agents drive through the main gate. That's when he finally removed the flak jacket and cleared the AR-15 that was beside him. As he was getting ready to go wake the girls, Bob flipped the switch to open the entrance to the Batcave.

Coming down the steps, Bob looked at Wyatt, then at the two women sleeping with the dogs. "It's over. You can all come out of the bunker."

Wyatt walked over to Bob and gave him a quick hug. "Thanks for the tablet to watch and hear. That was brutal. You alright?"

Bob returned the quick hug and rubbed his face. "Yeah, I'm okay. It was fucking brutal. Fred was a bad guy, plain and simple. But he was still a person, you know? Any death upsets me." Bob stopped talking because Gwenn had come into the Batcave and stopped to look at him.

"Fuck it," Gwenn said, before launching herself at him and kissing him. Hard and long.

Wyatt turned his head to give them some privacy and saw Tara standing there, with a matching smirk on her face.

"Well that answers that, doesn't it?" Tara chuckled, then led the dogs up the steps and outside for some fresh air, and potty breaks followed closely by Wyatt.

"Um, hi." Gwenn leaned back but didn't let go of Bob.

Bob kept his hands on Gwenn's hips and smiled. "Hi, yourself. So, that answers my question if you liked me."

"Really? You want to be a smart ass right after I kissed you?" Gwenn punched him in the shoulder, but smiled and led the way up the stairs and outside. "Oh, this feels so good. Help me get this thing off, will ya?" After Bob had helped her out of the flak jacket, Gwenn looked at him. "Fred was an ass, but he's still one of ours. That was nice of you to make sure he comes home."

"I promised him I'd make sure he got home. It was the right thing to do. The town doesn't need to know all the dirty details. It wouldn't serve any purpose at all." Bob rubbed Gwenn's shoulders to help loosen up the muscles from wearing the flak jacket all evening.

"I was so scared when you all rushed into that building. There was so much noise. How do you do that? It's not anything like they show on TV," Gwenn said, putting her hands on his hands, stilling his movement.

"No, it's not. But not one agent was hurt. Not even a broken fingernail. That's a good mission in any book. I'm going to go take an hour long, hot shower. Then I want coffee and food, and I'll tell you all what we found out about the dealer."

EPILOGUE

Two Weeks Later

It had been two weeks since the raid on the drug deal and the DEA agents were all packed and gone.

Bob had left and gone back to Washington D.C., and Wyatt was back in Ohio, after spending a week just relaxing with Tara and Gwenn after the drug bust.

Fred had been buried in a private memorial, and the town was starting to get back to normal.

Barb had decided to move to Montreal with her sister and had movers come to the property and pack up her house, which Gwenn laid claim immediately.

"This way, we each have our own space, and we don't have to incur the expense of building a place for me. It's perfect," Gwenn had stated as she had moved the few things she had a Tara's into her new house

So, Tara was now alone. Truly alone in her house. Of course, she had the dogs, but there weren't people in and out of her space. And she was thoroughly enjoying her space. She had finished putting the new ramps to the couches in the living room. Then with treats, she made sure each dog knew to use the ramp. "No more jumping you guys."

Now, she stood in the kitchen and looked at the monitor and waited. After what seemed like forever, she saw a car pull up to the gate. After verifying that the driver was who she thought it was, she went outside. Anxious and excited, she waited for the car to stop and for the driver to get out.

Walking over, she held out her hand. "Hi, I'm Tara. Nice to meet you in person. How was the drive? Any issues finding the place?"

"Hello. I'm Cecelia. Nice to meet you too. It was a very easy drive, and no, your directions were spot on. You ready to meet these two?" Cecelia said returning the handshake and smiling.

"Yeah, I am. Thank you for bringing them to me. I'm going to have to buy a van if I keep this up."

"Oh, no worries. I love this area. I'm so happy that they lucked out with a perfect retirement home." Cecelia opened the door to the back seat and unhooked Indy from the seatbelt. Lifting him up, she put him on the ground. "Meet Indy."

As soon as Indy's feet hit the ground, he dropped and rolled and wiggled on his back. Tara had a good chance to look at her newest boy. Indy was a sable Pembroke, like Peanut. Where Connal was red, Indy had reddish hair with black roots. He had the white socks on his feet, white chest and underbelly and two white areas over his shoulders. He also had the little nub instead of a tail. Since he was an older corgi, his face was mostly white, and his right eye was a permanent wink since he had lost that eye. After Indy got done with his rolling, he came over to Tara and sat down in front of her and gave her the best corgi smile.

"Well, hello baby boy. How are you?"

While Tara was on her knees petting and getting loves from Indy, Cecelia unhooked Annapolis from her seatbelt and put her on the ground beside Indy. "And meet Ms. Annapolis."

Tara turned her attention to Annapolis now. Unlike her brother, Annapolis came right to Tara for loves. "Oh, aren't you a pretty girl."

Annapolis answered with a lick on Tara's chin, which got

her more loves. Annapolis was red and white, much like Connal and she had white socks, white on her belly and chest. The white from her chest wrapped up her left shoulder and ended in the middle of her neck. Like Indy, her face was mostly white with just a little bit of a blaze between her eyes. On her left side, she had a large growth, which Tara had learned was a lipoma. It wasn't dangerous to her since it was just a collection of fat cells. The previous owner had tried to have it removed, but the lipoma had grown between Annapolis's ribs and muscle, and it was just too risky to continue with the removal. Tara made a mental note to keep an eye on it to make sure it didn't start to interfere with Annapolis's quality of life.

Tara stayed on her knees, petting and loving the two newcomers for another minute, before standing up. "Well, I'm just rude. Can I offer you a cup of coffee? Water? Bathroom?"

Cecelia shook her head. "Not rude in the least. Your welcome to these two alleviates any issues I might have had about leaving them here. I need to get back on the road. I have lunch plans with an old friend of mine about an hour south of here. But thank you for the offer."

Getting back into the car and putting on her seatbelt, Cecelia looked at the two dogs, then Tara. "Please keep me up on them. Maybe a post on Facebook about them every so often. I would love to see how they're doing. They really are sweet, little babies." Wiping a tear from her eye, she waved and left.

"Let's walk around a little bit, okay? Give you a chance to stretch your little legs and relax a bit before you meet your new brothers and sister. They're going to love you two," Tara said as she took the leashes off the two and let them wander around and smell and take care of business. Tara sat down on the grass and watched them as they explored their new yard.

Finally, they came back to her, and one sat on each side of her, leaning on her. Tara smiled and put an arm around each dog's shoulders to reach around and pet their chests.

"Welcome home, Indy and Annapolis. Welcome to Corgi Cove."

Just outside the view of the cove, there was a boat anchored. It looked like any other boat anchored, fishing on a beautiful summer day. But on this boat, Logan stood with binoculars while his brother Jake sat at the wheel of the boat.

When Logan raised the binoculars to his eyes to spy on the woman and the dogs in Corgi Cove, the Viking rune on his upper right arm peaked out from under the sleeve of his T-shirt and the scar at his elbow stretched.

Lowering the binoculars, he turned to Jake, and after looking at the matching tattoo on his brother's arm, signed, "Got to hand it to Fred, he took the fact that he wasn't the one that wrote the notes, did the break in, set the fire or did the walk around in the trees to his grave. He was smart to let us know that they thought that it was all him. He was a chicken shit and a dumbass, but he upheld the code, Family first. We'll remember him for that. He protected the secret."

Jake signed back. "Yes, he protected the secret. Now it's up to all of us to continue to protect it, as our fathers and their fathers before them have done for centuries."

As Jake slowly turned the boat back toward the way they had come, Logan finished putting on his shirt. Tucking it in, he made a show of straightening the sheriff's star over his right chest pocket.

Smiling, he walked over to Jake and thumped him on the back, then leaned over and made sure that the deputy sheriff's star was straight on the shirt that Jake had just put on. "Yes, we'll make sure the secret stays with only those that it belongs to. Let's go home and do our jobs, brother. Let's get back to Eriksport."

ABOUT THE AUTHOR

Dawn L Nolder lives in Fairborn, Ohio with her family and their dogs, Connal and Squirt. Dawn's interests include archaeology, in which she has a degree, along with genealogy, gardening, and corgis.

Readers and fans can follow Dawn online through her website, https://dawnlnolder.com/. Dawn is also on Facebook, https://www.facebook.com/DawnLNolder/ and Twitter, https://twitter.com/DLNolder.

Made in the USA
Middletown, DE
08 June 2017